What others are s

"I found [CHLOE'S SPIF

shed some tears…hard to

– Book Lover (Reader,

"I just loved [CHLOE'S SPIRIT]. Chloe and Marsh were incredible and Mary was just awesome…Such a great book."

– Trish Roberts (Reader, Amazon Kindle)

"…Ann Simas seamlessly intertwines an intriguing murder mystery [in CHLOE'S SPIRIT] with a budding romance [and] a love that spans beyond the grave… Fans of suspense, romance, and paranormal will be drawn to Simas's ability to create a well written, believable story [in CHLOE'S SPIRIT AFTERSTORIES]. She does a remarkable job developing her numerous characters."

–Stacie Theis, BeachBoundBooks.com

"The characters are so engaging [in FIRST STAR] that you won't want to put the book down."

– lfb68 (Reader, Amazon Kindle)

"FIRST STAR is a spellbinding romantic thriller that will leave readers on the edge of their seats and have them yearning for more."

–Stacie Theis, BeachBoundBooks.com

"[BLESSED ARE THE EAGLES] is a great mystery and love story with some interesting Hopi Indian folklore. Well written and good character development."

–Gary Wolfe (Reader, Amazon Kindle)

"Warning! [LOOSE ENDS] is very hard to put down! May be hazardous to your sleep…No joke…I was up till 1:15 this morning because I had to see how it ended!!!"

– Mary Geiger (Reader, via Ann Simas, Author Facebook page)

"Ann Simas has done it again. LOOSE ENDS is a dynamic mystery-love story…with many twists and turns right up to the end. Highly recommended!"

– Gary Wolfe (Reader, Amazon Kindle)"

"THE SUGAR CUP was delightful, with characters I rooted for, a puzzle that was fun to solve and the perfect blend of comedy, mystery and old-fashioned enchantment. I loved it."

– Eileen Dreyer, author of *Twice Tempted*

Available now…

CHLOE'S SPIRIT
RWA Golden Heart Finalist

CHLOE'S SPIRIT AFTERSTORIES
Second Chance & Foolish Heart

ALL'S WELL
An Eclectic Collection of Short Stories

FIRST STAR
RWA Golden Heart Finalist

BLESSED ARE THE EAGLES
RWA Golden Heart Finalist

LOOSE ENDS
A Sexy Thriller

▪

Coming soon…

HOLY SMOKE
An Andi Comstock Paranormal Mystery

HEAVEN SENT

▪

Also by Ann Simas
THE SUGAR CUP
(Written as Annie Sims, Harlequin Worldwide)

DRESSED

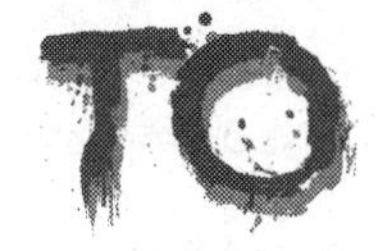
TO

DIE

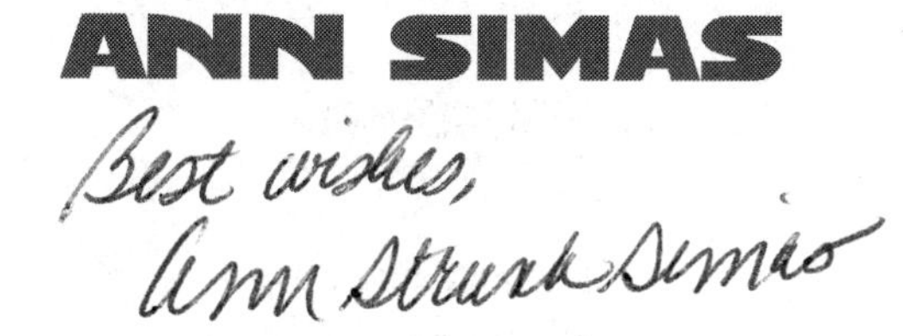
ANN SIMAS
Best wishes,

MAGIC
MOON
PRESS

DRESSED TO DIE

OCTOBER 2014

ISBN 978-0-9885460-7-3 (print book)

Magic Moon Press . POB 41634 . Eugene, OR 97404-0386

Editing by Nancy Jankow

Printed in U.S.A.

110314/11pthyph
CS4956233

This book is for
Judy Bolton and Nancy Drew—
two teenage gumshoes who
lived only in the pages of their
books and in the imaginations of
their authors and readers.
They provided me endless hours of
enjoyment and sleuthing in my youth.

Mille grazie to
Nancy Jankow for editing.

And to my readers, thank you.
I appreciate your support!

CHAPTER 1

GRACE GABBIANO THOUGHT she'd found a dead woman at first, but upon closer inspection, realized the corpse was a guy. The beard stubble gave him away.

Some might have questioned how she knew the body—dolled up in a crimson chiffon evening gown and a blonde wig—was dearly departed rather than a transvestite sleeping it off, but Grace had no doubts. She'd encountered death before, up close and personal. There was a look, a smell, that gave it away every time.

She quickly surveyed her surroundings. Acre upon acre of some of the richest farmland in the country sprouted every imaginable shade of green. Hovering over the northern horizon, all the way to the Coburg Hills, a smoky haze lingered from the previous day's field burning.

Above the haze, an upside-down bowl of blue sky stretched from the Cascades to the Coast Range, unmarred by anything remotely resembling a cloud. Several crows broke the peaceful morning silence with raucous *caws*, dive-bombing the corpse, hoping for a piece of the action.

This was home. Coburg, Oregon. Not a big city, like Seattle, where Grace had lived for the past six years, but a small town of not quite a thousand citizens. It had small-town problems like barking dogs and branches hanging too far over adjoining property fences and kids tossing water balloons at crusty old bastards who sat on a park bench, reminiscing better times or complaining about the cost of the new sewer system.

Grace turned her eyes back to the dead guy. *So, since Coburg is about as small-town as it gets without being totally off the map, what the freaking hell is a big-city problem doing here?*

God, she'd only been on the job for a week! She hadn't expected to have to prove herself so soon, but like it or not, this death belonged to her.

Instinctively, she sniffed the air, pervasive with the scent of thousands of mint plants. Today, the minty fragrance had another purpose. It almost, but not quite, disguised the stench of death.

Another annoying crow joined the fray, *caw, caw, cawing* brazenly as it circled and landed. Grace closed her eyes briefly, revolted by the idea of the bird pecking on what looked to be pretty fresh prey.

Meeting death, though it had happened before, was not a common occurrence, and she didn't think she'd ever get used to it.

Stepping carefully, she approached the body. The crow aimed a dark beady eye at her and fled as she knelt to confirm what she already knew. No answering pulse met the middle and index fingers she pressed against the man's carotid artery. Nothing. All gone. A DRT, dead-right-there. Probably since the evening before, if her limited experience with DRTs in Seattle had taught her anything.

Some welcome-home present.

She leaned back, contemplating what she could see of the dead guy's face.

A gentle breeze teased wisps of the wig across his five o'clock shadow. She dug into a pocket for her house key, using it to lift the strands that had strayed across his upper face. A squirming mass of insects happily devoured breakfast on the blank stare of his formerly dark eyes. She quickly averted her gaze, her throat working convulsively to fight back the inevitable gag response. The time would never come when she'd be able to handle the tiniest of God's creatures having their way with dead human flesh.

Several moments later, composed but still filled with dread, she looked back at the corpse. "Shit, shit, *shit*!"

Why did the DRT have to be Yeager Clausen, entrepreneur, land developer, town icon? Couldn't it have been a nobody, someone the media wouldn't give a rat's ass about?

"Why you couldn't just play dress-up at home?" she grumbled, only slightly ashamed of her peeved inquiry. The guy was, after all, dead.

Studying him from head-to-toe, an odd, unexpected sensation flared in the pit of Grace's stomach. She'd experienced an infusion of adrenaline like this only once before, but it was instantly recognizable.

She smelled a homicide.

Eight days! Holy crap, some people had all the luck. Back in Seattle, the thought of assisting on a death investigation would have thrilled her. Here in Coburg, she just wanted to settle in and do her job, unnoticed but appreciated, bypassing homicides altogether, thereby keeping herself out of trouble.

Her gaze swept the immediate area, then quickly flitted again over the body. A piece of paper, trapped beneath the arms folded across Clausen's chest fluttered in the light breeze. A suicide note? How odd. Egocentrics—filthy rich ones, especially—typically did not self-eradicate.

Grace replaced her key and stood, staring at the bloody froth, now dried, at the blue-tinged lips. Drug overdose most likely, but another scan of the immediate area and the body revealed no discarded syringe, no kit, and no powdery substance around his nostrils. No dead bugs laying around, either, that may have feasted one final time on his lethal stash.

If he'd been mainlining, the needle could still be in his arm, but a poke at his elbow confirmed that rigor had set in. If the needle was there, it would be up to the medical examiner to find it when he did his thing at the post-mortem.

The very thought of an autopsy made Grace shudder. She could've gone a lifetime without experiencing one, but given the deceased's age and the circumstances, it would be required.

Which brought her back to the suspicion that, cross-dressed or not, Clausen had not offed himself.

Every violent death she'd encountered while patrolling the streets of Seattle had been obvious homicide. Clausen in his evening gown wasn't so cut-and-dry. For one thing, nothing about him suggested traumatic death, yet….

Yet what?

She glanced again at the audacious murder of crows, as if their circling and swooping confirmed what that odd clench in her gut kept hammering at her.

If Yeager Clausen *had* been murdered, something would turn up, no matter how minute or seemingly insignificant, that answered how he had died and perhaps who had killed him, which would lead to the why of the crime. Grace had not an inch of doubt about that. Her fear was that the *something* might not show up in this lifetime, thereby leaving her looking like a fool if she proclaimed the manner of death a homicide before all the facts were in.

Jumping off the deep end again? Grace shook her head in disgust. Even as a kid, she'd always gone straight for the deep end. The shallow end was for sissies. The shallow end was for people who didn't like making waves. The shallow end was safe.

And thinking like that was exactly what had got her into so much trouble up north.

Grace planted her fists on her hips. "Okay," she said to the crows, ignoring her *gut feeling*. "Suicide it is, then. Murdered big shots are a pain in the ass, anyway."

She didn't like leaving the corpse unattended, but it was not yet seven a.m. The likelihood of the body being discovered by anyone other than scavenging crows this early on a Sunday morning was pretty slim.

Forcing the word *homicide* out of her head, she retraced her steps to the road with care and took off at a sprint. "Keep away from him!" she shouted over her shoulder.

Caw, caw, caw, the winged scavengers replied, which she translated into, *Peck, peck, peck his eyes out*. The gruesome thought made her cringe. "Quoth the raven nevermore." She panted, increasing her speed.

In a town the size of Coburg, and considering she'd been at the end of her run, it didn't take long to go from the mint field to her house. On previous mornings, she'd bicycled to work, but discovering a DRT in the field seemed to warrant faster transportation.

Grace quickly retrieved the keys for her VW Beetle and hightailed it to the new police station adjacent to the fire house. Occupied by CPD's six patrol officers and two clerks, it also accommodated ten volunteer reservists who provided part-time assistance, depending on their "real job" or academic schedules.

All the patrol cars were parked in the lot, including the one that should have been out on the six a.m. shift. Grace punched in the code on the automated key pad at the front door, breaking a fingernail in the process. She went directly to the dispatch desk, where the nameplate read TINA LOVE above ADMINISTRATIVE ASSISTANT.

Tina's work area screamed organized efficiency. On her first day, Grace had learned where contact phone numbers were located, how the filing system worked, and how to do data entry. Under Tina's watchful eye, she'd also read the *Policies & Procedures Manual* before lunch that day.

Despite being the new kid on the Coburg block, Grace's six years at Seattle PD had snared her a sergeant's rank. In the unlikely event of a death by suspicious or indeterminate cause, according to the *P&PM*, she would run the death investigation.

Suicide, she reminded her new Coburg self, but her old Seattle self insidiously whispered back, *Murder*.

Grace grabbed several tissues from the box on Tina's desk and blotted the sweat beaded on her forehead. Tick-tock. The weatherman had promised temperatures in the mid-nineties, and the sun was not a friend to forensic evidence of the outdoor variety.

She picked up the multi-line phone and dialed. "Tina, it's Grace. I need you down here right now."

A single mom, Tina finished up what was apparently a battle with one of her children over breakfast cereal versus Pop Tarts. "Marcus, you eat that, and I'll sew your mouth shut. I'll call my mom and be there in ten minutes, Grace. Or less, if I come in my jammies."

"Make it less and change here. I've got a body in Abner Nelson's south mint field. It looks like a suicide, but" —Grace hesitated— "it might be a homicide." *Now why the* hell *did I say that?* she wondered as the station door opened.

Patrol officer Deets Mallory walked in, nodded a greeting, and shuffled toward the coffee maker. Grace waved him over. "We've got a DRT."

"No shit?" Normally a man who took his time moving from place to place, Deets immediately detoured to the counter.

Grace finished issuing instructions to Tina. "As soon as you get in, call the new chief and let him know what's going on. The dead guy was a hotshot here in town and the chief may want to come out to the scene."

Deets mouthed, *Who?*

Grace held up her free hand, her gaze going to the reservists' work schedule posted on the wall. "Get Melody Jenks and Felix Montoya in to cordon off the road from both directions and tell them *no one* comes across that line except the EMTs, the deputy ME, and the call-car. And the chief, if he shows up. You'll be responsible for notifications. Make sure everyone knows it's an apparent suicide."

"I thought it was a murder," Tina said, her disappointment obvious.

Before her brain could stop her mouth, Grace said, "The scene doesn't quite add up to suicide, but there may be a suicide note." She glanced again at the schedule. "Wozinsky should have been on at six, but all the patrol cars are out front and no one's here."

"He got food poisoning from that greasy spoon across the Interstate," Tina said. "I warned him they deep fry road kill and pass it off as food over there."

Grace frowned.

As if reading her mind, Tina rushed on. "I called the Sheriff's office. They're taking our calls until Charlie Dillon gets in."

"And that'll be when?"

"Around eight."

Grace opted to forego a procedural lecture to the woman

who practically ran the office with her eyes closed. "Dillon can go ahead on regular patrol. Between Deets and me and the two reservists, we'll be okay on this call." Grace thought a moment. "That's it. Thanks for coming in on such short notice."

"Are you kidding?" Tina demanded. "A genuine possible homicide in Coburg. When do you think that happened last?"

Grace glanced up at her fellow officer, hanging over the edge of the counter. "Apparently, not for awhile, if the way Deets is drooling is any indication."

Tina chuckled. "Who is it, anyway?"

"Yeager Clausen, but I don't want that going out over dispatch or uttered to *anyone*. All we need is bunch of lookie-loos and reporters out there gawking, possibly destroying evidence, or worse, getting to the family before we do."

"My lips are sealed. Brandon, leave your brother's milk alone or I'm going make you drink it. He hates milk," she said, then disconnected.

Grace held the silent handset in her hand for a moment, wondering if Tina had learned her command success or been born with it.

"Yeager Clausen," Deets said, his tone a mixture of awe and excitement. "Homicide, huh?"

Grace felt compelled to list the overt signs of suicide, but left out mentioning Clausen's attire. No sense diluting Deets's reaction ahead of time.

He shrugged, gave her a quick scan, and glanced down at his own shorts and T-shirt. "Guess we'd better haul balls and get suited up."

"Speak for yourself," Grace said, and he laughed. After exchanging a coffee bet on who would be ready first, they headed for their respective gender-appropriate rooms to get into uniform. Grace needed a shower, but that wasn't going to happen. She hoped her deodorant lived up to its advertised promises. She managed the transition from runner to cop in three-point-five minutes, which allowed time to retrieve both cameras before Deets's prematurely silver head appeared in the men's room doorway.

"Just think, two weeks ago, I had to share Sunday shifts with that shit, Frey. McCrea did good bringing you on, Gracie."

Grace grunted and pulled her ponytail through the hole in her department-issued Coburg PD baseball cap. Corporal Jimmy Frey *was* a shit and she avoided him as much as possible. As the dickhead's supervisor, she had yet to figure out how to handle the situation without maiming him severely with her knee every time he let loose with another sexual innuendo.

Deets chuckled. "Don't ever play poker, Gracie. That expression of yours speak volumes." He buckled on his gun belt and grabbed a hand-held radio. "Why are you wearing shorts?"

"I'm still on bike patrol. My long pants are hanging in my closet at home."

"You could pedal out and I'll meet you at the scene in the cruiser."

"Pack up your bright ideas and let's roll."

He laughed, following her out the door.

Grace unlocked the trunk. CPD might be small, but it had the essentials. A quick check confirmed that everything needed for proper crime-scene evidence collection was right where it should be. She stowed the cameras and two extra rolls of film with the other gear, closed the trunk, and climbed into the vehicle. "Everything found at the scene is photographed, properly labeled, and logged in as soon as we get back."

"I get your meaning, and just so you know, it's not me who's been misplacing evidence."

Grace believed him, but the protocol reminder was good for both of them.

"You sure we need the film camera *and* the digital?" he asked.

"Better safe than sorry. Courts are still suspicious of digi prints in homicide cases."

"I guess you're right." He scratched his nose. "If it *is* a murder."

Maybe it *wasn't* a crime scene, but Grace had been well trained. Every unattended death had to be treated like it *might* be a crime. God and she both knew how *not* doing that had a way of coming back to bite a good cop right in the ass.

Tina pulled in as Grace backed out. They exchanged waves. Five-point-five minutes.

A moment later, Deets said prayerfully, "Sweet Jesus," He crossed himself. "A murder."

Grace shook her head. "One whole week on the job. I just have bad karma."

CHAPTER 2

"YOU EVER WORKED a homicide before, Gabbiano?"

Grace slid a glance in Deets's direction. "One or two, but not as lead."

Deets fingered the seatbelt constraining him. "I haven't worked a dead guy for over ten years. Not since I left L.A."

"Still miss your corpse du jour, do you?"

"Not really. Looking at dead people isn't my thing, but I like figuring out what got 'em that way. The challenge is like a straight shot of epinephrine."

Grace nodded. For her, forensics enhanced the mundane aspects of police work. She'd taken the job with the former chief's assurance that she'd be allowed to process some evidence for the department.

Chief McCrea had forgotten to mention he'd be retired by the time she reported for duty. She had serious doubts that the new chief would sanction in-house forensics, regardless of budgetary constraints. Hailing from the Portland Police Bureau, Aidan Cruz would be used to his lab work coming from state-of-the-art facilities, not a little room attached to his sergeant's house.

Grace braked to a stop. Chief McCrea's warning rang clear in her mind: "Don't say anything over the unit radio you don't want the entire Willamette Valley to hear, Gracie. Use the hand-held, unless you're damned sure you're ready for the consequences."

If Yeager Clausen lying dead in a mint field, in an evening gown, didn't qualify as something that needed to be kept confidential, nothing did. She picked up the hand-held and called in their location.

"Everyone's notified," Tina said. "Chief Cruz was already on his way. He just passed through Woodburn."

The woman worked faster than Superman. "Thanks." Grace clicked off for a second. "Remind Montoya and Jenks not to run sirens and only to use the hand-helds."

"Absolutely," Tina said. "Gotta go—if Chief Cruz stops by here before he heads your way, he might not understand me being at my desk in baby dolls." The airwaves crackled and went dead.

Grace exchanged a look with Deets, whose eyebrows jumped up and down. "Let's get this show on the road. You're not gonna believe what I found out here."

Deets, having been trained right in law enforcement, didn't rush over to the body for a close look. His howl of amusement was released from the roadside.

"It's funny, but it ain't that funny," Grace said, opening the trunk.

"The hell it isn't—the guy's wearing a dress. You should'a told me!"

"And miss your reaction?"

"It has shiny things on it," Deets said, wiping a tear from his eye.

"You're so astute! No wonder you've lasted this long as a cop."

"Up yours, Gabbiano," he responded good-naturedly. "A freaking dress! Men who wear Armani suits and Italian loafers don't usually end up in a field in a *frou-frou* dress. Holy Mary, Mother of God. The guys are going to love this."

Grace handed him a roll of yellow crime-scene tape. "That's twice you've prayed this morning."

Deets tugged on her pony tail. "Technically, crossing yourself is not praying, and for your information, I'm agnostic."

"Yeah, right."

They pulled stakes from the trunk and used them at six-foot intervals to wrap and string crime scene tape in a fifteen-foot radius around the body. Deets stood back while Grace painstakingly snapped pictures from various angles, first with the film camera, then with the digi, both on straps around her neck. She stopped a couple of times, just to study the corpse. She had the strangest feeling of familiarity. Not quite déjà vu, but almost.

Deets stared at the red dress and frowned, as if he were having a similar experience. A crow swooped in and landed next to the deceased's head. "Scat!" he shouted. The bird took flight.

"Okay," Grace said, "I see a nice big shoe print next to the body, so let's get started casting and gathering evidence before the EMTs or deputy medical examiner come in and destroy what little we have."

Deets considered the bag of plaster powder she extended to him. "I take it I'm in charge of that?"

"You have fabric on your knees. I don't."

He blew a raspberry and took the bag.

Grace reached back into the trunk to retrieve the evidence tent markers.

Deets said, "I'm really wondering why your call on this is a possible homicide. I bet that's a suicide note under his arm."

"I thought you were done with betting," Grace shot back.

Deets grinned.

"Okay, a fiver says it's not."

"*Five!*"

"This has got to be worth more than a cup of coffee," she said, her eyes back on the corpse.

Deets grunted. "I've known you less than two weeks and I'm ready to file bankruptcy."

She creased and placed the first evidence marker. "It helps to bet on the winning side."

"No shit."

Grace worried her lower lip, suddenly unsure of her abilities. Doubt left her feeling inadequate. "Should I call in the Major Crime Team?" Designed to pick up county-wide crime patterns and chatter involving criminal activity, officers from surrounding jurisdictions often participated in each other's violent crime investigations.

"Shit, it's Sunday morning. The MCT guys are at home screwing their significant others, or mowing the grass, or getting ready to watch pre-season NFL. They do *not* want to be called out. My advice is, consider this a suicide, unless the ME says otherwise."

"You're right." Her gaze fixed on the blue lips again, she said, "It looks like he asphyxiated from a drug overdose, but I didn't see a rig anywhere."

"Maybe he had a buddy out here with him. Clausen croaks, the buddy takes off. It's happened before."

"Who brings a buddy along for a suicide? Or a dress-up party?"

"Maybe he had terminal cancer or something and he needed his buddy to assist. This *is* Oregon, you know. It's allowed here. As to a dress-up party, ditto."

"Assisted suicide is only under a doctor's supervision, not a buddy's."

Deets scowled at her. "Unless his buddy is a doctor."

"Oh, please!" Grace itched to roll the corpse over to see if the body hid any clues. "Men like Yeager Clausen don't dress up in an evening gown and off themselves in a mint field." She marked shoe and foot prints with marker tents five through ten, putting down a measure and photographing each while Deets prepared the plaster. "Besides, I've known Clausen for a long time. His ego was way too big to be found looking like this on purpose, and until we know otherwise, he was way too young to be dying of natural causes."

"If you're still thinking of calling in the MCT and this yo-yo is a suicide, you'll never get an ounce of cooperation from them in the future. If he's not, they'll think you're some kind of brain trust when you solve the crime all by yourself."

"That's comforting." Grace worked her way around the perimeter, careful of where she stepped. "I was afraid I wouldn't reach genius status until my *third* week on the job."

She surveyed the plastic tents she'd left in her wake and made another notation. Deets prepped a second bag of plaster. "No high-heel prints." She pointed at Clausen's feet. "He came out here barefoot and ended up with those on."

"What are they, stilettos? They're obviously too small. Poor bastard never would've been able to walk in them."

"They're high-heel sandals, and you're right. They're too small. He seems to have a big foot for a man of his size."

Deets squinted at the corpse. "He's what? About five-nine? His foot looks about my size and I wear an eleven."

"What're you? Six foot?"

"Just over."

Grace walked back to the edge of the narrow road, put down another number tent and her ruler, then snapped several pictures from different angles. "Tire track here. Got enough plaster left?"

On his third bag, Deets said, "Just."

She flipped the page in her notebook and sketched the basic outline of the scene, then pulled her smartphone out of her pocket to get the temperature. She also made a note of the weather conditions.

As Deets finished his final pour, Grace pulled on latex gloves and began to walk a spiral path from the outside perimeter that ultimately took her to the body. She extended the tape measure and jotted down numbers at frequent intervals, but aside from the shoe, foot, and tire prints, the only items she'd noted in her pad were two gooey things covered with ants. One looked and smelled like chocolate, but the other had her stumped.

Reminded that the day promised more record-breaking temperatures, Grace scooped up the substances, each with a clean putty knife, and eased them into separate plastic bags. She sealed the closures, cutting off the ants' air supply before she labeled the bags. With any luck, by the time they reached the evidence room, the small beasties would be DRTs themselves.

She scanned the area again and spotted something with no legs—the distinct silver-gray color of cigarette ash. Placing the ruler beside the find, she snapped two pictures, then carefully creased a piece of paper into a pharmacist's fold and captured the ashes, placing them into another plastic bag.

Fearful she had missed something because of all the mint plants obscuring the ground, Grace went over the area again, but discovered nothing new. She tried once more to lift the rigid arms of Clausen's supine form. "He's got plenty of rigor. My guess is that he's been down about eight or nine hours already."

Collecting the last of his castings, Deets looked up. "You're probably right."

With a sigh, Grace extracted another container and went toward the evidence collection she'd been dreading the most: the crawlies in Clausen's lifeless eyes. Swallowing back her revulsion, she worked quickly, wishing she didn't have perspiration dripping into her eyes.

She screwed the perforated lid on the jar, labeled it, and put it with the evidence bags. CPD didn't have a crime lab, which meant no entomologist on staff. Did it even matter? In this instance, probably not. She was certain, in this case, that the question of how long Clausen had been dead mattered less than why he'd gotten that way.

The hand-held radio crackled. Melody Jenks's voice came through. "EMTs on their way. Fire truck was right behind them, but I'm holding them here. They're not happy about it."

"They'll get over it." Grace glanced at her watch. Nearly an hour had passed since Tina had called in the suicide. Too bad Coburg Fire, which could've responded in under five minutes, didn't have a Medic Unit or an EMT team to crew it. "Everything okay down your way?" She pulled off her cap and reached for a hand towel she'd tossed in the vehicle to wipe her brow. Nerves more than heat had caused her to break out in sweat.

"All quiet."

"Get shoe prints from everyone who comes back out, Mel, and keep an accurate log of who belongs to which one."

Melody's gulp could be heard over the hand-held. "Even the chief?"

"Yes. Deets and I will stop and do ours, too, and you'll have to add my running shoes when we get back to the station."

"Gotcha." A pause. "Is this something besides a suicide, Grace?"

"It's an unattended death."

"Right," Melody said.

"No media, Mel. Under any circumstances. Got it?"

"Got it. Uh, Grace?"

"Yeah?"

"What about other law enforcement personnel?"

"Like who? I haven't called anyone else in."

"Jimmy Frey," came the response, *sotto voce*.

Grace's finger hovered over the talk button. "God, give me strength." She glanced at Deets.

"Now *you're* praying," he muttered.

She rolled her eyes and depressed the talk button. "Exactly why would Officer Frey be headed this way?"

"I'm not sure he will," Melody said, "but he sleeps with his scanner and his hand-held…."

Grace grimaced. Reserve Officer Jenks could have discovered that little tidbit only one way.

"She seemed smarter than that," Deets said, bagging-and-tagging the last of the hardened castings.

Grace hit the talk button again. "The deputy ME should be along shortly and the call-car will be coming through to pick up the body, but no one else, unless you hear otherwise from my lips." She paused for just a moment, thinking of the other reservist she'd stationed up the road. "You listening, Montoya? All this goes for you, too."

"Hey, Grace," he responded, "I'm your slave, remember? You got a wish, I grant it for you."

"Forgive me, Felix. I *did* forget myself for a moment." She signed off, shooting a wry glance at Deets.

Two EMTs climbed out of the ambulance and gathered their medical equipment from the back of the vehicle. Grace stepped forward and introduced herself and Deets.

After a caution to tread carefully, one EMT approached the body, felt for a pulse, and said, "This guy's croaked." He stepped back to where his partner stood.

"Looks like drug overdose," the other one said.

Grace followed his gaze to the body. Everyone seemed in

agreement. The bloody froth at Clausen's blue lips almost certainly meant he'd died from asphyxiation as a result of an OD. "Looks like."

"How come it's marked out like a crime scene?"

Grace tried not to sound defensive. "It's an unattended death in questionable circumstances."

The EMTs exchanged a dubious glance and with no one to resuscitate, picked up their gear.

Wondering if she was being too cautious, Grace said, "Please stop at the checkpoint so Officer Jenks can get your shoe prints."

Two incredulous EMT gazes flew to the piece of paper on Clausen's lifeless chest. The EMT who had confirmed Clausen's croaked status said, "Are you fucking kidding?"

The other EMT elbowed him and said, "No problem." He looked like David Boreanz, who played Seeley Booth, the FBI guy on *Bones*. Grace liked him better as Angel on *Buffy the Vampire Slayer.*

Their skepticism weighed heavily on her shoulders. Her face burned as she raised her chin a defiant half inch. Suicide or not, she wasn't taking any chances on screwing anything up, or losing evidence. She was long past worrying about what co-workers, or EMTs in this case, thought of her method of operation. "I appreciate your cooperation, guys," she said, keeping her tone amiable. "Thanks."

Surprisingly, both men shrugged and smiled. The *Bones* guy said, "Our day is off to an interesting start. We don't get many calls on beauty queens."

Grace glanced at Yeager Clausen's brilliant crimson ensemble and wondered if he was, indeed, in drag.

CHAPTER 3

"LET'S ROLL HIM," Grace said.

Deets knocked away some of the crawlies with his gloved fingertips. The task of turning the corpse might have been more cumbersome if the body hadn't been so slight of build. Grace guessed Clausen didn't weigh in at more than one-fifty in his birthday suit.

"What do you call this style of dress?" Deets asked.

"It's a halter top over a flare skirt, for evening wear only."

"Wouldn't fit if the zipper was closed."

"Probably not. His shoulders and chest are fairly wide for his size, and his biceps are large. Looks like he worked out," Grace noted. "If he'd been dressed up in girl-clothes for his own reasons, seems like he'd have worn something that did fit. Can you hold him up while I snap a couple shots?"

Deets grimaced, but managed to keep Clausen's exposed backside to the camera. "Nice lividity. At least we know he wasn't moved after he died."

Grace photographed the open-zipper area.

Deets said, "No tighty-whities for Mr. Rich Guy."

She pursed her lips. The butt floss underwear didn't look practical or comfortable. Finished with taking pictures, she examined the ground one last time, but found nothing more of interest. "Okay, you can put him down."

"Still looks like it might be a suicide note," Deets insisted.

"Maybe it is, maybe it isn't."

"Obstinacy is one of your strong suits, huh?"

She gave the paper one more gentle tug. It wasn't going to budge without tearing. "Just so you know, both my parents are Italian. Being obstinate is obligatory in Italian genes."

She knelt, ready to remove the tiara tangled in the long-haired wig. The sound of another approaching vehicle drew her attention. Grace glanced up. The car had no markings, but it bore a license plate with an E prefix, which identified it as a government-owned vehicle.

"The deputy ME?" Deets asked.

"Probably."

A woman wearing khaki shorts, a tank top, and sandals climbed out of the vehicle, pulling latex gloves on as she approached the scene.

Grace searched her memory for the deputy ME's name and stepped toward the newcomer. "Dr. Riordan?"

The Deputy ME nodded and extended her hand. "Jade. And you are?"

"Grace Gabbiano and this is Deets Mallory." The feel of latex shaking latex always felt weird to Grace.

"And our dead guy?"

"Yeager Clausen."

"Bummer." The ME shook her head. "The man Coburg loved to hate."

"Yes, they did." Grace frowned. "I'd like to get him out of here before the media shows up and turns this field into a three-ring circus."

"Better hurry," Riordan said. "I heard it on my way up over the police band."

Grace ground her teeth together. "Someone put it out?"

"Frey, I think he said. Presumably, that's who the officer stationed at the checkpoint is trying to fend off."

"I'm going to kill that little shit," Deets muttered.

Grace scowled at him. "Take a number."

The Deputy ME pushed her sunglasses up on top of her head, her eyes back on the body. "Nice get-up. Silk?"

"Looks like," Grace said.

"Impressive. Threads this spendy are way beyond *my* means." She knelt next to the body and worked wig strands away to study the corpse's face. "Bloody froth. Looks like asphyxiation, possibly from an OD."

That made it unanimous, which still didn't come close to proclaiming Clausen's death anything but suicide.

"The call-car is right behind me." Riordan pushed to her feet, taking in the shoes, the tiara, the wig. "You'll be at the autopsy tomorrow morning, I imagine. Hacker starts at eight sharp. Given the circumstances, he'll probably do this one first."

Grace shivered, unable to summon even a grain of humor that the head ME's name was Hacker. Autopsy. She had managed to push aside the thought and now here it was, right back in her face again.

Riordan studied the body one last time. "You know, this may not be a suicide."

With a sigh, Grace said, "I know."

"If you'd like, I can do the death notification. I'm supposed to anyway, but most jurisdictions prefer to handle their own."

Grace thought about delegating the task, but growing up in a small town like Coburg had given her more than a passing acquaintance with Clausen's wife. Besides, judging by the way Riordan glanced at her wristwatch, she obviously had something—or someone—waiting for her. "Thanks for the offer," Grace said, "but I'll take care of it."

After the Deputy ME left, Deets collected the evidence bags and placed them in a box in the trunk of the cruiser. Grace made a few more notations on her scene sketch, then tried to lift Clausen's arm again. "I can't get this damned piece of paper out."

"You are one persistent broad."

Grace stared at the paper in question, her lips puckered. "Maybe if you help me, we can get his arm up a little."

"Gabbiano, I'm not sure I like you enough to do that for you."

"Don't forget, I'm the one who writes your performance

eval from now on."

Deets laughed. "Point taken." He leaned over and managed to work up the forearm just enough for Grace to remove the paper.

"'Now I am like them,'" Deets read, sounding disappointed. "What the hell does that mean?"

"He wanted to be a sprig of mint in his next life?"

Deets smirked. "Just occurred to me. This freak took the plunge near a paved road where he'd be noticeable."

Grace conceded he was probably right. Mint harvest was still a couple of weeks away. Clausen might not have been found until then if he'd been further out in the acreage. She turned the paper over. The note was written on the back of his company letterhead.

Now I am like them. What an odd message to leave behind. Grace slid the missive into a plastic bag, labeled it, and put it with the other evidence.

She kneeled and using her pen, eased strands of wig hair away from Clausen's face. "Look at his chin. Someone slugged him."

Deets gave her an amused glance. "You see a crime in everything?"

She shrugged. "Isn't that what they pay me the big bucks to figure out?" She clicked off two more shots with each camera, then made a fist with her right hand and lined up her knuckles with the three black-and-blue marks on his jaw.

"Well, hell, Gracie, I think you could be right. Someone must'a clipped him good to bruise him like that."

"Whoever did it might have some bruised knuckles, too." As she set about removing the red satin sandals and slipping them into plastic, she wondered if they might luck out and get a print off the leather insole, or maybe even the arched underside. "Let's bag his hands and feet, too. Even though there's no sign of a struggle, it's possible he scratched someone."

At the sound of more vehicles, Grace and Deets looked toward the road. Jimmy Frey pulled up in a patrol vehicle, in his civvies, a news van on his tail. Right behind them came the call-car, a nondescript white van sent out by the morgue to retrieve the body.

"Shit!" said Grace. "How the hell did a guy like Jimmy Frey ever get hired to work in law enforcement? He doesn't have the brain God gave a flea."

"My theory is he had something on Chief McCrea. If that's the case, he didn't need a brain."

"Chief McCrea didn't seem like the kind of man who could be blackmailed."

Deets shrugged. "Everyone has skeletons in the closet, Grace. Much as I liked McCrea, keeping Jimmy on was not his shining accomplishment."

Grace blew out a breath of frustration, glancing back toward Frey. She squared her shoulders. "I'll take care of our resident jackass."

She walked over to block Jimmy Frey's path. Last time she'd seen him, which had been the day before, his hair had been dark brown. Now it was bleached blonde. His new look kind of threw her. "No unauthorized personnel on this scene, Frey."

A good half a foot taller than Grace and buff enough for a weight-lifting competition, Frey took a menacing step forward. "Bullshit," he snarled, spraying spittle across her face. "I work for CPD just like you do and I'm the senior officer on the force."

Grace refrained from wiping the spit from her right cheek. Instead, she took a moment to slide her pen into the leg pocket of her cargo shorts. Frey had no seniority, either from age or rank, but leave it to the bully he was to try and manipulate her anyway. "As the sergeant and investigating officer, I'm telling you that on a crime scene, only necessary personnel are admitted access."

Grace cursed herself for even thinking the word *crime* in his presence, let alone uttering it.

"Crime scene?"

"I misspoke. It's an unattended death, apparently a suicide," she amended.

He peered over her shoulder at the yellow tape, the bagged evidence, and the victim. His expression darkened. "Are you saying I'm not necessary?"

"Not at this time."

"Who died and made you God?" he ranted.

"CPD's *Policy & Procedures Manual*."

"You're full of sh—"

"Problem?"

Frey spun around, his fists clenched, his face a mottled red. "Butt out, ass—"

Grace had no clue as to the identity of the newest individual on the scene, had not even heard his vehicle approach, but evidently Frey knew him. The stranger stood an inch or two over six feet, reducing Jimmy Frey's stature to that of shrimp. The look he gave Frey was enough, not only to quell the corporal's outburst, but to cower him.

"Grace," Deets said, peeking around the latest arrival. "Have you met the new chief yet?"

Grace swallowed the sarcastic comment perched and ready to fly off the tip of her tongue at the newest intruder. She sent Deets a grateful glance.

Ever the gentleman, Deets went on, "Grace Gabbiano, Chief Aidan Cruz."

Grace pulled off a glove as the chief extended his hand in greeting, then asked again, "Problem here?"

"Nope," she said, pulling off the other glove. "I just explained to Officer Frey who the investigating officer is on this case, and asked for his cooperation in vacating the scene."

To his credit, Chief Cruz waited until Frey stormed off muttering expletives, before he surveyed the scene. Only the slight movement of his left eyebrow as his alert perusal flickered over the corpse indicated that he'd seen anything strange.

He turned on Grace. "Just what the hell makes you think a crime has been committed here?"

CHAPTER 4

GRACE WASN'T THE least bit cowed by the scowling man looming over her, the long fingers of his big hands splayed firmly on his tight-end hips. He obviously thought he had the art of intimidation down pat.

"Having a bad day?" she asked.

"No, goddammit, I am *not* having a bad day. I'm not even *close* to having a bad day. Hell, I haven't even completed my payroll paperwork yet, and I get stopped for speeding at the Coburg off-ramp, and I have a freaking corpse to deal with, so why the hell would I be having a bad day?"

The absurdity of his morning, or at least the way he'd described it, tickled Grace. She tried not to grin.

"You think this is funny?"

Instantly sobered, she rearranged her features into what she hoped were lines of seriousness. She was speaking to her new boss, after all. "Not in the least. I've only been on the job for a week myself. I know exactly how you feel."

Aidan Cruz's scowl deepened. "Then I have to repeat my original question. What makes you think this is a homicide?"

"I never said it was a homicide." *Not to you, anyway.*

One by one, he took in the crime scene tape, the evidence markers, and the open trunk containing the box of labeled evidence bags. His dark glower finally landed on her again.

Geez, Grace, think before you speak! Any idiot could tell the scene had been treated as if a crime had been committed.

Grace cleared her throat, feeling both defensive and nervous about that inner feeling she had. "I'm not sure it is," she admitted. "At first glance, everything points to suicide from drug overdose, but there's no sign of any drug paraphernalia."

"You're going to have to come up with something better than that, Gabbiano. You've done some shoe-print casting, I see, so he had company here. You know as well as I do, when a user ODs, his druggie buddies don't hang around waiting to be arrested."

"Exactly! Why is there a note if Clausen had a buddy along with him?"

The chief's eyebrows furrowed as he mulled that over.

"Besides, if this is a heroin OD, he would've gone just like that." She snapped her fingers. "The syringe should still be in his arm—unless someone took it away."

Again the chief frowned. "Since you don't have an M.D. after your name, or a portable lab in your pocket, you have no way of knowing this is a heroin overdose."

"You're right," Grace said, willing to concede for the sake of convincing him her hunch had merit. "That's why I said 'if,' but I have seen a number of fatal heroin ODs and this looks the same." She snuck a quick glance at Deets. He gave her a quick nod that seemed to indicate she was doing okay, but she also read caution in his eyes.

"Who is this guy, anyway?"

"Yeager Clausen. He lives here in Coburg. He's a land developer. Extremely wealthy, I think. He's not the kind of guy who would go out of his own volition, in women's evening wear, and kill himself."

The chief pulled off a baseball cap advertising the Seattle Mariners and swiped his forehead with the back of his arm. "Weirdos come in every shape, size, gender, and tax bracket. Try again."

"Look at this," Grace said, unable to keep the excitement from her voice. "Help me, Deets." The two of them turned Clausen part-way over. The chief approached to see what all the fuss was about. "If he *chose* to play dress-up, he would have found a dress that actually fit. He couldn't even get the zipper up on this." They lowered his body and Grace lifted the bag containing the shoes. "And look at these heels. He's not a big man, but his toes were crammed in, literally. We found indications of bare feet, but no high-heel prints. These sandals went on after he was on his back and most likely after he was dead."

"How do you get that?" Deets asked, scratching his head.

"There are no butt-squirming indentations in the dirt," Grace said. "If you sit on the ground to put your shoes on, you're going to have some circular motion pattern left behind."

"Still doesn't prove he didn't kill himself," the chief said. "What else have you got?"

"Ego."

"So?"

"If he could answer, he'd tell you exactly how big."

Chief Cruz squatted to study the dirt more closely. His dark gaze traveled over the body and lingered on the tiara tangled in the wig, glittering in the sunlight.

Grace knew if she wanted to come to work the next day, she couldn't mention the feeling she'd gotten earlier. Instead, she tried a more concrete tact. "Boss, this is an unattended death with more than a few oddities about it. To be cautious, I recorded the scene and asked Deets to cast the shoe and tire prints. We looked for evidence and found cigarette ashes, a piece of something that looks like chocolate candy, and another piece of something that I haven't figured out yet."

"Evidence," Chief Cruz muttered.

"Just in case."

He straightened, piercing her with a look that warned her not to mess with him. "For now, this remains a death of indeterminate cause. I don't want you accusing anyone of murder…or making people afraid they're next on some killer's hit list."

Anger boiled up inside her. "I didn't just get out of the police academy, boss. I do know how to conduct an investigation."

"And I've read your personnel file, Sergeant Gabbiano,

so I have some reservations about that."

Grace's face reddened. She had lots of practice holding up under fire, but it was inexcusable for the new chief to disparage her in front of her co-worker and the call-car team who had come to retrieve the body. How many times did she have to go down this road?

Only the slightest touch of Deets's finger against her back kept her quiet. Chief or no chief, she sent Aidan Cruz a look that plainly said, *Drop dead!*

"And for the record," the chief went on, his brown gaze boring through her, ignoring her silent instructions to stop breathing, "there is *no* investigation unless the ME finds something tomorrow at the autopsy. Got it?"

Grace didn't trust herself to speak civilly so she nodded.

"Thanks to Officer Frey, the goddamned media is probably eating flesh up at the road block right about now." He looked southward, then back at her. "I'll handle the press on this case, understand? You say one word to a reporter and your ass will be standing in the unemployment line, again."

More humiliation flooded her cheeks. Despite his authoritative challenge, she opted not to retort that the *P&PM*—which Tina apparently hadn't forced him to read yet—mandated that he already *was* the only person authorized to talk to the media. Unless he officially appointed a designee, which seemed about as likely as Yeager Clausen getting up and walking away from the mint field under his own steam.

"You don't have to worry about me talking to the press." Except for her sister, a reporter for *The Oregonian* in Portland, Grace made a point of steering about a million miles clear of the media.

Chief Cruz studied her for several heartbeats and must have been satisfied that he'd made his point. He turned to Deets. "Mallory, tell Trina—"

"Tina," Deets corrected helpfully.

"Never mind," the chief bit out. "I'll tell her myself." He shook his head in disgust. "Unfuckingbelievable. Not even one day on the job and I have to talk to the goddamned press."

Grace got her first hint that maybe the chief liked the media even less than she did. The notion cheered her. She managed to smother her grin by biting her lower lip.

He motioned for the call-car driver and his assistant to approach with the gurney. "I'm going to schedule the damn news conference for nine o'clock tomorrow morning. You," he went on, his eyes and an index finger pointed at Grace, "will have been at the autopsy for an hour by then."

Grace's amusement evaporated. She gulped, hoping the chief wouldn't notice. "Yes, boss."

Was that her voice sounding so tiny, so shaky? *I can do it. I have seen blood-and-guts before, even if they weren't being excised from a lifeless body.*

"Want me to go with you to Ellie Clausen's?" Deets offered to Grace as the chief turned away.

The chief swung around, scowling. "Mallory, you take charge of getting the *evidence* checked in and locked up. I'll go with Gabbiano to the Clausen's after she gets back from the morgue." He aimed his displeasure at Grace. "Pick me up at the office as soon as you're through there."

"Yes, bo—"

"Stop calling me boss." His dark eyebrows dipped ominously. "It's either Chief or Aidan. Got it?"

"Yes…Chief."

Apparently satisfied that he'd delivered his orders effectively, Chief Cruz's long strides took him back to his vehicle. He climbed into a cherry-red Toyota Tundra, a color completely at odds with his dour mood but totally indicative of his fiery temperament. In a matter of seconds, he was nothing more than a confusing memory.

One moment, Grace was thinking, *Thank God I don't have to tell Ellie Clausen alone*, and in the next, she perversely resented how Aidan Cruz had taken over and told her to do exactly what she had planned to do anyway.

Grace asked Deets to bag-and-tag the wig and the tiara since she'd already removed her gloves. The two of them stood back while Clausen's body was wrapped in a clean white sheet and put into a plastic body bag.

The sound of the zipper closing seemed even louder than the swarm of obnoxious crows still circling the field.

"All you have to do now is get the DRT checked in at the morgue," Deets said.

Grace swallowed, hard. "Yeah. Checked in." Then less than twenty-four hours to psych herself up to go back for the autopsy.

"Chief Cruz is definitely not Chief McCrea," Deets commented as the two morgue attendants rolled the gurney to the call car.

A picture of the kindly retired chief flashed into her mind. A big man, equal to Aidan Cruz in height, but greater in girth and flabby where the new chief was solid muscle, McCrea was a jovial sort who almost always had a friendly twinkle in his eye. Aidan Cruz didn't look like he ever laughed, let alone twinkled, but there was something compelling about him.

Office gossip had him king of detectives in the Portland Police Bureau. His ex had re-married and custody of his preteen son had, for some reason, reverted to him. Unwilling to raise the boy in a large metropolitan area with a crime rate to match, he had landed in Coburg.

If the rumors were true, the dad could be a pain in the ass and his acorn hadn't fallen far from the tree.

CHAPTER 5

GRACE FOLLOWED THE call-car and got the body of Yeager Clausen checked into the morgue, or Surgery 10, as it was known in the law enforcement community. No one knew why.

Afterward, she picked up the chief and made the drive to Clausen's home with only the crackle of a radio call about a fender-bender on Willamette Street to break their strained silence.

Grace wondered if the chief had taken a curt tone with the media when advising them he had no comment until the news conference the next morning at nine a.m. sharp. Pity the reporter who showed up one minute late and expected a single syllable repeated.

At least Chief Aidan Cruz hadn't rounded out his tough-guy image by insisting he drive. One chauvinist on the force was enough, thank you, and Jimmy Frey already drew that paycheck.

"Nice digs," the chief commented as Grace eased through the open, ornate wrought iron gate and proceeded up a curved drive lined on both sides with flame ash, a lush carpet of grass, and hundreds of brilliantly colorful flowers.

She'd always found the faux-mansion ostentatious, but the grounds were a little slice of paradise. "Ellie's parents hate the rainy winters here. They moved to Palm Desert about five years ago and Ellie got the house."

"They must have some money."

"Her father, Patrick McCormick, broke into the RV business in its infancy. He made a bundle, sold the business, and retired before the market tanked. Between her family and her husband, they do okay."

"And you know all this how?"

"My Uncle Sal and Patrick McCormick are best friends."

"How did McCormick get along with his son-in-law?"

"According to Uncle Sal, Paddy 'tolerated' him."

"Specifics?"

"Without talking to Uncle Sal, I wouldn't want to say."

The chief knocked his knuckles against the door panel. "Your uncle lives here?"

"My entire family lives here, with the exception of my younger sister, who lives in Portland, and my older sister."

"Who lives where?"

Grace hesitated, silenced for a moment by the brief stab of sadness piercing her heart. "I don't know." She shut off the engine and reached for the hand-held radio. Had she really blabbed information to her new boss that she hadn't shared with most of the people who knew her well? And why was he even interested? "Dispatch, we're at the Clausen residence."

"Gotcha," dispatch replied.

Grace slid a sideways glance at the chief. His predecessor hadn't been big on formalities like Code 6 for "we're at" or 10-4 for "gotcha," but she wasn't sure how Aidan Cruz would take such relaxed radio communication.

He returned her inquiring gaze with a slightly raised left eyebrow, a trick she'd tried unsuccessfully to master herself over the years because it seemed to project authority. Already, she recognized that in Aidan Cruz, it meant *Don't try me.*

Grace shrugged and released her safety belt. "We're a small department. People are casual. It took me all week to come around myself." She thought she saw the corner of his mouth lift as he moved to unclasp his own seatbelt.

"So you'll ask him?"

"Him?"

"Uncle Sal."

"Oh. Yeah."

The chief climbed out of the vehicle. She followed an instant later, confused.

She closed the door of the patrol car and asked over the hood, "If I'm not investigating, why do you want me to talk to Uncle Sal?"

Chief Cruz took off his ball cap and massaged his scalp with long fingers. His hair settled into thick dark waves, despite the hat-band indentation. "I'm running on zip for sleep, then to be hit with a DRT first thing this morning…I'm impatient and out-of-sorts and it has nothing to do with you."

Was that a half-assed apology? Grace read between the lines and translated: Personal problem. "Okay, but—"

"Just leave it at that, Gabbiano. Give me a quick, *brief* rundown on the family."

God, another freaking hotshot paradox with issues. He could have asked his damned questions on the drive over instead of in the driveway. She glanced toward the double-entry doors. Through the obscure, full-glass panels, she made out the shape of a person. "Ellie and Yeager have been married for" —she thought a moment— "twenty years. He came from a poor farming family and earned a full scholarship to the University of Colorado. After college he came home, dated Ellie for the last three months of her senior year, and married her two weeks after graduation. He was on his way to being a real estate tycoon after only a year."

She waited for a question, but it never came. "They have two daughters. Caitlin is off to college next month and Lindsey is the family brainiac. She skipped third grade, and the middle school recommended she skip ninth, but maturity issues cropped up, so her folks said no."

"And Mrs. Clausen, does she work?"

"Not unless you count her volunteerism."

Chief Cruz slapped his hand against the top of the patrol car and said, "Okay, let's get it done. I'm going to let you take the lead, but if I think you're screwing up, I'll intervene. Are we clear?"

Grace nodded. She followed him up the walk, casting

about for a spot to latch her gaze that was not on his butt. Horrified that she'd even noticed it, let alone admired it, she stepped past him and rang the doorbell.

The door opened immediately. With cheeks slightly flushed, and her lips bracketed by little stress lines, Yeager Clausen's wife was petite and still gorgeous, dressed and groomed as if she'd just stepped out of an ad for Nordstrom's.

"Hello, Ellie," Grace said.

"I heard you were back in town, Grace. It's good to see you again."

"Thanks. You, too."

Ellie stepped back. "Come in, please."

Always polite, always gracious—at least as an adult. Grace, ten years younger than the fledgling widow, still remembered the hellion Eleanor McCormick had been, how she'd teased and tormented Grace for her tomboy ways at Uncle Sal's family gatherings. "Ellie, this is our new police chief, Aidan Cruz."

Ellie extended a limp hand to him. "I've heard good things about you, Aidan."

Grace almost laughed when the widow batted her eyelashes at him—talk about flirty brown-nosing!—then she noticed the bruises on Ellie's knuckles.

"Thank you," the chief said.

Grace zeroed in on the Ellie's briefly pinched lips. She might have a slack handshake, but the chief's was strong and firm. Her bruised knuckles were obviously fresh and still painful. Grace jumped to the conclusion that little Ellie Clausen had popped her dead husband a good one.

Despite her ebbing compassion, Grace managed to keep her voice gentle. "I'm afraid I have bad news, Ellie."

Ellie clenched her jaw. "You're here about Yeager." She closed the door and led them into the living room.

"Yes." After being raised by an Italian mother hen, Grace found herself more than a little surprised that Ellie hadn't automatically assumed the worst when two Coburg police officers showed up on her doorstep—that one of her daughters had been injured or killed.

“Can I get you something to drink? Coffee maybe?”

Miss Manners. Some things never changed. “No, thanks.”

“Something stronger?” Ellie suggested to the chief.

“No, I’m fine, thanks.”

“Please, sit down.”

Contemporary seating mingled with an eclectic assortment of antiques that included a pre-Civil War barrel desk, a Duncan Phyfe side table, and a William and Mary highboy. Grace had learned to recognize early quality furniture while working part-time during summer vacations at Rose o’ Sharon Antiques, where Ellie Clausen had spent a lot of money.

The low-slung upholstered pieces had probably been expensive, too, but they looked rock-hard. Grace wasn’t sure where to sit and the chief didn’t seem to be faring any better. All three remained standing.

“He’s dead,” Ellie said.

Grace narrowed her eyes. Had Ellie sounded relieved? “Either you’re psychic or you already knew.” She deliberately avoided eye contact with the chief. Men were such suckers for the poor little Ellies of the world.

For an instant, the widow looked startled, then she laughed. “Still the snotty little brat, aren’t you?”

Grace shrugged, unoffended by Ellie’s teasing. “If I have to be.”

“I knew because someone called….”

“Someone from CPD?” the chief asked.

Grace could almost hear him grind his teeth. God help the unlucky blabbermouth if he or she wore a CPD uniform.

Ellie’s expression became guarded and her eyelids flickered. The casual observer might have read it as confusion, but Grace immediately pegged it as evasion. “It was, um, a…friend. He, that is, my friend didn’t want me to hear horrible news like that from someone I didn’t know.” She dabbed at a solitary tear, a motion made all the more dramatic because of the dainty lace handkerchief that had appeared out of nowhere. “Apparently my friend is not aware that Grace and I are acquainted.”

“Apparently.” With the gender of the big-mouth idiot identified, Grace now had a good idea of who the *he* was.

She briefly considered pursuing the matter using the good cop/bad cop routine.

Even as she had the thought, the good cop said, “Move on, Sergeant.”

Grace nodded her acknowledgment, trying to keep her irritation from showing.

“My friend said Yeager was dressed in some kind of red dress,” Ellie said, then sank into a chair that had the shape and color of an unripened peach.

Ellie’s source had been helpful, but not close enough to get any details.

Grace envisioned wringing his neck with her bare hands.

CHAPTER 6

“I DISCOVERED YEAGER’S body on my morning run,” Grace said. “He’s been taken to the morgue at RiverBend for autopsy.”

“*Autopsy?*”

It was a gruesome procedure and not one relatives wanted to think about in connection with a loved one. “It’s the law, Ellie” Grace said, her tone gentled. “For all unattended deaths, especially someone of Yeager’s age.”

Ellie shuddered. Finally, some real emotion, but still she didn’t ask how her husband had died. Either she already knew, or she didn’t give a damn.

Grace shifted, just enough to assure she had Ellie’s attention. “Can you think of any reason Yeager might have wanted to kill himself, possibly with drugs?”

“Suicide? Yeager?” The widow began to laugh. “Yeager hasn’t done drugs since college. An occasional drink, yes, but drugs? My husband was far too much in love with his body to drug it to death.”

“He was wearing a red evening gown. Beads and silk, a halter top over a full, floor-length skirt. Is that the kind of ‘in love with his body’ you’re talking about?”

Ellie’s mouth dropped open, then she laughed again. “He wasn’t a cross-dresser, if that’s what you’re asking. What makes you think it was suicide, anyway?”

“There was a note.”

"A note? That would be especially uncharacteristic of him. My husband never told anyone what he was doing. Why would he document his death for posterity?"

"I can't answer that."

Ellie blinked at her.

From her pocket, Grace withdrew the photocopy she'd made of what appeared to be Yeager Clausen's last communication with the world. Ellie stared at the piece of paper, but made no effort to take it.

"Who would the 'them' be?" Grace asked.

Ellie looked up, an apparent frown of bewilderment on her face. "His parents have been dead for years and he's never had anyone else close to him die. This doesn't make any sense. That doesn't even look like his handwriting."

Grace frowned. "Are you sure?"

"Absolutely."

"So you don't think he was grieving for someone he wanted to join in the afterlife?"

"Don't be so dramatic, Grace. Why the hell would he kill himself? As far as my husband was concerned, *he* was the only reason for living."

Grace tucked the photocopy away, wondering if the chief had noted that the widow seemed to be corroborating the murder theory.

"Didn't you notice that Yeager never came home last night?"

"No."

"How could you *not*?"

Yeager's widow remained stubbornly silent. Grace waited her out. Five, ten, fifteen seconds.

Ellie jumped up and began to pace, agitated. Finally, she whirled on Grace. "We don't share a bedroom, okay? Satisfied?"

Well, that was a helluva way to have a marriage. "And you don't know where he was?"

"No, nor did I care."

Grace had a moment of shocked silence.

"Don't you want to know why?"

"No, but under the circumstances, I have to ask."

"We've been married in name only for most of the last three years. He had his life, I had mine. He took care of me and the girls financially, and I accompanied him to social functions for appearance's sake. Aside from that" —she shrugged— "we may as well have not known each other."

Grace glanced at the chief, who had his eyes narrowed slightly in Ellie's direction. "When you say Yeager had his own life, does that mean you didn't have sexual relations?"

Ellie snapped, "I just told you the extent of our relationship, Grace. Do you need me to outline it on a whiteboard?"

Silent for another moment, Grace decided to dive in all the way. "So, him being dressed in an evening gown was an indicator of the *other* life he had?"

Ellie approached, her frustration clear. "I just want to take you by the shoulders and shake you, Grace Gabbiano! Yeager was a sex maniac, but not for men. He probably screwed every female in this town, hell, in this county, at one time or another, except for you and your relatives." She took a deep, shaky breath. "Not that he didn't want to."

The admission sent a chill up Grace's spine. The thought of Clausen…well, it almost made her physically ill. Cautious as she moved on to other dark, uncharted waters, she asked, "What about…the girls?"

Ellie threw up her hands. "Jesus Christ, Grace, are you nuts?"

Even though she was a police officer charged with asking difficult questions, Grace nonetheless felt her face grow warm at Ellie's chastisement.

The chief crossed his arms over his chest. "Officer Gabbiano has to ask questions, Mrs. Clausen. It's part of the process to determine how your husband died, and why."

Envisioning shark fins all around, Grace rephrased her question. "Did your husband abuse your daughters, in any way?"

Ellie settled on the sofa, her narrow shoulders hunched. "Wouldn't it be wonderful if we had Indian Summer this year? Even if we don't, he can't ignore his children anymore."

Grace hated it when people answered with a nonsequitur,

but because Ellie's evasion churned her stomach with horrific possibilities, she let the question drop for the moment. She eased down next to Ellie on the sofa. "Does the dress I described sound familiar to you?"

Ellie heaved a loud sigh. "Honestly, Grace, even if I owned a dress like that, Yeager wouldn't have fit into it."

"No, he wouldn't, but then he didn't fit into this one, either." Grace glanced at the toe of her boot. A wilted sprig of mint was caught beneath the bottom lace. She looked up at Ellie. "So, was Yeager bisexual?"

Ellie pounded the sofa cushion with her fists. "Oh, for the love of God, he was a flaming homophobe! How many ways can I say this, Grace? Yeager was a male slut. He fucked anything that had a pussy!"

Shocked to hear that kind of language come out of Ellie's mouth—especially since Ellie's mother was a gracious woman who had raised her daughter not to cuss—Grace invited more sharks to circle her. "Except you."

Color rose high in Ellie's cheeks. "Yes, except me. Not that he didn't try, but do you think I'd risk getting some disease from him, just to keep him happy when one of his women wasn't available? My God, I've got two daughters to raise!"

Grace pulled out her notebook. Ellie obviously had some issues with her dead husband. Time to get down to business. And she didn't want a negative critique from the chief later just because he remained a silent observer.

"Where were you last night, Ellie?" Out of the corner of her eye, she noticed him take a seat on a low-lying loveseat that creaked under his weight and left his knees at an uncomfortable-looking angle.

The widow's spine straightened and her eyelids did that funny little fluttery thing again. "I met a friend for dinner, and then we took in a movie."

Some people just couldn't lie worth a damn and that spastic eyelid gave Ellie away every time. She'd been doing it quite a bit since opening the door, but Grace had seen it plenty of other times over the years. "The friend's name?"

Ellie jumped up from the sofa. "Marie Brewer. I don't

like the direction you're taking," she said, her tone suddenly haughty and angry as she glared at Grace.

Grace didn't miss the warning, either. With all sincerity, she said, "I'm sorry, but we already told you, questions have to be asked."

"Must you ask them right now?"

"The sooner, the better, the less likely you'll forget something important that you've seen or heard."

"Well, I don't appreciate it."

"You've made that perfectly clear. I'll need the name of the restaurant and the movie."

Ellie's glare intensified.

"Do you still have your ticket stub?"

"No." The widow stalked to the window.

Grace followed, anxious for another look at the dark smudges on her hand. Ellie had never been her favorite person, but she didn't like to see a woman black-and-blue, either. "How did you bruise your knuckles?"

Ellie's hand automatically went into the pocket of her linen shorts.

"Did you hit him?" Grace persisted, thinking it would be too easy if the other woman simply admitted it. After several moments of silence, Ellie surprised her by doing just that, then obliterated her moment of truth by closing in on the chief. Was she hoping for a me-helpless-woman, you-he-man-ally as she put a hand on his forearm?

"He got really angry and shoved me." Ellie leaned forward, pulling her honey-blonde hair aside with her free hand. "I hit my head against the cupboard. See, it left a huge egg."

Grace stepped over to see the injury for herself. She didn't blame Ellie for striking back, but it was obvious that something smaller than a hummingbird had laid this particular "egg."

Except for his flexing jaw, Chief Cruz's expression was inscrutable as he met her gaze and held it. It took a moment for Grace to figure out why. Ellie's blouse gaped where the top button had been left undone. The sly widow was offering the chief a free peep show of her impressive boob job. Poor guy didn't know quite where to land those pretty brown orbs of his.

Red flags began flapping in Ellie's hot air. Grace added another hash mark to the ones she had already placed beside Ellie's name on her mental list of suspects, more certain than ever that Yeager hadn't killed himself. "What were you arguing about?"

Her hand still on the chief's arm, Ellie asked, "Who said we were arguing?"

"He just happened to shove you for the hell of it? He was unprovoked?"

Ellie straightened, her eyes glittering as she reclaimed her hand. "Okay, we argued, but why we argued is none of your goddamned business, Grace."

In a surprise move (or not), Ellie crumpled onto the loveseat next to the chief. Practically on top of him. One hand clutched the dainty kerchief she pressed against her cheek, presumably to catch another stray tear, the other had somehow managed to attach itself to the upper part of the chief's thigh, very near his....

What a drama queen. And a bold one at that.

The chief jumped up as if he'd been launched from a jack-in-the-box, dislodging Ellie's hand in the process. It would have been comical if he hadn't said in that *tone* of his, "I think you can save the rest of your questions for later, Sergeant."

Grace's jaw dropped. Talk about an inopportune moment to take over the interrogation.

"I do think it would be best if you leave now," Ellie said. Miss Melodrama then reached up, grasped the chief's forearm again, and squeezed. "Thank you, Aidan."

The chief nodded, clearing his throat.

"Do you know what killed him?" Ellie asked of Grace.

Not who or how, but what. "His body had indications of a drug overdose."

"What do you mean?"

"Sergeant...."

Grace ignored both the chief and his warning tone. Ellie looked delicate, but she could squash bugs with the best of them. Hadn't he figured that out yet? "There was a bloody froth at his mouth."

Ellie looked skeptical. "That doesn't seem like enough to go on."

Grace shrugged. "In my experience, it is."

"I'm telling you again, no one loved him more than he loved himself. He had a physical exam two weeks ago, and in spite of a slightly elevated cholesterol, he was in perfect physical condition." Ellie fussed with the open button of her blouse, sneaking a peek at the chief to see if he she had his attention, no doubt. To his credit, the chief's eyes were directed over the widow's head.

Grace was starting to feel sorry for her new boss, but if the widow wanted to keep talking, who was she to stop her?

Ellie went on. "He exercised every day in a workout room right here at the house. He also ran, good weather or bad. The only drug he ever took was aspirin and the only reason he took that was to prevent a heart attack."

If you haven't shared a bedroom with your husband for three years, how do you know all those details? "Was he having financial problems?"

Ellie laughed. "Money flows freely in this household."

Of course, Ellie had a huge trust fund, so finances wouldn't be an issue for her under any circumstances.

"I'd like to verify that."

"Feel free. John Peck is his accountant, and his wife, Lila, manages Yeager's office. They're on their annual one-month summer vacation, but I believe they'll be back sometime next week."

Grace scribbled down the names. "And he didn't drink?"

"Rarely."

"Did he smoke?"

"No."

Grace shot a defiant glance at the chief. "One last question. Can you think of anyone in particular who hated Yeager enough to kill him?"

Ellie laughed, and her eyelids didn't flicker once. "You're joking, right?"

"A yes-or-no answer will suffice."

"Half the town hated my husband, Grace. Surely you haven't been gone *that* long."

No, she hadn't.

"Can you meet Sergeant Gabbiano at the morgue for an official ID?" Chief Cruz asked in parting.

"Do I have to?"

"Next of kin—"

"Oh, all right," Ellie cut him off, looking at her watch, "but I'll have to do it now. I want to pick up the girls and tell them before they hear the news elsewhere."

Taking a deep breath, Ellie said to Grace, "When will you know if my husband killed himself, or if someone else did it for him?"

I already know. Grace refrained from saying the words out loud in front of the chief, who even now, seemed to be staring daggers straight through her. "Soon."

CHAPTER 7

GRACE WASN'T HAPPY with her new boss. He'd insisted on accompanying her for the family death notification and knew questions would have to be asked. Yeah, okay, he'd basically said he'd just be along for the ride—read that, *I've got my eye on you, Gabbiano, and I'll be watching to see if you screw up*—but had any of the words coming out of his mouth been helpful?

Beside her in the patrol car as they drove back to the station, he seemed oblivious to Grace's ill temper. If only a lowly sergeant could say, *If you ever undermine me again, I'm going to kick you in the nuts,* to your chief and get away with it!

He was quiet until she put the vehicle into park so he could climb out. "You have a nice way with widows, Gabbiano," he said. "How are you with kids and old ladies?"

"I—"

"Meet her at the morgue for the formal body ID and don't harangue her anymore today."

Grace couldn't read his expression, shadowed as it was beneath the bill of his cap, nor did he allow her time to respond before he shut the door.

Really? The chief had let a pretty face distract him from the fact that, statistically, Ellie Clausen, wife of the victim, may have been his killer?

Glaring at his backside, she retorted, "At least I know when they're lying!" For a moment, his step faltered.

Oh, shit!

Disgusted, but belatedly thankful he hadn't heard her having to have the last word through the closed window, she made a U-turn in the parking lot and headed back to the RiverBend Hospital complex in Springfield.

An hour later, Grace finally managed to get to her brother's place. The former chief had established a contract with Rocco years before for photo developing and enlargements. The agreement saved staff from driving into Eugene and gave Rocco, who charged half what the photo shops did, an excuse to spend time in his darkroom.

Grace found her brother out front. He waved and shut off the mower. "I thought you were on bike patrol today."

She handed over three, thirty-six exposure film canisters. "When I went out for my run this morning, I found Yeager Clausen, deader'n a doornail in Abner's south mint field."

Rocco whistled. "No shit? Someone finally killed him?"

Grace sank down onto the lush green carpet of grass. She looked up at her older brother from beneath the bill of her CPD cap and smirked. "I might be the only one who thinks so."

Always ready to play Watson to Grace's Sherlock, Rocco flopped down beside her. "Oh, yeah?"

"Looks like an OD, probably heroin, but he had a goodbye note with him."

"That usually indicates a suicide."

As chief of the Coburg Rural Fire Department, Rocco should know and Grace didn't disagree. Usually. "Yeager wouldn't dress up in a woman's evening gown then go kill himself in Abner's field."

Rocco tossed one of the film canisters into the air and caught it, whistling in amazement. He eyeballed the roll and said, "Yeager Clausen outfitted in girl duds? This'll be some interesting film." He grinned. "You know, when I went down to the bank yesterday, Abner and Clausen were having words out front."

Grace stared at her brother. "Yeah? What kind of words?"

"Abner chewed his ass about buying farmers out for agricultural values, then rezoning the land for residential or commercial use." He stretched out, propping his head in one hand. "Old Abner promised to stop 'Mr. Land Developer' any way he could—even over Clausen's dead body."

"You're kidding! Abner said that?" Grace tried to picture the tall, almost gaunt farmer issuing threats to anyone. The image wouldn't gel. The Abner she'd known since childhood was a pacifist. Everyone in town knew it, including the creeps who'd vandalized his barn by painting COWARD on it during the Viet Nam war. Some of the letters were still visible.

"Knowing Abner, I'm sure he didn't mean he was actually going to kill that jerk, but you know his great-grandpappy helped settle this town. Every time he boasts about that, he lets you know he opposes what he considers to be Clausen's wanton destruction of our small-town ambiance. Abner's never made any bones about his opposition to Coburg being turned into an escape hatch for rich city folks who urbanize and destroy farm land in their quest for solitude." Rocco shrugged. "He even went down to the County Commissioners' offices to protest the new sewer. Hell, he walked around City Hall for weeks with a sign on a stick. His said, 'Grass grows greener over septic tanks.'" Rocco laughed. "He almost got himself arrested protesting the power plant."

Grace gave her brother a wide-eyed look. "Wow, when did Coburg become such a political hot bed?"

Rocco biffed her on the leg. "You make fun, but the old-timers and a lot of newbies don't want progress to visit Coburg—we're here, now close the gates. Look at how they were about getting downtown sidewalks and curb-and-gutter. And it's only been a few years since all those recall elections took place. Abner's pretty pissed that Clausen takes advantage of long-time residents who've fallen on hard times."

"That would piss anyone off, but Abner of all people should know that this is Yeager's vendetta against his own father—all the local farmers just happen to be in the way."

"Yeah, well, try not taking that personally when your

farm's been in the family for generations and some disgruntled shithead tries to close you down because he hated his own father."

"You think Abner is in arrears on his mortgage?"

"I doubt he has one, unless it's a second, but maybe he is on property taxes. We had a helluva year with all that flooding. He lost some crops and his barn needs to be rebuilt." Rocco shook his head. "The thing is, I can't imagine ole Abner knows how to get hold of drugs, let alone use them to commit a crime."

"Stranger things have happened." Grace pushed herself up.

"Ain't that the truth?"

"How about a six-pack of your favorite brewsky in exchange for a rush on this film?"

"Hey, I'm a public servant. I can't take bribes or gratuities."

Grace snorted. "In your own personal darkroom, on your on time? Right."

"Drop Top or Sierra Nevada." He grinned. "Or both. I hope you don't mean *rush*, like today."

"If this turns out to be a murder investigation, *rush*, like tomorrow or the next day, doesn't cut it, does it?"

"Always the smart ass," Rocco shot back, climbing to his feet.

"Not like you weren't an excellent role model."

"I don't mind telling you I had a dozen other projects going on today. If CPD would budget for some digital cameras, I could get some work done around here."

"We have one and I'll look at the jpgs as soon as I get back to my computer."

"What the hell?"

"I took both thirty-five mil film and digi—if this turns out to be a homicide, I want to have substantial documentation. You know digitals aren't welcomed in court one hundred percent yet."

"What did your new chief have to say about the double effort?"

She shrugged. "I haven't told him yet. The mood he's in

right now, with Clausen's death on his first watch, he'd probably shove the thirty-five mil down my throat."

"I'd be ticked, too, first day on the job."

"Hey! I've only been on the job a week myself, so he gets no damned sympathy from me!"

"Give the poor bastard a break, Gracie. I'll have negs for you by dinnertime, but don't expect any prints while the sun's still shining."

"I wouldn't think of it. How's the pond coming?" Grace couldn't remember a minute since he'd built his house that Rocco wasn't doing something else to it or the yard.

"Come see."

The week before, Grace had volunteered to help build up the banks. "Nice!" Since Thursday, he'd transformed several mounds of dirt and a variety of large rocks into a plant-and-water oasis. "This is great, Roc, and you've got fish! If you ever get tired of fighting fires, you can be a pond builder."

Her brother glanced ruefully at the blisters healing on his palms. "One pond per lifetime is enough, and a raccoon already got one of my koi."

"File a complaint and I'll arrest the little bastard."

"As I said, always the smart ass."

"Well, at least I don't bug you about getting married and giving me some nieces and nephews."

"Thank God for small favors. You'd think with three grandkids living underfoot now, Mom would be satisfied."

Grace laughed. "Maybe when she has three from each of us, she will be."

"At least she's eased up some since Delfina's kids are here." Rocco scowled. "Where the hell is she, anyway?"

"I wish I knew, but to tell you the truth, I'm glad Mom and Pop are taking care of those kids instead of Delfina and that loser she married. If Child Protective Services had intervened, things wouldn't be so good right now."

"Maybe, but on the other hand, Mom and Pop already raised their family—why should they have to raise a second one?"

"They didn't plan to have it this way."

Rocco blew out a frustrated breath. "I know."

"Delfina and Bobby dropping those kids off for an afternoon and never coming back for them was a new low, even for two drug heads."

"Yeah, well, if Delfina ever shows her face in front of me again, I'm calling you to arrest her for child abandonment and you'd better not say no."

"She needs help."

"She needs to grow up, divorce that jerk she's married to, and get herself some drug rehab—and not necessarily in that order. I worry about Madison every day—I'm sure Del did meth while she was carrying that kid."

Grace insides knotted up. Overcome with emotion thinking about her adorable three-year-old niece, she said, "I haven't seen any of the behavioral problems that you usually find in meth babies." She couldn't control the waver of her voice, or stop the sudden burning in her eyes, as she almost choked over those words, *meth babies*.

"The bad behaviors don't usually present until around five years, and Maddy is only three," Rocco said.

Grace wiped furiously at her eyes. "I pray to God Del didn't start using that crap until after Maddy was born. I just can't believe she's abandoned her children for drugs."

"Yeah, and what the hell is she doing to *get* those drugs."

Grace couldn't contain a shudder. Neither Delfina nor Bobby could hold down a job, so one or both of them had to be doing something illegal, and probably immoral, to get their fixes. Bobby was a lazy SOB and Delfina was a black-haired, green-eyed siren, which meant most men got an instant hard-on just looking at her. Bobby probably had her sleeping with a bunch of loser horny toads so they'd have money to buy their junk.

"Thanks a lot for cheering me up." Grace hugged her brother goodbye and climbed back into her patrol car.

Rocco squeezed her shoulder with affection. "Sorry, kid."

"Me, too. I just hope that someday Delfina…." Grace shrugged. "Thanks for the info on Abner."

"Tell your elf to bring a bag of chips with the six-packs."

"You drive a hard bargain."

Her brother grinned. "That, little sister, is something

you're the role model for!"

Ten minutes later, Grace sat down at her desk to review her notes. The phone rang nonstop, each time about the "mint-field corpse." Over and over again, Tina responded that a news conference would be held at nine a.m. the following morning. The chief would give the particulars.

Grace moved over to one of the three shared computers. How wonderful that the chief would even *know* the particulars by then. Still nursing a peeve from his earlier behavior, she almost wished he'd screw up at the press conference, but unfortunately, that would make her and the department look bad, too.

With the irony of that lingering in her mind, she put her password into the computer and turned her attention to the database program Chief McCrea had installed as his one big push into the electronic age. Less than an hour later, she was ready to pay a visit to Abner Nelson. Looking at the digital shots of the death scene would have to wait until later.

On her way out the door, she popped her head into the chief's office. Having already planned a means to thwart his no-investigation directive, she said, "I understand Abner Nelson had words with Clausen yesterday. I'm going to pop over there and see if he noticed anything odd about Yeager's behavior. After that, I'm going to grab some of the samples I collected, and head over to my lab to look at them."

With a distracted, "Okay," Chief Cruz never looked up from the file folder in front of him.

Grace hesitated, wondering if she should say something more about the lab. The agreement that she could do some forensic investigation, after all, had been between her and Chief McCrea. She opened her mouth, but a tornado-dark cloud seemed to descend over the chief's head—his features wrinkled into a scowl and she decided to leave well enough alone.

For all she knew, Chief McCrea had passed that information along to Chief Cruz.

For all she knew, it was her file in front of Chief Cruz, causing the thunder cloud.

CHAPTER 8

ON THE WAY to the Nelson farm, Grace realized she was hungry. The only fast food restaurant was clear over on the Interstate, but the market on Willamette Street offered fried-chicken-by-the-piece to keep starvation at bay. Munching a drumstick and sipping a Diet Coke, she took fifteen minutes to eat and rejuvenate.

Grace found Abner in the front porch swing of his farmhouse. The barest movement of his bony knee beneath worn coveralls explained his lazy back-and-forth motion. She couldn't remember ever seeing him wear anything but Carhartts. At his feet lay a big yellow dog, napping in the afternoon heat, undisturbed despite the presence of another person on his turf. "'Afternoon, Abner."

He nodded. "Good to see you, Grace. Heard you were back in town."

"It was time."

Never one to mince words, he said, "Dang shame that sister of yours is such a mess."

Grace had sat on that bony knee as a child, so she didn't resent in the least that Abner felt free to criticize her sister.

Years before, her grandfather had given up farming when it became apparent none of his children were going to carry on. Rather than sell the land, he'd leased most of it to adjacent farmers. Abner's father had taken the lion's share of the parcel. Farming it with his own, he'd made it pay. The legacy passed on to Abner, so in addition to being a tenant, he was also a family friend, which didn't make being at his doorstep any easier.

"I need to talk to you, Abner."

"Didn't think you came by just to sit in the swing, not with that uniform on." He stared at her, waiting.

His clear gray gaze was intelligent, though his eyes narrowed a bit with either suspicion or curiosity. Grace wasn't sure which. "I understand you had a verbal altercation with Yeager Clausen yesterday afternoon, in front of the bank."

The gentle motion of the swing came to a abrupt halt. "Verbal altercation, my ass! If you mean I called that no-good sonofabitch exactly what he is, then you're right."

If Grace knew one thing about Abner Nelson, it was that he was an upstanding man. Honorable, reliable, hard-working. But did that mean he couldn't commit murder? In Grace's experience, even angelic old ladies and ten-year-olds were capable of murder, under the right circumstances. "Tell me about it."

Abner pulled the ever-present pack of Marlboros out of his pocket and lit up without asking Grace if she minded. She stepped upwind to avoid having to inhale his smoke. "Not much to tell, Gracie. He's gobbling up the old-timers, one-by-one. Hattie Bingham got a letter from him on Friday, offering to bail her out of her 'financial constraints.' As if Hattie needs welfare from the likes of Yeager Clausen!"

He sucked in a long drag and blew out a huge plume of smoke, coughing. "Bastard tries to make it sound like he's doing this for purely altruistic reasons, when everyone in the Valley knows he's doing it to spite his dead father." He took another long drag. "God only knows how many more letters are out there that I haven't heard about yet. What the hell kind of man takes pleasure in other people's misery?"

Grace, remaining noncommittal, gathered that Abner had appointed himself savior of the Coburg flatlands. "You get one of those letters?"

The farmer's face reddened with rage. "He sends me one and that sonofabitch is history."

"So you don't owe any back mortgages or taxes?"

Abner pushed up off the swing and biffed his cigarette out onto some of the greenest grass in the Willamette Valley. The dog at his feet raised its head and gave a half-hearted *woof.* "I don't owe anybody anything, Miss Police Girl! I had a rough spring, but I pay my bills!"

Grace had never seen Abner so furious that his gaunt jaw appeared to be made of chiseled steel.

"Lots of folks in these parts were hurt real bad when the cannery went broke, Grace. Some of them had to sell out and a lot of others converted their crops to rye grass and mint. Some are even planting filbert trees, like there's not enough nuts growing up the McKenzie already! Me and my family managed to hold on to most of our other crops, but we converted to mint on about fifty acres."

He looked out over his land. "This is the best goddamned dirt in the United States, Grace. We got five feet of topsoil out there. It's pure black gold! Back before the cannery quit, we yielded as much as thirty tons of carrots an acre. That sure as hell is nothing to sneeze at."

"It sure as hell isn't," Grace agreed softly, wondering if this Abner, the insulted one spouting profanities, was capable of murder. His anger simmered so close to the surface, it didn't seem like it would take much to really set him off. Conscientious objector or not, she knew from her father and Uncle Sal that Abner Nelson had a temper. She'd just never seen it before.

"Since they put the sewer lines in, everybody and his damned brother from California wants to come up and buy a piece of the country life. Don't matter if land prices have sky-rocketed, Clausen wants to buy everybody out first, get the farmland rezoned as residential, then subdivide every goddamned inch of it for cracker-box houses with no room for a yard, or kids, or a dog!" His voice booming, he straightened his old bones, appearing to grow a couple of inches taller. "*He'll do it over my dead body!*"

The entire porch seemed to reverberate with his outburst. This time the big dog jumped up, barking in earnest. Abner quieted the animal with a one-word command, but the dog whined pathetically, indecisive about laying back down.

Abner yelled "Git!" then repeated it more loudly. The dog jumped off the porch and ran toward the barn.

Maybe, Grace thought, Abner did have something hidden deep within him, something dark. "Yeager Clausen died sometime late last night or early this morning, Abner. As you were heard to threaten his life in front of half the town yesterday afternoon, you've put me in the position of having to ask you straight out...did you kill him?"

Abner paled, his raw-boned features little more than a thin piece of skin over his skull. He sank back down onto the swing, almost missing the seat, even though he put his hands behind him to steady it as he landed. "Clausen's dead?" he asked, his voice a thready whisper.

She nodded. The old guy probably was not more than sixty-five, but he hadn't aged well. He looked a good ten years past that, and his reaction to her news seemed to add another decade, especially when he started to cough. He definitely did not look good, yet despite his momentary weakness, Grace knew he wouldn't welcome an offer of assistance from her.

"I didn't kill that sonofabitch, Gracie, but God strike me down for the thought, I'm glad if someone else did."

"He may have killed himself," Grace admitted reluctantly, feeling a little guilty for how her news had affected him.

He coughed again, a dry hacking sound that made Grace wonder why he continued to smoke. "That what they taught you up in Seattle, girl? How to bait a man with lies?" He pushed himself back up off the swing and went into the house. The screen door banged behind him as he left her standing there without a word.

Shamed, Grace walked over to the door, her hand raised to knock. Through the screen, she heard Abner's hacking cough and his wife's murmur of concern. She lowered her hand and turned and left the wooden porch.

Grace honestly didn't think Abner had it in him to kill Clausen, no matter how much he hated the land developer. She deserved her old friend's disgust, but she still had a job to do. That included adding Abner's name to a suspect list that, so far, held only one other: Ellie Clausen.

She bit her lip. Both of them had good reason to see Yeager dead, but why would either of them dress him up like a modern-day Cinderella? And then there was that other question rearing its ugly head: Where would either Abner or Ellie get the drugs and all the paraphernalia it took to cause the overdose? Or for that matter, the strength to coerce him into a woman's evening gown and then somehow force him out to the mint field?

Feeling like she'd made zero progress over the past several hours, Grace detoured to the still-burning cigarette in the grass. Using her thumb and index finger, she picked it up, careful not to touch the butt, or to burn her fingers. She held her breath as she rummaged in the trunk for a container. The only thing she could come up with was a bandage box in the first aid kit, so she dumped the Band-Aids out and put the still-burning cigarette inside, latching the lid to safely suffocate it.

In the unlikely event she might forget where and when she'd picked up one of Abner's discarded butts, she made a notation in her notebook and labeled the evidence bag that would hold the butt and ashes once they'd cooled.

The ashes found at the scene might have been there for a while, sheltered as they were under the mint, but even if they were Abner's, it still didn't prove anything. It was his mint field, after all.

Grace closed the trunk and climbed back into the patrol car. God, she was tired. She didn't even have time to wonder how the folks in Coburg proper were getting along without her cruising around on bike patrol. She took a moment to put her head back and close her eyes.

By the time she punched in the keypad code at the station house, everyone but Tina and patrol officer Mele Amaka had gone.

She found a note taped to her desk.

WHAT LAB?? I'll see you later about it. AC

With wisdom that comes from hindsight, Grace acknowledged, with or without the black cloud over his head, she should have gotten a verbal okay from Chief Cruz earlier about the lab.

If this turned out to be a murder, the budget would have to accommodate charges from the Oregon State Police Forensics Lab in Springfield. That might make the chief lean more favorably toward her doing some of the less complicated forensics in the lab adjoining her house.

Grace sighed, settling in front of the computer. If she'd been into ESP or aura-reading or something, she probably would've been zapped by the note's vibrations. Funny how two underlined words could tell you how pissed someone was. Again.

You're off to a great beginning with your new boss, Gracie.

Checking out evidence to take home to the lab might not be a smart move, but since she'd already informed the chief that's what she'd be doing…in for a penny and all that.

For the first time, she acknowledged that Harmon McCrea and Aidan Cruz were police chiefs not only of different eras, but quite possibly of different policy persuasions. Policies that didn't necessarily carry over from chief to chief. True, the lab wasn't all that elaborate or even technologically advanced by today's standards, but it had State of Oregon certification and for the types of examinations she and Chief McCrea had discussed, it would certainly suffice. And besides, as a private forensic consultant, her father still used it, so shouldn't that be good enough for Chief Cruz?

She frowned at the blinking cursor on the screen. In her mind, the lab problem was secondary to the chief telling her not to investigate anything until after the autopsy had been done. Grace huffed a breath of frustration. Lab or not, investigation or not, why had she been born so impatient? Not that it was her only failing, but as a fault, she considered it a biggie.

Even without promises of forensic investigation dancing in her head, she would have accepted the job at CPD. Big-city crime and peer backstabbing had taken a toll on her, and besides, her parents needed help with Delfina's children.

So far, she'd been too busy settling in and getting acquainted with her new job to assist much with the kids, though her parents continued to assure her they weren't overloaded or overwhelmed with being thrust back into the world of child care. Her cousin Gina, who was saving to buy a car, was helping out by babysitting over the summer, but once school started, schedules would change. Running little ones around from here to there was a lot different than sending them outside to play and Gina was an Honor student. With her International Baccalaureate studies, she might not have time to work in as many babysitting hours.

Grace glanced at Mele Amaka, who was logging off the Records system. She didn't want to risk the chief chewing anyone else's ass for signing out evidence to her. She'd assume sole responsibility for leaving the building with the ashes collected earlier, the possible melted candy, and the blob of something unknown, but she did let Tina and Mele know what she was doing. Better safe than sorry after a day like today, especially since evidence had been disappearing even before Grace came on board.

"What a day," Tina said. "I'm leaving."

"I'm headed over to the Interstate," Mele said. "Glad it wasn't me who stopped the chief this morning doing ninety."

Grace grinned. "The chief was *so* pissed."

Mele grinned back. "Dillon 'bout peed his pants when he saw it was Chief Cruz. The chief ripped him a new one later for letting him go."

"Ouch! Poor Charlie." Grace waved them off. "See you guys tomorrow."

First thing after the autopsy, she'd invite the chief over to see her lab. How could he refuse to utilize it after that, especially when she had one of the state's leading forensic experts living less than two hundred yards from her front door?

CHAPTER 9

CARRYING A SIX-PACK in each hand, Grace was surprised to find Chief Cruz sitting on her front porch when she arrived home.

"Chief," she said by way of greeting. "What are you doing here?" Surprised that he'd known where she lived and how to find the bungalow, and equally dismayed by her tactless question, she stood before him, leery of his answer.

"Nice to see you, too, Gabbiano," he said, his tone dry. He rose off the stoop, towering over her from where he stood. His eyes swept over the twelve bottles of beer. "Rough day?"

As if he didn't know! "Actually, it's a bribe to get my brother to put a rush on developing my film. Want one?" She took perverse satisfaction in letting him know she didn't plan to drown herself in hops and malt.

He shook his head. "I came to get a look at this lab of yours. McCrea apparently forgot to mention to me that he had okayed you doing some forensics work. I discovered it in your file after you went out to talk to Nelson."

So it *had* been her personnel file on his desk. "He put a clause about it in my hiring contract."

"Yes, that's where I found it."

Chief Cruz had said at the scene he'd already read her personnel file, so why was he re-reading it? Irked that he hadn't taken a minute to ask her about the lab earlier, in the office where such a conversation should take place, she frowned at him.

Exhausted, she craved a shower and cold beer before walking over to her parents' house for Sunday dinner. The last thing she wanted to do was argue with her boss on her own time. Blowing out a martyred sigh, she asked, "Would you like to see it now?"

He nodded.

"It's around back." She set the two six-packs on the porch.

He moved down the steps and followed her along the walkway. "I apologize for butting into your evening, but your comments about a lab didn't sink in until after you'd gone."

Grace faltered. In her experience, guys like him, at his level in the food chain, didn't apologize—period—and he'd done it twice in one day. Well, once and a half. "My family is used to police work taking precedence over…other things." She inserted her key into the deadbolt, opened the door, and flipped the light switch. The chief stepped into the room once she'd disarmed the alarm system.

He stood for a moment, appearing to absorb his surroundings. She followed his perusal of the room, wondering if he appreciated the value of the windowless set-up, no matter how simplistic it seemed compared to more modern innovations.

There were two microscopes side-by-side on a desk-height counter that ran the length of one wall. One was standard issue, the other a bifocal. A small portion of counter space had been set up for fingerprint examination and an old gas chromatograph that Pop had paid too much for at a bankruptcy auction years earlier was plugged in at the other end. A funky but functional light box her paternal grandfather had made separated them.

Various chemicals were visible behind the locked glass doors of an old oak medical cabinet on the end wall. An equally antique oak library table, overhung with a series of lights, dominated the center of the room. The top was strewn with measuring equipment and another light was clipped to the edge. Along the north wall stood floor-to-ceiling shelves filled with reference books, journals, and crime-related memorabilia. The wooden floor was scattered with several colorful throw rugs.

"I must be a little brain-dead today. Are you Joe Gabbiano's daughter?"

"I am."

He walked over to examine the giant fingerprint poster taped to the wall. Identification charts showing samples of arches, loops, and whorls hung below it. "He was on my interview board."

"One of the perks of being Police Commissioner," Grace said. "That's his print you're looking at. I grew up learning print ID by studying that exact example."

He turned back to her. "Small lab, but clean and functional." His glance raked the floor. "Even has decorator touches."

Grace ignored his facetious undertone. "More importantly, it's State certified," she said, just in case he'd missed that particular point somewhere in her file or hadn't noticed the framed certificate hanging on the wall.

"Does your father still use it?"

"Yes. He does consulting work periodically, usually for private individuals. I also use it. And my nephew."

The chief frowned. "Your nephew has access?"

"He's just learning the fingerprint characteristics," Grace assured him. Damn, why had she mentioned Kyle? What Aidan Cruz didn't know, wouldn't hurt him. "He's got the same bug I had growing up, and that Pop had before me."

"The boy's supervised when he's here?"

"Of course, and as I said, he's just learning fingerprint identification. Besides he's only ten—I wouldn't leave him here alone, and he doesn't have access otherwise."

A family of Hümmel-like figures chose that moment to come out of hiding and announce the half-hour to the tune of "Edelweiss."

The chief grunted. "Every lab needs a clock."

"It belonged to one of my grandmothers. It's a Black Forest clock and I was so taken with it as a child, she gave it to me not too long before she died."

"Nice memento."

"Yes," she agreed softly, "it is."

Aidan walked over to the bookcases and perused the titles. "You've got some old stuff here." He whistled. "Complete sets of Nancy Drew, Judy Bolton, and the Hardy Boys."

"Thanks to Mom and Pop."

"Amazing."

She searched for derision in his tone, but found none. "My grandfather—Pop's father—was a teacher, but he also rode in the Sheriff's Mounted Posse. You might say he indulged Pop's interest in forensic science, just as Pop indulged mine, and I intend to indulge Kyle's." She added with humor, "There's never been a cereal box, or an ad in the back of a comic book, that one of the three of us didn't order from if it related to detective work."

"Why didn't you just go straight into forensics, instead of law enforcement?" He leaned in for a closer look at her framed Dick Tracy badge and identification card.

"By the time I graduated, everybody wanted science-oriented majors, which I wasn't. I also didn't want to be stuck in a lab all the time. Not enough—" she shrugged "—excitement."

The chief raised that dark eyebrow in her direction.

Grace wished he'd stop doing that. "Okay, so Coburg isn't exactly a hot bed of activity, but you have to admit, a dead guy dressed up in girl clothes is far from boring."

A trace of a smile flashed her way. He moved on to examine a series of black-and-white and sepia-tone photos, ranging from shots of early Lane County Mounted Posses to hangings.

"My grandfather's," Grace said by way of explanation. "They've been on that wall for as long as I can remember."

"There's something particularly gruesome about old photos of dead people."

Grace glanced at the photo his eyes were on. "I wonder if putting the bad guy out for people to look at after the hanging deterred crime in any way."

"It would sure as hell make me think twice about it."

"Ditto."

"When you submitted your resignation in Seattle, you'd already taken and passed your detective's exam."

For the first time, Grace hesitated. Damn those personnel files. "Yeah."

"Why'd you do that? Why'd you come running back home?"

Grace's chin shot up in defiance before she had a chance to curb her reaction. "I didn't 'run' back home. Mom and Pop needed me here to help them with my sister's kids."

"The one whose whereabouts you don't know?"

Damn, did I have to chatter like a magpie about family matters? "Yes."

"You're a cop. If anyone can find her, you should be able to."

Grace didn't know him—or trust him—well enough to confide that she'd already accessed the police databases, both in both Seattle and Coburg, trying to locate her missing sister. Technically, she shouldn't have used the system for personal business, but since no missing-persons reports had been filed, either by the Gabbiano or the Sullivan family on Delfina or her dead-beat husband, she had few other options. "If we don't hear from her soon, we may have to hire a PI. We've run into a dead-end on our own." Grace gnawed her lower lip, debating how much to say. "Delfina's husband got a little too involved watching *The Sopranos*. He kind of thought that if he married into an Italian family, he should be able to live like…."

"The mafia?" the chief filled in helpfully.

Grace smirked. "Bobby isn't much in the brain-trust department."

"Umm. How old are the other kids?"

"Cassidy is seven and Madison is three."

Chief Cruz continued his perusal of the room, pulling out books, admiring the junior detective collection.

Getting back on track, Grace said, "So, as you see, I wasn't running away from anything, but *to* something." Then whether she should have or not, added, "Probably just like you were ready to get out of Portland."

His dark gaze narrowed on her. "News travels fast."

By now, Grace wanted a full accounting of Chief Aidan Cruz. He was a little brusque, but a personable trait peeked through occasionally. Still, any good interrogator knew when to ask and when to wait out. Not that the chief was in the hot seat, but now was the time to wait, except for one final question. "What do you think about the lab?"

Before he could answer, Angelina Gabbiano breezed through the door. She stopped dead in her tracks the instant her gaze landed on the chief, but it took her only a moment to recover. "Hel-*lo*," her mother said, extending her hand, casting an obvious side glance at Grace. "And who is this handsome young man you're hiding away from me in your musty old lab, Grazia?"

Instant heat suffused Grace's face. Warning flags started flapping in the breeze when her mother used her Italian name. She and all her unmarried siblings had been putting up with Angelina's maternal matchmaking for years. By rights, she should have been used to the suggestive tone of her mother's voice, but this time it was so blatant. She resisted the urge to whine, *Mother!* "Chief Aidan Cruz, Mom. Chief, this is my mother, Angelina. Patron saint of all unwed children over the age of twenty," she finished dryly. There, that ought to tell him to pay no attention whatsoever to her mother's romantic bent.

"A pleasure," the sucker in question murmured, and Grace saw that he meant it. But then, what man wouldn't? At fifty-three, Angelina Gabbiano with her still-dark hair and Sophia Loren-eyes made most women half her age look drab.

"I'm so glad Grazia invited you to dinner, Aidan. Joe told me just this morning that you start work tomorrow, and I should have thought to call you myself." Her hands, always moving when she talked, made a gesture Grace recognized as distress. "I've been so upset about Yeager Clausen. His poor children, losing their father that way. I spoke to Caity earlier. She's taking it pretty hard."

Grace only ran into the oldest Clausen daughter at Buon

Gusto, where she worked part-time for Angelina. While pleasant enough, she often seemed a bit aloof, like Ellie had been at that age. If Caity was broken up over her father's death, that would make her reaction a lot different than Ellie's.

Angelia gave Aidan's hand one extra squeeze, then turned and flew out the door, the skirt of her sun dress billowing behind her. "Dinner will be ready in fifteen minutes. Don't be late," she called over her shoulder.

Grace stood staring after her mother, mortified despite similar past experiences. Well, not *quite* so similar. Her mother had really been on a roll this time. Poor Chief Cruz.

She glanced at her boss. *Poor Chief Cruz, my ass!* After a sixty-second encounter with her mother, he didn't exactly appear besotted, but he definitely looked dazed. And she thought he'd fallen for Ellie Clausen's womanly charms!

"I wasn't fishing for a dinner invitation," he said, obviously stiff with embarrassment.

"It never crossed my mind that you were," Grace assured him. "Why don't you follow Mom over to the house? I need to lock up and have a quick shower and a change of clothes."

"Your parents live that close?"

Grace nodded. "I rent this place from them. It used to be a caretaker's cottage, back in the day."

He hesitated. "I think I'll wait."

He's afraid my mother will have him married off to me by morning. "How about that beer, then? The front porch is nice and shady at this time of day." She didn't want him in her house while she was showering, for God's sake. She'd never be able to look him in the dark eye again.

"Sounds good."

He preceded her out the lab door in silence and waited while she set the alarm and locked up. He followed her to the porch and sat, still without a word, as she went inside and grabbed him a cold beer from her own stash and put Rocco's six-packs in the fridge. For good measure, she shook a few pretzels into a bowl.

With a speed borne of growing up in a five-kid household with only one bathroom, she showered, pulled on a sundress that had been decorating a hanger all summer, added a dash of lipstick, and brushed out her hair. Thinking the loose style too hot, she pulled it back up into a ponytail, frowning at her reflection in the mirror as she tied a ribbon around the rubber band. No good. Her brothers would never let her live it down if she arrived in a dress, as if this particular dinner was important just because a sexy, eligible guy had joined them for dinner.

Quickly, she stripped and reached for a pair of shorts and a T-shirt that read *Bad Cop—No Donut*. Nope. Too casual. She ripped off the tee and pulled on a sleeveless cotton blouse instead. The sunny yellow color didn't send out signals of any kind, she decided as she slid her feet into flip-flops.

Just another Sunday-night dinner with family.

CHAPTER 10

THE USUAL FAMILY members were just sitting down at the table when Grace led Aidan into the dining room.

Her younger brother Dante, a law student at the University of Oregon, was there, along with Rocco, Uncle Sal and his wife Loretta, their daughter Gina, and her younger siblings. Uncle Vito was late and her parents' new friend, Jason Knox, had just arrived. Grace made introductions and considered sitting with the kids when she noticed the new seating arrangement at the grownups' table. She smelled her mother's fine hand at work.

By the time Uncle Vito arrived and took his usual spot, two empty chairs remained on one side of the big table and one on the other. Grace veered toward the single chair, hoping it wasn't obvious to her new boss that she didn't want to sit next to him. Aunt Loretta, who had been helping in the kitchen, saved Grace from her own rude behavior and Angelina's matchmaking by putting her arm through Aidan's, guiding him over to sit between her and Uncle Sal. Thwarted, her mother frowned. Pop said the blessing, with Angelina murmuring *sshh* only once to the children. Immediately after the "amen," Loretta winked at Grace, then turned to ask Chief Cruz a question.

Over spaghetti and meatballs, a hearty salad, roasted peppers and potatoes with Italian sausage, fresh bread, and a bold Chianti, Aidan seemed to meet the approval of everyone at the table. By the time her mother served *biscotti* still warm from the oven and coffee, he had established a rapport with her father and uncle, engaged Jason in an empathetic discussion about grass allergies, encouraged Dante to apply for an internship with the U.S. Marshal's office, and offered to help Rocco on another landscaping project that required muscle.

It was on this last point that Grace began to feel peevish—after all, she'd had sore muscles for three days after helping her brother for an entire day last week on his pond project. He'd never offered *her* a ticket to the first University of Oregon home game the following weekend in exchange for helping him.

Grace thought evil thoughts about Rocco for a full ten seconds before she remembered she didn't even *like* college football. For no reason, she laughed, drawing curious glances from her relatives and the two non-family members present. She felt her face suffuse with hot color and quickly excused herself to get more coffee.

Refilling cups, she noticed that even Kyle, Cassidy, and Maddy looked at Aidan Cruz with adoring eyes, no doubt imagining him as the father figure they'd never really had. And Gina…well, her cousin was seventeen. Her heart was throbbing madly on her shirt sleeve.

Grace dunked a chocolate *biscotto* into her coffee. God, could her mother cook! She munched the soggy cookie, studying her boss surreptitiously—he certainly didn't seem surly or unhappy at the moment. He'd eaten a hearty meal with all the gusto of a true Italian, complimenting her mother profusely along the way. He didn't even seem to mind her questions. They all now knew that he had three siblings, that his father was Portuguese and his mother, Irish. He'd been divorced for two years, and his son, Dylan, was eleven and already into his terrible teens.

Grace had never seen her mother in such fine form. She'd missed her calling for sure. She should have been the cop instead of Grace, the way she could squeeze information out of a police chief.

Aidan also flirted with Aunt Loretta, kidded with the

children, exchanged "stupid criminal" crime stories with her father, and listened intently to Uncle Sal's retelling of an encounter everyone around the table had heard just the week before. The story involved her uncle, a relentless squirrel, and repeated attempts to stock his bird feeder. Uncle Vito then gave him a detailed explanation on how to tell when wine grapes were ready for harvest.

After dinner, Rocco and Dante ushered Angelina and Aunt Loretta out to the front porch, where they settled into the comfy wicker furniture with a second glass of wine and put their feet up, exchanging quiet conversation about their week. Joe took Maddy upstairs to ready her for bed. Uncles Sal and Vito joined Rocco, Dante, and Aidan in the kitchen to finish off the *biscotti* and the wine.

Relieved to have a moment's respite before she tackled after-dinner cleanup, Grace freshened her coffee and went to the family room. Jason and Kyle had a game of checkers already in play. Cassidy and the cousins were "bowling" on the Xbox 360.

"Busy day," Jason commented, glancing up as Grace eased into a cushy overstuffed chair and raised her feet to the ottoman.

"And long," she said ruefully. "I don't think I'll have any trouble getting to sleep tonight."

Kyle looked up from the game board. "Mom always said coffee kept her awake."

"Trust me, kiddo, I never have that problem."

Jason studied the board, made a play. "I understand you discovered Yeager Clausen's" —he slid a look toward Kyle— "um, body, this morning."

News on the town grapevine traveled fast. "Yep."

Kyle considered the board with a intent frown. "What happened, Gracie?"

She thought about saying "nothing," but that wasn't the truth. "A man who lives here in Coburg died out in Mr. Nelson's mint field."

Kyle made his play, jumping and collecting Jason's piece, then looked up at her, his little nose wrinkled. "Did he smell like Spearmint gum?"

Jason chuckled and made another move.

For the short amount of time he'd been living with her parents, Kyle had already experienced the fragrance of the mint fields at their peak. She smiled. "Nope, he didn't smell like anything." She tacked on a silent, *Thanks to the plants*.

"How come he died?" the boy persisted.

"He may have taken some bad drugs," Grace said. "We won't know for sure until the autopsy is done."

Kyle's fingers hovered over a round black disk. "What's an autopsy? Is Mom going to have one of those if she keeps taking drugs?"

Grace almost choked on her coffee. How did Kyle know his mother took drugs?

She glanced at Jason, who gave her a hard stare. Was he telling her to shut up, or wondering how she was going to field her nephew's innocent inquiry? It wasn't the first time she'd drawn such a response when discussing her work. Most people thought kids were too young to talk about death, but Grace couldn't let either of Kyle's questions go unanswered.

Since her nephew'd had his tonsils out, he would probably understand the procedure from that perspective. "An autopsy is when a doctor does a surgery on the body to try and figure out exactly what caused the death. Anytime someone dies who hasn't been sick, or if circumstances surrounding the death seem peculiar, the law requires the Medical Examiner to do the autopsy."

She took a deep breath and went on, hoping her next statement wasn't a lie. "And your mom is not ever going to have an autopsy, because she is not going to die from taking drugs." And Grace, who didn't pray, and wasn't even sure she believed in God anymore, sent up a prayer: *Please, God, make it be so.*

Kyle went ahead with his move, jumping Jason twice. The older man winced good-naturedly and studied the board. "So this guy was peculiar when he died?"

Ah, the accuracy and naïveté of youth. Grace pictured Yeager Clausen, spread out on an carpet of earth and mint in his fancy red gown. "I guess you could say that."

She might have said more, but at that moment, she caught sight of Uncle Sal and the chief through the kitchen door. They were engaged in what seemed to be a serious discussion. Uncle Sal gesticulated vigorously, frowning. The chief nodded, as if in understanding.

Aidan spared a brief glance in her direction. *Uncle Sal must be giving him an earful about Yeager Clausen.*

She became peeved all over again. The chief had lulled her into a false sense of security over dinner, blending in as he had with her entire family. He didn't want her to investigate Clausen's death as a homicide. He did want her to talk to Uncle Sal and see what he knew about Clausen. He didn't want her to talk to the media. He did want her to go to the autopsy. He didn't want her to pick on widows and kids. He did want her interrogate Ellie Clausen, but only a little.

The man was just too confusing. Maybe she should ask him for a list of *do*s and *don't*s.

Boy, did she have a headache. She blamed it on the wine, but she knew damned good and well that she'd let Chief Aidan Cruz get under her skin.

That, plus for awhile, she'd totally forgotten she had to go the autopsy in less than twelve hours.

Kyle pleaded with Grace to let him tag along back to her place, since she had foolishly announced she planned to review the crime scene negs before turning in.

Aidan Cruz, upon hearing that pronouncement, made no demurring comment, so she figured he either gave his silent blessing, or he didn't think marking negatives for prints would compromise his new department. Or maybe he wasn't paying attention to her at all, but was totally engrossed in whatever Uncle Vito was saying to him and her brothers.

"Don't you have to go to bed?" she asked Kyle, wishing she'd asked Uncle Sal earlier to stop by before he headed home, so she could pump him about his conversation with her new boss.

"Nonna will let me stay up late. Please, Gracie. I wanna do my fingerprint—Tina said she'll blow it up to be almost as big as Poppie's. Ple-e-a-a-se!"

Grace glanced at the chief again. He studied her with that inscrutable look of his, but there didn't seem to be any censure in his expression. "Okay," she said, anxious to get away, "let's go." She held out her hand, forgetting until he glanced toward the men in the room, that he wasn't a little boy anymore. She ruffled his hair instead, grinning when he ran ahead. "'Night, everyone," she called out with a wave.

"Race ya," Kyle challenged.

"Not tonight!" Grace protested.

Kyle gave in with a good-natured grin. "Poppie says I remind him of you, when you were a kid."

"I bet he does," she said dryly. How engrossed she'd been in crime detection at an early age—even younger than Kyle. Anything and everything remotely detection-related had drawn her. Decoder rings, lemon juice for secret messages, whodunit puzzles. She'd even read every one of her father's turn-of-the-century crime-solving and forensics books, and now had a nice collection of her own.

More than one teacher over the years had been stymied, if not stunned, that her school projects dealt with topics that turned most people's stomachs. The murder-mystery treats she'd convinced her mother to help prepare for her eighteenth birthday during Civics class had been particularly inspired. To this day, she doubted if Mrs. Carson had recovered from her first glimpse of the realistic corpse, played by Rocco-the-stiff with "vigor mortis."

"Ee-yuk," Kyle said, glancing down the pathway.

"What's the matter?" Grace asked.

"It's that gross guy from your office." His *sotto voce* complaint carried loudly enough to be insulting, but when Grace saw who the "gross guy" was, she didn't bother to admonish Kyle.

CHAPTER 11

THE LAST PERSON Grace wanted to see, off or even on the clock, was Jimmy Frey, yet the douchebag leaned over her porch rail as if he had every right to be there.

"Kyle, why don't you go on inside the house and as soon as I finish with Officer Frey, we'll do that finger print."

Her nephew didn't look happy about the change in plans and glared at Frey as he passed him going up the front steps.

"Same to you, kid," Frey snarled at Kyle's back, then turned his version of a come-hither smile on Grace.

He didn't know her at all if he thought his treatment of her nephew or the mega-kilowatt porcelain gleam would woo her. "What do you want, Jimmy?"

"You shouldn't have put me off the crime scene this morning, Grace. Not only do I have more experience than you, but I know people in this town."

"Really?" Grace said. "You mean like Ellie Clausen?"

"Yeah," he blurted out, then apparently realized his error and said, "Of course. Everyone knows Mrs. Clausen."

"Of course," Grace agreed, amused and incensed at the same time. He had incredible audacity.

"It's obvious Clausen was murdered and I have some ideas on what happened."

Not for the first time that day, Grace regretted her inability to let go of the idea that Clausen's death was a homicide. Never, not in a million years, did she want to agree with

Jimmy Frey about anything.

Doggedly, he went on. "One way it could have gone down is that he and his fags were doing some smack and things went sour. Clausen croaks and his gay *cabañeros* take off so they don't have to answer any questions."

"Interesting." Grace wondered how he'd made it so far in life with his narrow-minded attitude. "But not likely."

"The other way it could have gone is that Abner Nelson followed through on the threat he made yesterday. Hell, everyone within two blocks of the bank heard the old buzzard. I could have had an arrest by now and you're still screwing around, doing nothing."

Grace wanted nothing more than to stick a big fat pin in his puffed up chest and pop all that hot air out of him. "What evidence do you have to back up your assumptions?"

"Assumptions, my ass. You know, *Sergeant*, just because they think you're some kind of hotshot from Seattle don't mean shit to me."

If she hadn't learned how to put up with assholes over the past six years, Grace might have taken exception, not only to Frey's accusation, but to his demeaning tone. "If you have a problem with the way I'm handling this case, Officer Frey, I suggest you take it up with Chief Cruz, who, by the way, instructed me to treat this as a suicide, until we know differently."

"On your back for him already, huh, bitch?"

Grace couldn't believe his foul mouth had actually uttered those words. She wanted to hit him in the worst way. Beat him over the head with something substantial, something like a baseball bat. She wanted to kick him in the nuts. She wanted to shove her fist down his throat. Instead, she took a step back. And if he leaned over the rail any further in his attempt to intimidate her, and fell flat on his ugly face, she wouldn't lift so much as a finger to help him.

"If you don't leave my aunt alone," came a threatening childish voice from the doorway, "I'm gonna report you to Chief Cruz, then you won't have a job anymore, and you might even go to jail!"

Grace felt like pumping her fist in the air at Kyle's bravado, but the stalwart little guy was on the porch where Frey stood, less than six feet away from him. She couldn't take a chance that the stupid bastard would retaliate, big man that he was, against a ten-year-old boy.

"It's okay, Kyle. Officer Frey was just leaving."

Frey took a step closer to the boy. "Keep your pie hole shut, you little punk, or you'll be sorry."

Kyle, who had grown up with a father constantly saying much worse to him, closed the distance between himself and Frey. "I'm not scared of you, mister. You're nothing but a bully and everyone knows bullies are shitheads!"

Grace leapt up onto the porch between them. Jimmy Frey obviously thought nothing of picking on a kid, and Kyle didn't have sense enough to be afraid of him.

What she didn't know was whether or not Frey was stupid enough to actually lay a hand on Kyle. Not only did she not want to find out, but she didn't want to have to kill Frey if he hurt her nephew, altering both her and Kyle's lives forever. "Get the hell off my property now, Officer Frey, or you're going to be singing falsetto next time you pick up the phone to talk to your girlfriend."

Frey took another step closer to Kyle, snarled, made a false jump at him. If he'd hoped to startle or frighten the boy, he had another think coming. Because his dad had done a lot more than *try* to scare him, Kyle put up his dukes as if to say, *Bring it on, jerk face!*

Frey muttered some choice profanities, some at Kyle, some at Grace, and stormed off the porch. He purposely knocked into Grace as he lunged past her, causing her to stumble backward.

Kyle grabbed her hand, helping to steady her balance. "He's not a nice man, is he, Gracie?"

"No, Kyle. What Officer Frey says and the way he acts is wrong. He has terrible manners and doesn't care how badly he treats people." She closed her front door and they headed for the lab.

"How come he's a cop then? Aren't cops supposed to talk nice to people who aren't criminals?"

Grace didn't know how to respond. "He's not your typical cop." She took a deep breath, not really wanting to chastise Kyle for his language, but knowing she had to. "Speaking of talking, you can't go around using language like, uh—"

"Shithead?" Kyle supplied helpfully.

"Kyle!"

"Well he is!" Kyle scuffed his sandal against the pathway. "He talks and acts like my dad when he's drunk."

"I know, but if you talk like that, well, you're still a kid. If you start talking like that now—"

"You think I'll be like my dad when I grow up. I'll never be like that, Gracie! I'm never going to yell at my kids, or hit 'em, or hit my wife, either. Honest, I won't!"

The speed with which anger at Delfina and Bobby consumed her shook Grace. She knelt down and hugged her nephew. "I know you won't, sweetie. You're a good person, you don't have it in you to be mean to people."

Kyle had tears in his voice. "I don't wanna be like my dad, Gracie. I just don't! I *can't* be!"

"Don't worry, Kyle, you won't. We're all in control of our own destiny, and if you keep away from drugs and alcohol and the wrong types of people, and remember to treat others like you want to be treated yourself, you'll grow up to be a fine man, just like Poppie, or your uncles."

"And Chief Cruz," he added, sniffing.

Out of the mouths of babes. Given the nature of the conversation, Grace agreed with her nephew. "C'mon," she said, wiping away his tears with gentle fingers. "Let's go do that finger print, then we'll sneak off to Dairy Queen for a treat."

With dark eyes that mirrored her own, Kyle perked up. "Nonna and Poppie will let me?"

Grace wasn't too certain about that, but she said, "I'm sure it won't be a problem." She thought longingly of the negatives she wanted to mark, and the cigarette ashes screaming to be put on a slide, but all that would still be there after Kyle shuffled off to bed. And besides, who said she needed sleep herself?

Grace turned on the light box and stuck the first strip of negatives under the holding bar. She grabbed the magnifying glass and went over the negs, one by one. There was so little to go on with Clausen's death, she hoped the photos, when developed and enlarged, would give her something more, something she'd missed. From the looks of the negs, however, that wasn't going to happen.

She hadn't found an opportunity to ask her father to stop by and give the ashes a quick glance, but he must have tuned in to her overt glances at dinner. Just as she made notes on the last neg, the door opened and he walked into the lab.

"Hey, Pop, thanks for coming."

"Maddy has a tummy ache, or I would have been here sooner."

"I'm so obvious, huh?"

"I see in you what I recognize in myself, Gracie." He planted a kiss on the top of her head and sat down at the microscope.

Grace retrieved two of the bags from the refrigerator.

Joe gave her a quizzical look.

"I'm pretty sure one is chocolate, and the other is a mystery, so I thought they should be chilled, to make them easier to work with."

"Sometimes, that can be the wrong choice," her father said. Carefully, he opened the bag Grace thought might be candy and lifted the small blob with a flat tool that resembled a miniature pie server. He put the object on a slide and viewed it through the microscope. "In this case, you got lucky, Gracie. Firming it up helps me scrape off the dead ants and dirt." Which he did carefully.

"I picked up cigarette ashes at the scene and I also got some ashes from a cigarette Abner threw into the yard when I went over to talk to him."

"Ah."

"You're impressed because I have two ash samples?"

Her father looked up at her and shook his head. "No, I'm impressed because you chilled this and it made it damned easy for me to see it has a nice white 'm' on it."

"An M&M," Grace deduced.

"And with a brown candy-coating, which is why it wasn't so easy to identify from the get-go."

Grace accepted the slide from him and replaced the candy in its bag, then scribbled in her notebook.

Her father ended up cutting a small section of the larger glob, dead ants and all, with a sharp, sterile knife before he smoothed it against a new slide with a frosting spreader. The tool had a strong resemblance to one that had mysteriously disappeared from Angelina's kitchen some years before. He centered the slide under the lens, working the adjustment.

"Can you tell what it is? It just doesn't look like candy to me."

Several long moments later, after repeatedly focusing the lens and making several adjustments to the slide, her father drew away, his expression one of concern. "You found this near Clausen's body?"

"Yeah." Grace straightened in her chair. "Why? What's up?"

"Honey, this definitely isn't chocolate."

He sat back, scratching his cheek in an absent-minded way he had about him when deep in thought. "I can't say with absolute certainty unless I take a cross-section, but I think what you've got here, *cara*, is a piece of skin and co-agulated blood."

"*Skin! Blood?*"

"Get it back in the fridge right now and take it to the morgue with you in the morning, Grace. Clausen has a piece of him missing somewhere."

CHAPTER 12

AT SIX A.M., Grace gave up trying to sleep and jumped into the shower. Her long, thick hair took awhile to dry, but she was still dressed and out the door in less than an hour.

All night long, tossing and turning, she tried to imagine where that bloody piece of skin had come from. A good portion of Yeager Clausen's head, torso, back, and arms had been revealed by the garment he wore, but she and Deets hadn't seen any visible injuries. The skin had to have come from somewhere, though. Or, from someone else.

Grace couldn't be sure if dread of her first autopsy had kept her awake, or the anticipation of possibly having a missing piece of the vic to present to the ME.

Even though her father had stressed to her she'd still need an analysis from the Oregon State Police Forensics Lab, she trusted his initial finding. He'd headed up the OSP Forensics Lab in Springfield for over twenty years and had another ten years in before that. He didn't need high-tech equipment to tell him what human skin and blood looked like.

After springing that surprise on him, her father had refused to take even a cursory look at the cigarette ashes she'd collected. He advised her to hand them over to the OSP lab, as well. She deferred to his judgment. She couldn't risk not having the evidence properly examined and tested.

Aside from a lack of sleep, the upcoming autopsy, and the damned piece of skin-and-blood, one more thing was bugging her. She couldn't shake the feeling of something familiar about Yeager's dead body in that fancy red evening gown.

Grace swung by Rocco's house first, handing over the marked negatives, the two six packs, and a bag of chips. With what she had decided to call The Blob cradled on ice packs in her father's smallest cooler, Grace pointed her VW Bug toward the police department, where she got into uniform and checked out a car.

She paced outside Surgery 10, thirty minutes early for the scheduled autopsy.

Though usually ravenous in the morning, she had skipped breakfast and her morning coffee. Call it ridiculous, but she didn't want to bolt for the bathroom during the autopsy, giving the ME the idea that she was weak. Which was not to say that, even on an empty stomach, she would be able to avoid upchucking.

At ten minutes before eight, a man dressed in blue scrubs and a matching cap unlocked the door from the inside to let her in. Visiting a morgue to deliver the body the day before was staggeringly different than getting intimate with all the equipment used to cut up and dissect that same body. Some implements resembled instruments of torture, while others looked exactly like tools in Pop's shed or her own kitchen drawers.

Grace swallowed, hard. The dissection of frogs and humans might be equivalent theoretically, but in reality, she finally understood that this was going to be much worse than the necropsy performed on the poor little green amphibian in tenth-grade Biology. Maybe if she hadn't known Clausen or his wife, it wouldn't be so personal. On the other hand, an autopsy wouldn't be pleasant, no matter who the cadaver.

"I'm Carmine Cichetti," the man said. "Folks around here call me Chick. I'm Doc's diener, or pathology assistant, as they call us now."

Ah, an Italian compatriot who assisted the ME with dead bodies all day. Fun. Grace extended her hand. "Sergeant Grace Gabbiano, Coburg PD."

"Hey, nice to meet you. I shop at your mama's store all

the time. It's worth the drive up there."

"It's only eight miles," Grace teased.

"Yeah, but for a guy who plays with dead people all day, it's a big adventure." He flashed her a wide grin. "Your mama cooks so good, I stock up on her specials on Saturday and save myself from starvation for the entire week."

Grace laughed, appreciative of the diener's effort to loosen her up.

"Doc's here. He'll be in presently." Chick shuffled over to the corpse, still garbed in the red gown, and lying on the clean white sheet. He slid a glance at Grace. "This your first?"

She nodded.

"Just think of him as an inanimate object," Chick said. "His soul's done gone to heaven already" —he shrugged, grinning— "or maybe he went the other way."

From what Grace knew of Yeager Clausen, he *might* have gone south. "I've spent a minute or two since yesterday trying to gear myself up for this," she admitted.

The diener's head jerked toward the door as he gave her directions toward the restrooms. "Just in case."

"Thanks."

"In the meantime," he said, handing her a stack of miscellaneous items, "here's your wardrobe enhancement for the morning. You can step over there and get yourself ready. While we're waiting for the doc, I'll finish taking my pictures."

Grace moved over to the corner he'd indicated, away from the body, and placed what he'd given her on the plastic chair. She set aside the surgical mask, goggles, and latex gloves and pulled on the apron, fastening the ties. Next she bent and pulled paper booties on over her work shoes.

"Good morning. I'm Dr. Hacker, and before you are tempted to make a crack about it," he said, his voice brimming with humor, "let's start off with first names—we'll both remain friends a lot longer. Call me Doug."

Grace straightened and walked over to him, her hand outstretched. "Grace Gabbiano." She'd heard horror stories about some MEs, but Doug Hacker seemed amiable enough.

"Ah, the famous Gracie."

Grace shrugged modestly. "You've been talking to my dad."

The ME grinned. "What can I say? Joe and I go way back. I tell him about my kids, he tells me about his. I hear you don't think our pretty boy did himself in."

He hadn't heard *that* from her father, which meant either the EMT grapevine must be alive and well in Lane County or Jimmy Frey knew the ME. "I think it's a possibility."

"At a glance, I'd say you're wrong, but get the rest of your gear on and let's see what we come up with." He pulled on two pair of latex gloves, and when he noticed Grace watching him as she pulled on her own, said, "If our boy was into an alternative lifestyle and contracted a communicable disease, I'd rather not share it with him."

"I don't blame you." Just the thought made her shiver.

"Measurements taken care of?" the ME asked Chick.

His diener nodded.

Dressed in identical blue scrubs, they looked like reverse images of each other. Grace choked back an hysterical giggle. Stress was a mean enemy.

"Now that our boy's nice and limber again, let's get his clothes off and bagged. Since Grace thinks this may be a homicide, we'll treat it as such until we learn otherwise." Hacker glanced at Grace. "Is this your first?"

No need to ask for clarification of first what. "Yes."

"Already gave her directions," Chick said.

Hacker grunted. "If you don't think you can make it, at least try for the puke bucket, okay?" He nodded toward a plastic bucket in the corner.

Grace felt her face flush with mortification.

"Relax, Gracie," the doctor said. "Since I can't rile the dead, I have to practice on the living."

His wink did little to ease her embarrassment. She forced herself to remember why she was there. As a law enforcement officer, she didn't have time to feel sorry for herself.

"I asked my dad to take a look at something I found at the scene yesterday morning." She opened the cooler and pulled out the baggie she had on ice. "Pop says it's skin and blood."

"You don't say?" Doug Hacker, M.D., considered the corpse with renewed interest. "Well, well."

"We didn't see any obvious injury yesterday, so wherever it came from, the wound is either concealed by the dress or the skin belongs to someone else."

"The plot thickens," Chick murmured.

"I always like a good mystery," the ME agreed. "Makes the day more interesting. Off with the gown, Chick, and let's see if this guy's missing a piece of himself somewhere."

The diener handled the garment carefully and with efficient dexterity to preserve any trace evidence left behind within the folds. He took equal care with the burgundy-colored thong. And then there was just Yeager Clausen, naked as a dead jay bird.

And missing his penis.

"Ouch," Chick said at the same time Grace said, "Oh, shit."

Dr. Hacker, the remaining professional among them, leaned over the corpse and murmured, "Well, well," again.

The sheet beneath the body that had been forgotten momentarily, was removed at last by the doctor and his diener. They continued to handle and fold it carefully to retain any residual evidence. Both items of clothing and the sheet were put into a large plastic bag Chick had already labeled.

Nothing could have confirmed the manner of death to Grace more aptly than a shorn penis, but the ME, a man of methodical medical precision, had to keep looking to find the *cause* of death.

"All-righty then." Hacker looked directly at Grace. "If you've always wondered about the inner workings of the human body, step closer. Otherwise, if you just want to observe in case I pull a rabbit out of his throat or something, step back a ways."

Grace couldn't read the ME's expression. Was he having fun at her expense? In the next instant, she heard a chuckle coming from the diener's direction. Okay, so Doug Hacker, M.D., ready to hack into his first body of the day, was a comedian. He and Chick were both a pleasant surprise. Maybe the next few hours would be bearable, after all.

Hacker began at what must be his usual starting point at the right side of the head, moving downward, noting for the microphone, the appendectomy scar on the abdomen, the writing callus on the middle right finger, the bites on the left calf that looked like they'd come from fleas, and other general and more specific comments about the overall condition of the body.

Grace nonetheless sensed a vibrancy in Hacker's demeanor that she pegged as eagerness to examine how Clausen's family sword had been excised from his family jewels. Impatient, she both admired and resented Hacker's strict, if time-consuming, commitment to procedure.

He continued to work his way around the body, finally arriving at the clenched left fist. He opened the fingers of the corpse's hand and exposed a blue plastic tube, about an inch long and less than a quarter-inch in diameter. "Well, here's the syringe cap," he said.

Grace leaned forward for a look. The ME handed the cap to the diener for bagging and continued his examination. For the microphone, he said, "Star-shaped tattoo between left index and middle finger at the inside juncture." He put his ruler against the marking. "Approximately one-eighth inch in diameter. Six point on the star. Dark blue coloration."

Hacker looked up at Grace. "I wouldn't take this for a gang tattoo, but I have to admit, I've never seen another quite like it."

Again, Grace approached the table for a closer look, then backed away so the diener could aim a digital camera at the marking. She made notes concerning the flea bites, syringe cap, and tattoo in her notebook.

The ME progressed to the inside curve of Clausen's elbow, frowning as he examined the skin. "No injection mark." He walked to the foot of the table, once more examining the area between the toes, then up the other side of the table for another look at the crook of Clausen's right elbow. "Bingo."

Grace moved toward that side of the table. Clausen had a lot of body hair and she had a hard time seeing the injection site. Hacker stood aside for her to get a better look, his finger near the mark.

"Intravenous injection," Hacker said, "to be confirmed during the post-mortem."

For some reason, no tell-tale minuscule drop of blood ringed the spot where the needle had entered the victim's body. Grace bit the inside of her lip. "I'm confused. I know for a fact that Yeager was right-handed, and you found his writing callus, so I don't see him trying to self-inject with his left hand."

"Drug heads don't always do things the way normal people do."

"Please, the guy's lost his Johnson. There's no way he self-injected."

"I'm with you on this, Gracie. Just give me a few more minutes, okay? We can't afford to miss anything else this obvious."

Grace stepped back out of the way and let the ME get on with his examination. He finally arrived back at the other side of at the head, noting the discoloration on the chin—which Grace explained resulted from the widow popping him—then examined the left ear and the inside of both nostrils.

"He doesn't seem to be a snorter. His sinuses are inflamed, but more like allergic-reaction stuff, maybe sinus rhinitis."

Grace made a note to ask Ellie if Yeager had allergies.

Finally, Hacker worked Clausen's mouth open. "Well, shit, this guy's just full of surprises. Hand me the tweezers, Chick."

The diener complied and leaned over for a closer look, the camera in his hand. He clicked off two shots.

"What is it?" Grace asked.

"It ain't a rabbit, but it is white." The ME extracted what looked to be a sateen-type fabric folded neatly into a one-inch square and held it up.

Chick snapped two more pictures then followed the ME over to the counter where he quickly laid out a sterile cloth. Using two pair of tweezers, Hacker began to unfold the square. When finished, he had one long piece, folded lengthwise, about two feet long. Meticulously, he worked a flat tool between the white folds and opened it up.

"Damned odd," he said.

"Both edges are bound. Looks like white ribbon from a spool," Grace noted. Why would someone fold a ribbon so meticulously and place it inside Yeager Clausen's mouth? "I know both the ribbon and the missing penis have to be in your report, but I'll trust you not to mention them outside this room."

At the mention of Yeager Clausen's penis, or lack thereof, three heads turned and focused on the groin area of the corpse.

"Do you think we'll be able to match the piece of, um, skin I found yesterday with the…?" Grace shrugged, at a loss for words. What exactly did you call the former home of a guy's dick?

"I can tell you today if it's a possible match," Hacker said. They moved back to the autopsy table and stared down where Clausen's penis had been. Doug Hacker put his gloved hand against the skin, moving it subtly. "It didn't come off with one cut—see how the skin is ragged here, and here? Whatever the killer used, it wasn't that sharp. It also came off post-mortem—no excess bleeding."

Grace considered that a moment. "So, possible dull shears or a serrated knife, something like that?"

Hacker nodded. "And he would have been flaccid, which would have made for a smaller circumference to cut."

"How long after death, do you think? I mean, there's bound to be some blood, right, if it was immediately after death?" She studied Clausen's groin area, confused. "He doesn't appear to have had *any* blood loss."

"Chick, bring the Luminol and Q-Tips and grab the UV light. Grace, will you hit the light switch by the door? Let's see what we have here."

For several minutes, the ME swabbed Clausen's groin, each time viewing the results under the black light, then making a note for the microphone while Grace did the same in her notebook. They pulled the clothing out of the plastic bag and repeated the process on the thong and the inside of the dress, in the area corresponding to Clausen's groin.

"Amazing," Grace said. "Nothing but a drop or two."

"We're not a crime lab here, Gracie. OSP will give you more definitive information, but we'll get you a blood type and I'm pretty damned sure it'll be a match for the vic."

She shook her head, dumbfounded. "Whoever killed him sat around and waited awhile before he cut that penis off."

Why would the killer do that? To keep from getting bloody? To work up his nerve? Or *her* nerve? Cutting off a guy's pecker seemed like it might be a crime of passion, something a woman—someone like the infamous Lorena Bobbitt—might do. If the dress meant anything, a territorial boyfriend might have done the same thing. Grace sighed, frustrated. Maybe it was something as simple as the killer just wanting to hang around and revel in the satisfaction of a penis well chopped.

"This is just freaking weird," Grace said.

Dr. Hacker and his diener murmured their agreement, then moved back to the table, ready for the part of the autopsy she had been dreading the most. In unison, they lowered their protective visors.

Grace made adjustments to the goggles as she fit them over the bridge of her nose.

"Sorry about the eyewear, but stuff flies around in here when we start sawing. You don't want to risk getting something nasty in your eyes," Hacker said.

Grace checked the adjustment for a snug fit, taking his meaning all too clearly.

The ME picked up his scalpel.

Grace hoped her gulp didn't sound as loud to the two men in the room as it did to her.

CHAPTER 13

"**CONGRATULATIONS ON NOT** spewing last night's dinner all over Doug-the-Hacker and Chick-the-Diener's shiny vinyl flooring," Grace told the pale reflection staring back from the mirror.

With one hand on the edge of the sink for support, she bent and put the other hand beneath the cold water, trying to capture enough to dampen her face. After several sloshes, most of which dampened the front of her shirt instead, she thought she felt sufficiently refreshed to straighten.

And then came the instant replay, in living color: the ME making a Y-incision in Clausen's chest, the diener pulling back the skin, folding it over the dead man's face so they could get to the organs. And later, the horrible whirring of the Stryker saw as Clausen's skull was cut before it was lifted off to reveal his poor dead brain. Dr. Hacker was so sweet, detailing every step and tool throughout the procedure for her.

Grace's stomach roiled and rebelled again. She rushed back to the toilet and heaved and heaved until her insides felt exactly like the cadaver's had looked. Afterward, she splashed more water on her face. When she finally peered into the mirror again and pronounced her reflection as presentable as it was going to get, she patted her face dry with a paper towel.

Her ball cap went back on next, the bill tugged down to

hide her eyes. She fumbled for her sunglasses, which hung dripping wet at the V of her shirt. She reached for another paper towel to dry them.

Hoping she wouldn't run into anyone, she pulled open the restroom door and headed for the exit. Chick and the doc had uttered a few words of sympathy as she'd left the autopsy room, apparently not fooled by her forced smile. Perhaps the fact that she had run out without the small cooler or the bag of evidence—or removing her protective autopsy gear—had given her away. At least she'd gotten the mask off before she barfed, and she hadn't had to resort to the puke bucket, either.

Resolutely, she did an about-face in the wide hallway and returned to Surgery 10, where Chick offered her a pat on the back and said, "Hey, you did better than half the guys who come in here for the first time. Doc was impressed."

"Thanks." Cooler and evidence bag in hand, she was anxious to be on her way.

Once outside, the flirty paramedic from the day before waved from a passing ambulance. Grace managed a smile and waved back, receptive to a personal moment of distraction after how she'd spent her morning.

The EMT—what had his name badge said? Ducey?—was cute in a macho sort of way, and his body language had definitely put out some vibes in the I'm-attracted direction. Not her type, really, but then it had been so long since she'd had a date, she wasn't sure she remembered what her type was anymore.

Thank God he hadn't been any closer. Except for her dark hair and the baseball cap, her mirror image had stared back like something straight out of *Night of the Living Dead*.

God, what was she doing having normal thoughts? She had to let the chief know that Clausen was missing his dick, then she had to get a team together to get to the mint field and find the thing before some crow carried it off—if it hadn't been dick-napped already.

She approached her vehicle, dismayed to find Chief Cruz leaning against the driver's side door. "Shit a brick," she muttered. So much for her plan to avoid contact with other life forms for the next twenty minutes. God, she didn't even have a stick of gum to put in her mouth to get rid of that horrible lingering barf taste.

"I didn't think you'd feel like driving back," Chief Cruz said, holding his hand out for her keys. "I had Mallory drop me off."

He looked her up and down, landing on her face. "Your color's gone, but otherwise you look okay."

Grace bristled. "You think because I'm a woman, I can't handle this?"

Aidan unlocked the unit. "Down, Sergeant. I just remember how I felt my first couple of autopsies. Both times, I puked my guts out before the diener even lifted the skin away from the chest cavity." His wry grin spoke of remembered disgrace. "The ME up there in Multnomah County took great pleasure in sharing that information with anyone who would listen for the next year, and believe me, there are a lot of people in the Portland metro law enforcement circles who want a good laugh at someone else's expense."

His confession gave her a little room for bragging rights. "I lasted until he put all the parts into a plastic bag and shoved them back inside."

The chief gave her a thumbs up. "Congratulations." He opened the door and hit the mechanism on the arm rest to unlock the passenger side. "You probably don't feel like eating anything, but how about a cup of joe? It will help get that taste out of your mouth."

Grace felt another instant of humiliation, then nodded. After yesterday, she didn't quite know how to react when the chief treated her like a human being. "Let's catch a drive-thru. I've got some news we need to act on right away."

He paused, the seatbelt in his hand inches from the clasp. "Please don't tell me we've got a murder investigation on our hands."

Feeling her little devil horns emerge, Grace said, "Okay, I won't. But we need to get back out to the mint field and find Yeager Clausen's penis before it's carted off by birds."

The windows in the patrol car were up, so Grace hoped the civilians getting into the adjacent vehicle couldn't hear

Chief Aidan Cruz roar, "*Fuck!*"

"Okay, people, we have a problem." Chief Cruz stood at the head of the table in the small conference room. His eyes met the intent gaze of every patrol officer and reservist who had been available on short notice, including a couple who'd left the graveyard shift just a few hours earlier.

Despite the "problem," the chief appeared calm. There was no indication that he had broken every speed limit from the McDonald's on Gateway to Coburg PD. No indication that a Sheriff's deputy had followed him the last two miles, then given him a stern lecture in the parking lot about passing on a double-yellow, when he could have used his lights and siren to get that dump truck to move over. No indication that he'd turned his back on the deputy, leaving Grace to soothe the guy's pissed off feathers.

"We have a probable homicide here," the chief went on. "I say probable because we have to wait for the ME's findings, but it's unlikely that Yeager Clausen" —he held up a finger— "a, injected himself with an as-yet unverified substance that most likely caused his death, b" —another finger went up— "dressed himself up in lady's evening wear, or c" —a third finger went up— "cut off his own penis."

Groans and gasps echoed off the walls, with a couple of *shits* and *yikes* thrown in for good measure.

"We're going back to the scene, where we will conduct a *thorough* grid search for the missing body part. Sergeant Gabbiano will coordinate that search. Mallory, Dillon, Frey, McPherson, and Taylor will be with her. Wozinsky, you still look like crap, so I don't want you in the sun, but you can coordinate getting the remaining reservists in place to block off the road, about fifty yards in each direction."

Grace was impressed that the chief knew names after only one day, but she was pissed that he'd assigned Jimmy Frey to her team.

"I want each and every one of you," the chief went on, stopping to make eye contact again with the each-and-everyone to whom he was speaking, "to think about and remember the oath you took, both as a patrol officer for this department and as a reservist. You have an obligation, morally and legally, to uphold confidentiality on this job. We've already had one breach on this case, and I'm telling you right now, if we have another one, the person responsible will be fired immediately. No questions asked, no excuses accepted. *And,*" he added, his tone hard as he looked directly at Jimmy Frey, "if I fire your ass, you can rest assured you will *never* work in law enforcement again."

His glance swept around the table. "Got it?"

Ten mouths opened and said, "Yes." Mouth eleven, belonging to Jimmy Frey, substituted a sullen nod.

Grace was surprised the chief didn't fire the little turd on the spot. If that made her a terrible supervisor, too bad. After less than two weeks on the job, she'd never seen one person more capable of ruining morale among the troops than Jimmy Frey. Daily, requests came in to partner with anyone but him. Grace obviously hadn't had time to talk to Chief Cruz about it, but the topic was first on her list of administrative to-dos.

"Okay," the chief said, apparently satisfied that his officers knew he meant business. "Get out there and find that goddamned penis."

"How'd we miss it?" Deets asked.

"ME says whoever did it, snipped it off after he killed Clausen," Grace said. "They did the Luminol thing and found just a few drops of blood. We couldn't see it on the red dress."

"Jesus." Deets squirmed against the seat of the patrol car. "What kind of sadistic bastard is this guy?"

Grace shook her head, frowning. "Look, I don't know if everyone has experience in a grid search, so I'll go over the particulars at the site, but I want you to keep an eye on Frey. I don't need any screw-ups on this."

"Figured he's the one flapping his jaws. What'd he do?"

"So far, all I know about for sure is that he called Ellie Clausen and told her that her husband was dead."

"What a fucking idiot."

"Exactly, which is why I need you to keep an eye on him."

"I'd rather be searching."

"I'd rather that, too. You have to do both."

They pulled up at Abner Nelson's mint field, a parade of three patrol cars and six searchers. Wozinsky had practically begged the chief to let him participate, swore his flu bug or food poisoning or whatever the hell he had, was almost gone. The chief had pulled him aside, told him that he needed an officer with experience, someone he could count on to get the reservists set up, someone who could facilitate proper roadblocks being put in place. Grace was still marveling at how well Chief Cruz had handled the situation. Wozinsky would be puffed up for weeks.

She reviewed how a radius grid search worked for her team. Each member would start from the point where the body had been found and move out ten feet with a string. There, he would drive in a stake, move to the left, and attach the string from his to the next person's stake. They would then get down on hands and knees to look for the missing penis in that first pie-shaped area. Once that section had been thoroughly searched, they'd go out another ten feet, widen the circle, and start all over again.

They'd keep looking until they had searched the entire field, and if they didn't find it there, they'd search the field on the other side of the road. If they still couldn't find it, they'd walk the entire length of the road in both directions, searching as far as deemed plausible for a dismembered penis to be tossed from a car. "If we haven't found it by then, we'll do it all over again."

"This is stupid," Frey said. "You should be bringing in a cadaver dog, or something."

"We aren't searching for a body, Frey," Deets intervened before Grace could open her mouth. "Got any other bright ideas?"

"Fuck off."

"Frey, if you don't want to aid in this search, go back to the station and report in to the chief. I'm sure he can find something else for you to do." Grace thought that might silence him, and it did. "Everyone understand how this is going to be done?"

Jamie McPherson moved forward, deliberately, it looked to Grace, bumping into Frey. "Let's do it," he said. "Let's find this guy's dick and let him rest in peace."

"Okay," Grace said, "I realize there are rocks in the field, so strap on knee pads and pull on your gloves. I'd like to do this without injuries or further contamination." She looked at each team member. "If you find what we're looking for, you will *not* touch your radio and broadcast it to the Willamette Valley. Everyone here know how to whistle?" The team nodded. "Let me hear." First Deets, then Dillon and McPherson, Taylor, and finally, after a long pause, Frey.

"What about you?" Frey demanded sarcastically.

Grace stepped over to the trouble-maker, put two fingers into her mouth and blew like her older brother had taught her more than twenty years earlier. Frey slapped his hands over his ears, cussing.

Taylor hooted. "You got the magic, Sarge!"

"Let's go."

The search was hot and tedious. After more than an hour, Tina showed up with two coolers filled with ice and water bottles. A third cooler held sandwiches. No one had eaten lunch, so in the time it took to guzzle a bottle of water, they also managed to down a ham-and-cheese on whole wheat. If they had to pee, which seemed doubtful, considering how many buckets of sweat poured off each person, they were out of luck. Or at least Grace was. The guys could relieve themselves behind one of the trees across the road, if necessary.

By the end of the third hour, Grace stood twenty-five feet away from where she'd found Yeager Clausen. She'd counted on the crows, or maybe even a turkey vulture or two, to be circling the spot where the killer had tossed the penis. The birds' absence seemed a taunting proof that the body part wasn't in the mint field, but Grace wasn't giving up. Not yet.

She went out another ten feet, pounded in a stake, then ran the string over to where Dillon had, only moments earlier, put in his next stake. Each step was taken with care to avoid accidentally stepping on the missing male appendage. Once back to the previously marked parameter, she got down on her knees and began another slow, methodical search. Damn, it was difficult to see beneath the mint. Abner was going to be furious that so many of his plants were being destroyed, but it couldn't be helped. They had to search, and the search had to begin in the most logical spot, in this case, where the body had been found.

Grace finished her quadrant, and feeling light-headed, headed for the cooler for more water, and honest to God, if she never smelled mint again, it would be too soon. She was half-way to the cooler when someone let out a whistle. Grace didn't recognize who the sound had come from, but Taylor and Deets were on the run toward Dillon and McPherson, so it had to be one of them. The whistle came again, and this time Dillon waved his arms like a high-wire artist who'd lost his balance.

In the back of her mind, she registered that Frey was nowhere to be seen. She took a moment to look around. The jerk seemed to be AWOL, but he might have stepped behind one of the trees to take a leak.

Grace turned and ran toward Dillon, who had half-disappeared into the leafy green foliage. "I hope this is it," he said, looking up at her, "because I have to tell you, Sergeant, I'm about to fry out here."

It *was* hot. Sometimes it happened that way in the Willamette Valley in August. One hundred degrees and eighty percent humidity. This morning's weather report said they might have rain by mid-week. Another reason she hoped Taylor had found Clausen's missing part.

She bent to examine the object. It sort of resembled a penis.

"It looks like the pecker's been pecked," Deets said.

No one snickered or even smiled. Of course not. Losing a penis was serious business to a man. The time for jokes was past.

"The crows were circling the body yesterday," Grace said, assigning blame.

"Nasty bastards," Deets muttered.

"Anyone seen Frey?" Grace asked once photos were taken of the dirt-encrusted glob of skin. As one, the group scanned the field and the three patrol cars. Jimmy Frey was MIA.

Grace handed the cameras to Taylor. "Don't let that thing out of your sight, Cam, and for God's sake, don't let any birds come near it. Jamie, I want crime scene tape strung about ten feet further out, all around." She turned to Dillon. "Charlie, get a drawing of this grid, complete with measurements. Everyone comfortable with task assigns?"

The three officers nodded.

Grace took a fortifying breath. "Deets, come with me."

She felt like a soldier marching off to war. Frey was in for it this time, and she wanted a witness in case she had to shoot him in self-defense.

"Where the hell is he?" she muttered. They checked inside each vehicle, which, even with the windows down, felt like a roasting ovens. They circled the cars, thinking Frey might have been looking for shade. Deets ran across the road to search behind the trees, then came running back.

"What?" Grace said.

"He's sleeping under that big cottonwood, on the backside."

Standing on the side of the road, her hands on her hips, her expression grim, Grace had an idea.

She went to her patrol car and reached in for the handheld. "Tina, Grace here."

"Hey, you guys doing okay for water?"

"Yeah, thanks, and thanks again for bringing the coolers out. Put Chief Cruz on, will you?"

"Did you find it?" the chief demanded.

"I think so, but it's a bit worse for the wear. Can you come out?"

"It's that bad?"

Grace closed her eyes briefly, picturing in her mind the appendage they'd found and the man sleeping under the tree.

She didn't need the chief for the desiccated dick, but she did need him for the sleeping one. "'Fraid so. I think you should supervise this collection."

He hesitated before he said, "I'll be there in two minutes."

Roughly two-point-five minutes later, Chief Aidan Cruz parked his car in the roadway ahead of Grace's. In dead silence, he followed her out to where three of her team members stood guard over the missing penis. Deets followed in their wake.

The chief knelt to examine the object without touching it. "Unfuckingbelievable. Clausen couldn't just be murdered, he has to be *mutilated* and murdered." He looked up at Grace. "Okay, bag it, get it on ice, as if that will make a goddamned difference at this point, and get it over to the OSP Forensics Lab immediately. You got the other piece with you?"

She nodded. "In the cooler."

"That goes, too. See if you can sweet-talk this into a priority without the expense that goes along with a rush job." He stood, surveying the field and the officers who had worked hard to find this missing piece of evidence. "I want this killer caught and this case off our hands and with the DA as soon as possible." His gaze went back over the team again. "Where's Frey?"

Deets pointed toward the cottonwood across the road. "He's sleeping under that tree over there."

"Yeah?" Chief Cruz planted his hands on his hips. "Gabbiano, get that thing bagged-and-tagged, then come with me," he barked.

Grace and her team worked quickly. Dillon held the cooler open and closed it as soon as she dropped the bag in. She hustled after the chief, who was already at the opposite side of the road.

Behind her, she could feel four pairs of eyes trained on the closest cottonwood tree, intent on the fireworks that were about to fly.

Flowing next to the trees was an irrigation ditch. Grace had played in that ditch as a kid, had almost drowned in it once when the rains had left the water high and swift. She hurried after the chief, but held back as he approached Frey, who slept reclining against the tree trunk, his hat drawn over his face.

The idiot's audacity and stupidity were unbelievable. Even as she had the thought, she noticed the chief had taken a icy bottle of water from the drink cooler. He unscrewed the top and emptied the bottle down Frey's neck.

Screaming and cursing, Frey came up swinging. The chief jogged left to avoid a sucker punch and Frey, still half-asleep, lurched forward, headfirst into the irrigation ditch.

Sputtering and turning the day blue with his profanities and threats, it took him a moment to realize whose mother he was insulting.

"Walk back," the chief called over his shoulder. "You'll dry out faster."

CHAPTER 14

GRACE STOOD BEFORE the chief's desk, her hands clasped loosely behind her back. His gaze swept her from head to toe, making her sorry she hadn't taken a minute straighten her sweaty hair and take a damp towel to her dusty clothes and dirty knees and elbows. At the moment, she definitely did not do her department proud. "Both pieces are checked in at the OSP Forensics Lab. They'll have something for us in the morning for blood type. If we want a DNA match, it has to go to the Portland lab. I also left the cigarette ashes."

"Do we already know Clausen's blood type?"

"A-negative."

"If the wiener comes up A-neg, we don't need DNA. What else do we know?"

"The ME found a blue syringe cap in his left hand. He was right-handed, so I don't think it's likely he tried to self-inject with his non-dominant hand."

"The needle mark was in the crook of his right elbow, and the guy was right-handed?"

She nodded.

"You're sure?"

"The ME found the injection spot and a writing callus on his right hand. Clausen wrote right-handed when he came in to file a vandalism report last week."

The chief gave her a thoughtful look. "What kind of vandalism?"

Grace glanced at the vacant chair facing her boss's desk, but thought better of taking it. "Nothing major—someone absconded with a small fountain Ellie had running near the front entrance to the property. Anyway, Clausen made notes with his right hand. I remember that distinctly, because he kept raising the hand he wrote with to shove it in my face to emphasize his point."

Grace shifted on her feet, suddenly overcome with exhaustion and feeling a little woozy. She couldn't remember the last time she'd had a day like this one. "I suppose he could have been ambidextrous, but there was no callus on his left middle finger."

"If he wrote right-handed, it's unlikely he'd self-inject with the less-used hand."

Grace nodded, even though she'd just said almost the exact same thing. "There's more. The doc pulled a piece of white satin ribbon out of his mouth. It was folded down to about a one-inch square. By the time he unfolded it, it was about three feet long and three inches wide."

Screw it, she was sitting down. The plastic seat squeaked a little as she sank down on it. She broke into a cold sweat.

The chief raised an eyebrow at her. "No bruises we couldn't see before?"

"No, and I've been puzzled about that. Even if he was with someone he knew, maybe someone he trusted, shouldn't there be *some* signs of resistance?"

"He could have had a gun pointed at him, but who injects with a lethal dose of anything to avoid dying by a bullet instead?"

"He might not have known it would be a fatal heroin injection—"

"We don't know yet that it was heroin."

Grace didn't feel she should have to remind the chief about the bloody froth around Clausen's lips. "*Assuming* it was, what if he thought he was shooting up something safe?"

His skepticism was evident. "Like what?"

She shrugged. "I don't know. A sedative?"

"And a smart guy like Yeager Clausen would believe that a sedative is injected into the crook of an arm?"

"Think about it—if you get a pain med in the hospital, they run the IV into the vein at your wrist. I think most people connect sedative to vein, regardless of which vein."

"You're grasping, Grace."

"Maybe, but there was *no* sign of a struggle. Everything points to him cooperating with his killer. There has to be some valid reason *why* he would do that." Grace frowned, thinking it through for about the hundredth time. "The killer may have been threatening Clausen's family in some way, or his business." She used the back of her hand to wipe her forehead.

"Possible."

"What are *your* thought processes when you're trying to figure out how things went down?" He raised that eyebrow again and Grace realized her tone may have been a bit strident. Her heart rate accelerated. *Shit, dehydration!*

As if he had all the time in the world, the chief picked up a Coke can on his desk and took a long swallow. He set it down again and met Grace's steady gaze with an amused one of his own. "Like you, I grasp."

Grace leaned forward, elbows on her thighs, her hands shaking. "Grasping aside, we know he wasn't alone out there. Or if he was, maybe one of those damned crows swooped down and took off with the syringe, too."

Aidan frowned. "When's the last time you drank some water?"

"When Tina brought the sandwiches out."

He glanced at his watch. "For God's sake, Gabbiano, that was over three hours ago. It's nearly a hundred degrees out there. You can't not drink water!" He stood. "Stay put."

He returned immediately with a bottle of H2Oregon. "Don't ever let me catch you being stupid about staying hydrated again."

Grace detoured home for a quick shower, tooth-brushing, and change of clothes, hoping the Clausen's ate late during the summer. She had more questions to ask of the mother and a few for the daughters.

For some reason, she expected the long drive to be lined with cars of friends and relatives stopping by to offer condolences, but there wasn't a vehicle in sight. Grace rang the doorbell twice before the oldest daughter, Caitlin, answered.

"Hi, Caity." She didn't know the girl well, but Grace offered her a hug. "I'm sorry about your dad, sweetie."

The fierce hug Caitlin Clausen returned told Grace the girl was in some serious need of affection and condolence.

"This is so creepy weird," Caitlin said, anger in her voice. She pulled back, wiping cheeks. "Do you…do you really think my Mom killed him?"

Genetics worked in mysterious ways. What the parents lacked in forthrightness, their daughter made up for in platinum. Still, she was surprised that Ellie had discussed being a suspect with her daughter, especially at this stage of the investigation. Grace thought about it a minute and decided not to lie to the girl. "I don't know, Caity. I hope not."

Caitlin wiped her eyes again. "You know, even though they were married, it was more like they were friends living together." She frowned. "Well, maybe not *friends*, but at least roommates who tolerated each other." Her frown deepened. "Well, maybe they didn't exactly *tolerate* each other, but I guess they got along well enough to cohabitate." She leaned forward, and whispered, as if imparting a secret. "They had separate bedrooms."

"I know," Grace said gently. "Your mom told me. Is she here?"

"Yeah, she's out in the solarium, reading, I think. Want me to get her?"

"Yes, please."

The teenager turned and walked away, her dark hair swinging loose almost to her waist. She had her mother's petite stature and her father's dark coloring, right down to the eyes. But Caity's were soft and warm, the total opposite of Ellie's icy blue or Yeager's calculating brown. Thank goodness Caity hadn't inherited her father's disposition.

Just as she reached the doorway, Caitlin turned and said, "Your mom is so cool, Grace. Do you know she brought dinner over for us last night and again today? Not one other person has stopped by to see how we are. No one. Did" — her voice caught— "did people hate him so much?"

This time Grace decided a white lie was in order. "I think it's more that people are so busy with their own lives, they don't have time to do for others. And sometimes, it's because, well, people don't want to acknowledge that something bad happened, because then they'd have to think about what it would be like if it happened to them."

Caitlin scowled. "So they're afraid it will somehow rub off on them?"

"Yeah, I think so. Violent death is like the flu to some people—they think it's contagious."

The girl's eyes blazed. "People are so fucking stupid."

"She thinks you did it!" Caitlin cried, hurrying along behind her mother as they both entered the front hall.

"Grace has a job to do, Cait."

"Fuck her job!" The girl advanced on Grace.

Gone was the sweet, grief-stricken daughter with tears in her eyes. Somewhere between the solarium and the front hallway, Dr. Jekyll had assumed control of Caitlin Clausen's body. The merger had resulted in the alien creature Sigourney Weaver had referred to as "bitch." Shocked, Grace wondered if more than grief was going on here, or had what she'd said to Cait just minutes earlier sent her off on a tirade?

The girl took another step forward, glaring at Grace, her fists clenched at her sides. Before Grace could decide how, or even if, she should address Caitlin's radical about-face to hostility, a smiling Lindsey joined them.

"I have a few more questions for you, Ellie, but I also need to talk to Caitlin and Lindsey, if it's okay with you, and if it won't interfere with your dinner hour."

Ellie glanced at each of her daughters. "It's up to them, not me, and we'll just heat what your mom brought over, or maybe we won't eat at all."

"I don't have another thing to say to her," Caitlin spat. "And it's none of her damned business if we're eating or not."

Maybe the kid is schizophrenic.

"I'll talk to you," Lindsey offered. "I think I want to be a cop when I grow up. Is it as exciting as it looks on *Law and Order*?"

Lindsey's previously stated career goals included cheerleading for an NFL team and working for NASA. Amused, Grace said, "Police work is not near as exciting as they show it on TV."

Lindsey shrugged, apparently unconcerned. "Murder is exciting, though." She turned and flounced off to the living room, her ponytail swinging behind her.

Bemused and confused by the varied reactions of the three Clausen females to Yeager's death, Grace followed her.

Lindsey settled in on the sofa cross-legged. "Investigating my dad's murder must be exhilarating."

"I don't know that I'd describe it quite like that." Grace turned to Caitlin, who had trailed behind them. "Maybe we can talk after your sister and I finish."

"Yeah, and maybe Kurt Cobain is really still alive and making a new album with Elvis," Caitlin said with a sneer. She stalked out of the room and made a big production of thundering up the stairs.

"She's always a raving bitch when she's on the rag," Lindsey confided.

Grace caught herself starting to grin, then remembered she was the grown-up in the room.

Lindsey jumped up off the couch. "I'm sick of being inside. Let's get something cold to drink and talk out on the terrace—it's the only really nice thing about this house."

The girl had a point. Living in the rainy Northwest, Grace never passed up an opportunity to be outside on a sunny day. She followed Lindsey to the kitchen, where the soul of the Clausen home should have been. Like the rest of the house, for what it must have cost, it lacked warmth, being stark white from floor to ceiling, including the shiny white quartz countertop. There wasn't even a colored magnet on the refrigerator.

The girl poured pink lemonade into tall glasses filled with ice and handed one to Grace. "Don't worry, it's not the powdered stuff." She grabbed a bag of potato chips and headed out through French doors. The house might be cold, but the outdoor living space and back yard were paradise.

True to summer in the Valley, the heat had peaked in late afternoon at one degree over a hundred. Clusters of strategically placed shade trees kept the patio area cool. Birds chirped from their feeder perches among a stunning array of leafy, blooming perennials, while a jay shrieked loudly as it played in the birdbath. Grace made a mental note to put up a feeder and add a bird bath to her small yard, even as she wondered if the recalcitrant hosta in her north bed would ever reach the proportions of Ellie's. "Your mom must have the greenest thumb in the county."

"What she's got," Lindsey said, "is a really cute gardener, and his color would be muscled bronze, not green."

A vision of Ellie's elegant manicure flashed into Grace's mind. Of course, the woman didn't do her own gardening.

Lindsey curled up on a chaise lounge and Grace settled into a chair at the glass-topped table so she'd have a place to set her glass and take notes, too.

"Is it true Dad was dressed up in some kind of fancy dress?"

Grace looked up from opening her notebook. Lindsey didn't meet her gaze, but was staring into the depths of her beverage. "Yes."

"Dad wasn't gay."

"I didn't think he was."

"He wasn't one of those—what do you call them? Trans…trans…."

"Transvestites?"

"Yeah. And he didn't, like, wear women's underwear, either."

Usually youngsters weren't privy to the most private aspects of their parents' lives. How could the girl be so certain her dad was straight? Did it even matter? An alternative lifestyle didn't pose a question mark, as far as Grace was concerned. Yeager Clausen hadn't hand-picked his death attire.

"Did you see your dad on Saturday?"

Lindsey shook her head. "I spent the weekend with a friend. Then yesterday morning, we went to U of O and got checked into the dorm for cheerleading camp. Mom came to get me yesterday afternoon, to tell me about Dad. I hadn't seen him since last weekend."

For the first time, the girl showed some emotion. Grace gave her a moment to surreptitiously wipe away a tear, but couldn't help speculating. Was Lindsey crying over her father's death or the missed cheerleading camp?

"How was he when you saw him then?"

"What do you mean?"

"Did he seem like he was in a good mood, happy? Was he well? Did he seem preoccupied in any way? Was he grouchy?"

Lindsey shrugged. "He was fine. He gave me my usual thirty bucks allowance, then took off for the golf course."

Thirty bucks! Money as a substitute for love? "And you didn't see him again all week?" she asked. What a strange family.

"Nope." Lindsey took a long drink from her glass and reached for the bag of potato chips. "Want some?"

"No, thanks." Grace looked down at her notebook. So far, she hadn't written more than *YC okay last weekend* under the girl's name.

Lindsey stuck her hand into the bag and came out with a fistful of chips. She crunched for a minute or so, apparently content with adding nothing to the conversation.

Grace put her pen down and casually leaned back in her chair. "I remember when I was your age—it always felt good to get away from home without my parents or siblings."

"Mom's okay. She nags sometimes, but…." Her shrug said she didn't consider that a big deal. "We didn't see much of Dad anyway, and when he was home, we tried to steer clear of him, you know?"

Grace was more saddened than surprised that Lindsey had leapt right through the opening she'd created. The girl stared at the yellow-and-white chip bag for several minutes, apparently thinking her words over carefully before she continued.

"Dad didn't go to school functions, or watch us play soccer and T-ball, or come to recitals when we were little," she said. "He was always too busy or in a foul mood." She took a deep breath, her lower lip trembling.

"Mostly, we didn't want to be around him because he never had anything nice to say to us." When she finally looked up, her big blue eyes, so like her mother's, were rimmed with tears. "Cait and Mom and me, we could never do anything right, you know? Dad criticized the way we looked, our grades sucked, our friends sucked. No matter how hard we tried, nothing pleased him."

The girl's lower lip trembled again. "Are you sure he was murdered and he didn't kill himself? We had a horrible argument last week because I wanted to go to Hawaii with one of my friends and her family for a week before school starts."

"Kids and parents argue all the time," Grace said. "It's part of growing up, and your dad definitely *was* murdered."

"Probably because he was a bastard," came Caitlin's vehement declaration from the doorway.

"Cait!" her sister cried, casting a half-embarrassed, half-dismayed glance at Grace.

"And he wasn't just in a foul mood some of the time, he was in a *shitty* mood *all* the time."

CHAPTER 15

CAITLIN'S EYES WERE trained on Grace.

Grace met her gaze steadily and without condemnation.

"We have a lot of *stuff*, you know? Everyone thinks we have it so great because we have *stuff*." Caitlin's voice roughened, but no tears fell. "Having every material thing you want doesn't mean shit if your father is hateful and manipulative about giving it to you."

Looking distressed, Lindsey cut it. "Mom said we're not supposed to say bad things in front of—"

"You think anyone in this stinking town *liked* Dad, Linz? He never did a damned thing that didn't benefit *him*. Look what he was doing to those hick farmers, telling them he was looking out for their best interests. He laughed all the way to the bank when they sold out to him."

Wow, Grace thought, *this kid lives with her ear plastered to walls*. What else did she know about her father's business?

"He's probably down there in Hell right now, Linz, laughing 'cause you're sitting here feeling guilty about him dying."

Grace sensed Lindsey wasn't the only one feeling some guilt, but before she could offer Caitlin a word of kindness, the older sibling was gone again, rattling the glass in the French door when she slammed it behind her.

"I'm going to kill myself if I grow up to be like her,"

Lindsey promised.

"Don't do anything rash," Grace said dryly. She didn't remember having PMS as a teenager, but she supposed each girl was different. She made a couple of quick notes in her book. "Did you talk to your dad at all during the week?"

"Like he'd want to talk to me!" Lindsey said. The girl leaned forward and her voice dropped, but she couldn't meet Grace's eyes. "I was in the hallway outside Mom's bedroom when Mom told Dad she was shipping me off to cheerleading camp this week and that Caity was going down to Stanford for freshman orientation next week."

Grace waited, feeling Lindsey's pain, wanting to throttle both the girl's parents. Had Ellie actually used the words *shipping off*?

"Dad said, 'Good. I'm sick of having them around the house all the time.'" Their eyes finally connected. "That was rich, considering Dad was hardly ever home anyway."

Grace felt her heart crack. She couldn't imagine a father speaking of his daughters that way, yet she knew from years of working on the street that it happened all the time, regardless of class status. Was there anything she could say that might soften those horrible words for this child? "Just because parents say things like that doesn't mean that we're lacking in any way," she said, hoping Lindsey didn't take it for a platitude.

"Grownups *always* try to make everything they do wrong seem right," Lindsey shot back. "Caity and I both pull a four-point. We wouldn't mind spending more time at home, but instead, we take as many extracurriculars as we can to avoid Dad. Mom volunteers for everything that comes along, so even though she always does school stuff with us, she's never around the rest of the time."

Grace flipped her notebook closed and stood. In a moment of compassion, she crossed over to Lindsey and squeezed her shoulder. "I'm sorry for your loss, Linz."

The girl look up, agonized. "I called to talk to Mom Saturday night and Dad answered the phone. He said he didn't know where she was and that he had company, so he couldn't talk."

Grace tried to curb her exasperation. "I thought you said you didn't talk to him."

"You asked about during the week. That was on the weekend."

The literal interpretations of kids. Grace dug out her notebook again. "What time was that?"

"Around eight-thirty, I guess. It was right before we walked over to Dairy Queen. We wanted to be back in time to watch *Dirty Dancing* and that started at nine."

"Did he say who was with him?"

Lindsey shook her head. "I just figured he brought one of his women home. I caught him doing that once, you know." She hung her head, as if in shame, and her voice lowered even further. "When I heard he was in a red gown, I remembered something else…."

Grace's pulse accelerated, as if it knew Clausen's daughter finally had a lead for her. "What, Lindsey?"

"He said, 'Tell your mother I picked up her crowning glory, the red dress.' And then he hung up, without even saying goodbye." She took a deep breath and blurted out, "Mom doesn't own one red piece of clothing, Gracie. Not one! Red isn't her color."

Grace's initial instinct was to reassure Lindsey Clausen, possible future Girl Detective, that this latest bit of information meant nothing. But what if Clausen mentioning the red dress to his daughter *did* mean something? "What did your mom say when you relayed the message to her?"

A frown creased Lindsey's forehead. "Actually, I never told her. She came to pick me up at camp yesterday and when we got home, everything was all screwed up around here. Mom was crying, talking to Gramma and Grampy on the phone, trying to reach her friend Marie." The forgotten bag of chips spilled onto the terrace. The girl clutched the sides of the chaise so tightly her knuckles whitened. "Am I in trouble?"

"No," Grace assured her. "Not at all."

"Was Dad trying to tell me something?" Lindsey leaned forward, her tone and expression earnest, pleading. "OMG! Maybe he wouldn't be dead now, if I'd been smart enough to understand he was trying to tell me he was in trouble!"

Grace was torn between anger at Yeager Clausen and empathy for his daughter. What had gone wrong with the world that a fifteen-year-old girl knew so much about her father's indiscretions, then felt torn by guilt because she thought she was indirectly responsible for his death?

"Smart has nothing to do with it, Lindsey. You could no more have prevented your dad's death than you can estimate how many pieces of potato chips just fell out of that bag." She knelt so she could meet the girl eye-to-eye. "Even if he was giving you a clue, he wasn't doing it to be saved."

Grace had an epiphany. *He was leaving a clue to the killer's identity.* "Was the call disconnected, or did he actually hang up?"

Lindsey looked at her with confused, teary eyes. "What difference does it make?"

She was a sad-looking little waif, trying to be grown up, but her floppy ponytail stood askew on the side of her head and black mascara dribbled down her cheeks. "Maybe none," Grace said. "Maybe all the difference in the world."

The girl wiped the back of her hand against her eyes, smudging mascara everywhere. For several moments she said nothing, just sniffled. "Now that I think of it, it seems like he was still talking when the phone went dead."

The budding detective didn't know it, but she may have provided a substantial clue. Now all Grace had to do was figure out what it meant and who'd been there with Clausen.

She asked Lindsey a couple more questions, then left her staring off into space on the terrace. She stepped inside, taking a moment to think before she sought out Caity.

Had Clausen been wearing the red dress when he left the house Saturday night? Grace thought back to the scene. A few foot prints in the dirt and not many crushed plants indicated little activity. It was possible, though unlikely, he'd changed clothes in the roadway. The killer wouldn't have risked being discovered like that.

The high-heeled sandals had gone on after he died. She was sure of that. He wouldn't have been able to walk in them, as confirmed by the barefoot prints on-scene. Even with a gun or some other weapon trained on him, the killer must have spun a helluva convincing story to get him out into that field.

Given what she'd learned about the Clausen familial relations over the past two days, she ruled out a threat to Ellie or the girls. He didn't care about anyone but himself. His ego had let him be tricked into believing he was injecting with something benign. She was sure of it.

Lindsey claimed she hadn't passed the message about the red dress on to her mother. Ellie hadn't mentioned it, but Grace still needed to confirm Lindsey's story.

God, she hated knowing all this stuff about Clausen's family. Even as screwed up as her own family could get sometimes, they were nothing like this one. It was sickening and sad all at once. Almost overwhelmingly so.

Grace found Ellie in the solarium off the dining room, her perfectly manicured fingers clutching a magazine. It was obvious from the upside down print that she wouldn't be picking up any useful tips on how to make Martha Stewart's cover wreath with leftover garden goodies.

She didn't have the heart to grill Ellie after what she'd learned from Lindsey, but if Clausen had been killed for his marital infidelities, the sooner she caught the widow lying, the better.

"Get the goods on me from my daughter?" Ellie asked, her tone sardonic, her vernacular totally un-Ellie-like.

"I wasn't trying to," Grace said. "Mind if I sit?"

Ellie inclined her head toward the matching wicker chair across from her. "You wanna know more 'bout what a wunnerful father he was, or what a prince he was as a husband?"

Grace flipped open her notebook. "You choose."

Ellie's venomous expression softened. "My girls are intelligent, pretty, and personable. What's not to love 'bout them?" she demanded quietly.

Under the umbrella of Ellie's pain, Grace was willing to forgive Caitlin her Jekyll-and-Hyde routine earlier. "Nothing. You've done a good job raising them."

Ellie reached for a glass that Grace suspected wasn't

straight lemonade. The deduction had less to do with Grace's detecting skills than to Ellie's sudden candor, though the diluted pink beverage, the rosy tinge of her cheeks, and the slushy way her words came out were also a dead giveaway.

Ellie toasted Grace, then took a huge swig. "Thank you," she said, indelicately wiping her mouth with the back of her hand. "I 'preciate that you did not give the credit to the bashtard who sired them."

Grace had no first-hand knowledge of Yeager's ability or inability to parent, but so many pain waves radiated throughout the Clausen household, she had little doubt he should have had his family jewels tied off, rather than using them to father children. She looked Ellie square in the eye and said as gently as she could, "I let you off the hook yesterday, Ellie, but now you've got to be straight with me. Was Yeager sexually or physically abusive to the girls?"

To Ellie's credit, she didn't flinch at the question. "If it had been less damaging on their psyches, I would have preferred it," she said bitterly. "But he never laid a hand on 'em. His swords were verbal and visual. The bastard loved playing with their emotions." She raised her chin in defiance. "Both my girls are shtronger than me—they learned early how not to cry."

That didn't sound like an achievement to Grace, who had grown up in a household with an abundance of love and emotion. That meant tears flowed as easily as hugs and tempers, and that was okay.

Unable to get either of the girls out of her thoughts, Grace wondered if the widow had tunnel vision where her daughters were concerned. How could she not know Lindsey was shedding tears of guilt and Caitlin was in some serious need of counseling?

Feeling only the slightest remorse for questioning Ellie while alcohol had control of her mouth and brain, Grace asked, "Who was Yeager having an affair with?"

The magazine forgotten, Ellie clasped her drink with two hands. This time she drained half the glass, dribbling it down the front of her finely-woven embroidered white shirt, a garment that probably cost more than Grace made in a day.

"My huzzban was not having *an* affair."

"I have it on pretty reliable authority that he was."

"Well, you're wrong. He was having *sev'ral* affairs." She took another long sip. "All at once, and more of them over the years than I can count on my fingers...and toes."

Geez, more than twenty? When did he have the time? "Is that what you were fighting about on Saturday?"

Ellie polished off her drink. "Thass none of your business." She emitted a very unladylike belch, then squinted at Grace. "What makes you think we had a fight?"

"The bruises on your knuckles, remember? You said you slapped him. Last I heard, people don't *slap* each other for no reason."

Ellie grunted, as if trying to remember something. "Still none of your business."

Grace sighed. You couldn't squeeze blood out of a turnip and you couldn't squeeze answers out of a drunk. The conversation with Ellie was effectively over. All other questions would have to wait. Except one. "Do you own a red dress?"

Despite her insobriety, Ellie managed to look indignant. "Certainly not! Red is for shluts."

"Lindsey said she called here Saturday night and your husband told her to let you know he'd picked up your 'crowning glory,' a red dress."

"My ash!" Ellie cried. "He wouldn't know where to buy a dress if you drew him a map."

"Would he pick up something for you at the dry cleaner?"

"I told you, I don't own a fucking red dress. Red is for shluts."

"Okay. What's the name of the dry cleaner you use?" Grace intended to verify whether or not Clausen had picked up a red dress last Saturday and made a note of Ellie's response. She wondered if the two red dresses hanging in her own closet had slut-like attributes.

"What about the autopshy?"

Ellie wasn't in any condition to hear or retain any information of a technical nature, so Grace opted for the standard response. "The ME has to wait for test results."

"Drugs," Ellie spat. "I tol' you he didn't do drugs anymore! You people are barfing up the wrong tree."

Considering she didn't seem to be taking her husband's death all that hard, drunk or sober, Ellie Clausen was adamant that the *cause* of his death was not drugs. "When he did do drugs, did he inject anything?"

Ellie hiccupped, waving a hand through the air. "He smoked or snorted his poison. Yeager din' like needles."

"A phobia?"

The widow smirked and narrowed her eyes. "He passed out once when he had to have a bud—blood test."

"Blood test for what?"

"AIDS, of course. You think I'd have sex with a man before I knew if he was clean?"

"I thought you said you weren't having sexual relations with him."

"I wuzzin. That was b'fore I knew he screwed" —she belched again, waving her hand through the air— "can't 'member their names…."

Grace sighed. "The Deputy ME will give you a call, let you know when Yeager's body will be released."

Ellie's lower lip jutted out stubbornly. "Better call shoon. Gotta go…." She frowned.

Up to that point, Grace had been willing to overlook Ellie's inebriation. She was, after all, in her own home. "You're not driving anywhere in your condition, Ellie."

The other woman shot her a haughty look, but the effect was spoiled by her glassy, unfocused eyes. "My condishun?"

"You're drunk," Grace said bluntly. "You drive and I'll arrest you. I don't think you want a DUI heaped on you at this point."

"I'll drive," came a voice out of nowhere.

"Good," Grace said, thinking the wrong daughter wanted to be in law enforcement. Caitlin Clausen was the one who had a career involving stealth ahead of her.

"I'm having him cremated, y'know." Ellie's tone held a bit of a challenge, but she also sounded a little gleeful. "I want him to burn, jus' in case he din' go straight to hell."

Caitlin crossed to Ellie, putting a protective arm around her shoulders. Grace couldn't discern who had the most agonized expression on her face, the mother or the daughter.

Yeager Clausen might be in perdition right about now, but Grace wondered, as she let herself out, exactly what kind of living hell he'd created for his family on good old terra firma.

CHAPTER 16

MIRACULOUSLY, AND DESPITE what she'd witnessed earlier at the autopsy, Grace's appetite had returned. Monday night, her mother worked the dinner-hour shift at Buon Gusto, which carried Italian-related products. Grace stopped in fifteen minutes before closing for a salami sandwich, an apple, and a Diet Coke. The line was almost out the door. She people-watched while she waited her turn.

With the last customer served, Angelina flipped over the closed sign and joined Grace at a small table.

"Your hair looks great, Mom!"

Angelina patted the new style self-consciously. "You think so?"

"Absolutely. Has Pop seen it yet?"

Uncharacteristically, her mother fidgeted with a piece of salami she filched from Grace's sandwich. "No."

Grace grinned. "You're scared!"

"I am not!" She popped the slice into her mouth.

"Mom, he's going to love it."

"He loved my long hair. He'll hate this."

Grace laughed. "Mom, you look more like my sister than my mother! You don't have a gray hair on that gorgeous head of yours—how could he possibly hate it? This new style looks even better on you than that twist thing—no one even knew you *had* long hair when you did that every day."

Angelina turned her head to examine her reflection in the

window glass. "You think so?"

This was a mother Grace had never encountered. "I'll bet you your next grandchild that Pop'll ravish you the moment he sees you."

"Is that any way to talk to your aging mother?"

"Aging, my patootie."

"You'll never get out of giving me grandchildren that way," her mother said, then added slyly, "That Chief Cruz, he's quite a looker, huh?"

"He's also my boss, Mom. Office romances don't work, remember? I have the experience to prove it."

"Still, you wouldn't want to work after the babies start coming."

Grace shook her head. "You're about as subtle as cruise missile, Mom."

Angelina leaned close and whispered, "I bet he's a magnificent lover."

Grace's mouth dropped open. "Mom!"

"I do know a little about things like that, Grazia." Angelina's expression altered meaningfully. "How do you think you and your siblings got here, anyway?"

"Pop always said by stork."

"Listen, my little smarty-pants *bambina*, you are almost hopeless in the marital department. At work, however" — she put her fingertips to her lips, then blew a kiss to the stars— "*cara mia*, you rock. With that in mind, Marilou over at the beauty shop said something to me this morning about that *bastardo* Yeager Clausen fooling around on his wife. I think you should stop by and talk to her—she probably knows more gossip than anyone else in town."

"Thanks, I will. I'm going to talk to Harley over at the newspaper, too." At the door, Grace turned back to her mother. "If you and Pop want me to watch the kidlets tonight while you fool around, I'll be happy to oblige."

Laughing, she pulled the door closed an instant before a bag of pasta hit the glass.

The landline answering machine greeted Grace when she

walked through her front door. The only reason she still had a landline was because of the alarm in the lab. She depressed a button and listened to one hang-up dial tone and one message from her father.

"Gracie, tried your cell, but it went straight to voice mail, so I'm guessing you have a dead battery. Uncle Sal and I are going fishing tomorrow, and you know we have to be on the road before dawn to catch anything, so I'm turning in early." So much for her parents having a night of wild sex. "I wanted to talk to you about that piece of skin, but I guess we'll catch up later." He chuckled. "I'm sure it's an interesting story." A short pause, then, "I hope your first autopsy wasn't too hard on you, Grazia. I wouldn't have wished that on you for anything." Another pause. "Sleep well, *cara*. Love you."

Grace listened to the message once more, just because her father represented the normal part of her life, then deleted it. She really did want to talk over the case with him, and she hadn't asked the chief yet if he'd wiggled any information about Clausen out of her uncle.

Grace remembered to put her smartphone on the charger before she also called it an early night. She awoke by six-thirty and was on her bike, headed for the station, by seven. A stack of messages awaited her from the previous day. Those that could be dealt with in the office, she took care of immediately. The remainder required her to be out on the street making face-to-face contacts. She got into uniform, mounted her police bike, and took off.

Just after five, hungry and thirsty, she locked her bike in the secure cage on the south side of the building. Wiped out from dealing with all the previous day's problems, she was reminded that small towns could be a royal pain in the butt.

Her mother had dropped a sack lunch off at some point during the day. Grace grabbed it off the corner of Tina's desk and plopped down at the computer where she opened the Clausen case file to enter her notes.

"Jason Knox stopped in to file a police report," Dagne Nelson said, handing her a pink square of paper. "He asked me to say 'hello' to you."

Grace glanced at the work study student. "What happened?"

"Someone stole one of his animals."

Even though Jason was her parents' friend, he was a relatively new acquaintance, made only a year or so before. Grace hardly knew the man and knew even less about him, except that he and Pop were evenly matched on the golf course. She'd never heard anything about him having animals. "A dog?"

Dagne, CPD's work study student, scowled. "You wanna see the report?"

"No, thanks." Grace opened her pasta salad, wondering why Dagne was always so surly. Perhaps this time, it was because her uncle, Abner Nelson, was on a suspect list for murder.

Dagne went to the next message and extended her hand with another pink sheet. "You also got a call from Harley, over at the *Weekly*."

"Wasn't he at the press conference yesterday morning?"

"How should I know? I didn't come in until four."

Grace sighed, curbing her impatience. She glanced at her watch. Harley lived and breathed the newspaper. He'd be there late tonight, because he had to go to press tomorrow. Grace mentally calculated how long it would take her to finish the case notes. "Would you please call him back and let him know I'll be over around six-thirty?"

Dagne frowned and mumbled something Grace hoped was an affirmative.

Tina appeared out of nowhere. "Dagne, Connie wants to go over your work assignment for tonight."

The girl's face scrunched up with displeasure and she stomped away.

"I don't think I'm her favorite person," Grace said. She popped the tab on her can, then dug into her salad. "I just don't know why."

"That girl needs a good swift kick in the ass, if you ask me," Tina said. "She used to be a sweet kid and now she just mopes around all the time."

"Maybe she has boyfriend troubles."

"If she's a sourpuss like that with a guy, I wouldn't doubt it." Tina cast a speculative glance after Dagne. She looked back at Grace. "Jimmy Frey tried to get into the evidence room today."

"Tell me you didn't let him."

"Like I would! He hasn't logged in anything he should be looking at for over a year."

Everyone in the office knew that Tina took her designation as Evidence Clerk as seriously as she did her martial arts class. The key was in a locked drawer in her desk and the key to the drawer was always on her person, until she left at five, then it was handed over to whoever worked the swing shift. Frey managed to avoid working swing, so even though everyone suspected him of being responsible for the missing evidence, no one knew how he'd managed to remove it.

"Only new evidence is the stuff you brought in from the homicide."

Grace couldn't fathom his motives. "I wonder what he's looking for."

"Beats me. The dumb shit grabbed for the key just as the chief walked in." Tina grinned, her violet-colored eyes sparkling with mischief. She patted the chain around her neck where it disappeared beneath her CPD T-shirt. "I believe the boss thought Jimmy was trying to cop a feel."

"I'm sure you disavowed the chief of that notion."

"As soon as Jimmy picked himself up off the floor, he tried to make it straight with the chief by saying I was showing him a move I learned in self-defense class."

Grace laughed. "Well, I guess that much was true. Where is the little weasel now?"

"The chief sent him over to the jail with Wozinsky to book a guy who flashed his weenie at a couple of ladies doing their laps around the park."

Grace almost choked on her soda. "A flasher? In Coburg?"

"What can I say? First a dead guy with his weenie missing and now another one wagging his. We're getting to be big-city for sure. At least The Little Prick is out of our hair for a while."

"What?"

Tina lowered her voice. "You know, The Little Prick. Don't tell me you haven't heard that yet."

"Who on earth are you talking about?"

Tina whispered, "Jimmy Frey."

Grace took a moment, trying—and probably failing—to look appropriately stern. "You shouldn't be assigning nicknames to co-workers."

Tina considered her for a moment, then shrugged. "Okay. By the way, our quick-acting chief is starting to do some reassignments. Mele is the new Evidence Clerk, thank God. That part of the job has been making me a little crabby by the end of the day, especially" —she put her hands on the flare of her hourglass hips— "when I have to put up with groping. I doubt Jimmy will try to take the key off of Mele."

Grace didn't think so, either. Mele Amaka, a former shot-putter of Hawaiian–Samoan descent, was five-eleven, two-thirty, and built like the proverbial brick shithouse. Frey would end up flattened if he so much as thought about making a grab for the key.

She quickly considered logistics. In a small jurisdiction like Coburg, even if Mele wasn't in the building, no one would have to wait long if they needed access to evidence. It also guaranteed him day shifts for a long time, which meant that Officer Frey would have to rotate to swing shift. Too bad.

"The chief is mulling over how to handle evidence on weekends."

Chief McCrea had left a written confidential report, eyes-only, for her and Chief Cruz. Alone, she hadn't been able to do anything about the missing evidence, but with Aidan taking the problem seriously, they should be able to put a halt to the problem and put the screws to the culprit.

Tina leaned over and whispered into Grace's ear, "Mele says if Jimmy gives him any shit, he's going to fry his *huevos* for breakfast."

Grace could think of only one response. "Bring on the bacon."

Grace went in search of Mele to open the evidence room. "Nice chain," she said to him when he pulled a key from under his shirt.

"So nice of Tina to let me use it." Mele flashed some dimples and a smile that seemed incredibly white against the rich darkness of his skin. "I invite Officer Frey to come after it any day of the week."

She gathered what she needed from the room and thanked Mele. She hadn't seen the need to take the clothing over to the OSP lab, but she did want a closer look at it and the other items.

With the evidence bags in-hand, she went to the conference room, where she spread a clean white sheet across the long table. By the time she had the red gown laid out, Tina and Connie Benz, the half-time data entry clerk, were *oohing* and *aahing* over the garment.

"Silk, you think?" Tina asked.

All the labels had been removed from the dress, but Grace was betting the fabric was exactly that. From a back seam, where the dress had ripped below the zipper, she snipped a single thread and held it with tweezers over a match flame. The fiber left behind a trail of ash, confirming that its parent was a silk worm.

"Glass beads on the bodice?" Connie guessed.

"Looks like it."

Tina whistled. "This is one expensive dress. Must be a designer gown, don't you think?"

"Honestly, I don't know." Grace made a quick decision. "I'm going to drive up to Seattle on my days off. I have a good friend up there who's a walking fashionista encyclopedia." She grabbed the digital camera and clicked off several pictures. She held out little hope that Ellie's dry cleaner would recognize it, but she had to ask.

Once Tina and Connie had left for the day, Grace began to go over the dress more carefully. It was in excellent condition, except for being ripped at the bottom of the zipper. The satin sandals with three-inch heels held no identifying marks, either. Grace gauged them to be a size eight, but when she held one next to her size eight, upsized her guess to a nine. Both the dress and the shoes looked brand new, other than the soil smudges on both.

The rhinestone tiara was pretty but bore no remarkable characteristics. Several hairs that might or might not have been from the wig were caught in the settings. She plucked them out and transferred them to a labeled plastic bag.

After rewrapping the dress, Grace laid out the wig, working her way through the long strawberry blonde strands with gloved fingers. “What have we here?” she murmured, reaching for the long-nose tweezers.

With care, she separated the hair strands and extracted an object of the deepest sapphire-blue. She held it up for inspection.

What the hell was a bird feather doing in the wig?

CHAPTER 17

GRACE GLANCED AT her watch. Ten minutes late. Harley Jacoby rewarded punctuality. He made it a point never to acknowledge visitors if they made the mistake of showing up too early, but show up late and you might as well be a wart-hog with extra long tusks and bad breath.

Harley had been putting out the *Coburg Herald Weekly* for over thirty-five years. On the Tuesday before deadline, he'd be glued to his computer, editing, egging on his carpal tunnel, daring his spine to protest from the god-awful curvature he'd forced upon it for over three decades.

A serious journalist who hated big cities, he was, no doubt, writing the story of his career, with a headline reading, *Murder in a small town*. Harley loved intrigue with a dash of sensationalism sprinkled on top. Grace was willing to bet twenty bucks the subhead would be something like, *Prominent businessman dressed to die*.

"Grace!" boomed a big voice, considering the size of the man it came from. "Quit lurking out there and come tell me what you know about Clausen's death."

Grace stepped into his office, wondering why he wasn't yelling because she was late. "You know I can't discuss an ongoing investigation, Harley." Contrary to literary and film portrayals of harried small-town newspaper editors, Harley's office was immaculate.

"Ah-ha, so you admit it was foul play!"

Uh-oh, blooper. The press conference had occurred before homicide had been confirmed and wily old Harley had wormed it out of her in less than a minute. "It's an unattended death, Harley. SOP—we always look into unattended deaths."

"Oh, so you just came over to talk about my new Apple iMac, huh?"

"Hey, you're the one who asked to see *me*."

"Hmmm, so I did, but since I didn't hear back from you, I didn't expect you to come by until tomorrow morning. You know darned good and well I'm going to be one of your best sources of information." He puffed up just a little bit, and added, "If not *the* best source."

Grace frowned. "Dagne didn't call to let you know I was coming over at six-thirty?"

Harley shook his graying head. His wild curls went bouncing. "Nope." He scowled. "That means you're late—what's up with that, little lady? You know I'm on deadline."

Even as she had an uncharitable thought about the work study student, Grace said, "Hey, if you didn't know I was coming, you don't get to be mad because I'm a few minutes late."

Harley turned back to his computer. "That's what you think!"

"And, of course, I know you're on deadline—that's why I'm here right now, instead of in the morning."

He nodded, his eyes squinting in satisfied approval as he pushed his half-glasses on top of his head. "What have you got for me?"

"You tell me what you know and I'll tell you what I know."

"Glad I taught you *something* when you were a know-it-all teenager working for me."

"My mother says ten Hail Marys for you every night, just to thank you."

Harley laughed. "Your sister didn't fair so well, or Angelina would be saying twenty for me."

"Mikey says *The Oregonian* decontaminates reporters to get rid of all the stuff they learned before they got there."

"Hunh!"

Grace liked Harley and the twinkle in his intelligent hazel eyes. His ethics were legendary, despite his chosen profession, and his nose for gossip even better. If it happened in Coburg, Harley knew it, almost ahead of time.

He nodded toward an old wooden chair.

Grace eyed it with skepticism. She remembered it being rickety fifteen years earlier.

"Homicide or suicide?"

She hesitated. "Off the record?"

"Gracie, Gracie, Gracie."

"Off the record this week, Harley. Maybe by next week's edition, it won't be."

His eyebrows beetled in displeasure at her. "Agreed."

"It is."

"It is what, a homicide?"

Grace nodded. "Sorry, I can't do any better right now."

"What *can* you tell me?"

Grace reached for the dish of jelly beans Harley always kept on the corner of his spotless desk. "Apparent asphyxiation due to drug overdose."

"Lab results will be in when?"

"The ME put a rush on them."

Harley glanced at his computer screen, scratching his head. "I have friends in high places. I could make a phone call."

Grace knew he meant his old buddy, the governor. "A well-placed phone call never hurt anyone." She popped a purple candy into her mouth, then a red one. Harley always swore they didn't have flavors, but Grace knew better.

"I wonder if one of his girlfriends offed him?" Harley mused, his attention back on her, even though his eyes remained unfocused, as usually happened when his thinking wheels were in motion.

"I believe it was someone he knew." Grace pulled out her notebook and lifted a pen from Harley's desk. "Let's start with his latest amour."

The editor half-rose from his chair and grabbed the candy dish, filling his palm before putting it back within Grace's reach. "Carolyn Haas. Financial wizard of the Willamette Valley. Quite a looker under that executive get-up she wears."

Grace translated that to mean Ms. Haas wore bland tailored suits, a severe hair style, and probably eye glasses. She didn't interrupt to confirm. Harley was on a roll.

"She and Clausen were an item for over a year. Probably longer than he ever stuck with any of his flings. They split the sheets about six months ago."

"An amicable parting?"

"Depends on whether you were the boy or the girl."

"Did she threaten him?"

"Not that I heard, but she did hope to reconcile." He grinned at her. "Isn't that the proper buzz word these days?"

Grace tossed a few more jelly beans into her mouth. "Far as I know. Who told you she wanted back with him?"

"The lady handles my retirement investments and she isn't exactly keeping it a secret." He shrugged. "She's smart with numbers, but not so much with matters of the heart."

"An old and common story."

"Carolyn comes across as a pretty tough nut, but I don't know if she's got what it takes to kill."

"You didn't like him, either?"

Harley laughed and almost choked on his candy. "I printed anything I could that might clue folks in to the kind of asshole he really is. I mean was."

Grace decided to catch up on back issues of the *Weekly* and wondered if her former boss should be a suspect. "Clausen wasn't involved recently?"

"Not just with one woman." Harley held up a hand to forestall any questions.

He sat back in his chair, a leather job meticulously conditioned with regularity, gazing at the ceiling for a moment. "He did Jessica Bennett for a few months just prior to Carolyn. Before and since, he also did Terry Moore, Dorrie Kelso, and Liz Dominy. The last two are best friends." Harley wiggled his eyebrows. "I think they had a little threesome going on with him."

"Kinky."

He shrugged. "To each his own, Grace."

"Any more?"

"I'm sure there are others I don't know about."

If Ellie's fingers-and-toes count was correct, Harley was right. "You said Carolyn Haas was vocal about wanting to get back with Clausen."

Harley shook his head, as if disappointed. "Didn't I teach you something about human behavior when you worked for me, Gracie?"

"You only let me work on ads," Grace reminded him. "Mikey got to be your reporter and gaze into your crystal ball. I did, however, get the highest marks in my class at the academy for report writing. What's your point?"

He squinted at her again, not saying anything.

The sneaky old fart *knew*, because she was a cop, that she'd already talked to Ellie. "Okay," she said, "Ellie knew the 'what,' but not the 'who.'"

"Too many *Who*s in Whoville," Harley commented, "and too many *Who*s of whom to be ignorant."

"Is that Confucius or Will Rogers?" Grace mocked. "So you think Ellie knows who they were?"

"I can only speculate, but I hear tell women usually do know these things."

She wondered if some female insight had rubbed off on him after being married for over forty years to the same woman, or if he was simply spouting a Harleyism. Those were always tinged with sarcasm and the observations of an armchair journalist/behavioralist watching human nature in action. If he was right, Ellie had lied to her. Again.

"I heard Clausen was dressed in some kind of evening gown."

"We're still off the record?"

Harley glowered at her. "For once I get to cover something besides recall petitions and protests against power plants and you're torturing me like this."

Grace rose, snagged another jelly bean, and tucked away her notebook.

"Okay," he groused. "Off the record."

"It was a fancy red thing, expensive, no labels, didn't

quite fit."

Not much surprised Harley, but Grace could tell this had. His eyes bugged a little. "Something familiar about that."

Grace frowned. "I thought the same thing, but I don't know why."

Harley shook his head, as if to clear it. "You know, rumor has it Ellie is fooling around, too."

"*Ellie?*" The woman with ice water for veins, unless she was soused? Then she remembered something Lindsey had said. *What she's got is a really cute gardener.* Call her naïve, but Grace had taken that as a teenage-girl-crush kind of remark, not an Ellie-screwing-the-gardener comment. Slightly stunned, she waited for Harley to elaborate. When he didn't, she prodded, "Are you going to name the lucky guy?"

"I don't know." He spun around to face his computer screen. He pulled his glasses back down and settled them on his nose. "Depends on what else you might have to tell me that I can use in my article that's *not* off the record."

First and foremost, Harley was a journalist, but Grace wasn't above a little extortion herself. "Mikey was down last Saturday and brought her high school scrapbook. There's one picture of you and Louise—"

"Hamm Starr!" Harley bellowed. "Two *r*s." He swung back around. "Shame on you, the daughter of good Catholic parents, resorting to blackmail!"

Grace grinned, unabashed. Two could play at Harley's game.

The editor rubbed his desk fondly. "I told Louise I heard the click of a camera that day." His expression turned sly. "She might like a copy of that photo, Sergeant Gabbiano. Maybe compare the stud I am today to the stud I was then."

"Harley!"

"Hey, you started it."

"I think not, and I'm not going to be the one to finish it, either." Teasing her old employer about a photo taken in bad light that revealed two unidentifiable lovers atop the smooth oak surface having a quickie was one thing. Handing that photo over to someone who admitted he was the male in the picture was something else entirely. "Hamm Starr," she said, back to the job at hand. "Is he related to Zelda Starr?"

Harley nodded, not bothering to hide the smug look on his face. "He and Clausen went to high school together and palled around with Jack Dellenbach. All of them were in my oldest boy's class. Clausen didn't always treat Hamm well, but that apparently didn't stop them from being best friends. The three of them even went off to college together—University of Colorado, if memory serves—but I recall they split to different schools the summer before senior year. Hamm just moved back a few years ago. He's an artist."

For a name that didn't ring any bells, it set off loud peals. In Grace's mind, a new scenario began to unfold.

An ill-treated friend.

A best friend's wife.

An affair to remember.

CHAPTER 18

GRACE KNOCKED ON the door of Good Hair Day. Visible through the full-panel glass door, Marilou Perkins sailed over to flip the lock. Attractive and about thirty-five, she wore lots of jewelry and trendy, baggy clothes over a slim figure. A huge mass of dark hair was caught up in a haphazard twirl on the back of her head. She reminded Grace of a gypsy.

"Thanks for seeing me on such short notice." Grace had noticed the lights on from the newspaper office and placed a call to the salon from the sidewalk outside the *Weekly*.

"Hey, my pleasure. For once, maybe all those 'secrets' I hear every day that aren't really secrets will be worth something." While her tone was conspiratorial, her eyes sparkled with humor. "Of course, I may not be able to divulge my sources…."

Grace played along. "Of course."

"Want something cold to drink? I have Coke or Snapple Lemonade."

The latter sounded good to Grace, who settled into a rattan settee. Marilou made her way over to a small fridge and extracted two bottled beverages, the second of which was a microbrew. "You're on duty, or I would have offered you one of these."

Grace pulled out a pen and her notebook. "I'll take a rain check."

Marilou shot her a impish grin. “You’re on.”

“You’re not from around here,” Grace said.

The owner of the Good Hair Day unscrewed the cap of her bottle and took a long swallow. “I migrated from North Carolina a few years back. I guess this drawl will always give me away.”

“I went to Asheville once, drove over the Blue Ridge Parkway. The Smoky Mountains are beautiful.”

“Yeah, sometimes I miss it, especially when it rains here for forty days and forty nights. Or more.”

Grace laughed.

“I’ve had a helluva day. Four colors, two perms, and six cuts, one of whom left crying because I’d cut half an inch too much off the back, when I actually cut less than the inch she instructed me to cut.” She tipped the bottle up to her mouth again. “Some days, it just doesn’t pay to get up in the morning, ya know?”

Grace did know. She’d had days like that herself. Just yesterday. And the day before. “I hear you may have information about Yeager Clausen.”

“Your mama was smart to send you to me,” Marilou said, sinking down into the rattan chair matching the settee.

Grace’s smirked. Why deny what was exactly right? “I’ve heard rumors that Clausen may have been cheating on his wife. Do you know anything about that?”

Marilou leaned forward, her huge dangly earrings sparkling as they brushed her cheeks. “Honey, that man had his pants unzipped so often, he’d have made a porn star look like a choir boy.”

Grace wished she were the one drinking the beer. “Any names to go with the rumors?”

“Rumors suggest unsubstantiated fact,” Marilou said, “and there was nothing *maybe* about that Casanova making the rounds.” She repeated the names Harley had already provided and added two more.

Grace met the other woman’s gaze and asked, “Were you one of his affairs? Is that why you’re so certain?”

“Me and that little pipsqueak? Honey, I like my men big, in both body and brain, and, well, you know—down *there*.

The only things big about Yeager Clausen were his ego and his bank account."

Everyone sang the ego song in unison. "What about Ellie?"

Marilou took a long swig from her bottle. A delicate little burp followed. "Ellie's not a customer of mine—I'm not ritzy enough for her, you know—but I do Hamm Starr's mother's hair and she told me herself, 'My boy is doing that Clausen woman.'" She grinned. "I shouldn't say this, but if you can imagine a wrinkled-up prune screeching from under a hair dryer, you'll understand the look of disapproval on Zelda's face when she told me that. I swear, every customer in the shop nearly keeled over laughing."

Had she not known otherwise, Grace would have conjured up visions of the Wicked Witch of the West wearing a dome-shaped plastic helmet, both the woman and the dryer spewing hot air. However, having already made the acquaintance of Hamm Starr's mother on a peeping-Tom call, Grace knew her to be a spitfire, but hardly a witch, and definitely not a prune. "Have you ever heard Ellie's name paired with anyone else?"

Marilou hesitated. "It's a circuitous-route sort of rumor, but…."

Grace tried out the chief's trick and raised an eyebrow in the other woman's direction.

Marilou shrugged. "Some rich guy named David Kirk. Lives in Portland. That's all I know."

"You're sure no one else?"

"Nope, just the Hammbone."

"Hammbone?"

Marilou drained her brewsky and stretched like a very contented cat. Her unusually green eyes danced with mischief. "I guess you could say, I've done more than Hamm Starr's hair."

Grace's tail drug the ground by the time she returned to the station. She'd been at work for over twelve hours already, but she wanted to get her latest case notes entered into the electronic file while they were still fresh.

The main lights were on inside, as well as those in the chief's office. His closed door indicated *do not disturb*.

Grace entered her notes, then reviewed the log of the day's calls. Finally, almost against her better judgment, she knocked on the chief's door.

"Come!" he snarled from the other side.

Grace fervently wished she'd just left well enough alone and gone directly home.

"I don't want you racking up a lot of overtime on this case, Gabbiano," he said in lieu of a greeting.

How did she respond to that? Budget was an issue in a small town like Coburg. She knew it. God knows, the entire world knew it after years of budget crises and embezzlement had made her home town the daily news in regional papers, but this was a murder investigation. She wanted to ask, *You're kidding, right?* Instead, out came, "How much is 'a lot'?"

He pushed back in his chair, making it squeak. Grace thought the swivel mechanism could use some WD-40. "Let's see, you probably came in an hour early this morning, right?"

She blinked, not wanting to confirm or deny his guess.

"And it's now after eight."

She blinked again, trying not to squirm.

His eyes narrowed on her. "You're not done yet, are you?"

"I'd like to take a look at the hair strands from the tiara, compare them against some from the wig. Also, Rocco developed the negs, so I'd like to review the enlarged photos."

"In that lab of yours?"

She nodded.

Aidan studied her for several moments more without speaking.

Grace was no mind reader, but she could practically hear the wheels grinding in his head, and they didn't sound good.

"When do you plan to sleep?"

Grace opened her mouth and snapped it shut almost immediately. Against her brain's better judgment, her mouth opened again and asked, “When do you?”

“When I sleep has no relevance to this discussion, Gabbiano. I’m not the one trying to balance an investigation with my bike patrol and other duties, including supervision of my patrol staff.”

Grace felt her face grow hot. She’d gone out on bike patrol and taken care of all the non-emergency calls from the day before, and it was true, she hadn’t been much of a supervisor today, but wouldn’t her officers have come to her if they needed something? “I’ve already read through everything that got logged in,” she said. *Note to self: keep closer tabs on the reports coming through the office throughout the day, instead of holding them for review at day’s end.*

“I won’t authorize more than ten hours of OT on this investigation. And you’re going to have to keep up bike patrol.”

He sighed, though whether from disgust or resignation, Grace couldn’t tell.

“From what I’ve heard, the citizens apparently like seeing an officer on a bike. It makes them feel safer and connected.”

“Connected?”

He leaned back over the desk and picked up his pencil. “Don’t ask me. That’s the message I got from Tina, who says office staff took a number of calls today from folks who wanted to know where you were yesterday.” He stared at her intently. “You’ve apparently made a ‘connection’ with people in the short time you’ve been here. Some of them were worried about you.”

Grace stared back, startled and feeling warm again, but this time from a feeling of satisfaction. The people she encountered in Seattle on a daily basis had probably hoped she was dead if she didn’t show up on her patrol route.

“That’s nice,” she said, sounding lame even to herself. “I mean—”

“No more than ten hours,” he repeated.

Grace frowned and almost opened her mouth to offer to do the work on her own time, then thought better of it. Any evidence she acquired, any leads she developed, would hold up a lot better later on if they were on the clock.

"Log everything back in first thing tomorrow morning, with a full report on my desk by nine. What you checked out, what you found."

Grace caught herself just before she opened her mouth to ask why he was so pissy. "Thanks, Boss," she said instead.

He swore under his breath. "You call me 'Boss' again, and we're going to have some trouble. Got it?"

She nodded, his strident voice having stopped her in her tracks as she tried to make an exit. "Sorry, it just slipped out."

"Look, I'm not worried about the goddamned budget, okay? I need you rested so you can get your job done, not so haggard you don't know which end is up. Understand?"

Again, she nodded. "When are we going to officially declare this a homicide investigation?" Grace could swear he growled.

"When you bring me that report tomorrow morning, I'll let you know what I've decided." He looked back down at the paperwork on his desk. Thinking she was dismissed, she turned toward the door. Grace didn't understand his vacillation, but he was the boss, uh, chief. She made it almost to the threshold when his voice stopped her again.

"And Gabbiano, you screw up, even remotely like you did in Seattle, I'll have you out of here so fast, you won't know what hit you."

Grace squared her shoulders and turned to meet his steely gaze with one of her own. "I didn't screw up in Seattle," she said with all the dignity she could gather on such short notice.

"I read your file—"

"Everyone's read that file," she shot back, "and no one believed me about what really happened, not even after I put my side of it down on paper. It probably never even *made* it into my file." She turned back toward the door. "If you're ever interested in my version, let me know. I had the foresight to keep a copy of it."

Grace thought her exit from the chief's office might have been more impressive if the tread on her boot hadn't stalled on the nap of the carpet. She lurched, but managed to catch herself on the doorjamb before she went sprawling.

Afraid that Aidan Cruz would come after her and say he'd changed his mind about her taking evidence home to her small lab, she hurriedly changed clothes. She'd made prior arrangements with Mele to check out the evidence she wanted to examine. In short order, she grabbed the key from its new hiding place, noted in the log what she was taking, and high-tailed it out the door. All the while, her cheeks burned with heat from both anger and shame.

How long did she have to pay for something she hadn't done?

Grace chastised herself for being every kind of fool. The debacle in Seattle had taught her several hard lessons. Never get involved romantically with a co-worker, especially one who has more clout than you do. Never do anything on the job without documenting it meticulously. And never, ever, trust your department to stick by you.

She should have known learning those lessons late would follow her wherever she went.

It was just too bad that Chief Cruz seemed to be watching her every move under the assumption that she'd fucked up royally on her former job.

CHAPTER 19

ROCCO ARRIVED HOME from the fire station at the same time Grace pulled into his double driveway. “Debris burn got out of control,” he said. “Gotta get this smoke off of me.” He went for a quick shower and came back in clean shorts and a T-shirt.

Still fuming, Grace opened a bottle of Sierra Nevada for him and one for herself.

“What’s got you all riled up?”

Grace almost choked quaffing the icy microbrew. “Same ole shit,” she said, wiping her chin. “That incident in Seattle is going to haunt me to my dying day.”

Her normally unastute brother jumped to the correct conclusion. “I take it Aidan is in this mix somewhere.”

“He reads my personnel file and thinks he knows everything about me.”

“Simmer down, Gracie. When he gets to know you, he’ll understand that tripe Dave Mackey put in your record was nothing but vindictive bullshit.”

“Yeah, right,” she said, unable to keep the resentment from her tone. “And yet I’m down here now, instead of still up there, working toward detective.”

Grace wanted sympathy, but Rocco had none to give. “Little sister, you made a conscious decision to come back to Coburg to help out Mom and Pop, remember? You could have stayed and let your union rep help you duke it out with

Seattle PD, but you were sick of that rat race, remember? You've got a fighting streak a mile wide running up that stubborn hide of yours and it's not yellow—if you'd really wanted to stick it out up there, you would have. No one could've made you quit."

"Everyone was glad I left."

Rocco *tsk-tsked* her. "Having a pity party, are we?"

Grace glared at him.

"You know damned good and well your ass would have been fired immediately if the charges brought against you were true. Internal Affairs did their investigation and cleared you."

"Cleared," Grace murmured, feeling bluer by the minute. "With a fucking big black cloud over my head forever."

Grace gave herself a stern talking-to during the short drive from her brother's place to the little house she now called home. Aidan Cruz, Rocco had pointed out, was a man with personal problems that probably left him out of sorts. Add a murder investigation to the mix, and you got more than a little grumpy.

The first thing that surprised Grace about the observation was the fact that it had been made by her brother. In her estimation, none of the males in her family was particularly observant—or empathetic—when it came to emotional turmoil. That said, they all knew when to back away and give the females a wide berth.

Secondly—and this actually made her laugh, lightening her mood considerably—Rocco's *grumpy* came about as close as Pluto in defining her boss's often surly attitude. Descriptives like irascible, pain in the ass, and butthead, maybe, but not grumpy, which brought to mind happy guys like the Seven Dwarves.

Grace suddenly realized that two missed meals had left her hungry. She opened all the windows and changed into a short cotton nightie. In the kitchen, she sliced some cheese, washed some green grapes, and loaded both onto a tray with some fresh-baked calamati olive bread from Buon Gusto. A glass of Uncle Vito's Dago Red wine would seal the deal.

The table-for-two on the front porch was perfect for a single diner—one chair to sit in and the other to put her feet up on—although sometimes, she longed for a mate to be sitting in that other chair.

Grace took a long sip from her glass, puckering up at the strong, raw taste of Uncle Vito's wine, even as she enjoyed the satisfying after-bite. She settled into the soft floral cushions lining the wicker chair, her food momentarily forgotten as she gazed skyward.

The evening had pretty nearly ended up perfectly. As usual in the Willamette Valley, the heat of the day that peaked around six p.m. had dropped to a comfortable seventy-five degrees. By the time she finished in the lab, and closed all but her bedroom window, she'd at least be able to drift off without sweating to death.

Being this far north, the sun had set not too long ago, leaving the sky a dark lavender. The noxious smoke clouds from late-afternoon field burning had drifted south, painting vivid red slashes in the western horizon. She could still smell the scorched grass, and as usual, grass ash littered the surface of her little bistro table.

The field burning worried her because of Kyle. He had asthma and even with a rescue inhaler, a nebulizer, and his Advair discus, he'd still been in for medical treatment several times over the summer. Last time, her mother had come home with an EpiPen, which everyone in the family now knew how to use.

Poor little guy. It was an asthmatic's curse, living in the Willamette Valley. Mold in the rainy season, pollen from grass and trees in the spring, smoke from burning grass fields in the summer and fall.

A short time later, Grace opened the first evidence bag and removed hair fibers that had been gathered from inside the wig cap. She placed them, one at a time, on a slide, bemoaning the lack of a comparison microscope so she could look at them side-by-side against the sample of Clausen's hair she had taken at the morgue.

Her notations were brief. *Sample 1, wig cap, 2 strands:*

black, healthy, dyed, fine. Sample 2, wig cap, 1 strand: brown, healthy, fine. She looked at Clausen's hair and matched it to Sample 2. So, who did the black strands belong to?

She snipped from the wig. This time, she wrote *Sample 3, wig, 2 strands: blonde, dyed, coarse, human.*

The killer had used a lush human-hair wig that couldn't have been cheap. Grace made more notes, then repackaged the samples, wondering about the tiara. She hadn't brought that along, though memory said it wasn't cheap glass, but pricier rhinestones. She made a note to check Rose o' Sharon for a ballpark value and maybe even have it dated.

Grace placed the hairs she'd extracted from the tiara on yet another slide, expecting them to match one of the three samples she had already catalogued. Instead, she discovered that she had yet a fourth type of hair to toss into the mix. *Sample 4, tiara, 3 strands: blonde, natural, fine.*

"What the hell?"

Morning came too damned early, but Grace dragged herself out of bed, showered, grabbed a banana, and biked off to the station. Her morning ritual of getting into uniform quickly completed, she transcribed her lab notes into the computer and printed out a copy of her updated report. She left it on the chief's desk, along with photocopies of several photos she planned to add to the file.

Instead of toe-tapping until he came in, she opened the binder containing a hard copy of the case file and inserted the original labeled pictures into plastic sleeves. That done, she flipped back to the first page and began to reread the file. By the time she'd finished, the office had begun to liven up. Deets and Mele were hanging out over the coffee pot and Tina was working on a flyer for a cop meet-and-greet scheduled for the end of the month in the park.

Coffee cup in-hand, Mele waved her over toward the evidence room door. Grace grabbed the handle sack she'd used to transport the evidence bags.

With all the evidence properly returned and logged back

in, she stood for a moment examining another item in the case box she hadn't yet dealt with—the blue bird feather. She put it on her mental list of things to ask her father, who had encyclopedic knowledge of who had what expertise throughout the Pacific Northwest.

"Gabbiano!" bellowed the chief.

Grace started and returned the bird feather to the box. She left the evidence room, with Mele locking up after her.

Within seconds, she stood inside Chief Cruz's office. "Yes?"

"Okay, you're investigating a homicide. I know this is asking a lot, but try to work two hours of bike patrol in daily. You choose which two."

Asking lot, my ass! It was a ridiculous request. "Yes, sir."

He scowled at her formality. "I want updates on everything you do, about everyone you talk to. Got it?"

"Loud and clear."

His scowl deepened. "Are you messing with me, Gabbiano?"

"No, Chief. I just want you to know that I understand what you're telling me."

"What's on your agenda today?"

"I have an appointment with Marie Brewer, the woman Ellie Clausen is using as her alibi, then I'll talk to Carolyn Haas, Clausen's last known love interest, who is also an investment broker. She may have some information about his financial affairs. Then I'm going to the dry cleaners with a picture of the red gown. After that, I hope to have the tiara identified and dated at the antique—"

"Enough," the chief said, his hand raised. "Get out of here, Gabbiano. Close the door on your way out."

"Don't worry, Chief, I'll get my two hours in on the bike somehow." She pulled his door closed before he could comment on her sardonic assurance.

Grace managed to make it to her appointment with Ellie's Saturday-night alibi with five minutes to spare.

Marie Brewer seemed the exact opposite of the widow Clausen. Tall and curvaceous, warm and friendly, she welcomed Grace with a pleasant smile on her face.

"Thanks for seeing me," Grace said.

"No problem. Ellie warned me you'd be calling."

Grace took no offense. Marie Brewer had a twinkle in her eye that said she was teasing. She and Ellie were the original odd couple, all right. Even as a youngster, Grace had wondered at the incongruity of their friendship.

"Coffee?" Marie asked.

"Yes, please."

"Let's go into the kitchen. It's much cozier there."

Grace wasn't sure she wanted a cozy interview, but the kitchen was a dream come true. Warm cherry cabinets, oak flooring, rustic tile countertops, and tasteful, homey country decorating accents. It was much like the kitchen in which her mother created miracles.

"How do you take it?"

"Black, thanks."

Marie set out a plate of *biscotti* with the coffee. "From Buon Gusto."

Grace picked one up and dunked it into her cup. "I'd recognize Mom's handiwork anywhere."

Marie picked up a cookie and copied Grace. "How did I not know these are for dunking."

"That's why they're so hard," Grace said. "They don't fall apart on the way to your mouth."

Marie laughed and repeated the dunk.

Grace wiped her lower lip with the napkin her prime suspect's alibi had provided. "Ellie says the two of you had dinner on Saturday night, then went to a movie."

Marie nodded, but averted her eyes. Early on, Grace's maternal grandmother had told her if you could read a person's eyes, you could see into the soul. Even using Braille, Grace would have known Marie was lying. It was as clear as that flickering eyelid thing Ellie did.

"I know you and Ellie have been friends for a long time, but you won't be doing her any favors if you don't tell me the truth. In a murder investigation—"

"*Murder*?" Marie sputtered, spewing wet chocolate crumbs across the table. What was left of the forgotten cookie floated for a moment in her cup, then sank. "Yeager was *murdered*?"

Grace nodded.

"Oh, my God. Ellie said you thought he died from a drug overdose, but she never mentioned murder." She dropped her head into her hands. "I can't do this. I detested that sonofabitch and the way he treated Ellie and the girls, but I just can't do this."

Grace got her notebook ready.

"Ellie was meeting someone, and I was supposed to say she was with me, just in case, you know, her husband should ask."

"And that someone was?"

Marie looked miserable as she raised her head. In a small voice, she asked, "Do I have to say?"

"I can't force you, but it will go a lot better for everyone, if you do."

Marie threw back her head and jammed her hands into her hair, ruffling it before she slapped her hands palms down on the table. "Christ, how did it ever come to this?" She leveled her gaze on Grace. "You think Ellie killed him!"

"I don't know who killed him—yet. I'm sorting through things now."

"Well, it wasn't Ellie, though God knows she had reason enough." She squeezed her eyes shut, then opened them, full of remorse. "I shouldn't have said that, and I shouldn't speak ill of the dead."

"You won't be," Grace assured her.

After a couple of false starts, Marie opened up: the affairs over the years, the treatment of Ellie and the girls that, given a name, would have to be called emotional abuse. "He used to hit Ellie, too, though she'd never admit it, not even to me."

"So how do you know, then?"

"He wasn't careful where his fist landed sometimes. He must have been so angry he'd forget to keep his aim below the neckline."

Grace made a note, thinking about the bruises on Ellie's knuckles. Were there others beneath her chic clothing? "So Ellie retaliated with an affair of her own, with one of his friends?" Adultery didn't justify adultery, but she tried to keep her expression neutral, her tone nonjudgmental.

Marie's mouth dropped open. "You already know about Hamm?"

The woman looked so distraught, Grace reached across the table and gave her hand a squeeze. "You're not the first to give me his name."

Grace watched, helpless, as Marie dropped her head and began to sob. She wondered if Ellie knew exactly how good a friend she had in Marie Brewer.

Coburg was growing, but still lacked a few amenities. A dry cleaner was one.

Grace stopped next at the dry cleaner Ellie used. Their computerized records indicated that Mrs. Clausen, a regular customer, hadn't left anything, and no one from the Clausen household had picked up anything, for the past week. No one remembered ever seeing her husband in the store, and no red gown had ever come in for cleaning. Even when Grace pulled out the photo of said evening wear, the dry cleaning staff remained definitely, *absolutely* certain the dress had never been in their shop.

So what clue, exactly, had Clausen hoped to leave via his youngest daughter? The red dress he'd mentioned and the red dress he'd been found in had to be one and the same, but beyond that, what?

CHAPTER 20

HARLEY WAS RIGHT. Carolyn Haas epitomized the term "career woman." In her expensive, stylishly cut gray suit, she looked like something directly out of an executive high-fashion magazine, only not quite as tall. The hem of her skirt hit just above the knee. Her hair, a honey blonde, was long enough to be shaped into a sleek French twist. She probably could have worn contacts, but chose trendy black horn-rimmed glasses instead. If she thought they concealed her red, puffy eyes, she was sadly mistaken.

Grace wondered if the brief dossier she had compiled on Clausen's former lover was anywhere near accurate. Two-point-five mil seemed like a lot of money, but maybe for an investment banker, it wasn't a lot of worth.

"Thanks for seeing me," Grace said.

"Not a problem," the distraught former lover said. "I know you want to talk to me about Yeager Clausen, but since he's a client, I'm not sure there's anything I can discuss about him that isn't confidential." She moved behind her desk and indicated the chair opposite for Grace.

"This is a murder investigation, Ms. Haas. The victim—your client—doesn't really have any confidentiality issues now. If you prefer, I'll get you a letter of release from his wife...."

Carolyn's face went white and she collapsed into her chair, unquestionably in shock. "Murder? *Victim?* Yeager's dead?"

Apparently, Carolyn-the-financial-wizard didn't climb out of her investment portfolios often enough to know that her ex-boyfriend was past tense. How, in a community where bad news spread quicker than the Asian flu, had the woman missed hearing the news?

"I'm sorry," Grace said sincerely, cursing herself for not picking up on the fact that Haas had been talking present tense. She had assumed her red, puffy eyes were the result of hours spent crying over her dead lover, when instead, she might have allergies, or another lover had dumped her. Or maybe she was faking it and had killed the jerk and cried from remorse.

"My God, how did he die?" Carolyn's voice cracked on the last word as she broke into inconsolable sobs. "He can't be dead!"

Grace rose and filled a glass from the water cooler in the corner. She also grabbed the box of tissue from a table strewn with financial magazines.

Carolyn removed her eyeglasses, oblivious to the streaks of mascara and eye shadow left behind as she scrubbed at her eyes. After several nose-blows and an equal number of eye-swipes, she reached for the glass and drank until she drained it. Water dribbled down her chin onto her expensive suit. Her face looked like she was coming off a one-week bender.

"How is it you hadn't heard the news yet?" Grace asked.

"I've been out of town. In Chicago, meeting with a group of investors on another project. I took the red eye into Portland and drove down to Eugene this morning. I went home, took a shower, got into some clean clothes, and came directly here. I haven't read a local paper for a week."

That, at least, explained her bloodshot eyes. Lack of sleep, not tears.

"You know we were lovers, or you wouldn't be here," Carolyn said, leveling a watery gaze on Grace.

For a moment, all Grace could think was, *Finally, someone who appears to be genuinely grieving over the SOB.* "I've heard rumors. You just confirmed them."

"Call me stupid, but I thought we might get back together." She slumped down in her leather chair. "I haven't spoken to him in six months. He emails me his portfolio instructions." Tears continued to run down her cheeks onto her suit coat and the silk blouse beneath. "Ohmygod, I can't believe he's dead! How did he die?"

"Probably asphyxiation due to drug overdose," Grace said.

"Yeager didn't do drugs!"

Another vote in for no drugs.

Haas frowned. "You know he didn't do drugs, and that's how you know it was murder."

Smart lady. "Something like that. We're still waiting on results from the lab."

"Then how…why…?"

"I'm sorry, we don't give out details in a homicide investigation."

Haas lifted a shoulder.

"Was he in to anything, any investment, that might have gotten someone's dander up?

"Not financially, at least not with his own investments. But the way he treated others…."

"You mean like the foreclosures?"

Carolyn blew her nose again. "You've been busy, Sergeant."

"The trail gets cold if you don't work fast."

"He must have pissed off half the town of Coburg at one time or another."

Grace gave herself a mental kick. She should have had Deets going through Clausen's office already.

They spent a few minutes discussing some of Clausen's shadier, yet totally legal deals and Grace marveled at how much the woman knew. During a year or so of pillow talk, he'd probably told her more than his wife had ever known about his business in twenty years of marriage.

Haas dabbed beneath her eyes with tissue until she seemed satisfied every bit of mascara had been removed, then slid her glasses back into place.

"I know this is sensitive," Grace went on, "but did he

have any proclivity for kinky sex."

She actually laughed. "Yeager? My dear, he was quite adventuresome, but kinky? No."

"Would you elaborate?"

Apparently back in career-woman-made-of-steel mode, Haas narrowed her eyes on Grace. "He liked the missionary position, doggie style, vibrators, porn flicks, edible panties, screwing in the shower, and even a quick fuck in the back of his car. To my way of thinking, none of those qualifies as 'kinky.'"

Grace mostly agreed. "What about dressing up in women's clothing?"

"Yeager? Absolutely not. He had a normal, healthy sexual appetite. His other performance—the one that involved principles—that's where he was lacking."

"Would you mind explaining?"

"He took advantage of our relationship by capitalizing on some information I had."

"Like insider trading?" Grace asked.

"Exactly, only worse, because he'd snuggle up after a good fuck, and fool that I am, I told him whatever he wanted to know, gave him promises of financial support."

"The breakup was not your idea?"

Haas sighed with a look of self-disgust. "Stupid, isn't it? I've got an MBA, and I used to have some pretty healthy bank accounts before we started sleeping together. He was doing at least two other women, not including his wife, while he professed to love only me—and I would have taken his sorry ass back in a nano second."

Stupid didn't quite describe what Grace thought about it, especially since she'd never found Clausen even remotely attractive or sexy, but then, who was she to judge after her one and only serious and disastrous love affair? "Would you mind telling me how he affected your financial situation?"

Haas pushed away from her desk and went to the window, her previously straight shoulders stooped. "In matters of the heart, I suppose you could almost expect a woman to make mistakes, but financially, I should have known better than to cave into his pleas to invest in his hare-brained schemes. I lost over a million dollars in a deal he had cooking with a developer from Seattle. I might as well have taken the money and used it for a bonfire." She looked over her shoulder at Grace. "It would have been more satisfying."

"And there were other instances like that?"

"Several, on a smaller scale, but overall, just as devastating."

"One last question. Did you ever sleep with Hamm Starr?"

Haas spun around, her mouth gaping in obvious disbelief. "He was Yeager's best friend!"

Coming from a woman who had no compunction about sleeping with another woman's husband, the response and implied denial struck Grace as ironically absurd.

She left with a list of the bad investments Haas's lover had talked her into, mentally placing the financial wizard's name next to Ellie's on her Suspect #1 list.

Grace rested her head for a moment against the steering wheel. All the unasked and unanswered questions she had for Ellie were bugging her beyond belief.

If she didn't ask those questions today and get some answers, it wouldn't matter how tired she was tonight, she'd never sleep.

Back in Coburg, Grace drove through the fancy gate, parked, and called in her location. She dragged her booted feet up the Clausen sidewalk.

She wasn't particularly religious, and would never admit to her mother that she had purposely asked for weekend shifts to avoid being dragged off to mass, but exceptions existed for everything. She sent up a small prayer: *Please don't let Caitlin answer the door.*

With grim determination, she pressed the doorbell.

The widow herself responded. Her hair was disheveled and hanging in her face, her simple, but expensive summer dress was soiled from God-knows-what, and her breath would have failed the Breathalyzer from ten feet away. From smell alone, bourbon was today's beverage of choice.

Probably, Ellie's defenses were down and as Grace had experienced the day before, it was almost impossible to get any information out of the inebriated woman, but she had to try. "I need to ask you a few more questions, Ellie."

"Shuure." She wobbled backward, spreading her arm wide. Unfortunately, it was the arm attached to the hand clasping her highball glass. Liquid flew over the rim of the glass, splashing everything in its wake. Ellie liked her whiskey straight.

Grace had always hated the smell of bourbon. It was a leftover thing from childhood and the time her mother had soaked a cotton ball with it to soothe a middle-of-the-night toothache. "Are your girls home?" she asked, trying to breath through her mouth.

Ellie frowned, as if thinking about that. "Nope. Linz went back to cheerleader camp and Cait is down at your mom's shtore." She glanced down at the mess she'd made, then leaned forward, tottering as she whispered, "They didn't wanna be around a drunk."

For the first time ever, Grace felt a pang of sympathy for Yeager's wife. "How about if I make you some coffee, Ellie?"

"Okay," Ellie said agreeably. She wobbled on unsteady feet, somehow missing the bourbon puddle and headed for the kitchen. Her erratic path left her looking like a toddler just learning to walk.

In a matter of minutes, Grace had the coffee brewing. Ellie drained her glass before Grace could get it away from her. She sat at the table, quietly spinning the empty tumbler with her fingertips. *Please don't let her pass out before I get some coffee down her throat.*

Unwilling to wait out the drip machine, Grace stuck a cup under the spout and filled it. She grabbed an ice cube from the freezer and floated it in the cup, cooling it enough that Ellie could drink it without burning her mouth.

Once the pot finished brewing, Grace repeated the routine. Ellie drank half her second cup before Grace threw out her first question. "Did Yeager have a habit of not coming home at night?"

Damned if Eleanor Clausen nee McCormick, drunk or not, didn't still have that way of looking down her superior nose at a person. "Pershonal business is none of your concern."

"Don't give me any shit, Ellie. This is a murder investigation. Answer my question."

Ellie's lips compressed, even as she picked up the cup to take another sip.

"I already know that you know he had affairs, Ellie. Lots of them. You told me so yourself, remember?"

"Then what the hell are you bothering me for?"

"It's my job. I get paid to bother people."

Ellie drained her cup, sounding a lot less drunk than she still looked. "So I knew. What are you going to do about it? Arrest me?"

"What did you and Yeager fight about? Why did you slug him?"

"I told you. I slapped him."

"You don't get bruises like that from slapping someone. You slugged him, and you slugged him good."

Ellie looked down at her hand, her expression one of satisfaction. "I did, didn't I?"

"Ellie, please...."

Ellie finally looked up, her chin tilted in a prideful manner. "I threatened to leave him," she said, staring at Grace with slightly more focused eyes. "I finally got the balls to leave the bastard, but we had that fucking contract...."

"A prenuptial agreement?" That threw Grace for a loop. Ellie had been the one with the money, not Yeager.

"No. The sonofabitch talked me into putting all the real property into his name a year or so ago. Said he needed it as collateral for some deal he had cooking with a firm out of Seattle."

Twice on the Seattle thing. "What about your personal assets—did he get you to sign those over, too?"

"He used a sizable portion of my trust to invest in some high-tech deals overseas."

"I can get a court-order to look at your bank accounts and investment portfolio."

Ellie slammed her fist against the table. "*The lying bastard!* All those years, he made me believe we were going to be rich beyond our wildest imaginings. My money would come back quadrupled, or more. I'd be able to leave him, take care of the girls without him—do it all, *everything*, on my own." Tears welled up in her eyes. "How could I have *believed* that worthless piece of shit?"

"Is anything left?"

"The college funds my parents set up for the girls, a little account I've been stashing over the years." She shook her head in disgust. "I might be able to live a year on it, if I budget carefully." She hung her head, staring blindly at the table. "I have to wait until the accountant gets back before I have a more accurate picture of what Yeager had that I know nothing about. And I suppose I'll have to talk to that bitch he was screwing, the one who did investments for him."

"Carolyn Haas?" Grace confirmed.

Ellie nodded. "He was such a prick!"

Being a public servant, Grace couldn't commit herself openly, but she certainly agreed with Ellie's estimation of her dead husband.

Ellie got up on steadier feet for a third refill.

"How long have you been seeing Hamm Starr, Ellie?"

The widow straightened, her spine stiff with disbelief. "Oh, my God! I can't believe Marie told you! She *promised*!"

"You friend takes no heat for this," Grace said. "I heard it from two other people before I ever talked to her."

Ellie actually flushed. "Two?"

Grace nodded.

Ellie slid down into the chair, defeated, her coffee and stubbornness both forgotten. "I don't know how it started. Yeager has had one woman or another on the side for years, and one day I just got sick of it. I was lonely, I was horny. Hamm showed an interest in me, probably because he was always competing with Yeager in some way, but I didn't care why. He's drop-dead gorgeous and he had a penis that stood up when he looked at me…." She shook her head, as if to clear it and focus her thoughts, then she narrowed her blue gaze on Grace. "Does it shock you, to hear me speak so frankly?"

"You'd have to be a lot more candid than this to shock me, Ellie," Grace said, though in fact, she was slightly stunned because Ellie had always seemed so prim and proper, just proving you definitely shouldn't judge a book by its cover. Or a woman by her upbringing.

"Hamm and I have been sleeping together for about a year."

That was about the same timeframe he'd been getting it on with Marilou Perkins of Good Hair Day fame. Geez, the man, like his friend Yeager, must have been hornier than a three-peckered goat.

"So, you're still seeing him?"

"Yes."

"Do you think your husband knew?"

"How could he?"

How could he not? Grace wanted to ask back, but refrained. If Clausen and Starr were as close, as competitive, as Harley and Ellie maintained, the two buddies probably told each other everything, trying to outdo each other.

Ellie, finally bordering on sober, must have reached the same conclusion. "Jesus, he must have known," she said, her voice barely above a whisper.

"How long were you with Hamm Starr Saturday night?"

She rose and went back to the coffee pot. "From about eight until around, ah, two, two-thirty."

Ellie was in danger of floating soon from beverage consumption. "Hamm's not going to give me a different story, is he?"

"No, of course not."

"I *will* be talking to him," Grace said, wishing she could see Ellie's eyes, "just so you understand. I don't want you pulling the same alibi stunt again that you tried with Marie."

But Ellie was on a different wave length. "No wonder Yeager seemed so cocky when I told him I wanted a divorce."

"How so?"

"He laughed, reminded me I would have nothing when he

got through with me. Not my home" —her voice broke, and she had to set down her cup to support herself against the counter— "and not my daughters, even though he couldn't have cared less about them."

She threw back her head in apparent anguish. "Why is it acceptable for a man to sleep with anything in skirts, but a woman better never play around, or she's screwed—literally and figuratively?"

"With his history of infidelity," Grace said gently, "I doubt any court would have given him *your* house or custody of your daughters—the girls are both of an age where they would have had a say about that." The moment the words were out of her mouth, Grace regretted uttering them. Personal opinions had no place in a murder investigation, but she felt so sorry for the pathetic creature standing at the counter.

On the other hand, Ellie had a much more potent motive than infidelity—Yeager had apparently held her captive in a loveless marriage. With no means of escape, no hope for happiness in her future, had his wife finally taken matters into her own hands?

Grace tamped down her sympathy and steeled herself to sound gruff. "Did you kill him, Ellie? Did you kill your husband?"

"I wish I had!" Ellie cried, whirling around. "I wish to God I'd had the courage to kill that lying, unfaithful piece of shit before someone else beat me to it!"

CHAPTER 21

GRACE HAD ONE more stop to make before she checked in the patrol car and put her mandatory two hours in on bike patrol. Really? What the *hell* was the chief thinking when she had a murder to solve?

She worried that Rose Callahan at Rose o' Sharon Antiques might not have time to talk to her during the noon hour, but as she drove through town, lines of hungry people trailed out the doors of both the café and Buon Gusto, waiting to get in for lunch.

Grace parked in the lot behind the antique store and entered through the rear. She exchanged greetings with Rose, who had been a friend of Angelina's since childhood, then explained why she was there.

"Well, it's a beauty," said Rose. While she examined the tiara, she asked, her tone deceptively casual, "How's your uncle?"

Rose's crush on the oldest brother in the Santarelli family, Angelina's brother Vito, was a well-known infatuation that had lasted for almost five decades. It was also a topic Grace hoped to avoid when within ten feet of Rose. "He and Mom are both fine," she said pointedly, steering the conversation back to the tiara. "Is it valuable?"

Rose shrugged and smiled. "Let's give it a closer look." She handed the tiara back to Grace and spread a jeweler's cloth out on the glass countertop. Grabbing a magnifying glass and a jeweler's loop, she nodded for Grace to set it down. "The stones are perfect and all there. The silver is clean."

"Sterling?"

Rose nodded. "Looks like it, and whoever owned it, kept it immaculate."

"Really?"

"Well, sure. It's not tarnished at all, and see this stuff right here?" Rose used a sharp pencil to point out a miniscule amount of greenish substance. "That's a cleaner."

Grace couldn't believe she'd missed it, but then she hadn't put a magnifier on the tiara yet. "Like from one of those little jars with the sponge inside you can buy at any grocery store?" she asked, remembering all the hours she'd spent as a youth cleaning her grandmother's silver.

"Yes, or something similar."

"How old?"

"Um, maybe twenty-five years. Thirty tops."

"Not new then."

"Definitely not, but not an antique either."

"So how much is a tiara like this worth?"

Rose tilted her head, turning the tiara this way and that. She picked up the loop and examined some of the stones. "For one thing, it's not actually a tiara, it's a crown. See how the band goes all the way around, and you've got these four rings inside?"

Crown. Clausen had left a message for his wife about her "crowning glory."

"Those are silver-plated and they're for holding the crown in place so it doesn't fall off the head. If I were to place it in the shop, I'd ask about three-fifty for it, maybe four. It's got a lovely lotus pattern in the front and a navette design around the band."

Grace knew what a lotus was, but a navette? "What's that?"

Rose explained, "Just another name for a marquis, or an oval shape that's stretched out to have points at both ends. In this case, the navette runs horizontally."

Grace hurriedly jotted some notes down in her book.

"And all that makes it worth so much?"

Rose gave the crown another critical look, pointing to the lovely array of stones. "As I said, you've got some really beautiful crystals here, and a lot of them. All the settings are impeccable, and every stone is in place. Also, the silver frame is hand-wired. You hardly ever see that. It's fairly large, too—probably nearly six inches in the front."

"Does that mean anything?"

Rose set the crown back down on the cloth. "Usually, you don't see this size worn for a wedding or other special occasion. And if it's on royalty, well, then it's encrusted with precious and semi-precious stones." She looked expectantly at Grace. "Figure it out yet?"

Grace gave her old family friend a blank look. This guessing game was payback for not dishing out more information about Uncle Vito.

"Grace, come on. What was the big event on TV every September when you were growing up, what every little girl in America wanted to be?"

Totally clueless, Grace shook her head.

"Miss America?" Rose suggested.

It took about three seconds for the light bulb to go off over Grace's head.

Crown. *Crowning glory.*

The white ribbon in Clausen's mouth.

"Oh, shit!" she said.

Grace was starving, but food would have to wait. She had to get back to the station.

Her tires spun gravel in Rose's parking lot, and she almost hit Deets head-on when she pulled into the driveway at the station. She gestured wildly to him to reverse direction. Her radio crackled an instant later. "Can't. I'm on a call. Back soon."

She depressed the button on her hand-held and said, "Okay. Find me, no matter what."

Grace grabbed the bagged crown, showing it a little more respect, not because of it's purpose, but because of it's value.

She locked the patrol car, and ran through the station door, calling for Mele.

"He's out on a call," Tina said.

"I need into Evidence! Where's the key? Shit, this new system isn't working already!"

"Don't freak!" Tina pulled the key out of her cleavage. "I'm anointed backup if it's urgent and Mele's out."

Within seconds, Tina had the door to the Evidence room unlocked. Grace reached into the Clausen evidence box and pawed through the bags until she located the one with the white ribbon in it. Next, she grabbed the red dress and the high-heeled sandals. "I'm not leaving the building, so I'm not logging this stuff out."

"Don't worry about it." Sensing intrigue, Tina trailed Grace like a shadow to the conference room. "You, I trust."

Grace carefully removed the gown from it's bag and spread it out over yet another clean sheet. She placed the crown above the bodice, then reached into the bag containing the ribbon, unfolding it with her gloved fingers shaking with anticipation.

She laid the strip of white satin at an angle across the bodice of the dress and positioned the heels at the hem, then stood back.

"Holy, crap," Tina said.

"Exactly," Grace agreed.

A long whistle came from behind her. Grace turned around.

"Okay, Gabbiano, you've established that the killer has a statement to make about beauty queens," Chief Cruz said. "Now how the *hell* does that relate to Yeager Clausen?"

Grace's brain pedaled faster than her feet as she made her bike rounds. Maybe the chief had done her a favor, after all. This case was getting more interesting and more confusing by the moment. Time on the bike was time to think, unless today turned out to be one of those summer afternoon's when everyone had something to say, and they absolutely *had* to say it to her.

As it turned out, most of the residents and antique shoppers she encountered were satisfied with a wave, but by the time she wheeled into the Buon Gusto parking lot two hours later, she shelved her thoughts on the murder and let them wander to a *panino* made on a nice big slice of warm *foccacia*.

For sure, her brain hadn't been productive thinking about the motive behind Clausen's murder. She still had to get Deets into the victim's office to find something more on the "Seattle deal." What kind of call was he on, anyway? She still hadn't heard a peep from him.

Try as she might, Grace simply couldn't connect any dots between financial dealings or love affairs to Clausen's death. Still, the fact that he was dressed in a beauty queen get-up did speak to a crime of passion.

Even though Coburg was a small town, Grace took a moment to lock up her bike. She was surprised to see her mother's car at the far end of the parking lot. "Mom, how come you're here? I thought you'd hired more help so you could have Tuesday and Wednesday off."

"Pinky called in sick and Bradley doesn't come in until four. Between me and Caity, we're doing okay." She gave her daughter a hug, whispering, "Lunch was a bitch, though. I'm glad I'm anal retentive when it comes to organization, or we'd have been up *cacca* creek."

Grace gave her mom an extra squeeze, laughing. "I hope there's something left for me, if you were that busy."

"Fresh bread coming out of the oven now."

"Where are the kids?"

"Gina is watching them, but she has paper due tomorrow, so I hope your father gets back soon." Grace's cousin Gina, a recent high-school graduate, was taking summer classes at UO on a fast-track to college graduation.

Something in her mother's tone sent up Grace's radar.

"Today is school registration for Kyle and Cassidy. It's too much for Gina to take all three of them."

"What about Aunt Loretta? Surely since Uncle Sal is fishing with Pop, she can—"

"Loretta is at her quilting class today."

Grace knew what was coming next and instantly felt guilty for what her response had to be. "Mom I can't take time off to watch Maddy today. I'm sorry."

"*Nessun problema,*" Angelina said breezily. "You just go by and pick her up and take her to work with you for an hour. She's such a little sweetheart, she won't be any trouble."

Grace groaned. *No problem.* Right. Chief Cruz would crucify her. "Mom, I'm still on probation. My boss—"

Angelina rolled her eyes and clasped her hands dramatically over her heart. "What a hunk, Grazia. Just the type of man I need for a son-in-law and you need to father your children."

"Mom, don't start!"

"I'll start, if I want to. You are twenty-nine years old. Practically old enough to be a grandmother yourself."

"Gee, thanks."

"You have to worry about biological clocks and things like that."

Her mother was definitely not a women's libber. "I haven't heard any ticking yet, Mom. Besides, when the alarm goes off, it won't be my boss I'm considering to make it stop."

Angelina frowned. "That might be a problem. I'll have to think on it."

"Don't you dare do anything I'm going to regret!"

Her mother reached over to pat her cheek. "Don't worry, *cara,*" she said, as if an Italian endearment would soften her daughter up. "I will be totally discreet."

"If you'd mind your own business," Grace said with good humor, "you wouldn't have to worry about being discreet."

"What do you want for lunch, my darling daughter?" Angelina asked, ignoring Grace's comment.

Grace relayed her cravings and watched as her mother sliced a large piece of foccacia in half, then proceeded to layer it with salami, provolone, and roasted red peppers. "Geez, Ma, that's big enough for two people!"

Angelina shot her a sly look. "Maybe you can share with someone."

"You're impossible."

"You want a coffee?"

"Yes, please. Iced. Jason was raving about your coffee the other night. I think you've made another convert."

Angelina waved a dismissive hand in her direction. "That man is too picky about his *caffè*. Do you know, when we go out to eat, if we can't get coffee from fresh-roasted beans, he won't order it?"

"It's the Northwest way of avoiding bad java." She pilfered several extra napkins. "It's also why you only brew from fresh-roasted beans."

Busying herself at the espresso machine, Angelina muttered something unintelligible about mouthy daughters. "I made you an iced latte. You don't get enough dairy."

Nonplussed, Graced accepted the plastic cup her mother handed her, complete with lid and straw.

"So, you'll take Maddy?"

Defeated, Grace said, "Yes, Mom, but I'm on my bike, so tell Gina to drop her off on her way. I need you to *promise* you'll pick her up by four, at the latest. I'm still new on the job and regardless of how hunky you find the chief, he won't think favorably of me baby-sitting at work."

"I'm sure Aidan will admire your loyalty to family."

Knowing it was impossible to reason with her mother, Grace closed the door on her final comment.

Somehow, she was going to have to figure out how to deal with shared family responsibilities, her guilt when she didn't feel she was holding up her end, and work, that small inconsequential part of her life that paid the freaking bills.

CHAPTER 22

ANY HOPE GRACE had of her niece arriving in the office unnoticed was dashed the moment Jimmy Frey screamed at Maddy for taking a piece of candy from the community candy bowl.

Frey's voice escalated several decibels in an effort to make sure the chief, in his back office, knew a child had invaded the inner sanctum.

"We offering a daycare service now, Gabbiano?" Frey hollered.

"Forget your hearing aid?" she shouted back, wondering why the hell he'd chosen this of all days to frequent the inside of the station.

Her retort silenced him, but only for a moment. "A police station is no place for kids," he retaliated, even louder.

"Really?" Grace snapped. "You're here."

"Why you—"

"I'm on my lunch hour, Corporal. If you have a problem, take it up with the chief." And with that, Grace led Maddy, who had observed the entire episode with wide eyes and a quivering bottom lip, on a nonchalant stroll to the office she shared with Deets.

Her colleague raised an eyebrow in her direction, but said nothing about Frey's outburst.

Maddy was not so reticent. "Bad man," she said, shaking her small, curly head woefully.

"Amen," Deets muttered, picking up his CPD ball cap. "I'm off to Armitage Park. Someone's using picnic tables for firewood."

"I thought you were going to radio me when you finished your other call."

Deets gave her a baleful look. "That guy you just had the yelling match with? I had to clean up another one of his messes. I walked in the door about one minute ago."

Grace didn't require any further explanation. "After you hit the park, I need you to check out Clausen's office, see if anything…interesting turns up."

"Sure. We got a key?"

"I called. The building manager occupies the adjacent office. She knows you're coming and Ellie's already okayed it, so we don't need a warrant."

"Something specific I'm looking for?"

"See if you can find anything about a big deal out of Seattle that involved a million-dollar investment from Carolyn Haas and Clausen hocking just about everything his wife owns."

Deets whistled.

"My sentiments exactly. I also need you to check out Carolyn Haas's alibi for Saturday and Sunday." She slid a piece of paper across to him on which she'd written the name of the conference Haas said she'd attended. "Mind if I sit Maddy at your desk?"

"Only if she knows how to file," Deets joked.

"Can't file," Maddy said seriously, after he'd left and she'd been perched on top of two phone books.

"Don't have to, sweetie. You can color Deets a nice picture and that will make him the happiest man in the office."

Maddy smiled her angelic little smile and set to work doing just that. She only looked up once during the next hour to repeat that smile on Chief Cruz, who stuck his head in, but said nothing except, "Hi, sweet pea," to the little girl.

Grace thanked her lucky stars she'd had time to brief the chief on everything she'd learned so far today *before* Gina dropped Maddy off.

The office was fairly quiet until the five-foot tornado roared in.

Grace recognized the voice of the invader immediately, but thanks to Marilou Perkins, she couldn't help but envision Zelda Starr as a human-sized prune. Which wasn't fair, because despite her evil-sorceress-sounding name, Zelda was actually kind of pretty. If you ignored the dark, gray-streaked frizzy hair that always looked as if it resulted from a finger having been stuck in a light socket.

Her second day on the job, Grace had been sent out to Zelda Starr's place. Her co-workers' laughs and snickers had echoed behind her as she left the station house. They hadn't been laughing an hour later when she'd come back with two smart-ass teens in tow.

No one had believed Zelda on any of the previous five occasions they'd been called out to find an elusive peeper. Not until Grace, who managed to corral *two* peepers. She stepped out into the reception area to see what had Hamm Starr's mother all riled up.

"Hello, Zelda," she said to the woman who had informed her almost two weeks ago that her mother-in-law's name had been Mrs. Starr. She was Zelda. "What's going on?"

"This," screeched the petite fireball, waving a piece of paper under Grace's nose.

Gently, Grace clasped Zelda's wrist and managed to extract what appeared to be a letter. While everyone in the office, including the chief, stood at the ready, apparently in case Zelda went postal, Grace read the letter.

"It's not true!" Zelda ranted when Grace finished. "I don't owe a penny to anyone. I own my land free and clear."

"Mr. Clausen doesn't actually say you have any delinquent payments, Zelda."

"Bastard!"

"He just says that if you find yourself in a financial bind over your property ownership, he'd like to talk to you about purchasing—"

"I lease out what land I don't live on for farming. Not

likely I'm ever gonna have a money problem!" The tiny tyrant tossed the chief a belligerent stare. "What're you doing, letting a dead man write letters, anyway?" she demanded. "Didn't I tell him not to send me no more letters last time I talked to him!"

Aidan plucked the letter from Grace's fingers. His eyes scanned the document, then moved back to the head of the letter again. "It looks like this was written and mailed on Saturday."

No wonder Zelda had freaked. "You don't have anything to worry about," Grace said soothingly. "Not now."

"I told my boy not to hang around with the likes of Yeager Clausen." Zelda snatched the letter out of Chief Cruz's grasp. "Been telling him that for years. Deserved just what he got, Yeager did. Terrorizing old folks like me. You know, old Jeremy Bacon killed himself over one of Clausen's damned letters!"

With that, she stormed out of the office, leaving center-of-the-storm quiet in her wake.

Grace looked at the chief. "Maybe Hamm Starr had more than one reason to want Clausen dead."

Grace began to toe-tap the instant the clock confirmed her mother was five seconds late. Clausen had been dead for over forty-eight hours. What little trail existed was threatening to get mighty cold. She had a schedule to keep for the rest of the afternoon to ensure that it didn't.

Not to mention, the chief wasn't likely to allow a child in her office for more than an hour.

Exasperated with her mother's tardiness, she picked up the phone and called Harley. "What do you know about the death of a man named Jeremy Bacon?"

"I'm fine, Gracie. Thanks for asking." He paused, apparently in thought. "He owned a small parcel west of town. Filbert trees. Died about six months after his wife went."

"Suicide?"

"No, he had a heart attack. What's up?"

"Just checking out a lead."

"You're only working the Clausen case. How is that related?"

"Thanks for the info, Harley. Bye."

"Grace—"

"Maddy, *bambina*, your Nonna is here."

The little girl squealed. Grace whirled in her chair. "Mom, you're late!"

Angelina cast her daughter a stern glance. "Is that any way to greet your mama?" She looked around. "Is Aidan in? I'd like to say hello."

"He's busy, Mom. You can't just barge in on him."

"Of course, I can, Grazia." She praised Maddy's "art," then herded all three children together.

Before she could divert her determined mother, Tina called out, "Hey, Gracie, I've got a DV with no one to cover."

"No one?"

"Uh-huh."

There goes my afternoon, Grace thought. Why'd it have to be a domestic violence? The disagreements that ensued from a domestic squabble could take hours, not to mention they had the potential to turn violent for the responding officer. They weren't supposed to go out to DVs, except in pairs. "Mom," she called across the room at her mother's back, "I have to roll on a call. I'll catch you later."

"All right," Angelina said. "Kyle's due for his allergy shots, then we're going to the toy store. Your father should be home by then."

The mention of the toy store brought yelps of delight from the three children.

Grace reminded them, "Hey, guys, keep it down, okay? People are working here."

Ignoring her, the siblings chattered on, but moved to the chairs near the front door and sat as their grandmother instructed.

"You're spoiling these kids, Mom."

Angelina took time to level a stern glance on her middle daughter. "Remember what they've been through," she said.

"How could I forget?" Grace lowered her voice. "Delfina

and Bobby won't be able to compete with this spending spree of yours when they come home, will they?"

Angelina whispered back. "Listen, Grazia, if Delfina and that good-for-nothing husband of hers ever come around here again, they're in for the fight of their lives getting these children back!"

Shocked, Grace stood mute as her mother beelined for the door marked CHIEF.

"Grace," Tina called out. "That DV?"

Pushing this latest familial development momentarily to the back of her mind, Grace grabbed a bottle of water. "Okay, I'm going. See if you can't raise someone to meet me there." She took the piece of paper Tina extended with the address on it.

"Aidan, how wonderful to see you!" her mother could be heard to chirp.

Grace hurried out the door, wondering if it was too late to adopt out to a different family.

CHAPTER 23

THE DOMESTIC VIOLENCE turned out to be stranger than Grace had anticipated.

"You gonna arrest him?" shrieked the self-reported victim.

Grace noted the blood streaming from the alleged abuser's head. "Did he hit you?"

"He wanted to."

"It looks like you got the first blow in, Mrs. Stockton."

"So what. He threatened me with that big-ass ham fist of his, so I hit him with the frying pan first."

"Big-ass ham-fist, my ass!" Mr. Stockton roared. "You gotta quit watching that Letterman guy, Minnie. He's givin' you too many weird ideas."

Grace had to bite her cheek to keep from laughing. "I'm afraid you can't assault someone just because he threatens you, ma'am." She turned to the stunned Mr. Stockton, who, indeed, sported a big-ass ham fist, in addition to his wound. "Do you need medical assistance, sir?"

"Huh?"

Grace couldn't tell if he was dazed or drunk. "I'll be happy to call the EMTs to see to your injury." Without touching him, she leaned forward to get a whiff of his breath and a look at the wound. She estimated he had about five or six stitches in his immediate future, and judging by the amount of alcohol exhaled with each breath, he'd already imbibed plenty of anesthetic.

"Hurts," he said, not quite whining.

"I'm sure it does." Grace depressed the button of the radio attached to her shoulder and asked Tina to dispatch a Medic Unit to the DV address.

"Don' wanna go to jail," the big man mumbled.

"You don't have to go to jail, sir," Grace assured him, "but you have the right to press charges against your wife for hitting you with the frying pan."

The big lug actually smiled, and turned into a pile of mush as he gazed lovingly at his spouse. "Minnie don't mean nothing by it. Hell, it was just a love tap."

Grace sent up a silent prayer, asking for light traffic, so the ambulance could arrive quickly, and she could be on her way to actually fight some crime.

By the time the EMTs transported their reluctant patient to the ER, the air outside was dotted with charred wisps of grass. The sky to the north had already taken on the grayish pall that accompanied hundreds of acres of grass fields north of town being burned off. The pungent odor made Grace's lungs burn. How in the world, she wondered, were people like her nephew supposed to breathe under these conditions?

She pulled her smartphone out and speed-dialed her parents' house. "It's me," she said, when her father answered. "The field burning is horrible today. Do you think Kyle will be okay?"

"Your mama called from the allergy office. The doctor said as long as he's kept inside until the sun sets, he should be fine. They'll come straight home after the toy store, and we have plenty of movies in the Netflix queue for them to choose from."

"They ought to stop it."

"Someday they will. The farmer's are finding out there are other ways to clear their fields."

"Yeah, well until then, they ought to come down here and be forced to breathe it like we are!"

Her father chuckled. "You're just the woman to invite

them. In the meantime, call the Air Protection Agency and complain."

Grace rolled her eyes. *Like that would do any good.* "Later, Pop."

Yeager Clausen's physician, Dr. Richard Mattson, looked like Doogie Howser.

"Thank you for seeing me," Grace said, shaking hands.

"No problem. I'm sorry to hear about Yeager. Quite a shock. His wife said drug overdose?"

"That's what we think. Lab results aren't in yet." She withdrew her notebook and took the chair he indicated. "Any signs he was using when he came in last week?"

"None. The guy is, I mean *was,* a health freak. He drank very little, mostly socially, if he was honest on the form, but no drugs, not even tobacco."

"How did everything check out? Anything crop up that might cause him to take his own life?"

Doogie laughed. "He'd only been my patient for the past year, but I don't see a guy like that doing a number on himself. If you wanted to know how cool he was, all you had to do was ask him. His overall mental health certainly seemed good."

"So, no terminal illnesses. Anything else out of the ordinary?"

The doctor checked the file he had up on his computer screen. "His cholesterol was two-ten. Not exceedingly high, but borderline. I advised him to watch what he ate a little more closely, since nothing he named in his regular diet seemed out of whack. Probably genetic. He was hooked on chocolate, and he might have been one of the unlucky few whose blood cholesterol was affected by too much of it."

He leaned back and crossed his arms over his chest, started to say something, then with a little shake of his head, apparently decided not to.

"What?" Grace asked.

Indecisive, the doctor said, "Maybe I shouldn't even repeat this, but since you're conducting a murder investigation, it may have some relevance. At the time, I remember thinking, TMI."

Too much information? Curious, Grace tilted her head at him, wondering why a doctor who'd probably seen just about everything had suddenly gone beet-red.

"He, umm, bragged about using chocolate during, umm, sex."

Grace blinked at him. "Chocolate. During sex."

Doogie nodded.

"Can you be more explicit?"

He sat forward and put his finger inside his collar, as if to loosen it. "Yes."

Grace waited and finally he began to describe several games Yeager Clausen had played with his partners that involved bite-size chocolate candies and various female orifices.

Fascinated and repulsed at the same time, Grace managed to jot down what she heard. As she drove back to Coburg, she thought Clausen's murderer had chosen the wrong way to do him in—drowning him in a vat of hot chocolate might have been more fitting.

TMI, indeed.

If Grace had been tired before, her brain felt like mush by the time she returned to the station. She entered her case notes for the DV, then set to work on transcribing her interviews with Marie Brewer, Carolyn Haas, Rose Callahan, Clausen's doctor, and the latest Ellie conversation. She also included her brief encounter with Zelda Starr and her follow-up call to Harley about the deceased Jeremy Bacon.

A quick radio contact with Deets told her he was still at Clausen's office. Grace made arrangements to meet with him first thing in the morning to go over his findings. She also asked him to check out Yeager's insurance policy for a suicide exclusionary.

Her cell rang. Thinking it was probably her mom, she pulled it out of her pocket. LC Medical Examiner showed on the readout. "Grace Gabbiano," she said.

"Hi, Grace. Doug Hacker here. I'm getting ready to fax over the autopsy report on Clausen, but I wanted to give you a head's up on one last peculiarity I discovered after you took off."

How much more weirdness could there be?

"Our guy had M&Ms shoved up his butt."

Shocked into silence, Grace's jaw dropped.

"You still there, Gracie?" Doug asked.

"I saw his doctor earlier. He said Clausen liked to put bite-size pieces of chocolate in female orifices when he…."

Hacker laughed. "Sorry. It's just that we get all kinds of freaky stuff though here, so it always surprises me when I'm surprised."

"I guess that explains the stray M we found at the scene. Thanks for letting me know."

The ME disconnected, still chuckling.

Grace stuck her head in the chief's office. She gave him a rundown of what she'd learned over the latter part of the day, not particularly thrilled with having to discuss with him Clausen's perversions with M&Ms, and where some of those Ms had ended up.

Back at her desk, she made a list for the following morning of things she wanted to get done before she left for Seattle. The chief had okayed her day off as overtime, indicating the previously authorized ten hours of OT was history. Once up north, she planned to see Clausen's disgruntled business associate first. Afterward her friend Abby, who taught fashion and costume design at UW, would take a crack at the evening gown. Before she headed to the locker room to change clothes, she left Mele a note telling him she needed to check out the red gown for two days.

At home, she took time for a quick shower, then walked over to her parents' house. After a short discussion, it was decided the air had cleared enough that Kyle could go out, so Grace rounded up her nieces and nephew and took them to Dairy Queen. There, she ordered a burger and onion rings for herself and various ice cream treats for the kids, who had long-since eaten dinner.

It was a mundane, relaxing, entertaining hour. Thoughts

of dead men dressed up in evening gowns, adulterous spouses, frying-pan-wielding wives, and vindictive co-workers were pushed aside. It was just her and three kids who'd been abandoned by their parents. Yeah, right. Mundane.

Back at their grandparents' house, the children hurried up the stairs, the girls to get into their PJs while Kyle gathered his stuff for a sleepover. Grace headed back to her little house and sat on the front porch in the gathering twilight, idly pushing herself in the swing.

"Hey, Gracie."

"Pop!"

"Sorry, I didn't mean to startle you."

"I should have heard you coming—I guess I'm too engrossed in my thoughts."

"Of the crime or the new chief?"

"Why doesn't Mom expend this much energy on Rocco's love life?" Grace groused.

Her father laughed and joined her on the swing. "Aidan seems like a good egg. I think he can handle a little of your mother's meddling."

"I hope so." Grace frowned. "He doesn't seem to like me much, as it is."

It was Joe's turn to frown. "What makes you say that?"

"He keeps making references to Seattle, and he's not very subtle about it."

Her father grunted. "Maybe I should talk to him."

"Maybe you should just keep out of it," Grace said. "I don't need Mom trying to marry me off and you trying to protect me from dragons, especially if both of you have my boss targeted as the victim. Besides, I already offered him a copy of my rebuttal to the charges, if he's interested."

"I think he's a fair man, *cara*. You might be bent out of shape a little, too, if you'd been hit with all this your first day on the job. I hear he's also got problems with his kid."

"Oh, yeah? I heard that, too. What kind of problems?"

Joe shrugged. "If he wants us to know, he'll tell us."

Grace gave the porch swing another push.

"Sorry you missed those trout for dinner," he said, folding his hands over his belly in contentment. "Nothing like fresh fish to make a man feel manly and to make a woman bitch because her kitchen smells fishy."

Grace happened to know that her mother loved fresh trout, so she didn't take her father's comment as anything but a love note.

"Well, gotta get back." He looked toward the north. "Glad that wind came up this afternoon. Cleared the air nicely."

Grace nodded her agreement.

"Mom's putting the little ones down and Kyle will be over soon. Waiting for this meteor shower has been almost unbearable for him." He smiled down at his daughter. "Reminds me of you in more ways than one. Your brothers and sisters always fell asleep before it was time to watch, but not you. He loves those detective stories, too."

"He wants to grow up to run the crime lab, like you."

"Or be a cop, like you." He leaned down a planted a kiss on the top of her head. "Have a good evening, Grazia. Enjoy the time with Kyle. Your work will still be there tomorrow."

Grace reached up and gave her dad a hug. She had more to say to him, wanted to tell him where the blob of skin came from, but he was right, the work would still be there tomorrow. "Take some of your own advice and enjoy your evening with Mom."

Her father grinned. "I plan to."

Kyle passed her father on the walkway. "Gracie, I'm ready! Got my PJs, my sleeping bag, my binoculars, my Nintendo 3DS."

"Everything you need for a meteor sleepover," Grace agreed, "but save the Nintendo for later, or you'll miss the show. Can you set up the chaises?"

"Sure. Nonna sent birdies, too."

Grace's mouth began to water. The Italian cookies, which she and her siblings had dubbed birdies because *i ciglipini* was too hard to pronounce, were usually reserved for a Christmas treat. A delectable filling of semi-sweet chocolate, sugar, nuts, raisins, and red wine was wrapped inside a half-moon shape of sweet dough, then baked to perfection. "I can't believe Mom turns on the oven when it's almost a hundred degrees outside," she murmured. "Who's she trying to impress?"

He handed her two plastic baggies and kept one for himself. "She said she was trying to cover up the smell of fish."

Grace groaned. "Aidan" was written in fancy script across a decorative label on one of the baggies. *Mom, you never give up, do you?* If the way to a man's heart was through his stomach, Angelina had apparently decided on that path to capture the chief for her daughter.

Grace set the chief's bag of goodies on a side table by the front door so she wouldn't forget them in the morning. Kyle quickly spread out his sleeping bag in the living room, which he preferred to the spare bedroom because it had the TV, and lined up his belongings within easy reach.

Within minutes, he also set up their meteor-watching station on the front lawn, but they still had an hour to go before it would be dark enough to see anything. They decided to spend the time in the lab, fingerprinting.

Fifteen minutes of instructions flowed into half an hour, but both Grace and Kyle were satisfied that he had the single-roll motion down pat. "On TV, they show the cops rolling the finger back and forth," Kyle said, a slight scowl of disapproval on his face.

He looked so like his mother in that moment, Grace had to take a deep breath to regain the composure she lost when thinking about Delfina, and how much she missed her. She nodded. "I always cringe when I see them do it wrong. Watch this. If you rock the finger back and forth, all the lines become obliterated."

"Ob-what?"

"Obliterated. Mushed up. The finger becomes a little paint roller that keeps covering up everything it did before, including all those nice, clear lines you need to see to make a positive identification."

The boy squinted at the giant fingerprint on the wall he'd been studying for weeks. "Poppie had his done right. There's no smudges or anything."

"Someday you'll be able to roll a print perfectly, too. For tonight, you've done great. Go clean your hands, then you can take a quick look at your thumb print."

Kyle hurried to the sink. He returned a minute later, reaching for the magnifying glass. Her nephew bent over the desk, examining every line intently. His kind of focus seemed to be genetic in her family.

When he finished, they locked up the lab and headed to the front yard. Kyle plopped down on one of the chaise lounges, while Grace headed inside to make a cup of coffee for herself and a cup of hot chocolate for Kyle to drink with their birdies. She grabbed a sweater for later while the tea kettle boiled. For such a hot day, it had turned surprisingly cool with the evening breeze.

Hands full, she pushed the screened door open with her rear end just as her cell phone rang. Half-tempted to ignore it, she stepped out onto the porch, then back inside again. Likely, it wasn't her parents, but it might be important.

She set the two cups down on the table by the door. "Hello?"

"Gabbiano, it's me."

CHAPTER 24

GRACE COULDN'T SUPPRESS a wry grin. Aidan Cruz seemed pretty sure that's all he needed to say by way of greeting. "What can I do for you, Chief?"

"One of my neighbors needs some instruction in the fine art of neighborliness."

"Someone using you for target practice?"

"In a manner of speaking."

Had he actually growled? "You want me to come out there and arrest him?" Wherever "there" was.

"I want you to come out here and scare the piss out of the little shit—when I find him, or them."

Grace glanced at the stained glass mantel clock her mother had made during her craftsy phase. "Right now?"

"No, sometime next week."

Grace wanted to ask more questions. *Why me? Why right now? Why can't you do it yourself? You're much scarier than I am.* Instead, she said, "I'm kind of tied up right now, Chief. Can I talk to this felon in the morning?"

Over the phone line came a rumble. It might have been the chief exploding. "If this could have waited until morning, I wouldn't have called tonight, goddammit!"

Whoa!

"I need you to get out here as soon as you can."

"I'll have to bring my nephew with me. We're having a meteor party."

She could almost hear the chief sizzling through his silence. "When you get here, make sure the boy stays in your vehicle." He gave her directions on getting to the parcel where he'd parked his motor home. "Bring a handcuff key with you."

Intrigued, Grace wanted to ask why, but dared not.

"And, Gabbiano?"

"Yes, Chief?"

"Breathe a word of this to anyone after you've been out here and there won't be a job you'll be able to get anywhere in law enforcement except scrubbing toilets at the jail."

Whoa, Nellie! Whatever had the chief's dander up apparently wasn't dangerous, or he wouldn't have allowed Kyle along. On the other hand, it must be something sensitive, or he wouldn't be issuing so many threats.

"I'll get there as quick as I can. I have to lock up, and I'll have to stop by the office for a key, since I don't carry one."

His long-suffering sigh felt like something warm and real blowing in her ear. "Just get here as soon as you can, okay?"

"Sure." Grace hung up, curiosity eating at her. What on earth?

Grace poured the hot drinks into travel mugs and put the chief's bag of cookies into a carry-sack.

"We gonna be back in time to see the meteors?" Kyle asked, obviously worried.

"I think so, but if we miss them tonight, they'll still be good for the next two evenings."

"Poppie and Nonna probably won't let me be up that late two nights in a row. And besides, you're going to Seattle tomorrow."

"Well, let's not count our chickens before they're hatched."

"Huh?"

"That just means, let's not think the worst before it actually happens."

"Oh." Kyle accepted the travel mugs while Grace locked up. "Whaddya think's wrong with Chief Cruz?"

"I haven't got the slightest idea, but I do know he doesn't want us talking about it, whatever it is. When we get there, you're to stay in the car, and if you can avoid looking out the windows, that might be a plus."

In the car, Kyle fidgeted with his seat belt, excited about the adventure. "Is he like a spy, or something?"

"No."

"Maybe he's naked!"

"I hope not!"

When she came out of the station with the handcuff key, he said, "I wonder why he called you. Isn't there another officer working at night?"

Grace wondered the same thing. Within minutes, she had her answer.

Coburg's new police chief made quite a spectacle as she drove onto his property. No wonder he'd demanded confidentiality. Of course, who would believe this story, anyway—the chief handcuffed to a hammock and the hammock wedged at an odd angle against the side of the motor home where the door opened out.

Kyle looked at Grace, and Grace looked at Kyle. Despite the chief's orders, they climbed out of the vehicle together and approached him. Simultaneously, they burst out laughing.

By the time Grace unlocked the handcuffs connecting the chief to the hammock, her boss had cooled off considerably. Maybe it was having Kyle there, or maybe it was the ridiculousness of the entire situation, but Aidan actually had a sheepish grin on his face.

"You been robbed?" Kyle asked, helping right the hammock before he pulled it away from the motor home.

"No, someone just had a little fun at my expense," Chief Cruz said. "I was exhausted when I got back here. I had a beer and decided to take a quick nap before the mosquitoes came out. The cuffs were pressing into my back, so I dropped them and my keys onto the ground."

He glanced north, toward the Howard farm. Anyone who'd lived in the general vicinity for more than twenty-four hours knew the Howards had six kids who loved to get into trouble. "My guess is, one of those punks who've been skulking around here for the past two days dropped by to say 'hello.' Lucky for me, I didn't leave my weapon out."

Grace shuddered at the thought. "Want me to go over there and put that scare into them now?" The chief must have really been tired not to hear or feel a thing while he was being handcuffed to the metal frame of the hammock.

"No." He scratched his neck. "Damned mosquitoes got me, anyway."

"Umm, how did you end up, you know" —her gaze slid to the open door of the motor home— "over there?"

"They conveniently removed my cuff key from my key ring. I thought maybe I could pick the lock with something inside, but as you can see, the door wasn't quite wide enough to get the hammock through. Fortunately," he added ruefully, "my cell phone was just inside on the counter where I could reach it."

He glanced from Grace to Kyle. "I have your word, *both* of you, that this is just between the three of us?"

Grace and Kyle casually put their hands behind their backs. Angelina, mother and grandmother, would have recognized the gesture, but the chief didn't know them yet, so he didn't. Fingers crossed, they both nodded solemnly.

Grace and Kyle ended up watching the Perseid meteor shower from Chief Cruz's "front yard." Aidan set out a lawn chair for himself, apparently having had enough of hammocks for one evening. As for Grace and Kyle, they took the hammock so they didn't have to crane their necks for the display, which boasted some of the brightest, longest meteor tails Grace had ever seen. Even Aidan seemed fascinated by the show. Munching on Angelina's fresh-baked cookies, he sipped a cup of coffee and proclaimed he'd never had a better dinner.

Grace silently moaned, wondering if her mother's incessant matchmaking schemes would put a damper on her career in law enforcement, or end it altogether.

Kyle fell asleep on the way home, but awakened long

enough to stumble into the house, where he flopped fully clothed on top of his sleeping bag. Grace removed his shoes, wondering, yet again, how his mother could have given up moments like this.

She eased out the front door and went to the lab to retrieve the magnifier and the extra set of pictures Rocco had printed for her. Uncomfortable with leaving a sleeping child alone while she examined photos in the lab, she locked up tight and went back to the house.

After changing into a sleeping T-shirt, she curled up in the chair in her spare bedroom with the door closed so the light wouldn't bother Kyle. She positioned the floor lamp over her shoulder for optimal lighting.

Rocco had done an outstanding job of developing the negatives. His photos always seemed clearer, more defined, than those processed by photo shops.

Inspecting each picture carefully, Grace again experienced the sense of déjà vu she'd had at the crime scene. Something was unsettlingly familiar about the victim being trussed in an evening gown sizes too small for him.

She went to bed a short time later, tired, but unable to sleep. After tossing for an hour, she finally dozed off in a tangle of bedcovers. Not long afterward, she dreamed of Yeager Clausen, walking down some kind of pathway in the beaded silk gown, alternately popping chocolate candies into his mouth and puffing madly on a syringe-shaped cigarette. Grace jerked awake.

Unable to get back to sleep and bathed in sweat, Grace turned on the fan, then dialed her younger sister.

"Someone better be dead!" Michaela snarled.

"Someone is," Grace said, hurriedly assuring her, "but no one in our family." She related the details of Clausen's death, hoping to probe Michaela's memory. "This all seems vaguely familiar to me, Mikey. I think I read something about a similar case recently, like maybe within the last year, but I can't remember where it was or who it involved."

Grouchy at being awakened from what she informed her sister was a "hot" dream, Michaela finally agreed to do some checking. "Don't expect any miracles," she warned, yawning. "I've got two features that come first and the only thing that keeps my paycheck coming is how many clicks my articles get on the website." She yawned again. "Besides, you're the cop. Investigating is your thing."

"Yeah, but you're the reporter and you'll get the scoop when I bust this case wide open."

Her sister responded with a sleepy growl of laughter and severed the connection.

Envying her sister's "hot" dream, Grace finally tumbled into dreamland.

She didn't expect to wake up all hot and bothered the next morning with her own dream sizzling through parts of her body in ways she'd never experienced before.

Damn, she absolutely, positively *had* to make her mother stop trying to hook her up with Aidan Cruz!

CHAPTER 25

GRACE HEARD THE front door slam as she climbed out of the shower. Great, Kyle was going to spread the word bright and early this morning about their evening adventure. The chief was going to kill her.

No sooner had she slipped on her sandals than her father knocked on the door. "Gracie, you up?" he called, already inside.

Grace finished brushing her hair and pulled it back into a ponytail. "Good news travels fast."

Her father laughed as he moved around her kitchen preparing coffee.

Drawn more by the aroma of fresh-brewed French Roast than the thought of the conversation ahead, Grace finally wandered into the kitchen.

"You need to impress upon Kyle that he can't tell anyone, or I'm dead meat."

Her father regarded her sternly. "The way I heard the story, your fingers were crossed behind your back, too."

"Yeah, but you don't see me blabbing it at seven o'clock in the morning."

"I'm not sure I approve of you and Rocco and Dante teaching my grandchildren the finger-crossing rules," he said, doing his best to remain serious.

"Yeah, right, Pop. You're the one who taught us—cross

your fingers behind your back when you promise not to tell, then you can then tell *one* other person the secret without breaking your promise."

"It seemed reasonable when I learned it as a child." He shrugged. "As a parent, I realized it was a good way to keep track of what my kids were doing."

"So you used it as a method for us to rat each other out without feeling like we'd betrayed anyone?"

Her father nodded.

Grace stared at him, awed. "Brilliant. I never suspected your subterfuge!"

"Just remember it when you have kids. It'll save everybody a world of grief."

"Well, at least Kyle has told his one person, so I think I'll be able to keep my job—unless you had your fingers crossed when he told you."

"It would be totally unethical and unprofessional for me, as police commissioner, to even *think* about repeating a story like this one." Joe's eyes glittered mischievously.

Grace silently recounted the discovery of her boss handcuffed to the hammock and grinned. Behind her, the coffeemaker gurgled its grand finale. "I wish you could have seen him, Pop. This big, bad police chief reduced to…." She started laughing so hard, she couldn't finish.

"Grazia, Grazia," her father admonished, laughing with her. "It's not good to know something like this about a superior officer."

Grace wiped away a tear. "Why not? It might come in handy sometime."

Joe gave her a look.

From out of nowhere, an image of former Chief Harmon McCrea popped into her brain, followed immediately by thoughts of Jimmy Frey. A forewarning? Uneasy, but able to shake it off, she poured a cup of coffee for herself and one for her father. She joined him at the table where he was already munching on birdies he'd brought along.

"You hear any buzz from the OSP Forensics Lab?"

He pushed the cookie bag toward her. "None."

"Not even a little gossip about what I dropped off there?"

"Only that there are a lot of other jobs in front of yours."

"Ah-ha! So, you at least *tried* to get some information."

"*Mea culpa*."

"That's my pop," she said with pride. She grabbed a birdie, took a bite, then blew on her coffee. "I found this really blue feather in the wig. I don't suppose the OSP lab would take a look at that for me?

"Like from a blue jay?"

"No, it's bigger and really vivid." She thought about it for a moment. "More like a tropical coloration. It's got a brilliant hue."

"I'd send it to Fish and Wildlife in Ashland. They have a bird specialist down there." Grace jumped up and grabbed a pen and notepad from her junk drawer.

"Thanks," she said, once her father had written down the contact name. "You're not going to believe where that skin came from."

"Try me. I've seen everything."

Grace raised an eyebrow at him.

"I have," he insisted.

Grace shrugged. "His pecker."

Joe ended up with coffee spewing out of his nose. "Jesus Christ, kid, give your old man some warning before you drop a bomb like that!"

"Sorry, Pop." Grace jumped up to get the dish cloth. "But you were insistent that you'd seen everything."

"Well, yeah, but not with people I know." He used a napkin to blow his nose, then got up to throw it away. When he sat back down, he said, "Shit, this puts a whole new spin on things."

"Ya think?"

"Do you have a theory about what happened?"

"Not really." She told him about the hunt for the missing penis, then gave him a rundown on the tiara that was actually a crown, the white ribbon, and the M&Ms. "So far, I have four suspects, none of them all that good, and two more to interview this morning who may make the list. Clausen didn't climb willingly into that dress, or give himself a lethal injection, or cut off his own—"

Joe held up a hand to forestall her. "Someone either had a weapon pointed at him, or held some other threat over his head."

"Exactly." Grace finished off her birdie and grabbed another one. "But even then, wouldn't you think he'd struggle, at least a little?"

"Like all murders, it's more complicated the further you get into the investigation."

"Yeah. Things would have been a lot simpler if he'd killed himself."

Grace bundled up Kyle's belongings for her dad to take back to the house and gave him Abby's number where she would be staying in Seattle.

Deets was already in the office by the time she arrived, having a phone conversation with Clausen's life insurance company. Several neat stacks of file folders and other paperwork were laid out on the top of her desk. From the beginning of their work association, she had discerned and appreciated his organizational skills.

While she waited for Deets to finish his call, Grace rifled through a thin folder on the SeaTac Development Corporation, then went back to the beginning and began to read in detail.

Clausen had kept meticulous records. Grace jotted down the phone number for a man named Grayson Hanover, who was listed in the file as CEO, and made copies of several documents involving large sums of money and a legal agreement that didn't seem to be in Hanover's favor. The other folders in the pile were labeled DELINQUENT TAXPAYERS, FINANCIALLY INSOLVENT, and DEAD WEIGHT.

"Cocky bastard," Grace muttered under her breath.

Deets glanced over from his desk, nodding his agreement. Into the phone, he threatened the next person in the food chain. "If the information I want isn't faxed over here about thirty seconds ago, the court order I'm going to get will involve more than just looking at the particulars of Clausen's life insurance policy."

Grace gave him a thumbs up and went back to reading. She wasn't particularly surprised to find names of several prominent Coburg farming families in the DELINQUENT TAXPAYERS file and a number of senior citizens among the FINANCIALLY INSOLVENT, along with a couple more farmers. But in the DEAD WEIGHT file, the arrogant, conniving Mr. Clausen had listed everyone from his father-in-law, to the former police chief, to Zelda Starr, and….

"Good God!" Uncle Vito! What the hell had he done to incur the wrath of Yeager Clausen?

A retired priest, Vito was the only family member who enjoyed farming. He cultivated a small parcel of land his father had set aside for him years before. It included a greenhouse that not only supplied Buon Gusto, but gave the family a constant and tasty source of garlic, plum tomatoes, herbs, and other fresh produce. On the parcel next to that, he tended the Zinfandel and Sangiovese grapes, which grew on vines her grandfather had planted more than fifty years earlier. Following tradition and his father's recipe, Uncle Vito used them to make Dago Red wine. He produced around eight hundred bottles a year, selling most of it under the Santarelli family label. He proudly displayed his gold- and silver-award medals in his small winery tasting room. Grace hoarded several bottles in her cupboard.

She pondered the significance of the DEAD WEIGHT file as she stepped into the conference room to use the phone. Within moments she had appointments set up with SeaTac Development and Hamm Starr and obtained permission to ship the bird feather to Fish and Wildlife in Ashland for identification.

Deets stuck his head through the door, letting her know he was ready. He hadn't learned much from Clausen's office, but promised to review the files again in case they'd missed something. "Run background checks on every name he's got in those folders," Grace said.

"Including your uncle, the priest?"

She sighed. "Yes."

"I take it I can get some help on this?"

Grace cocked her head at him. "Anyone except Dagne or

Frey. She's not giving her all to the job and Frey's likely to fuck up the assignment just out of spite." She didn't miss the look of relief on Deets's face. "Maybe Felix? He's a financial whiz kid, isn't he?"

Deets nodded.

"One last thing." She told him about the feather and asked him to have Tina ship it overnight to Fish and Wildlife. "Here's the woman's name and mailing address. Make sure it's sent certified, return receipt."

"A feather? Man, this case just keeps getting kinkier and kinkier."

CHAPTER 26

HAMM STARR'S STUDIO was almost all windows. Grace had an urge to put her sunglasses back on, the room was so bright. She dropped her hand to pet the black Lab that danced a welcome around her feet. "Friendly dog," she said. The canine rewarded her with a drooly lick.

Hamm shrugged. "What can I say? Blackie likes women."

Just like his master. "I appreciate you seeing me at such an early hour," she said, remembering the old adage about catching more flies with honey. She went one step further in browning the tip of her nose. "I know, as an artist, this is the best time of the day for you, so I'll be as succinct and quick as I can." She glanced around with only half-feigned appreciation. "You have some remarkable work here."

Almost preening, whether from the compliment about his work or because he was a man on the prowl, he flashed her a seductive smile. "You obviously have an eye for good art and a sensitivity for the artistic mind."

Grace refrained from rolling her eyes. "I've always admired those who can put thought to canvas and make it look like something." Her gaze wandered to a portrait in progress of a woman, so voluptuous, so naked, Grace felt her face flush.

"Would you care for a cappuccino?"

"No, thanks."

"It's no trouble. I have one every morning at this time. Won't take me a minute to prepare." His eyes roamed up and down her body in a way that left little doubt what he was thinking.

This wasn't the first time she'd been hit on while working, but it never got easier. Grace cursed her own lack of foresight. She should have considered that "Hammbone" might not have come on quite so strong if she'd arrived in uniform for the interview. Even though she was heading for Seattle directly afterward, she shouldn't have worn a sundress.

"Follow me. We can talk while I foam things up."

Definitely attractive, subtlety apparently didn't rank high with him, and the lack of it detracted from his appeal. The ubiquitous leather thong held back his gleaming coal-black hair. A skin-tight black T-shirt, covering a well-muscled torso and impressive biceps, was tucked into equally skin-tight black denims that emphasized the muscles of his legs and his perfect ass. This guy worked out. Religiously.

She followed him to a small kitchen tucked into a back corner of his studio. He pulled a chair out for her at a small chrome-and-glass table. She looked over her shoulder at him and caught herself swallowing hard, snared by the intensity of his blue, blue eyes. Sexy, but calculating.

She started in surprise when he reached out and trailed his fingertips up the side of her neck and around to her jaw, where he cupped her chin and tilted her head up. The pads of his fingers were rough, probably from working the various small sculptures around his studio. She jerked her head away, unable to suppress a shiver of response.

His eyes flared with satisfaction. "I would love to paint you."

Her gaze went straight to the nude he had underway. "Not in this lifetime," she responded, her tone as dry as she could make it.

He shrugged and with a self-deprecating smile, moved to the counter where the espresso machine sat. "You can't blame me for trying. You're a beautiful woman, Sergeant."

Grace took a calming breath and thanked him for the

compliment. Good lord, no wonder Ellie and Marilou—and God knew who else, including the babe with no face on the in-progress canvas—were ga-ga over Hamm Starr. She would've had to be dead not to have some reaction to him.

Blackie nudged his cold nose against her hand, begging for another rub, which she obliged. Apparently satisfied, he padded over toward a bank of windows. He circled several times, his nails clicking on the vinyl flooring before he settled into a round ball, closed his eyes, and went to sleep. Grace grinned. So much for doggie adoration.

She pulled her notebook from her shoulder bag. "The lab tests aren't back yet, but the cause of Clausen's death appears to be asphyxiation from drug overdose."

Hamm half-turned toward her. "Yeggs hasn't done drugs since college."

"Yeggs?"

He shot her a devilish grin. "Hamm 'n Yeggs...leftover nicknames from our days of carousing."

As if you're not still *carousing*. "So, no drugs since college?" Those who knew him seemed so certain about that.

"Trust me, none. He and I and Jack, well, we quit the drugs after our junior year. We made a pact."

"Jack Dellenbach?"

He nodded, but seemed surprised that she knew who he was talking about.

"What prompted that?"

He turned back and scooped ground beans into a small metal cup, which he then fitted into the machine. "We just decided it was time to grow up."

Grace wanted very badly to see his face. His body language, at least from the rear, said he'd either left something out or altered the truth. "You all grew up so much that you split to different schools for senior year?"

That brought him around. "You've been busy."

"Yes, I have."

He considered her for several moments before he spoke. "We moved on to different schools. We thought part of growing up was not relying so heavily on one another." He filled a small pitcher from the sink and poured the water into the machine's reservoir.

"Usually, life-changing decisions like that have some sort of deep motivation."

"Do they?" He pushed the red ON switch.

Grace made a note to check on Hamm Starr's educational background, along with that of his two friends. "You must have lost a lot of credits, transferring your fourth year."

"A few."

"Where did you go?"

"Columbia University."

"That's a long way from Colorado."

"Yeah, but they had a great art school."

"And yet you came back here, and so did Clausen." She watched him for some sign that this meant something. "But not your friend Dellenbach."

"No." He turned to the espresso machine for a moment. "Jack didn't want to come back here."

Most college students would walk on hot coals, rather than take more classes to graduate, yet these three friends had done exactly that. "What about Clausen and Dellenbach, where did they finish up?"

"Yeggs went to U-Dub and Jack went to UTEP."

Washington, Texas, and New York. Interesting that they'd each gone to a far side of the country. Of even more interest was why at least one hadn't stayed at CU.

"You have a star tattoo between your left index and middle fingers."

He glanced down at his hand, which had gone into an odd-shaped fist. "We all got one. Mine came first, a star on account of my last name. They had to have one, too. During our drinking days. Buddies for life."

He seemed to favor the hand slightly, as if there was some disability involved. Was it recent, or longstanding? "'We' being you, Clausen, and Dellenbach?"

He nodded.

"Where is Jack Dellenbach now?"

"Dunno. Haven't heard from or about him in" —he grunted, as if surprised— "nearly twenty years."

"Does he still have family here?"

He shrugged. “They moved away the summer before we started college. Went to San Antonio, I think.”

That might explain why he never came back to Oregon. “Did you injure your hand recently?”

His expression registered shock, then quickly smoothed out. “It’s from a car accident, in college.”

“While you were at CU?”

He nodded, but the affirmative response came slowly, almost, it seemed to Grace, unwillingly. She scribbled *Check Boulder PD records*.

“When was the last time you talked to Clausen?”

“I guess I saw him about a week ago.” He went to the lone cabinet over the counter and withdrew two cups and two saucers. Once he had them arranged to his satisfaction on a tray, he turned to face Grace.

“You guess?”

He leaned against the counter, frowning at her. “Okay, I *did* see him a week ago. He came by.”

“So you saw him last Wednesday?”

The handsome artist’s frown deepened. “I guess it was Friday.”

Grace stared at him, waiting for him to make up his mind.

“Yes, it was Friday.”

“Are you sure it wasn’t Saturday?”

“No, I mean, yes, I’m sure. It was Friday.”

“He had several fresh flea bites on his leg.”

“He didn’t get them from Blackie!”

Grace’s gaze swept the floor where the dog snoozed, her astute eye examining the dust bunnies laden with dog fur in the corners.

“Despite my housekeeping, or lack thereof,” Hamm said, his tone stiff, “I take excellent care of my dog and he doesn’t have a single goddamned flea on him.”

For some reason, Grace believed him, so she moved on. “Ellie says she was with you Saturday night. Would you mind telling me from when to when?” For good measure, because she had a rotten feeling Ellie had already prepped her second alibi, she added, “Please keep in mind, this is a homicide investigation, and I’d hate to find out later that you haven't given me the correct information."

He looked so horrified, Grace considered it fortuitous that the counter offered him some support.

"*Homicide!* What are you talking about?"

"I take it that you haven't talked to Ellie." The widow certainly played nasty with her friends and lovers.

"Not since...Saturday, uh, I mean yesterday." He released his death grip on the counter behind him and tried to ram his fingers through his hair, even though the strands were tightly constrained. Was it the pull on the roots or something else that had turned him stark white? "Fuck. Murdered. *Fuck!*"

Assured that Romeo finally got that she was dead serious, Grace said, "What time were you and Ellie together on Saturday night?"

He didn't answer for at least a minute. Grace waited him out. Finally he said, "She came over about eight and left around midnight."

"You seem to be having a hard time remembering days and times. Did you and your girlfriend have a little talk with her husband Saturday night, maybe kill him to get him out of the picture?"

"*What?* Are you crazy?" he demanded, obviously incredulous. "Ellie left here at midnight, so I can't speak for her, but I sure as hell know *I* didn't talk to him."

Hickory, dickory dock, the rat lied about the clock. "I did ask her. She says she was with you until two or two-thirty."

"No way! She wanted to stay later, but I had to meet…I mean, I had to take care of something else."

Grace wondered how Ellie would take the news of her lover's cheating ways. "Her name?"

He tried to feign puzzlement and failed. "Ellie Clausen. You know that."

"Don't jerk me around, Mr. Starr. You know I want the name of the woman you saw after Ellie left." She made a notation in her notebook. It was actually a star doodle, but he didn't have to know that. Let him sweat. "Your own alibi will have to be verified."

"You're shitting me?" His voice rose at least an octave and almost cracked.

"I never shit anyone. If you can't verify who you were with, then…." She lifted a shoulder, as if to say, *There's nothing I can do for you.*

"Christ! This is unbelievable. Why would I kill my best friend?"

"For the same reason you were sleeping with his wife?" Grace suggested.

He glared at her. "Little Girl Scout turns bitch."

"Just a cop doing her job. Sorry if that makes you uncomfortable. Her name, please?"

His internal debate was quite entertaining. When finally he reached a decision, Grace gave herself a mental pat on the back for having avoided a confrontation involving necessary threats.

"Jennifer Sousa."

Grace gave him the eagle eye. If he meant Jennifer Sousa, daughter of Manny and Rosa Sousa, then he'd better be prepared to face a statutory rape charge. "She lives on Eighth?"

He nodded, suddenly wary.

"She's seventeen, you jerk."

He paled even further. "Twenty-two."

"Maybe in your wet dreams."

Every inch of cockiness drained from him. Cappuccinos forgotten, he wobbled over to a chair. "Seventeen?"

"You grew up in Coburg. Didn't you go to school with Manny and Rosa? They're your age."

"Seventeen?"

"Yeah, you know, a teenager. She still goes to high school, baby-sits for one of the women at the station."

"Christ."

Grace glanced at her watch. She'd heard enough from Hamm Starr. If she hurried, she might have time to talk to Jennifer before taking off for Seattle at nine. "Unless you want me bringing you up on charges of having sex with a minor, don't pick up that phone to call either Ellie or Jennifer."

"I'll have to talk to Ellie at the funeral tomorrow," he said, his tone sulky.

"Tomorrow?" *Gee, thanks for telling me, Ellie.*

"Yeah, at Armitage Park. Actually, it's a memorial service. She wants to drown his ashes in the river afterward." His muscles tensed, as if he had blabbed something else he shouldn't have.

"What time?"

"One-thirty."

That certainly put a kink in Grace's plans. She hadn't planned to return from Seattle until Thursday evening. Now she'd have to come back first thing in the morning. Great. She shoved her pen and notebook back into her purse and rose. "Just remember what I said about contacting either one of them."

She got to the studio door and turned. "And Mr. Starr, if I were you, I wouldn't finish that nude by adding Jennifer Sousa's features to the face."

As Grace climbed into her VW Beetle, she wondered if Ellie Clausen needed a special permit to pollute the McKenzie River with her husband's ashes.

Jennifer Sousa was a striking teenager. Petite, stacked, beautiful. Her Portuguese heritage shone through every healthy pore and every strand of waist-length hair. What red-blooded male would be able to resist her, looking, as she did, a good five years older than she claimed to be?

Grace was surprised to find her engaged in the mundane activity of watering a bed of petunias. "I'm here about Hamm Starr."

The girl's mouth clenched stubbornly, even as she quickly cast a furtive glance over her shoulder toward the front door. "Yeah, so?"

"This conversation is just between you and me, not your parents."

Jennifer relaxed, marginally.

"Were you with him at any time over the weekend?"

"I don't have to tell you anything."

"No, you don't, but if you don't answer my question, I'm taking you to the police station, where you will be questioned in the presence of your parents, and afterward your father will go beat the crap out of Hamm Starr, and then I'll arrest him for assault and Hamm for statutory rape, and you can take them both cookies at the County Jail."

Jennifer apparently didn't like that scenario. "He never *raped* me. We met a little after midnight on Saturday. At his studio." She tossed her head, flaunting her attributes. "He's painting me."

"Yes, I saw. How long were you together?"

The girl's defiant gaze skittered around the yard. "I left around one."

"Really?"

"Okay, I was there all night. Does that make you happy?"

"Only if it's the truth. And if you use condoms."

"It is the truth and it's none of your damned business if we use rubbers or not."

"You're right, but it is *your* business. Of course, I guess you already understand that you sleep with everyone your partner sleeps with."

"He's not screwing anyone but me!" the girl protested. "We meet every Saturday night. Every. Single. One."

Grace decided on a nonverbal comment. She rolled her eyes.

"I'll kill him!"

"Please don't. It's not worth ruining your life over a man." She jotted down a couple notes and turned to leave. "Thank you for your time, Jennifer."

"Wait!" The girl put out a hand to her. "You're not going to tell my parents about me and Hamm are you?"

"Not unless I have to."

"What do you mean by that?"

Grace looked the teenage sex goddess straight in the eye. "If I find out you lied to me, your parents will know everything I know in a New York minute."

CHAPTER 27

FORTUNATELY, SEATAC DEVELOPMENT Corporation was located south of Seattle, closer to Tacoma, or Grace wouldn't have made her appointment on time.

It wasn't much as corporate offices went. The building was old, the furnishings shabby. If they'd shown a profit recently, they certainly hadn't put any of it back into the cosmetics of running the company.

Only the name of the man she was to meet parlayed the apparent dilapidation into success: Grayson Trenton Hanover III.

She opened her badge wallet when he asked for identification. He then checked the sleek Rolex on his wrist before he sat down behind an obviously vintage solid cherry desk, leaving her standing.

Okay, Grace decided, pulling out her notebook, she could play his game. "I understand you had a partnership with Yeager Clausen of Clausen Enterprises, Coburg, Oregon."

"We've had a few investments together," GTH III concurred.

"Mr. Clausen was murdered over the weekend, Mr. Hanover. While interviewing people in connection with his death, your company name came up several times as a failed business co-venture."

The man tapped his fingers, one of which sported a gold ring with a diamond bigger than a pea, against the leather blotter on top of his desk.

Grace waited him out.

Finally, “Your point, Sergeant?”

“I’d like to know if the deal went belly-up because of you or Mr. Clausen?”

Hanover blustered. “Because of him, of course.”

Grace pointedly gave the office a once-over. Despite the quality of the furnishings in his inner sanctum, the pieces were old and worn.

“Believe me, what you see here does not reflect the financial standing of this company in the business community.”

Grace made a note to have Felix Montoya utilize his knowledge and resources to check out Mr. Hanover and the shoddy-looking SeaTac Development. If Felix, who had just earned his B.A. in Economics, lived up to his own hype as a financial wizard, he should shine on this assignment.

“Clausen and I planned to develop a piece of land near the Interstate, on the north end of Coburg. He assured me he had jumped through all the land-use hoops, glad-handed all the right public officials, schmoozed all the planning people. He’d gathered investors. We were set to go.”

“And?”

“He used the money to fund another deal overseas that bankrupted almost before it even got started. He had counted on the short-term investment tripling before putting the money into the Seatac project.”

“How much did you lose?”

“Three million.”

Plus the one million Carolyn Haas had lost. Despite GTH III’s assurance to the contrary, Grace guessed it to be an amount he couldn’t afford to lose, just as it had been for Haas. “Enough to kill over.”

“Perhaps for some. For me, I had another way of dealing with him.”

The guy was practically a refrigerator. “Which was?”

“Ruining his reputation. A man like Clausen would suffer more with a tarnished name than he ever could by dying. He had his pride, but beyond that, he had a gigantic ego.” He shook his head with something that seemed like sorrow. “I was almost ready to level my attack. Too bad he's dead. I would have relished watching him sink into the muck."

Grace believed him. The pompous owner of Seatac Development Corporation honestly seemed to savor revenge over death.

To save time, Grace met her friend, Abby Sloan, at the university. Grace used gloved fingers to spread the crimson gown over a clean white sheet she'd brought with her.

"Dior," Abby said immediately.

"You're sure?"

"Absolutely. Circa 1993."

"Any idea where it might have been purchased?"

"Any high-priced dress shop, definitely big-city type." She rattled off the names of several such shops in the Northwest. "It'll be impossible to track and it might not have even been purchased in Washington or Oregon."

Using work hours to track down the dress would take valuable time from her investigation. Time Grace didn't have. Granted, the gown was a good clue, but she had other leads to follow that might be more productive.

Several students wandered in to admire the dress.

"Everyone swoons over it," Grace told Abby as they walked toward their respective vehicles to head for a favorite hangout, where they planned to have dinner with mutual friends.

"Silk, bugle beads, the epitome of *haute couture*. Who wouldn't? Whoever bought it had some bucks."

"Yeah? Like how many?"

"Dress like that, even twenty-some years ago? Probably several thousand."

Grace shook her head, amazed. "Nobody seems to care that it was bad luck for the man who wore it last."

Grace swore at the obnoxious alarm emanating from her smartphone. It couldn't be morning already! After three unsuccessful attempts, she managed to silence it. She showered, dressed, and sat down to coffee and toast with Abby.

"I wish you could stay longer," her friend said.

"Me, too, but I have to be at that memorial service. The killer might jump up and make a confession." She smirked. "I'd hate to miss *that*."

"Lack of sleep must be affecting the reasoning part of your brain."

"Probably, but just the same, murderers do show up at funerals."

"Don't you ever get tired of being a cop? Everything just seems so…tedious."

"It is sometimes, but this homicide involves an interesting group." Grace chuckled. "I had forgotten what small-town living is like." She glanced at her wrist watch. "It's almost seven. I'd better go. I have to allow time to go home and change clothes."

"Don't get any speeding tickets hauling ass out of town," Abby teased, giving her a hug.

"I still have connections on the force. Not everyone up here hates me."

"No one hates you. You've blown that part of the story way out of proportion."

As she drove away, Grace wondered if her friend might be right.

And then she remembered how Dave Mackey had betrayed her and knew that at least one person and his cronies *did* hate her.

Grace observed the small gathering at the riverside service from behind her Gucci-knockoff sunglasses. Chief Cruz had situated himself beside her, making no secret of his perusal of the attendees.

Aside from the widow and daughters, Harley was there for the newspaper and Jimmy Frey crowded in next to Ellie, confirming to Grace once and for all that his big mouth *had* delivered the bad news of Clausen's death to her over the phone.

Marie Brewer stood on the other side of her friend, and Ellie's parents, Patrick and Kathleen McCormick, hovered protectively behind their granddaughters. Carolyn Haas and three other women Grace didn't recognize were positioned as far from Ellie as they could get and still hear the minister. Hamm Starr stood conspicuously apart from everyone.

Mayor Samuelson had come, as well, along with Bill Prior from the bank, Hank and Donna Defore from the real estate office, and Jason Knox. Grace's uncles, Sal and Vito, Aunt Loretta, and her own parents stood midway between the Clausen family and the recent Clausen extra-marital affairs, with Rose Callahan sidling ever closer to Uncle Vito.

No other friends or relatives had shown and Grace wondered if they even knew about the service. Ellie wouldn't have invited Clausen's girlfriends, so word of mouth had played a part in the notification process. Of all the women present, only Carolyn Haas shed any tears. Considering how Clausen had treated her, Grace surmised that love is definitely blind.

She had texted the chief about the service after leaving Starr's place, but she was still a little surprised to find him in attendance. Did he think she couldn't handle scrutinizing the mourners? Better that than the other option, she decided as she watched him watch the widow who watched him back. *Surely not!*

Grace forced herself to listen as the minister rambled on—and on—about Yeager Clausen and his virtues. Pillar of the community, devoted husband and father, philanthropist. Thankful she had on dark glasses, she found herself amused, despite the occasion, as she glanced from expression to expression. To a person, each listened to Pastor Goode with obvious astonishment. Was there anyone in town who had seen the glowing picture of the deceased that Pastor Goode painted? Perhaps he felt his eulogy had to live up to his surname.

Continuing to covertly study each face as the good reverend wound down, Grace almost gasped aloud when her gaze landed on Jimmy Frey. The pure hatred radiating from his eyes nearly threw her back a step. She knew he resented that she had come on staff at a higher rank, but did that really justify his behavior? She quickly glanced at the chief. He had slipped on his own dark glasses, so it was impossible to tell if his focus was still on Ellie, or if he, too, had witnessed Frey's rancorous, silent message to Grace.

Ellie stepped forward to accept the urn containing her husband's ashes. Grace honestly expected her to leave with her daughters and Yeager's remains, but with a word to her daughters to stay put, the widow walked briskly down the path to the river, exactly as Hamm had said she would.

"You can't throw that into the river," said Chief Cruz.

"Oh, really?" Ellie demanded coldly. "Watch me." And with that, she hurled the ceramic container into the water with an aim as deadly as Nolan Ryan's. The urn crashed against a rock jutting through the surface, spilling what was left of Yeager Clausen into the McKenzie River.

"She should have flushed him down the toilet," Jimmy Frey said, coming up behind Grace.

"What a charitable observation."

Frey tensed and reddened. "Listen, you bitch," he began, his voice low, his hand grasping her upper arm painfully, "mind your own fucking business and leave Ellie alone."

"Take your damned hand off me, Corporal, or be prepared to find out if Ellie likes eunuchs."

"Don't 'corporal' me, Sergeant. I'm on my own time."

"Oh, yeah?" Grace pushed up her dark glasses with her free hand and looked him up and down in his CPD uniform. "Well, I'm looking for a killer and I'll be talking to whomever I have to, to find her…or *him*."

His grasp tightened, but then Ellie marched up the path and right past him, gathering up her daughters and her parents, leading the posse to the silver sedan parked in the lot.

Frey gave Grace's arm one last painful squeeze, hustling after them. By the time he reached the parking lot, Ellie had already started up her Lexus and sped away without a backward glance for him.

"I take it there's no reception at the house later," Aidan said, his tone droll.

"I guess not." Rubbing her bare arm, Grace glanced over her shoulder and up. Only moments before, the chief had been following Ellie down to the river bank and now he was within a foot of her backside. He moved quickly and quietly for such a big man. Had he come to her rescue and frightened Frey away? She glanced at the other mourners, who stared after the departing Clausen family.

Harley approached her, a bemused expression on his face. "No one quite seems to know what went on here this afternoon."

"Just one in a series of events." Grace quickly added, "Off the record."

He examined her upper arm. She glanced down, surprised to find the shape of a big red thumb print forming

"You've got four more on the backside," Harley said. "I suppose that's off the record, too. What the hell, Gracie! That guy should be in cuffs. You gonna stand for this, Chief?"

"No."

A man of few words.

"Aidan Cruz."The chief put out his hand.

Harley looked like he had reservations about shaking it.

"Chief, I'm sorry," Grace said. "This is Harley Jacoby, editor of the *Coburg Herald Weekly.*"

Harley finally grasped the chief's hand. "About the assault on Grace…."

"Harley!"

"Off the record," the editor said.

"I'll deal with it," the chief said.

"I'll take care of it myself," Grace said.

The chief's expression hardened and his gaze went after Frey, racing to catch up with Ellie's vehicle. He turned back to Harley. "I like your paper, Harley. You've got a good mix of news and you did a good job of reporting Clausen's death."

Harley grunted. "Didn't have much choice. You and your sergeant here were mighty stingy with the details."

The chief gave Grace a look. "She's good at what she does."

"I'll buy that," Harley said, rubbing his hands together. "Time to get back and start doing some digging." He glanced out at the river where the urn had hit the rock. "And some writing. Just don't know how much I plan to use of what I find, though. Clausen was an asshole, but I haven't got anything against the rest of the family." He looked once more at Grace's arm, gave the chief a harsh, silent appraisal, then headed for his car.

Grace looked around, surprised to find everyone else gone but Hamm Starr. He had walked down to the riverbank and stood with his head bowed, as if in prayer.

His eyes on the lone mourner, Chief Cruz said, "I know it's your day off, but I need to talk to you. Do you mind meeting me at that café on Willamette? Neva's?"

Grace chewed on her bottom lip. *Need to talk.* That sounded serious. She noted, however, that he hadn't been dumb enough to suggest Buon Gusto. Her mother would have reserved the church if they'd gone in together for lunch.

The chief pushed up his shades and rubbed the bridge of his nose with two fingers. "I hope you don't mind doing this outside the office. I missed breakfast *and* lunch. I'm hungry." Right on cue, his stomach provided a back-up rumble.

"No problem." She took a leap. "Is something bothering you?"

"Did I say I was bothered?"

Never one to leave well enough alone, Grace said, "Well, you have furrows in your forehead and you're rubbing—"

The chief slipped his glasses back into place. "Skip the analysis, okay? I'll meet you there in ten minutes."

He followed Harley to the parking lot and jumped into his big red Tundra, leaving a cloud of dust in his wake.

Grace followed at a slower pace, wondering what the hell she'd done now.

CHAPTER 28

GRACE'S EMOTIONS PELTED her from several directions. Jimmy Frey had managed to catch her unaware, so the chief had witnessed her inability to fend for herself against a co-worker. A co-worker about whom she had some serious concerns. If Frey could hurt her like that—and he *had* hurt her—was he capable of harsher violence, like murder?

She'd be engaging in a little of that herself if he ever laid a hand on her again.

Grace glanced at her watch. Once she'd known she had to come back for Clausen's memorial service, she'd offered to help Gina supervise the three little ones at the Amazon pool for an hour or so. Afterward, she would take Kyle for his allergy shots and Gina would take the girls home. She made a quick call, apologizing to her cousin for bailing at the last minute because she had to meet with the chief.

"Chill," Gina said. "They've been monsters all day! I was just getting ready to call and tell you that I cancelled swimming as a consequence for not minding me."

Gina's grownup response left Grace admiring her and feeling guilty at the same time. "I'll get there as soon as I can to spell you, Gina. Maybe you can tie them to the oak tree in the meantime."

"I wish!" Her cousin laughed. "Don't hurry. Uncle Joe just came back, so the law of the land is about to change."

Grace couldn't help grinning as she hung up. Pop loved

his grandkids, but no one in the house could be firmer with them, or get them to settle down faster, than he could.

Grace arrived at the café first. The chief had gone on to park at the police station and walked over. She let him choose the table, figuring he'd pick a corner if this was to be a serious discussion, or a window seat up front, where it was brighter, if it wasn't.

He surprised her by choosing the vacant patio, which was just fine by Grace, since Neva's didn't have air conditioning. Most customers avoided the outside tables because of the noisy exhaust fan, and even though Neva had recently replaced it with one that was fairly quiet, everyone mostly still ate inside. Not even the draw of speakers piping easy listening music to the patio could lure them out. Crazy.

They ordered—Grace hadn't eaten lunch, either—but didn't speak until Neva, today in a lime green uniform, bright yellow tennis shoes, and an electric orange apron, served Aidan's coffee and her iced tea.

Aidan shook his head in amusement as Neva walked away. "It hurts me to look at her."

Patience wasn't one of Grace's strong suits. "Am I in trouble?"

Chief Cruz arched that damned eyebrow at her. "Should you be?"

"With you, I can't tell," she replied honestly.

He picked up his coffee cup, frowning. "I want my officers and staff to do what I tell them, but I don't expect them to abide by my rules because I scare them."

"You don't scare me," Grace said, this time not quite so honestly, "but I like my job. I want to do it well and I don't want to get into trouble while that's happening."

The corner of his mouth lifted. "Rest easy, Sergeant, you're not in trouble—this time."

Grace looked at him uncertainly. "Okay." She ripped open a Splenda packet and dumped it into her iced tea.

He put down his cup and leaned forward on his elbows. "I've re-read your file, Gabbiano, and I want to take you up on your offer. I want to see your rebuttal to the allegations."

Grace froze, her long-handled spoon hovering over the

glass of tea. To give him credit, he *had* cut her some slack by referring to the charges against her as allegations, which in fact, they were. She'd never had a review hearing. No disciplinary action had ever been taken. The big question was, why couldn't this have waited until the next day, when she was on the clock? "I appreciate that. Thank you."

His mouth went up a little at one corner. "Don't thank me yet."

Neva arrived with their food and put a hamburger and fries down in front of Grace. Chief Cruz lifted his arms off the table to make room for his club sandwich.

He took a bite, accepted a refill on his coffee, and shoved down a few fries. "Do you mind giving me a rundown of what you've been doing since I saw you yesterday morning?"

Already halfway through her burger, Grace obliged. She started with Hamm Starr, editorialized about his relationship with an underage girl, bemoaned Ellie lying to her again, and finished with what she had learned about the red evening gown.

The chief picked up the last quadrant of his sandwich.

Grace had the sudden suspicion that he was no longer listening to her, so intent was he in staring at the contents of his coffee cup as he chewed. She decided to test her theory. "I'm thinking of having a bidding war on the red gown. Raise some money for the department. Maybe throw a big party with free booze for all."

"Sounds good."

Grace started laughing.

Startled, Aidan looked up. "What?"

Grace shook her head. "You're not listening to a word I'm saying!"

"I heard you. The dress is a Dior, sold in the early nineties."

Well, at least she knew when he'd left the conversation.

His expression turned rueful. "My apologies. I have a lot on my mind besides work. I guess my thoughts wandered."

You *guess*? Grace was itching to ask what those thoughts were, but she didn't dare. She really didn't know the chief well enough to get personal with him.

He settled it by saying, "I'm going to pick up my son Dylan this weekend. He's not thrilled about the move."

Grace wasn't sure how to respond. She tried to keep it safe, noncommittal. "Coburg will grow on him and school starts soon. He'll make friends in no time."

The chief made a grunting noise and polished off his coffee. He pulled out his wallet, holding up his hand when Grace reached for her purse. "I'll get it," he said. "Consider it payback for giving me a briefing on your day off." He put a twenty down on the ticket and stood.

"Thank you." Grace gave him points for leaving Neva a hefty tip.

"You're welcome."

The woman who wore her clothes straight off the brilliant-color rack winked at him as they left. "Hope everything goes okay with the kid coming, honey."

Grace did a double-take. Neva calling the chief *honey* and making a personal comment about his kid meant he'd eaten more than a meal or two at the café since Sunday. Neva always had been one to lend a sympathetic ear.

Which made Grace wonder if the mighty oak had wanted to say more about his little acorn coming to town, but decided at the last minute to keep it to himself.

Stuffed and ashamed of herself for shoving all that greasy food down her throat, delicious though it was, Grace decided her penance would be a run. Not until later, though, when it was almost time for the sun to go down and it had cooled off some. Then she might stand a chance of outdistancing the mosquitoes.

Not fanatical about running, she did it anywhere from zero to three times a week and never when it rained or if temperatures soared up or down. Now that she had bike patrol, she felt pretty comfortable with her daily level of exercise.

Despite Gina's earlier assurance that Pop would get the kids to tow the line, he most likely had dropped in only to pick up something he'd forgotten. On Thursdays, he helped Uncle Vito at the vineyard. In exchange, when the wine was corked, he got six dozen bottles of Dago Red *gratis*.

If the kids had been ill-behaved all day, Gina was probably pulling her hair out by now. Grace still planned to spell her cousin, but she couldn't take the nieces along to the allergist's office. Time to get creative in her thinking.

She pointed her Beetle toward Rocco's. Her brother also had Thursday off, and he couldn't tell her otherwise. Hadn't she spent last Thursday performing chain-gang labor for him on his pond? He owed her. He owed her big.

After several minutes spent alternately arguing and bartering, he finally agreed to watch the girls. "It's the lesser of two evils," he growled at Grace's back. She laughed. Offering him a choice of babysitting the nieces or taking Kyle to allergist had been a stroke of genius, but she'd mistakenly thought he'd choose to take Kyle for his shots. No sane man ever offered to baby-sit.

Grace rolled down her car window and eyed her brother with suspicion. He flashed her an angelic smile.

Pollen had been heavy in the Willamette Valley all summer. After sensitivity testing, Kyle's immune system had reacted ferociously to grass, trees, dust mites, molds, and to a lesser degree, about fifteen other allergens prevalent in the area. Visiting the allergist's office every four-to-seven days to build up the serum so he could get on a monthly schedule had been too much for Angelina's schedule. Everyone in the extended family had taken turns getting the boy into Eugene, but this was Grace's first time.

Today's visit would leave Kyle just one shot shy of reaching his maintenance level. Her nephew checked himself in at reception, where they gave him his file to take to the shot counter. Unexpectedly, undergoing allergy shots had given Kyle some equilibrium in his life by allowing him to take charge of doing something that was solely about him.

"Wanna watch?" he asked Grace.

Grace expected an impish grin, but instead, he turned serious eyes on her. Her mother had already warned her that Kyle didn't like needles, but he stoically submitted to his shots. Guessing he was silently asking for her support, she said, "Sure."

While they waited, another patient went behind the counter to use the phone on the wall. "Hi, honey," the woman said to whomever answered, "I'm just about ready to leave the allergist's."

The remainder of the conversation was lost when the nurse arrived at the counter and greeted Kyle by name. Grace liked the young woman immediately, giving her extra points for remembering a boy who had only been a patient for a short time.

The nurse made some notes in Kyle's shot chart, then pulled his extract from one of two refrigerators. She opened the box and pulled out two bottles, which she held up for him to inspect.

"They want me to check every time to make sure those are my bottles," he explained to Grace. "So I don't get someone else's stuff."

"I see." Grace bent to examine the labels on the bottles herself.

The nurse swiped each bottle top with an alcohol-soaked cotton ball before she pulled two syringes out of a box. She removed a blue cap and inserted the needle through the rubberized top. Pulling the plunger to fill the tube, she then tapped her finger against it to get rid of the bubbles. She did the same thing with the next one.

The nurse had obviously completed the task thousands of times, but this was the first time Grace had seen it. The first time she'd seen needle-and-syringe setups with little blue caps.

Little blue caps exactly like the one Yeager Clausen had been clutching in his fist at death.

The nurse swabbed alcohol on Kyle's upper arm and administered the shot. She repeated the procedure for the other arm. Kyle held a piece of cotton against each injection site and nodded when the nurse glanced at the digital clock and told him the time. "I gotta wait twenty minutes," he told

Grace.

"Right." Grace looked around. "Why don't you grab two chairs over by the window? I need to talk to the nurse."

"Okay." He tossed the cotton balls into a bio-hazard container and whipped out his Nintendo.

"Do you have a minute?"

The woman whose nametag read Linda glanced again at the clock on the wall, then toward the door. "Looks like Kyle was our last shot patient for today, so sure. What can I do for you?"

Grace introduced herself, explaining her position at CPD. "The cap on the syringe, the blue one? Can I see it?"

Linda grabbed a full setup and held it up.

"How easy would it be for someone to abscond with a couple of these?"

Linda shrugged. "Sometimes we're really busy with patients in back, so I suppose it's conceivable that someone could take one." Her head inclined toward the reception desk. "We have a video camera on the shot counter, but no one's constantly watching the monitor in the nurses' station."

"While we waited for you to come to the counter, one of your patients just walked around to use the phone. She didn't ask, and no one questioned her, she just did it."

The nurse tilted her head at Grace. "Not all our patients have cell phones and everyone knows it's okay to use our landline."

Grace nodded, wondering if other allergists' offices were set up similarly. She made a mental note to have one of the reservists find out. God, she was tired. Having brain- overflow with mental notes only made her more exhausted. "Would it be okay if I keep this syringe?"

The nurse bit her lip.

Grace slipped her badge out of her purse. "You can take my contact info, if you want. This is relevant to a case I'm working."

"I guess so." She wrote down Grace's information and badge number.

"Thanks again," Grace said, sipping the syringe into the

side pocket of her purse before she went to join Kyle.

She personally knew at least ten people who got allergy injections. Clausen hadn't, but one of his daughters did.

Talk about trying to find a needle in a haystack!

CHAPTER 29

DESPITE HER ALMOST uncontrollable urge to set Buzz Wozinsky immediately to work on the possible allergy syringe aspect of Clausen's murder, Grace refrained from going anywhere near Coburg PD.

She and her brothers (Rocco had conned Dante into watching the nieces) took the kids for pizza. They were more interested in the indoor playground than eating, but that was the point—to wear them out and have them deeply asleep by the time Joe and Angelina got home. Grace hoped her parents were having a romantic evening out. Alone.

Rocco and Dante begged off at the doorstep, assured by Grace that she could handle putting the children to bed. She lucked out. No one argued, begged for water, or devised other, more creative reasons to stay up later.

The closing highlight of the evening was a call from Sean Ducey, the Angel-look-alike EMT who had responded to the Clausen scene. He invited Grace to a movie Saturday night. Since she hadn't had a date in over eight months, she accepted. Later, she wondered how he'd gotten her cell number.

She fell asleep watching *Suspicion* on TCM, but roused long enough to wobble home when her parents came in. She stripped and tumbled into bed, pleased that she hadn't given so much as thought to Yeager Clausen and his merry band of girlfriends all evening. Upon waking, she wasn't so pleased with the path of her nocturnal wanderings. Her and the chief doing the nasty in his hammock? Really?

At the station, Grace immediately went to put a sealed copy of the rebuttal the chief had asked for on his desk. Just being in his office caused her face to flush from renewed remembrances of dream passion. Had he been there and noticed her telltale color, she would have claimed rosy cheeks from riding her bike to work.

At her own desk, with *only* the murder victim on her mind, she compiled a list of the items needing attention. To keep things professional, she used the computer, instead of writing it out longhand.

1. Contact CU, U-Dub, Columbia, UTEP re Yeager Clausen, Hamm Starr, and Jack Dellenbach – Tina
2. Contact Boulder, CO PD re traffic accident, circa 1992-3 – me
3. Verify arrival of bird feather at Fish & Wildlife lab – Tina
4. Talk to Ellie re: Hamm, Kirk, fleas, Lindsey's shots – me
5. King County, WA CHC on Grayson Trenton Hanover III + financial standing – Montoya
6. Jimmy Frey sleeping with EC? – Mallory
8. Background checks, interviews, alibis: Clausen's girlfriends – Carolyn Haas, Terry Moore, Dorrie Kelso, Liz Dominy, Jessica Bennett. Any with cat/dog? – Jenks
9. Allergy offices – Wozinsky
10. David Kirk – Cruz

Grace sat back, considering the list. Thank God she had people to help out! She went to the photocopier and made six duplicates. One she handed to Deets as soon as he walked in. Tina got the second copy and Montoya the third.

Grace had a private chat with Melody Jenks when she assigned her the girlfriends. Maintaining eye contact, she said, "These women will be on the defensive and maybe even confrontational. Stand your ground with them, Mel, threaten obstruction charges if they don't cooperate and make sure you get complete information about alibis so you can accurately substantiate everything."

Melody's chin went up. "I can do this, Grace. You can count on me to keep these bitches in line."

The reservist's look of determination was all the guarantee Grace needed. "Hit the road, then."

Wozinsky had taken a call at the nursery, where several dozen small potted trees had been mowed down during the night by someone driving a four-wheel ATV. His assignment would have to wait until he returned to the office.

That left the chief for the final item on the list. Grace knocked on his door, opening it upon his *Enter* command. She handed the list over. "Can you use one of your contacts at Portland Police Bureau to check out number ten, David Kirk? He's a known fling of Ellie's before Hamm Starr."

Chief read down at the list, then looked up at her. "I think I can handle that." He glanced at the sheet of paper again. "You're methodical in your approach, Gabbiano. I like that."

"Thanks, Chief." She couldn't help noticing that he hadn't opened the envelope with her rebuttal yet, but she decided not to ask why. "I'm heading over to Ellie's after I contact Boulder."

His eyes back on the paperwork she'd interrupted, he lifted a hand in acknowledgement.

Grace had promised everyone beer and eats at her place after work if they came through by five. As usual, Jimmy Frey was nowhere to be found and for once, it didn't piss her off. Though she'd really like to give him a good, swift kick in the nuts for leaving her arm black-and-blue, she didn't want a confrontation with him about why he'd made the being-investigated side of the list. She also didn't want him at her home later.

She called Boulder PD, who accessed their computer database and informed her the crash had occurred outside the city limits. They referred her to the Boulder County Sheriff's Office. Grace jotted down the number, said thank you, and redialed. After two transfers, she was connected to a records officer who identified herself as Dana Roberts. The woman, polite, but firm, said, "We're incredibly short-staffed right now—everyone's out trying to get their summer vacations in before school starts, you know?"

"I understand," Grace said, "but I need this information for a murder investigation I'm working."

"And you need it immediately."

"You got it."

After a long-suffering sigh, Officer Roberts said, "Okay, give me the information and I'll see if one of the clerks can research it for you."

"Thanks." Grace recited what she had, along with phone and fax numbers at Coburg PD and her email address.

"I'm not making any promises," Roberts warned.

"I understand."

"Nineteen ninety-two or -three is a long way back."

"I know. I owe you big time."

"Everyone owes me big time. No one ever pays up."

Before Grace could assure the officer that *she* would, the woman hung up. Grace had a bad feeling nothing would be coming from Boulder County SO anytime soon. Well, she'd give it until Monday, maybe Tuesday. In the meantime, maybe her sister Michaela would score something.

Grace couldn't decide whether to call Ellie Clausen for an appointment or just show up at her door. Opting for unannounced, she dutifully got on the patrol bike and pedaled over. The round trip could go toward her two-hours.

Caitlyn opened the door. "I am *so* looking forward to freshman orientation next week!" she said to Grace, in lieu of a greeting.

Grace murmured something unintelligible in commiseration. "Is your mom home?"

"She's upstairs, throwing all of dad's stuff away."

"You mean she's donating it, like to Goodwill or something?"

"No, I mean she had a big trash thing delivered this morning and she's throwing stuff out the window into it."

Grace looked up toward the landing. "Okay if I go up?"

"Go ahead. I love her, but I'm sick of listening to her yelling at him when he's not even here anymore."

"Which room?"

Caity flounced through the front door. "Just follow the noise," she called over her shoulder. "I'm going down to Buon Gusto to see if your mom will let me work today!" She stopped halfway down the front steps and turned to Grace. "I'm sorry I acted like such a bitch the other day. Mom says it's hormones, and maybe it is, but I think it was just me sucking!"

"Thanks, Caity. I appreciate the apology." She watched as the girl climbed into her Honda CRV and drove away. Maybe there was hope for her, after all.

Grace closed the door and turned toward the stairs. Following the "noise" was simple enough.

"Bastard. Two-timing piece of shit! *Asshole!*"

With the windows open, the widow's imprecations could probably be heard by half of Coburg. "Hi, Ellie. Want some help?"

Ellie swung around, her jaw set with anger, her eyes filled with tears. Why she'd bothered to apply eye makeup that morning was anyone's guess. What was left channeled in black rivers down her pale cheeks.

The widow finally appeared to be grieving.

"Got a match?"

"I don't think my brother would appreciate responding to a fire here, just because you decided to burn up your husband's things." She looked around the bedroom with interest. It was bigger than her two bedrooms put together and as richly appointed as the rooms below. The king-size four-poster bed tossed with Laura Ashley's best was particularly impressive.

"Knowing Rocco, he'd probably tell me to put it out myself." She sniffed. "What do you want now?"

"Are your parents still in town?"

"No, they left this morning."

Grace watched Ellie move purposefully around the room. "I thought you and Yeager didn't share a bedroom."

"This is shit he didn't move to the other room. I should have tossed all of it out a long time ago."

For the first time, Grace realized she was actually concerned about Ellie and her daughters. You couldn't live with someone, even if you hated him, and not mourn when he died. It wasn't normal. Besides, didn't you have to love in order to be able to hate? Bemused by the three Clausen females' ability to hide their true emotions, Grace said gently, "I have a couple more questions."

"I have a feeling you'll always have a 'couple more questions,' Grace. Ask away." Ellie heaved another armful of men's clothing out the window. It landed with a soft *thunk* below.

Grace settled on an Art Deco-style chaise that seemed out of shooting range. "Do you have any pets in the house? A cat or dog that might have fleas?"

Ellie shuddered. "My God, no! Fleas? Are you insane? That's exactly why I'd *never* have an animal in my house." She narrowed her eyes at Grace. "What's *this* all about?"

"The ME found some bites on the back of Yeager's calf. He thought they looked like flea bites, which usually come from dogs or cats. Do you know who he may have visited on Friday or Saturday who may have had pets?"

For a change, Ellie seemed to be considering the question seriously and without animosity. "He went to the DAC for lunch on Friday afternoon, but I don't suppose they have animals there."

"The Downtown Athletic Club? I wouldn't think so."

"Maybe one of his girlfriends, then."

A girlfriend with fleas? How appropriate. "We're checking."

Ellie sucked in a breath. With renewed vigor, she grabbed a shirt and piled it full of men's toiletries that looked as if they had never been used. A few other personal effects from bedside table followed. Ellie tied up the arms of the shirt, then that bundle, too, went sailing out the window. This time, the sound of breaking glass echoed back.

"You might want to have a seat for the rest of this," Grace suggested.

"We're moving to interrogation mode?"

"You might say that. It'll happen each and every time I catch you lying to me."

CHAPTER 30

ELLIE PICKED UP a pair of expensive, tasseled leather loafers that looked brand new and sent them flying through the open window. "I take it you've talked to Hamm." For good measure, she picked up a pair of boots in like condition and heaved them out, too.

"Did you really think he'd lie for you when I'm investigating a murder?"

Ellie shrugged her slim shoulders in defeat. "A girl can hope, can't she?"

Grace wanted to tell her, *Not when it's a man like your husband or his best friend*, but managed to quell the personal commentary. Civil servants gathered facts, she reminded herself. They didn't preach, no matter how strongly they felt about certain subjects. A little demon inside her head reminded her that she often deviated from that protocol.

"I wondered why Hamm avoided me at the funeral service." A self-deprecating laugh rattled out of her. "Silly me. I thought he was protecting my reputation, but he was just covering his own sorry ass."

She dropped a running shoe, her expression stricken. "Ohmygod! Yeager put Hamm up to screwing me!" The other shoe fell. "He did it so I'd be the one to ask for the divorce. I walked right into that little rat bastard's trap. He played me. *They both played me!*" She threw Grace a look of anguished despair. "*I* had to be the one to press for a divorce.

He had to come out looking like the injured party."

From what little Grace knew of the undearly departed, the deduction sounded plausible.

"Bastard!" Ellie said bitterly. "How could he?"

Which bastard was Ellie referring to? "So, where were you *really* after you left Hamm?"

"He was so anxious to get rid of me, I knew he either had another woman coming in or he was going to meet her somewhere else." She sank to the floor, leaning against the footboard of the bed. "It was a little girl, a kid the same age as Caitlin. She's been to my house before. I *knew* her."

"So you hung around there?"

"I was going to wait until she left," Ellie admitted, picking frantically at the hem of her shorts, "but she never came out. At three o'clock, I gave up and came home. I wanted to confront him, but I had my pride." She met Grace's gaze directly, her eyes filled with tears. "I didn't want him to know how deeply he'd hurt me."

It was obvious to Grace that Ellie cared a great deal more for Hamm than she had her husband. Maybe even loved him.

"I have never in my life fallen for the right guy." Ellie hung her head and began to sob in earnest.

Grace gave her space. Women in that much pain wanted to be alone with it, not be patted on the back and told, *There, there, it's going to be all right.*

Using one of her husband's discarded shirts to wipe her eyes and nose, she mumbled into the expensive cloth, "I'm so fucking gullible. Hamm said he wanted to marry me, then half an hour later, he's screwing that girl, that *child*." She took another swipe at her eyes and nose, then tossed the shirt into a growing pile. "I haven't had sex with Yeager for two years. He wanted to sometimes, but I couldn't risk getting AIDS or some other STD because he couldn't keep his pants zipped." She sniffed loudly. "Then I end up having sex with his best friend, and it turns out he can't keep his dick zipped up, either."

Ellie raised her chin either in defiance or self-protect mode. "You must think I'm a pathetic moron. Can't choose 'em, can't keep 'em."

"Men can be real bastards," Grace agreed quietly. "I think every woman alive learns that at some point, one way or another."

Ellie nodded. "Don't you even want to know who the girl was?"

Grace hesitated, not surprised that Ellie wanted to tattle.

"You already know, don't you? Isn't there some kind of law about screwing underage girls?"

"That's a separate issue right now, but there is something else I need to know."

The widow threw up her arms. "Of course there is."

"It's Jimmy Frey. I know he's the one who called you. And he stood over you like a bodyguard yesterday. Are you also having an affair with him?"

"Contrary to what you or the town may think, I only sleep with one man at a time. Jimmy is under the misconception that I'm interested in his overtures. I've told him repeatedly that I'm not, but he doesn't seem to get it."

He wouldn't. "If he starts bothering you to the point where he frightens you, call Chief Cruz directly and report it. He'll make sure Frey gets the message."

"I will."

"Did Yeager ever take Lindsey for her allergy shots?"

Ellie laughed, incredulous. "You're kidding, right?"

Grace glanced down at her notebook. "You said you only sleep with one man at a time. Not counting your husband, who are the men you slept with during your marriage before Hamm?"

Ellie glared at her. "I swear you are a bitch, Grace Gabbiano!"

"I'm not going to apologize for doing my job. I could care less who you sleep with, but if it's possible that one of your former lovers thought he'd have a clear path to you by killing your husband, then it becomes part of this investigation."

Ellie hiccupped on a fresh sob. "I only slept with one other man."

Had Ellie placed an slight emphasis on that last word? What the *hell* did that mean?

"David Kirk?"

Ellie's jaw literally dropped. "I fucking hate living in Smalltown, America!" She got to her feet and leaned against the footboard.

Grace sighed. "Tell me about him."

Ellie's chin wobbled and more tears fell. "He lives in Portland. I only saw him when I went shopping up there."

"How did you meet?"

"He's…."

"He's what?"

"He's into finance. I met him once at dinner with Yeager, several years ago. He was with his wife."

"I take it he's still married."

Ellie nodded.

"Do you still see him?"

"Not since I started seeing Hamm."

"If I recall, that was about a year ago."

Ellie nodded again.

So, the other affair wasn't that cold. "We'll be discreet when we talk to him." Grace scratched out some notes, then proceeded cautiously with her fishing expedition. "I got from what you said a minute ago that you might have had an affair with someone other than a man."

Ellie's eyelid began a wild flicker. "Leave it alone, Grace," she begged. She glanced frantically toward the door.

"Caity went over to Mom's store to see if she could work today," Grace said. "I'm not prying for enjoyment, Ellie. This is a murder investigation. I'll guarantee confidentiality on anything you tell me."

Ellie gnawed on her lips. "It's…oh God!"

Grace had a feeling what was coming, but she let Ellie set her own pace.

"It only happened a few times, Grace. You've got to understand. I'm not a lesbian. It's just that, well, I was in a situation, and it just *happened*." She started to cry again.

Grace felt sorry for her, but dammit, Clausen's death had been a crime of passion, and maybe the passion had come from a woman.

"I only explored it because men are such pricks!"

"I need a name, Ellie."

Ellie's sobs grew louder. "Liz Dominy." She clutched the poster of the bed with white-knuckled hands. "And Dorrie Kelso."

"You had affairs with each of them?"

Ellie choked out, "No."

Grace had a jaw-dropping moment. "Both of them? Together?"

"Yes," Ellie wailed.

A threesome for a first foray into bisexuality? Did Ellie even have a clue that Liz Dominy and Dorrie Kelso had been fucking her husband? Maybe even seduced her to get back at him for some reason?

"Give me some dates, Ellie."

Grace jotted down more than a *few* dates.

Ellie grabbed a corner of the pretty floral sheet and scrubbed at her face, clearing away more tears. "Is there anything else, or can we be done now?"

"Yeah, we're done, but how about letting me send an officer over to help with this before you get too far along? There may be something in Yeager's personal belongings that will give us a clue as to who killed him."

Ellie looked around the room, shoulders slumped. "I doubt you'll find anything, but have at it. You may find something in his room, or his office downstairs, but more likely, his office on Willamette will be the goldmine."

Grace already knew that to be fact. "Thanks."

Ellie grabbed her arm as she turned to go. "Don't judge me, Grace, please! With my luck with men…I just thought maybe I'd chosen the wrong gender, that maybe life had something more to offer me the other way. I was wrong. I'm screwed up, I know it, but I can get myself back together again. I have to, for my girls."

"It's not my job to judge you, Ellie." But it was hard not to pity the pathetic, insecure creature Ellie had become.

Torn by feelings that seesawed between compassion and distaste, Grace pedaled to the end of the drive. She gave serious thought to what Ellie had said earlier, something that may have been Yeager Clausen's method of choice for blackmail. *Had* he been worried about his standing in the community if he divorced Ellie and left two daughters with nothing? Had he tried to orchestrate it so his wife would be the one to file? Or was something else going on?

Grace pulled out her phone and speed-dialed Melody Jenks. "Hey, Mel, have you seen Dorrie Kelso and Liz Dominy yet?"

"Headed to Kelso's now. Hitting Dominy after that."

"Okay, listen." She instructed Melody to make a discreet inquiry of both women, not only about their threesome with Clausen, but their liaisons with Ellie. "Don't discuss this with anyone but me, Mel. I mean it. *No one* in the office hears a word about this, okay? Not even the chief. And find a way to make it clear to Dominy and Kelso that they better not be talking to anyone—including each other—about this, either."

"I read you loud and clear, Gracie. Man, this whole case is stuff they never teach you about at the academy."

Grace disconnected and activated her shoulder radio. "Wozinsky, you free?"

The radio crackled. "Headed back to Coburg now, Grace. What's up?"

"See me at the entrance to the Clausen property, ASAP."

In less than five minutes, Buzz Wozinsky pulled up outside the gate separating the Clausen home from the main road.

"What's up, Sarge?"

Grace explained what was going on inside and asked Wozinsky to do a thorough search of Clausen's bedroom and office. "Be meticulous," she told him. "Even if you have to come back tomorrow to finish the job. You're looking for anything that might give us a clue as to who he was with Saturday night, and why he died. You'll have to go through the stuff in the Dumpster first, then Ellie's room. When you're done there, it's okay to help her finish heaving his crap out the window."

Back at the station, she heaped another assignment on Tina, asking her to check property records through the county assessor's website, and recorded transfers through

Deeds and Records. Just because Yeager had convinced Ellie he owned everything, didn't mean it was true.

Grace sighed, conflicted about a case like she never had been before.

Whether it was true or not that Clausen owned everything, it still made a helluva motive for Ellie to kill the sonofabitch.

CHAPTER 31

PARCHED FROM HER speed ride back to the station, Grace went to the fridge in the tiny kitchen for a bottle of water. She was dismayed to find the eight-pack she'd put in to chill three days earlier nearly gone—and she'd been off for two days.

"I told The LP not to drink your water," Connie Benz said, coming up behind her.

Ever since Grace had suggested to Tina that derogatory nicknames not be assigned to co-workers, Jimmy Frey, The Little Prick, had become The LP.

"He's such a shit," Connie went on. "He just laughed and said you got paid more, so you could afford to share."

Grace grabbed the last bottle and decided from here on, she'd refill her empties. Frey didn't strike her as the kind of guy who'd chance drinking her unsterilized backwash, but if he did, too bad.

Connie scavenged around for something and finally pulled out a yogurt. "I'm just lucky he hates healthy food, or I'd never have anything to snack on." She straightened, grinning. "If he ever *does* touch my food, I'm going to sic Stevie on him."

Grace gave her a fist bump, grinning back.

Connie, the office vegetarian, was the all-American soccer mom who worked half-time to supplement the family income. Her husband, Stevie, a potential star running back for the Seattle Seahawks until his knee gave out, did sports broadcasting for a local TV station. Connie had met him in an English class at UO and they'd been together ever since. In addition to doing data entry, she was a natural wordsmith and in high demand for anyone in the office who wanted something written right.

Grace wandered over to Tina's desk. "Have any luck?"

"I thought I had 'til five."

"Oops." Grace turned to walk away.

"Hey, get back here! Your feather arrived and they're looking at it. They'll call this afternoon with findings." She rifled through some papers. "I got Clausen's social security number from his wife and Hamm's from the man directly." She made a wry face. "He didn't want to give it up, but I convinced him otherwise."

Grace half-way wanted to know exactly what Tina had on Starr to make him talk. Probably Jennifer Sousa.

"U-Dub verified Clausen attended during the time you noted. Same for Starr at Columbia. Couldn't get any more than that without a mandate from God."

"Starr thinks Dellenbach's folks moved to San Antonio."

"I'll start looking. Here's the property records info."

Grace reached for the printout Tina held out to her. "I can't believe you got everything done so quickly."

Tina shrugged, grinning. "Wonder Woman."

"Obviously." Grace scanned the document. "Ah, shit."

"That's what I thought. Guess it does make Ellie your number one suspect, huh?"

Grace finished entering her latest case notes into the computer, then went to the bathroom. She splashed cold water on her face and used the towel she had stashed in her locker to dry.

On her way out the door to complete what remained of her two hours of bike patrol, she had one last question for Tina about the whereabouts of the persistently missing Jimmy Frey.

The phone rang before Grace had a chance to ask.

Tina listened in silence, then turned to her keyboard. Her fingers flew over the keys. "Gotcha," she said into her headset. "Did you call OSP?" She rolled her eyes. "Okay, I'll have some people over there pronto."

"Armed robbery at the truck stop on I–5 . Several truckers heading south on the Interstate are in pursuit of the suspect vehicle, an '85 or '86 extended-length white Dodge van with California plates." She looked at the screen and read off the numbers. "Suspect is a white male, about thirty years of age, long brown hair pulled back in a ponytail, wearing a blue Yankees baseball cap, white Nike T-shirt, blue jeans, and sandals. His right ear is pierced and he has a 'weenie man' moustache." She looked up, grinning. "I'm just quoting the guy who called it in. The suspect is armed with a semi-automatic pistol, they thought might be a Glock. The vehicle is rusted in places and both the driver and front passenger doors have been painted over in a circular shape."

"Radio Wozinsky and tell him to get over there," Chief Cruz said from the doorway of his office. "This came in as regular phone call, not nine-one-one?"

Tina nodded.

"Get OSP and the Sheriff's Office on this, too. Gabbiano, you're with me. I'll drive."

That was fine by Grace. She'd done the driving course, and she'd done it well, but she'd never actually been in a high-speed pursuit.

Deets exited the men's room, a newspaper in his hand.

"Saddle up, Mallory." The chief issued one last command to Tina. "All reservists on duty to the truck stop."

"What about Frey?"

"If we need him, I'll let you know."

Grace glanced over her shoulder and caught Tina smartly saluting the chief's back.

Once their vehicles were on the road, sirens blaring and lights flashing, they made the Interstate in less than two minutes. Wozinsky radioed that he'd been next door at the McDonald's buying lunch, so he was already on scene. Grace wondered about that, since she'd left him at the Clausen house, but the guy did have the right to a meal.

Wozinsky reported one injury—a customer hurrying out of the perp's way had tripped and fallen, probably breaking her arm. Buzz had already called for EMTs. He also reported that two reservists were pulling in and he'd have them start interviews immediately. Mele Amaka, who'd been ticketing speeders on I–5 at the Coburg exit all morning, radioed that he was clear to assist. Grace instructed him to join Buzz at the truck stop.

The next call came in seconds later from an OSP officer who'd picked up pursuit of the van at the 30th Avenue exit in Eugene. Aidan kept to the outside lane, swearing at idiots who were slow to move over. Grace stopped checking the speedometer when it shot past ninety.

Aidan barked at her to have Tina broadcast a cautionary on the CB to the truckers on the van's tail. "Tell them to back off—the suspect is armed, and the police are in pursuit."

Behind them, Deets kept pace and from the right, a Lane County Sheriff's vehicle shot down the onramp at the I-105 interchange. A white Mustang from the Traffic Safety Team, along with two more OSP vehicles, joined the chase at the Oakridge interchange.

With all the law enforcement traffic barreling down the Interstate, sirens wailing, southbound traffic mostly kept to the far right lane or pulled over entirely. Pissed at the number of drivers who refused to obey the law, Grace jotted down plate numbers and vehicle makes-and-models. A citation for nearly three hundred dollars would serve as a reminder for a law all drivers should already know.

The radio crackled. "Be advised, southbound trucker took a swipe at the suspect vehicle. Vehicle is off the roadway, flipped over, wheels up, in the median strip." The unknown officer paused a moment, but the radio was still on. Squealing brakes and earsplitting sirens screamed over the airwaves. "Suspect is out of the vehicle." *Crack. Crack.* A instant later he shouted, "*Shots fired!*"

"Jesus." Aidan maneuvered closer to the jersey barrier to bypass the roadblock LCSO had put in place. "I hope they got the northbound lane closed in time.

Within minutes, he pulled their vehicle in behind the original OSP unit. He shut off the siren, but left the lightbar going. Grace scrambled out just as Deets pulled in behind them.

The chief joined them in seconds. "No goddamn vests," he muttered as they hunkered down.

Deets said, "We've had a lot more excitement since you two came to town. Never needed Kevlar before, that's for sure."

Grace had to admit she liked wearing a uniform a lot better without the stifling vest, but when you needed it, there was no substitute. At the moment, she felt incredibly exposed and underprotected. She reached back inside the vehicle, took the keys from the ignition, then squat-walked toward the trunk. Awkwardly, she unlocked it and withdrew the binoculars.

"Don't get your fool head blown off," the chief growled.

The suspect, Grace soon discovered, was probably closer to twenty than thirty. Blood streamed from a cut on his face, but other than that, he appeared unharmed from the crash. He moved in a circle, waving his weapon erratically.

Without warning, he positioned himself behind the overturned van and began firing again at vehicles stopped in the northbound lane just beyond the police barricade. Then he took aim at the uniforms. An officer exiting a newly arrived cruiser from Cottage Grove PD fell to the ground. Grace hoped CGPD's budget had included bullet-proof vests. Several more shots rang out. The shot pierced the window of a civilian SUV.

Grace used the binoculars to assess the damage and gritted her teeth. "He's hit someone in that car—or the window glass did some damage. Either way, it's a head injury. We're going to need more than a couple of ambulances down here."

"I'll call it in," Deets said.

The joint city–county SWAT team had already been summoned, but private citizens were in jeopardy, not to mention the police. Taking cover behind a semi pulled over at the side of the road, officers from the various jurisdictions discussed the situation. They broke off as more shots were fired. “He must have a goddamned arsenal over there,” Aidan said.

Grace peered around the front of the semi through the bins. “He’s hit another civilian. Some guy who climbed up on top of his car to watch. Stupid idiot.”

“We can’t wait for SWAT,” Aidan said.

The LCSO deputy who had kept pace with them on the freeway spoke up. “I’m a member of the team. I can take him.”

“Alive?” one of the OSP officers asked.

“Not if he’s still shooting people.” Another shot punctuated his statement.

“Officer down!” came a shout from across the highway.

“Do it,” Aidan said to the deputy. As commanding officer in the jurisdiction where the original crime had been committed, he’d obviously made his decision. Grace thought it was the right one. They had no idea how many others the suspect may have already injured, or how many he still might.

The deputy quickly retrieved a high-powered rifle from his patrol vehicle. He turned his hat so the brim faced backward and moved forward to position himself behind the OSP vehicle for better visibility. He steadied on his target. The first shot hit the mark and the gun-waving van driver went down.

After a moment of eerie silence, the uniformed officers crouched low as they approached the downed man. The suspect still had a weapon, though no one knew yet if he was still alive to use it.

Without exception, every officer fell prone to the ground when the screams began. “Fucking pigs!” Over and over again.

“What the hell was that?” someone cried out.

“There must be someone in the van,” said the LCSO deputy.

“Kill the motherfuckers! Fucking pigs.”

Aidan came scooting back on his belly. “Get me a bullhorn.” Grace located one in an OSP unit.

“The press is here,” she said as she handed it over to

Aidan.

"Jesus H! Mallory, get a couple of OSP or LCSO people to the vultures back." He put the bullhorn to his mouth. "You in the van, identify yourself."

"Fucking pigs!"

"A regular goddamned poet," Aidan said.

Grace lifted the binoculars, scanning the van. Nothing moved. She glanced over her shoulder at the rumble approaching from the north. The SWAT guys had finally arrived. Two ambulances followed and behind them, several more patrol units.

"Identify yourself," Aidan yelled again.

"Bullshit! Kill the motherfuckers!"

Grace raised the binoculars again. Something didn't quite jibe with a cohort in the van.

"Shit, shit, shit!" whoever it was squawked.

"It sounds like a woman," the chief said.

"It sounds inhuman," Grace corrected. "Screeching doesn't make it a woman."

As if to prove her wrong, the voice sang out, literally, "Pretty baby, pretty baby…won't you come and let me rock you in my cradle of love."

Grace leveled the binoculars on the van once more and through the rear side window observed a brilliant blue flutter. Confused, she took a leap. "Chief, I think it's a talking bird."

Aidan took the binoculars from her and focused on the vehicle. "She's right," he said, effectively quieting the snickers her statement had elicited. "There's a goddamned bird in that van."

The oncoming sirens finally ceased. SWAT team members, armed and in tactical gear, poured out onto the roadway. The team leader ordered everyone to stay back while his men approached the vehicle. In a matter of minutes, they signaled the all clear. One of them confirmed, "Bird on board."

Everything passed in a blur for the next three hours. EMTs responded to injuries and police officers took care of redirecting traffic in both directions to nearby detours. The

HazMat team was called in to deal with the van, which turned out to be a traveling meth lab. Firefighters cleaned up the spill from the ruptured gas tank. Deputy ME Jade Riordan arrived, along with Assistant DA Paul Thompson and DA Investigator Chris Bellois, neither of whom Grace had met before.

Animal Control arrived to corral the injured bird for transport, a chore that took almost thirty minutes. The three-foot-tall creature, flapping its uninjured wing at every opportunity, clearly resented each moment spent getting it under control. The press, forced back by OSP officers, focused on the bird for their story. It screamed obscenities, the likes of which most people only heard in newer action movies, then, with the sweetest voice, it would switch to songs from the '30s and '40s.

Grace particularly liked its rendition of "Blue Moon."

As she watched the two men from Animal Control coax the bird into a cage, she bent to retrieve a couple of feathers left behind in the fracas. "What have you got?" the chief asked, coming up behind her with Deets.

She turned and held it up for inspection. "Look familiar?"

Deets reached out and ran his finger down the edge of the feather. "Like I said, this job hasn't been this exciting, ever. You two really have a way about you."

Aidan looked from the feather, to the captured bird, to the body being zipped into the plastic bag. "I suppose it's too much to hope we've found our killer."

"Nothing ever comes that easy," Grace said, wishing that for once she'd be proved wrong.

CHAPTER 32

JOHN "CAPPIE" CAPPLAND. The name meant nothing to *anyone in Oregon, including Clausen's widow, but it meant* quite a lot to the authorities in California. Even before his fingerprints came back from AFIS, the Automated Fingerprint Identification System, a criminal history check showed several outstanding warrants for manufacture and sale of drugs in the state to the south, as well as Arizona and Texas. Meth, heroin, and marijuana were his drugs of choice, but he wasn't opposed to selling a sheet of LSD to school children, if they had five bucks.

Cappie apparently had adopted the I–5 corridor as his store front. Buzz Wozinsky also discovered that he spent the night at the motel across the freeway every two weeks. "Except this time, he was there just a week ago."

"What about the bird?" Chief Cruz asked.

"Animal Control agreed to have a vet look at it, but they don't want to house it beyond the weekend," Grace said.

Melody Jenks sank into a chair and put her feet up on the conference room table. She took a long swallow from a can of Diet Coke.

Felix Montoya sat down next to her. "What bird?"

Deets had everyone laughing by the time he finished relating the story of Animal Control trying to remove the creature from the upside-down van. "The Haz/Mat team drew the line at extracting the bird. Animal Control had to suit up to protect themselves from the meth chemicals inside the vehicle, and man, were they unhappy about it. It must have been a hundred degrees inside that van, and maybe another thirty degrees inside those suits. Poor bastards. That goddamned bird did not go peacefully."

Tina appeared in the doorway. "Here's the report from Fish and Wildlife, Grace."

"Hey, remember that old guy who came in to file the missing-bird report the other day?" Felix asked.

Tina froze, a dumbfounded look on her face.

Felix pressed on. "Didn't he say it was something exotic? Something blue?"

Tina smacked the side of her head in an I-could've-had-a-V8 moment. "There's been so much excitement around here, I forgot all about that!" She hurried out of the conference room, returning less than a minute later. She handed a file to Grace. "I bet your bird today is the same one Jason Knox reported stolen.

Grace quickly scanned both pages. "Dagne said Jason reported a stolen animal. An exotic bird worth twelve-K is a pretty big deal. Doesn't Dagne know that yet?

Tina reviewed the paperwork over Grace's shoulder. "She didn't even list what kind of bird, so I guess we must have heard Mr. Knox say it was exotic. She didn't even record the color." Tina straightened, frowning. "Looks like I need to have a talk with Dagne. If she can't get more complete information than this, she can't be taking reports."

Jimmy Frey sauntered in, as if he hadn't been missing all day. "What's going on?"

"Where have you been, Frey?" the chief asked.

"Out working, Chief. Took a call at the RV plant and another one up at the nursery. Busy afternoon."

No one said anything and Grace couldn't believe the chief didn't fire him on the spot for lying. Not only had someone else taken the nursery call, but how had an officer, purportedly in the field responding to calls, missed hearing the second biggest call of the decade over his patrol radio? He would have jumped into the fray with his usual lack of finesse if he'd actually been working.

Frey looked at each of them with a hint of dare-me on his face. "Time to clock out, too."

Grace thought it rather harmonious of the others that no one bothered to clue him in about what he'd missed.

Ignoring Frey, Deets took the report from Tina and scanned it.

Grace had little doubt that Frey's parting mutters, which cast aspersions on the intelligence of the anuses of everyone in the room, were heard by all as he turned and left the room.

Wozinsky lifted a middle finger after Frey.

Deets shook his head. "Unbelievable."

"Unbelievable is right," Felix agreed, his eyes trained on the door.

Grace glanced at the chief. His jaw flexed, but other than that, he showed no emotion.

Connie rose to leave. "I'm going to head out. See you all on Monday."

Just as she reached the doorway, Grace had a thought. "Connie, would you mind dropping off the feather we got today at the Gateway post office on your way home?"

"Not a problem. Certified, return receipt?"

Grace nodded.

Tina jumped up. "I'll get it for you." She returned waving a single sheet of paper. "The Fish and Wildlife bird lady says the first feather is from a macaw, with a flower-sounding name…geez, I can't even read my own writing." She squinted at the page. "Hyacinth, that's it!"

Grace rolled that around in her brain. "Hyacinth does sound exotic. I wonder if it's the same bird."

Deets shook his head. "I can't believe all this shit went down in quiet little Coburg today."

Chief Cruz pushed back his chair and stood. "You all did an impressive job."

"You did," Grace agreed. "It's been quite a week."

Aidan stretched. "I hear you're having FAC at house, Gabbiano. I move we adjourn to that location to finish this discussion."

"FAC?"

"Friday Afternoon Club."

"Ah." The chief inviting himself along kind of threw her for a loop. She eyed each person in the room. "Depends on whether or not my team came through for me, in spite of the freeway chase."

Melody leaned forward in her chair. "Have I got some stories for you from Clausen's ladies."

Montoya laid his hand dramatically over his heart. "Don't worry, Grace. You wanted information, I got it."

"I got a lot of nothing, but I can report it just as well at FAC," Buzz said.

"How about you, Deets? Get anything out of" —Grace tripped over her tongue because she'd almost said The LP "Corporal Frey?"

"The boy does like to brag," said Deets. "I agree with the chief. We meet at Gracie's in twenty minutes to discuss it."

"I have to beg off," Tina said. "My mom's got bingo tonight and I promised her I'd be home on time."

"Okay, thanks, Tina. Have a good weekend."

"You too. 'Bye all."

Deets sighed and glanced at Grace, a forlorn expression on his face, as the others filed out.

She opened her mouth, but he forestalled her with a raised hand. "When I want advice from Dear Gracie," he said, tweaking her nose, "I'll ask for it."

Grace wondered if he was some kind of mind reader.

They turned the office over to the night shift, which consisted of Dagne Nelson, the work study student, on dispatch and data entry, and Officer Charlie Dillon and Reservist Ted Reiker, both driving patrol. Tina had a talk with Dagne in private before she clocked herself out.

Dagne shot looks designed to maim at Grace when she came out of the women's changing room.

Grace walked directly over to the girl and said, "We count on you to get the facts straight, Dagne. If you can't do that, or you don't want to, say so now and you're out of here. No hard feelings."

The girl's eyes narrowed and her expression grew stormy.

She managed to bite back whatever it was she obviously wanted to say to Grace.

Grace stared her down until the student worker finally turned in a huff and sat herself down at the data entry computer.

Chief Cruz watched the exchange in silence, then preceded her out the door.

Grace had ridden her bike to work, so he offered to put it in the back of his Tundra and give her a lift to the market. "Unless you already have beer and snacks on hand?"

Grace picked up several bags of munchies, but only three six-packs. She didn't want anyone driving home from her place under the influence. At her house, Aidan unloaded her bike while she grabbed a couple of baskets from the cupboard and filled them with chips, crackers, and nuts. The chief came in and offered to do something more, so she sent him back out with two chairs from the kitchen table to supplement the pair of wicker chairs at the bistro table on the front porch. Those, along with the wicker stool, the front steps, and the porch railing should suffice for seating.

When Deets arrived, she instructed him where to find the cooler and had him dump in the bag of ice she'd picked up with the beer. Felix was dispatched with the tray of snacks.

Grace joined her co-workers on the porch. Melody arrived with a box of crispy fried chicken from the market. "Just in case anyone's super hungry," she said, grinning impishly as she tore the top off the box and passed it around with napkins.

Felix opted for the top step, where he could lean against the porch rail. The chief took one of the oak kitchen chairs and flipped it backward to straddle. Deets claimed one of the wicker chairs and she took the other. Melody said she was too wired to sit, then immediately took the stool.

"Where's Buzz?" Grace asked.

"On his way," Mel said. "He was going into the market as I was coming out."

"What a day," Deets said.

"No shit," Felix agreed. "Man, I been here, what? Three months and I get action like this." He grinned. "No one's gonna convince ole Felix he's working in boring Smalltown, U.S.A."

They all raised their bottles in silent salute to that profound statement.

"So," Melody said eagerly, "who goes first?"

"I will," Felix volunteered. "My stuff ain't gonna be near as spicy as what you and Deets have to say."

"Money's sexy," Grace assured him.

"There is that," he agreed, "but there's one thing sexier."

Grace rolled her eyes. "Move on, Felix."

Wozinsky arrived at that moment. "Brought corn dogs," he said. "Can't have beer without 'em. He placed the bag on the table and tore it open before he reached for a bottle.

Grace grabbed a corndog and a mustard packet. "We're just getting started. Go ahead, Felix."

He washed down some chips with his beer. "So, this guy, Grayson Trenton Hanover III, is worth about twelve mil. Even after Clausen stiffed him." He shrugged. "I guess he might have wanted to kill him for the three mil he lost, but I doubt it."

"Then the shabby state of his office doesn't mean anything?"

"Nah. According to *NW Business News*, his folks survived the depression, so he learned how to live conservatively. Like a lot of the super rich, he doesn't believe in flaunting what he has. And no record, by the way, but if he told you he was going to publicly humiliate Clausen, believe it. He's done it twice before to others."

"Wow." That confirmed, she hoped, one suspect off the list. "Thanks, Felix."

"I'd better go next," Melody said. "I'll be laughing so hard when Deets gets through talking about The LP, uh" — she peeked at the chief— "I mean Jimmy, I won't be able to talk." She dug into her back pocket. "Let's see. Terry Moore got married about six months ago, hated Clausen's guts, isn't sorry he's dead, and hopes his wife had a big insurance policy to collect on."

"Motive," Deets said.

"Yeah, except she really didn't give a shit about him.

She's married to this knock-out guy and they're going to have a kid. Aside from the fact that she didn't like Clausen, there was no reason to kill him. They were only involved for the sex." Melody's brow knitted. "I don't get that. Better to like the guy you're screwing, but to each her own, I guess."

"Next," Grace said.

"Dorrie Kelso and Liz Dominy. I lump them together because Harley was right. They live together half the time, have sex together, shower together...you get my drift?"

"Huh?" Felix said.

"Wake up, Montoya," Deets said, laughing. "They're a bisexual twosome. *They* used Clausen."

"Oh," Felix said, then, "Oh!"

"Forget it, Felix," Melody advised. "These chicks are *way* out of your league."

"Yeah," Felix said, "but man, oh man, girls gone wild!"

Everyone laughed. Felix was a devout Catholic, had a steady girlfriend, and a wedding date set for the following spring. He was CPD's pseudo-lothario.

Mel grinned. "They say he was into anything and everything and they're really going to miss him and his M&Ms."

"I bet." Grace moved on. "What about Jessica Bennett?"

"She's what you'd call a socialite, if Eugene had socialites. Mommy and Daddy have a lot of money, Clausen wanted some of it for a venture he was putting together, she said no, he stopped screwing her."

"Those were the three at the memorial service?" Grace wanted to know.

Melody nodded. "They said they were there."

"Any of them have a cat or dog?" Aidan asked.

"Moore has a husky, an outside dog she swears has never even seen a flea, the bi-girls don't like animals except of the two-legged variety, and Jessica has a tabby."

"I suppose her cat is too rich to have fleas," Grace said.

Melody laughed. "She says *Giselle* goes to the kitty beauty salon once a week."

Inexplicably, Grace remembered she was about a month past needing a hair trim. "What came back on their background checks?"

"Clean on everyone except the girls gone wild. They had a little run-in with the law a couple of years ago. Seems that they were peddling their wares in a local hotel bar and had the misfortune of soliciting an off-duty detective." She looked up. "They pled no contest and got probation. Nothing since then."

"Any of them come up with any suggestions as to who might have wanted him dead?" Grace asked.

"Nope. He was good in the sack, but otherwise, he was an asshole. Could have been anyone."

"That narrows it down significantly," Aidan said, his tone sardonic.

Grace grinned. "Guess we can at least cross them off our possible suspect list. Thanks, Mel. What about David Kirk, Chief?"

"Married, family man with three kids. Wealthy, but not filthy rich. His office is next door to one of the downtown Portland hotels, and Nordstrom is nearby." He shrugged, but his eyes danced with humor. "Mrs. Clausen apparently liked the convenience of shopping and sex being close together. My old partner Pete said the guy wigged out when he walked in and started asking questions. Kirk was adamant the affair has been over and done with for about a year and he's been on the straight and narrow since then."

"Yeah, I bet," Mel commented.

Grace polished off her corndog. "His timeline agrees with Ellie's, though. Thanks, Chief. Buzz, what have you got?"

Wozinsky shook his head. "I meant it when I said I got nothin'. Mrs. Clausen said he never worked from home. No computer, no filing cabinet. Same with his bedroom. Slept there, got dressed there. That's about it. Went through the Dumpster, checking pockets, looking for stray pieces of paper or whatever, and it was all just clothes, underwear, shoes, and personal-care items." He grimaced. "And for the record, if I stink it's because some of the bottles she threw away broke. I thought I was gonna die in that Dumpster with those fumes!"

Everyone laughed and Mel leaned over to sniff him, then pretended gagging.

"Stuff it, Jenks." He wadded up his napkin and threw it at her.

Grace reached for her beer. No wonder he'd whizzed through the task so quickly. "Thanks, Buzz."

Deets set his bottle on the table and rubbed his hands together.

"Are we ready for this?" Grace asked dryly.

"I'll make it short and sweet, and for the benefit of the ladies here, I'll keep it cleaner than Jimmy did. He didn't want to be a kiss-and-tell boy at first, but I convinced him to talk." He paused for a moment, making eye contact with each of the others, his expression confirming he was hoping to build the suspense. "He's been boinking the widow for years. Now that Clausen's out of the way…." Deets wiggled his eyebrows suggestively.

"Don't be such a pain in the butt," Grace said.

Deets shrugged, enjoying himself. "Leaving out all the intimate details, now that Clausen is history, he and the widow are gonna get hitched."

"My ass!" Grace said. "Ellie says he's been making a pest of himself for months and doesn't take her hints to get lost. She says she only does one guy at a time and right now it's Hamm Starr, and it'll never be Jimmy Frey." She blew out a breath heavy with resignation. "For once, I believe her."

Which meant Jimmy Frey really could be a suspect, and one she wouldn't mind carting off to jail.

Deets shrugged. "Frey's adamant that they're an item."

"He's a lying little shit," Mel said.

"And he's delusional if he thinks I'll believe him over Ellie," Grace said.

Felix whistled. "That's pretty bad for him, since she's your number one suspect."

Grace fiddled with her corndog stick. "What about the insurance?"

"Clausen's agent said there was a suicide exclusion. He faxed me a copy of the policy to confirm."

"Any double indemnity clause?"

"Nah, just boiler plate stuff."

Grace played with the sweaty label on her bottle, peeling

it away from the glass.

"I thought we weren't looking at suicide," Melody said.

"We're not, but since someone tried to make us think we are, it doesn't hurt to consider everything." She glanced at Deets. "How much?"

"In keeping with the size of his ego, a cool two mil."

Buzz whistled. "Nice nest egg for his daughters."

"Two million doesn't go far today," Melody said.

"Invest it right, and you could parlay that into a really pretty retirement package," Felix tossed in.

"All this information is well and good," the chief intervened, "but what about Mr. Cappland and his bird?"

A bit disconcerted by the chief's redirection, several moments of silence ensued until Melody spoke up. "Well, if that blue monster is the same one Mr. Knox reported stolen, Cappland must have had some idea as to the bird's worth."

Aidan tapped a finger against his beer bottle. "It would be odd, a guy like that knowing the value of an exotic bird."

"We don't know that he did. Druggies will steal anything they can sell for a couple bucks. He probably thought he could pull a fifty for it," Grace said. "What I'm wondering is, does finding that feather in the wig mean he killed Clausen?"

"Hell," Wozinsky said, "It was Knox's bird. Maybe *he* killed Clausen."

"Very funny," Grace said.

"Moot point anyway," Deets said. "Knox stated that he first missed the bird on Saturday, but didn't report it until Monday because he thought it would find its way home."

Wozinsky asked, "Are macaws like homing pigeons or something?"

No one had an answer.

CHAPTER 33

GRACE STOPPED BY the First Christian Church early Saturday morning to talk to Pastor Grimes.

"I hate to be blunt, sir, but I need to know if any of what you said on Thursday at Yeager Clausen's funeral service was true."

The minister appeared taken aback. "My dear young woman, Yeager has been a member of my congregation for years."

"I understand that, but everything you said about him being a dedicated father and husband, pillar of the community, humanitarian…."

Pastor Grimes sighed, then took off his glasses and made a production of cleaning the rimless lenses. Grace waited with her notebook poised.

"Sir?"

"I'd heard rumors, but when you're asked to officiate a funeral, you do not bring up a person's...weak points." He fixed the glasses back into place. "I do know that he made donations to worthy causes." The old gentleman slumped back into his well-worn, highback leather chair. "It's really the only thing I know about him to be true, and even that, God forgive me for saying so, was probably because they resulted in a tax break."

Grace checked off yet another name from her to-be-interviewed list and rose, extending her hand. "Thank you for your time, Pastor. You've been a big help, and I sincerely doubt you have to ask God's forgiveness for speaking the truth in this particular instance."

Grace really did like bike patrol. It gave her an opportunity to rescue little old ladies like Gunny Spriggs, who roved the street in her nightgown, asking folks what time the jitney left for Eugene.

About the same time she spotted Gunny, her shoulder radio came to life. Gunny's wandering had been reported by a neighbor. Maybe the one who was trying to urge the old woman back toward her house. Grace reported her location and announced she had Gunny in her sights.

"Hello, Gunny." She aimed a friendly nod at the neighbor. "'Morning, ma'am. Thanks for your help."

Grace locked up her bike to the nearest stationary object, then moved back toward Gunny. "Nice morning, isn't it?"

The old woman, three-quarters of a century in years and frail beneath the yards of flannel she wore, shook off the neighbor and squinted at Grace.

Several inches taller than the old woman's five feet, Grace positioned herself so the sun wouldn't be in Gunny's eyes. "Can I walk back home with you?"

"Waitin' for the jitney," Gunny said. "Got to get to Eugene."

Grace had been out on Gunny calls twice before. After the first time, she'd picked up a book on Alzheimer's. It damned near broke her heart to see Gunny, her favorite grade school teacher, end up with the same horrible disease her grandfather'd had. Back then, the illness had been called severe senile dementia. Some people had considered him just plain nuts and made him the butt of their cruel pranks. "I don't think the jitney runs on Saturday, Gunny."

"Impertinent," Gunny snapped. "Show some respect to your elders. Of course it runs on Saturday." She studied the park and said, "Train stops here, too. Oregon Electric. I can take the train if I miss the jitney."

Grace wasn't even sure how long it had been since a train

had run the route through Coburg, but it hadn't happened in recent history.

Gunny squinted at Grace again. "You're one of the Eye-talian girls. Angelina, isn't it?"

"That would be my mother," Grace said, keeping her words slow for Gunny's benefit. "She asked me to give you her regards next time I saw you, so I'll say 'hello' for her now. I'm Grace. You taught me fourth grade. I loved your history lessons."

"Taught everyone history."

Grace nodded. "You sure did. History was my favorite subject because of you. It was actually fun."

"Wasn't supposed to be fun," Gunny declared, and then she smiled and the vivacious, intelligent woman Grace remembered came back. "Better to have fun, than not."

"True," Grace agreed. To the neighbor, she said, "Mind if I leave my bike locked to your fence while I walk Gunny home?"

"Not at all." Obviously relieved to have someone else take over the chore of redirecting an old woman who didn't want to be redirected, the woman said goodbye and hurried on her way.

"Did I say you could call me Gunny?"

"You did. Last week. Do you remember?" Grace put her arm through the old woman's and started to move her down the block toward home.

"Maybe. Someone's been in my house again! Took my pots and pans, cleaned out my Frigidaire. I'm hungry!"

She looked hungry. Nothing but skin and bones beneath the flannel, yet a week ago, Grace had checked Gunny's kitchen and it was fully stocked. "I'll see if I can find them for you."

The old woman shuffled along beside her. "Someone on my roof last night. Took something off my porch, too." She stopped walking. "What was it? What did they take?"

"Once we get back to your house, I'll look and see if I can figure it out. Come on now, let's keep walking."

"My boy cheated me, you know. He took all my money. Spent it on…on…he needs to give it back. I can't afford to live anymore."

After Gunny had said similar things before, Grace had been ready to skin Gunny's son alive. She'd had Felix check out Jasper's financial situation, only to find he ran a wildly successful software company in the Portland area and paid all his mother's living expenses. She'd read that along with paranoia came delusions and extreme distrust of loved ones. "I'm sure Jasper will make sure you have everything you need to live, Gunny. Please don't worry about that."

"He took my money," Gunny wailed. "I need it for my jitney fare."

Grace tried to soothe her. "No jitney today, so you won't have to worry about that." A few more feet and they were at Gunny's house. "Can you make it up the steps okay?"

The old woman turned clear, confused eyes on her. "I hate being like this. My words don't come out right. Nothing's right anymore."

Grace swallowed to hold back her tears. "I know, sweetie. It's hard. I'll help you as much as I can." *If only you can remember that.*

Gunny reached up and patted her cheek. "You're a sweet girl, Angelina."

Grace got the old woman into the house, filled the teapot and set it on the stove. A short time later, Gunny sipped her tea and ate the scrambled egg and toast Grace prepared.

Grace picked up the phone and hit the speed dial for Gunny's son.

"Hi, Jasper, it's Grace Gabbiano."

"Is she okay?" he asked immediately.

"Oh, yeah, she just went out for a walk this morning in her nightie, but she's fine. I'm feeding her now. She's having a confusing day. Said someone was in the house." She glanced at Gunny and smiled. "We've made sure everything is back in the cupboards and refrigerator, but she insists there's something missing off the front porch."

"I'll be down by noon, Grace. I'm sorry you had to worry about her."

"It's no worry, Jasper. Really. Look, once you get here and have a look around, why don't you give me a call and let me know if anything is missing, all right?"

"Sure, and thanks again, Grace. Tell Mama I'll take her out to lunch."

Grace cleared away Gunny's breakfast dishes and washed up, leaving everything to dry in the rack on the counter. "Jasper will be here by noon. He's going to take you out to lunch."

"Oh, goodie," Gunny said, smiling. "We can ride the jitney into Eugene and eat at…." The old woman trailed off, a look of intense confusion on her face.

Grace offered to help Gunny dress, but as if a cloud bank had lifted, Gunny's mind cleared and she assured Grace she was perfectly capable of dressing herself.

Grace gave the old woman a hug and said goodbye, holding back her tears until she walked out the front door.

Traffic on Willamette Street was beginning to pick up. Some folks were in town to shop for antiques, others were passing through, headed north to hit the fruit-and-vegetable stands or the nurseries further along. Others went straight to the flea market.

For all the negative hoopla they had generated, Grace thought the curbs, gutters, sidewalks, and new pavement on Willamette were wonderful. Coburg still had its small-town atmosphere, but now pedestrians and school children could walk on the side of the road without fear of being run over or breaking an ankle in a pothole.

There were other new additions, too. A bank with Saturday hours, a bed-and-breakfast in a building that in year's past had housed, among other things, a restaurant and a needlework shop. But above all, Coburg was heaven on earth for antique lovers.

Grace eased her bike into a rack at the park and pulled out her cell phone. To save time, she had programmed the number for Animal Control. The woman who answered told her the incarcerated Hyacinth macaw was doing fine.

"Are you sure?"

"Of course, I'm sure. The obnoxious thing has been

screaming obscenities for hours."

Of *course* it had to be. It would be too weird to have *two* exotic birds involved in this case. "No, I mean about the *kind* of bird."

"The vet says so. He also said he knows who it belongs to."

"Jason Knox," Grace said. A startled pause told her she got that right. "Have you notified him yet?"

"No, my supervisor said not to until we talked to you, since the bird is involved in police business."

"Thanks, I appreciate that. I'll talk to him myself. When can the bird be released?"

"The vet says it can go home anytime." The sound of rustled papers came over the line. "Do you think Mr. Knox will be amenable to paying the vet's bill?"

"I'm sure he will. Thanks for your help." Grace disconnected, wondering how the hell Jason Knox's bird had ended up in a drug dealer's mobile laboratory.

Several workers at the truck stop had told Wozinsky that Cappland filled his tank, then parked his van in the lot for an hour or so before initiating the hold-up. A check with the motel across the interstate confirmed he hadn't spent the night. Why had he altered his pattern?

Maybe the bird was driving him crazy with its singing and squawking and he wanted to return it.

But then why instigate an armed robbery in a place where dozens of truck drivers congregated at any given moment?

Both the guy and the bird must have been high on meth fumes!

CHAPTER 34

GRACE PUSHED OFF, pedaling idly down Willamette, then east on Pearl, north on Miller, around to Emerald, Mill to Diamond, back to Willamette. It was enjoyable, chatting with people she hadn't seen in years, cooing at babies, admiring the bloom of summer flowers, getting a peek at interesting window displays. She even climbed a small tree to retrieve a frightened kitten for a distraught six-year-old. That was something she never would have done in Seattle.

And in between talking to town citizens, she had time to think about who'd killed Yeager Clausen.

Ellie obviously had the most to gain, not monetarily, but in terms of her freedom. Tina had confirmed that title to all Ellie's real property had been transferred to her husband. The bad news was, he had sold it to Carolyn Haas for one dollar, probably to repay her loss in investment. Presumably, Ellie didn't know that yet.

She'd probably set fire to the house when she found out.

What a rotten bastard! And why had Haas kept that information back?

Even Clausen's investments were held singly. The possible reasons for Ellie killing her husband read like a multiple choice test: a) a fit of passion over infidelity, b) theft of everything Ellie had legally owned, c) being trapped in a go-nowhere marriage, or d) all of the above.

Grace would have assigned a different yet similar motive

to Carolyn Haas: jealously over abandonment. Abner was off the list, but Jimmy Frey had taken his place. Passion, money, power. He had a lot to gain if he thought the widow needed a new husband and he was available.

And what about Hamm Starr, allegedly the victim's best friend? Did he have anything to gain? As far as Grace could tell, he had no skin in the game except his pecker. Either he was screwing Ellie to best Yeager in a rivalry that apparently scanned decades, or Ellie was right, and he had colluded with Yeager in a scheme to get her to seek divorce. Free of her, Clausen could continue doing his own thing without the albatross of a family around his neck. Come to think of it, Starr got to keep doing his own thing, too (case in point, Jennifer Sousa). He could continue to string Ellie along forever, with no intention of every marrying her.

Another liar outed in a case already brimming with them.

Grace shook her head. It was hard to understand why some people lived the way they did.

Killing Yeager didn't seem to fit Hamm's artistic MO, but that didn't mean he *hadn't* done it.

Suspects were back to Ellie, Carolyn, and Jimmy. And, okay, *maybe* Hamm.

Unless Ellie was the best actress she'd ever encountered, Grace was inclined to discount her. And if Carolyn hoped to win her lover back, what purpose would there have been in murdering him?

That left The Little Prick.

Grace eased up to a stop sign and put her foot down to balance the bike.

Jimmy Frey was obnoxious, offensive, and a general pain in the ass, but was he the kind of guy who would force another man to dress up in evening wear and kill him in the hopes that the man's widow would marry him? Or was that scenario wishful thinking on Grace's part because she disliked Frey so much?

She checked for traffic, then pushed off.

Her radio hummed to life. "Jason Knox is here to see you, Grace. Are you close enough to bike in?"

Grace depressed the response button. "I'm only a couple

of minutes away. Can he wait?"

After a moment's silence, Dagne Nelson came back on and said, "Yes. Out."

Stopping once to tell two ladies out antiquing that they couldn't park tail-in on Willamette Street, even for loading, Grace made the station house in less than five minutes.

Jason, standing tall and distinguished in a polo shirt, pleated pants, and leather loafers, always looked like a fashion plate for a gentleman's magazine. With his good looks, intelligence, and personable charm, no wonder her matchmaking mother was trying to hook him up with someone.

She extended her hand. "Hi, Jason. Nice to see you."

He nodded, offering his own hand. "I understand you have my bird in custody." He offered her a wry grin.

Grace chuckled. "We don't actually have it here. Excuse me just a moment." She hurried to her office for the Clausen file, where she'd put the digital printout of the blue beast. "Does this look like your macaw?"

He glanced at the photo. "It looks exactly like my macaw, because it *is* my macaw. If she sings 'Blue Moon,' 'September Song,' or 'Teacher's Pet,' you'll know it's Cyan."

"I believe, among other things, we did hear some 'Blue Moon,'" Grace admitted, reluctant to comment on the bird's extended vocabulary.

"I play some of my favorite early- to mid-twentieth century music for the birds. It keeps them happy." He smiled, looking a little self-conscious by the admission. "Will you please authorize her release from Animal Control? Today."

"Absolutely. The vet says she's in good health and her wing should be fine soon." No need to tell Jason yet that his feathered friend might somehow be involved in a homicide. "Animal Control is hoping you won't mind paying the veterinarian's bill. Apparently, the vet recognized it as your bird right away."

"That won't be a problem."

"I have a couple of questions for you." Grace glanced around the office. "Let's step into the conference room."

He hesitated, then nodded.

"Please, have a seat," Grace said. She thumbed through

the file until she came to his stolen bird report. Having read it once, she knew the basics, but she took a moment to review the details.

She looked up at him. "At the time you filed the report, you stated you had no idea how someone got into the locked aviary to take the bird."

He looked momentarily disgruntled.

"I'm sorry to have to ask you questions you may have already given answers to," Grace said. "Our work study student isn't completely trained and I'm afraid she left some information out of the report."

Obviously irritated, Jason tapped his fingers on the arm of his chair. "That's correct, but there was a picture of the van in which you found Cyan—and Cyan herself—in this morning's *Register-Guard*."

Grace hadn't read the paper yet, and wasn't sure how it related to the break-in.

"I recognized both my bird and that van. It was parked on my street over the weekend. There were magnetic signs on the doors for a landscape company."

The information fit with what the HazMat team had extracted from the vehicle along with the drugs and drug paraphernalia. Apparently, Cappland had tried to blend into the neighborhoods he cased by posing as Capp Landscaping.

"Did you question any of your neighbors about the van?"

"No, I didn't think to."

"Most landscapers work during the week, and they don't have out-of-state plates on their vehicles."

"I admit, I didn't notice the license plates, but many of my neighbors have jobs during the week. I just assumed someone was getting an estimate for work to be done."

"No one came to your house that day?"

Again Jason hesitated. "I was on my way to Eugene when I noticed the vehicle. Obviously he came to my house, or he wouldn't have been found with my macaw."

"Obviously," Grace agreed. "I was surprised when I learned the value of the bird. Do you think the bird-napper knew, or are you inclined to think it was it a random bird-napping?" She bit her lip when the urge to giggle hit her.

Jason shook his head. "Some of my neighbors don't approve of my aviary and complain about the noise. They want me to get rid of my birds." He shrugged. "I've explained that you can't just 'get rid' of a hundred thousand dollars worth of birds, but they don't understand. I've glassed in the sides as a concession, but the top has only a wire cover. I can only imagine that the birds were noisy that day and whomever this man in the van was seeing complained and repeated what I'd said about their value."

"You're certain the aviary was locked?"

"Yes."

"What's the access?"

"I can get in from the house, and of course, that door isn't locked."

"No outside exit into the aviary?"

His gaze darted left for an instant. "No."

"What kind of locks do you have?"

"Deadbolts."

Any thief worth his salt could do a deadbolt. "There was no sign of entry to the house itself?"

"Not that I could see. I also have an alarm system, which was on in my absence."

"The monitoring system covers the aviary?"

Jason paused. "It's supposed to, but now you've got me wondering."

Grace scribbled some notes. "Okay, I'm going to send someone over to have a look around."

"I would have appreciated that happening on Monday when I came in to make the report."

"I know, Jason, and I'm sorry it didn't. The clerk you talked to has been thoroughly instructed again about complaint procedures, though I know that's not much consolation to you now." She closed the file and her notebook. "There may still be some evidence we can gather that will tell us how he got in. Has anyone else been around your house this week?"

"Landscaping came on Wednesday. I saw the meter reader on Thursday. The paperboy comes every morning. Your parents were there for dinner with the children on

Wednesday evening. We ate on the patio."

"Anyone else?"

"Not that I can think of."

"Do you have a housekeeper?"

"Yes. She cleans on Monday, Wednesday, and Friday, but she's been on vacation this week, visiting family in Medford."

Grace stood. "Okay, thanks. I'll give Animal Control a call and let them know you're on your way."

Jason stood, as well. "Thank you. I appreciate it. Cyan doesn't do well in unfamiliar surroundings."

"I should warn you, she's picked up some new words."

"Profanities, no doubt."

"No doubt," Grace agreed. "Too bad Mr. Cappland didn't survive his escapade so we could ask him how he got the bird."

"Yes," Jason said. "Too bad."

CHAPTER 35

GRACE CALLED ANIMAL Control while Jason was still at the station. She was told he needed to come sooner rather than later to get his macaw. The bird was driving everyone crazy, including the animals who were howling and yowling nonstop.

After Jason left, she called Ellie Clausen to ask for a meeting later that afternoon. No one answered, not even voice mail. Jimmy Frey was next on the list. Same story. Grace briefly considered that they were together, then blew the idea off as ludicrous.

"Who's in the field?" she asked Dagne. She could have looked at the schedule herself, but this was sort of a test for the student worker.

"Mallory, Jenks, and Montoya."

Thank goodness. The group who, for some reason, liked weekend duty and worked well together.

She bit her lip, wanting to light into Dagne for not taking a more comprehensive report from Jason, but refrained from doing so since Tina had already spoken to her about it. "Okay, thanks."

Grace hit the button on her radio and instructed Deets and Melody to get over to Jason Knox's place on the stolen-bird break-in. "That *was* the bird our drug guy had in his van yesterday."

She bit her lip a little harder. Did she dare have Montoya

bring in Jimmy Frey? Better check with the chief on that one, and he was gone to Portland to pick up his kid.

"Keep trying Ellie Clausen for me, will you?" she asked Dagne. "Here's her number. When and if you reach her, please set up an appointment time. I can be there whenever." She belatedly remembered her date. "Up until about six-thirty anyway."

"Anything else?"

Grace narrowed her eyes at the young woman. Did she detect a note of snideness?

"Nope, thanks. I really appreciate your help."

Dagne scowled.

"Is there a problem?"

The phone rang, saving the girl from having to answer.

The door opened and Jasper Spriggs walked in. "Hello, Grace."

"Hi, Jasper."

"Mama laid down for a nap, so I thought I'd come over in person. Talking on the phone might wake her. You got a minute?"

Grace motioned him to follow her to the conference room. "How's she doing?"

"She seemed a little out of it, but sometimes sleeping helps."

"Did you find anything missing?"

He nodded. "The old wooden rocker on the front porch. Daddy bought it for her fifty years ago. I couldn't decide whether to help her remember what was missing or let her stew about it. Either way, it was a tough call."

Grace murmured sympathetically.

"I decided to tell her, but I don't know if she understood that I'd try to get it back." He leaned forward earnestly. "Do you think there's any chance we might?"

Coburg was a small town, but Grace couldn't go door-to-door searching for a fifty-year-old rocker. "We'll try, Jasper, that's all I can promise. Let's make it official and file a report. That way, I can get it on the computer for other officers to see."

Once they had that taken care of, they went back to the

conference room and he slumped down into a chair. "I have to figure out what to do about her." His anguished gaze skittered away. "If it was up to me, I'd have her come live with us, but my wife and I, we're having some problems right now. Empty-nest problems. Mama would require a lot of care and I need to focus on keeping my marriage together."

"I understand," Grace said, and she did, but Gunny was near the point where she needed someone around twenty-four hours a day. "Have you considered adult care?"

"No nursing home!"

"No, I mean something like an Alzheimer's care facility. I've read that some are set up in a tiered structure, with the level of care dependent on the stage of progression. Early-stage residents have a little apartment of their own, but without a kitchen, and they eat family-style with the other residents at meal time. There must be something like that in the Portland area. You could have Gunny evaluated, see where she would fit in the tier."

"I suppose that's a possibility."

"It's just a thought. Certainly, it would be much easier for you, not having to travel so far each time something comes up." Not wanting him to know she'd already run a background on him, she asked, "Are finances a consideration?"

"No. I can afford it. Daddy left Mama well settled, and she's got retirement from working at the school district, but I don't touch those accounts." He drew a deep, sorrowful breath. "When her doctor diagnosed her, I knew we'd need that money sometime down the road for her care."

Grace was relieved that Jasper had foresight concerning his mother's future. It would mean all the difference for the level of Gunny's care later. "Have you discussed any of this with your mother?"

"It's hard to talk about," he admitted. "She's always accusing me of stealing her money."

"That's common in people with Alzheimer's, Jasper. Are you already her guardian and conservator?"

"I have her power of attorney."

"That's a start. I know the courts are resistant to taking

away the rights of the elderly, but your mother could be in danger if she continues to wander like she does. You should see about getting the court to appoint you both guardian and conservator. Power of attorney just isn't enough at this point."

"I know." He sighed. "I'll discuss the living situation with my wife, see what she thinks." He sighed again. "I wish I had siblings, so they could help me out with this."

Thankful for her own family, Grace knew exactly what he meant.

Grace pedaled through all the new subdivisions. Children played in the yards, shot hoops at the curbs, and ran screaming through sprinklers. They weren't really supposed to have hoops in the public right-of-way, but Grace didn't have the heart to make anyone move them. Considering the temperature, a surprising number of people were out gardening. A few others aimed their hoses alternately at their cars and their kids. Grace could've used a soak herself. The thermometer was going to break one hundred by the end of the afternoon.

Dagne radioed twice, once for Bobby Beaudet's barking dog, for about the umpteenth time, and once to settle an argument between two neighbors over who owned the apples once the fruit had fallen from the tree. According to Tina, who had broached just this topic earlier in the week, September was the start of an annual feud between these particular neighbors that lasted for months. Apparently it was heating up pre-season this year.

The third time the radio rasped, it was Melody. "Your sister just called. She's faxing an article. She wants you to read it and call her back right away. She's going somewhere for the rest of the weekend where cell phones don't work."

Why had Mikey had called the station instead of her cell phone? "Thanks, Mel. I'll be back shortly. I'm just south of town, but I see a traffic infraction I have to deal with first."

"She sounded really excited—was that because of what she's faxing or the guy she's going away with?"

Grace laughed. “Probably a little of both.”

Half an hour later, Grace finally parked and locked her bike in front of the station house. She took a moment to check her smartphone. It had a charge, but no messages and no missed call. Who could figure out the workings of Mikey’s mind?

She beelined for the fax and found the tray empty. Quickly, she checked her in-box, but nothing had been put there, either. Dagne was sitting at the data entry computer, but no one else was in sight.

“Dagne, did you see a fax come through for me?”

“No.”

“Where’s Mel?”

“Getting a soda.”

Grace waited an impatient ten minutes for Melody to return.

“No fax came through that I saw,” Melody said when Grace asked. “Your sister was so excited, I thought it was coming immediately.”

“Could something be wrong with the machine? Dagne, would you mind helping me check it out?”

“I do mind. I’m busy.”

Grace exchanged a confused glance with Melody. Angry and puzzled by the girl’s behavior, she walked over to where Dagne sat, entering case reports. “What’s your problem?”

The work study student turned to glare at her.

“I take that to mean you *do* have a problem. Would you mind telling me what it is?” She initially assumed Dagne, being Abner Nelson’s niece, was holding a grudge because Grace had questioned her uncle about Clausen’s death. But this nastiness went beyond that kind of hostility, and once Grace thought about, she realized it had been going on almost the entire time she’d been at CPD.

“Yeah, I’ll tell you,” the girl snapped. “You think you’re so hot, but I’m warning you to stay away from my boyfriend.”

“Boyfriend?” Grace quickly considered the guys she worked with who might be in the twenty-year-old’s age range. Amaka, Dillon, Wozinsky? Surely none of the reservists—Felix, who already had a fiancée, or Taylor or McPherson, who were both married, or Bobby Wright, who'd started the week before she had?

Puzzled, Grace said, "I don't—"

"Don't play dumb!" Dagne shouted, tears forming in her eyes. "Jimmy told me you'd deny it, but you just leave him alone, you hear?"

Grace almost fell over in shock. She shared a look of disbelief with Melody, who was choking on her Diet Coke. "For one thing," Grace said, "Jimmy Frey is old enough to be your father, and for another—and I don't mean to insult your ability to choose boyfriends—but I'd sooner enter a convent than resort to dating Jimmy Frey."

"He's not too old!" Dagne's lower lip quivered and she frowned with uncertainty. "How old is he, anyway?"

"Thirty-nine," Melody interjected. "And believe me, I know, because he hit on me long before you got here, kid. The only thing good looking about the SOB is his face, and he has a nice bod, but everything inside is about as ugly and stupid and mean as it gets."

"You're just jealous," Dagne accused.

"So jealous I'd knock Gracie over trying to get to that convent if he was the last man on earth left to date."

Considering what a bitch the girl had been over the past two weeks, Grace surprised even herself when opened her mouth to dole out some motherly advice. "It really isn't any of my concern since you're of age, Dagne, but just be careful. He's not the kind of guy who's willing to give you happily-ever-after."

"You're right. It's none of your business!" Dagne swiped at her tears. "Besides, you can't just come in here pushing your tits in guys' faces and think you can have whoever you want!"

Grace reared back as if Dagne had slapped her.

"You're out of line, Dagne," Melody said in a voice that told Grace exactly why the other woman had reputation for resolving disputes. "And if your boyfriend is so hot for you, why is he telling anyone who'll listen that he's going to be marrying Ellie Clausen?"

Nothing could have shut Dagne Nelson up faster. Grace could tell from Melody's expression that she desperately wanted to call back those final words, but once uttered, there was no chance of that.

"You're a lying bitch, just like her!" Dagne screamed, jumping up from the computer.

God, they did not need this internal strife in the office. And all because of Jimmy Frey. Grace hadn't seen a discordant note among her staff anywhere that didn't involve him. If she had to handcuff the chief back to his hammock herself, he *would* hear her out about this as soon as he was back in the office on Monday.

"Call me a bitch again, and you'll be swallowing teeth," Melody warned.

Of an equal stature, the two women faced off. Where Dagne was soft and feminine in ruffles, Melody, while not buff in the true sense of the word, definitely had some muscles on her, not to mention skills in the fine art of self-defense. Despite all that, Grace was certain that the look in Melody's dark eyes put Dagne off like nothing else could have. Grace didn't even have to intervene by shouting, "Time out!" but she did it anyway.

Melody took a step back, reclaiming her soda, which she'd left on the corner of Dagne's desk. Dagne sniffled a few times, backing away two steps to Melody's one. The girl's immaturity flashed like a red warning light. She was too blinded by love, or infatuation, or whatever she was consumed with, to see the true picture.

"Look," Grace said. "If you're unhappy here, you don't have to stay. We can get along without you."

Dagne glared at her. "Yeah, well, I can't get along without you. I'm getting class credit for this gig, and if I walk out the door now, I might as well flush my grade down the toilet."

"Okay, then we have to figure out a way to get along. I can't tell you not to have a relationship with one of your coworkers, but I can tell you that you'd better not let it affect your job performance, or you *will* be walking out that door." She met Dagne's glare with a stern look of her own. "Are we clear on that?"

The girl opened and closed her mouth several times, like a fish taking in oxygen. Grace could almost see the retort forming, dared it to come.

Melody cleared her throat, ending the glaring contest between the sergeant and the work study student.

Dagne pulled down her too-short skirt and said, "I'll take a look at that fax machine now."

"Thanks." Grace was her mother in many ways. She put her hand out to give Dagne's shoulder a squeeze, but the girl jerked away.

While Dagne examined the fax machine, Melody pulled Grace into the conference room. "I am *so* sorry, Grace! I don't know why I said that. That's confidential information."

"Don't worry about it," Grace said. "I'm sure Dagne reads every report that's filed—I've caught her at it several times when she's supposed to be doing data entry. She signed a confidentiality agreement when she came here at the beginning of the summer. If she wants to keep earning her class credit, and if she wants a good recommendation from us, she'll keep her trap shut."

Dagne appeared in the doorway, her face a stone mask. "It's got paper, it's online, and it has toner. Something must be wrong at the other end." She turned and walked away.

"Great," Grace muttered. She reached into her pocket and withdrew her cell phone. Mikey's work number was tenth on speed dial. Grace had the choice of leaving a message in her sister's voice mailbox or hitting zero for operator assistance. She chose zero and after several minutes was transferred to someone in the crime-beat section.

Grace explained her problem.

Sounding harried, the man said, "Our fax is broken. She sent the stuff to you and left without waiting to see if it went through."

"Can you get it to another fax machine in the building? I really need that information today."

"No," he said, "I can't. I'm the only one here. I'll leave the originals and a message on Michaela's desk for you, but that's the best I can do."

"Do you have time to read it to me?"

"Are you kidding?" He hung up without saying goodbye.

Frustrated, Grace disconnected and dialed her sister's cell phone. It rang six times then went to voice mail.

Grace let out a shriek of frustration. Typical of Michaela to go someplace incommunicado!

She spent the rest of the afternoon at her desk, updating case notes on the Clausen file, checking the fax machine, waiting for Michaela to return her call. In between times, she responded to several small incidents in the downtown area involving kids on skateboards. Periodically, Dagne informed her she hadn't been able to reach Ellie Clausen to schedule the appointment.

At the end of her shift, she heard the main phone ring several times from the women's changing room. Buttoning up as she stepped out to see why Dagne hadn't picked up, Grace was surprised to find the girl gone. From the looks of things, she'd left for the day, clocking out sixty minutes early.

Disgruntled because she wanted a little extra time to get ready for her date, Grace consulted the patrol schedule. McPherson, Reiker, and Trudeau were on shift. She went to the radio. "Jamie, you there?"

"Yeah, Grace. What's up?"

"Dagne split early and no one's minding the store. Can you or one of the others come in for an hour?"

"Reiker's catching speeders and Trudeau's at a fender-bender out past the nursery. I can be there in a few, if you can wait long enough for me to grab some grub."

"I can. Thanks, Jamie."

At six-thirty, Grace finally got on her own bike and headed home. Hot and sweaty, she had exactly thirty minutes to shower, wash her hair, and get ready for her evening out. There wasn't a second left over for pampering.

She hoped Sean Ducey hadn't decided on some date-night movie.

She definitely was *not* in the mood for mush.

Sean Ducey, a good-looking, intelligent Irishman, had a sense of humor and he loved telling jokes in an Irish brogue. He was pretty good at it, too, and fun to be with.

Grace was certain, by the end of the evening, he hadn't thought the same of her.

They'd gone to see a Bruce Willis movie, so that, at least, had been action-packed.

Afterward, when they'd both admitted to missing dinner, he'd treated her to a burger at Red Robin. As usual, the restaurant was noisy, and Sean liked to talk, so she mostly just listened. At her door, he gave her a quick peck on the cheek and said he'd call, but Grace knew he wouldn't.

Sean was a nice guy, but as she watched him drive away, she knew he'd make a better friend than a boyfriend.

As she hurried inside to check her answering machine, hoping that Michaela had been responsible and checked her voice mail, she pulled out her own cell phone, which she'd set on vibrate for the evening. No messages on either.

Disappointed and a little angry, Grace tried phoning her sister once more, yelling into the phone when Michaela's voice mail picked up. "Where the hell are you?"

CHAPTER 36

GRACE AWOKE AGITATED and in no mood for a run. With considerable effort, she forced herself out of bed and into running clothes.

Exercise was touted to keep not only the body, but the mind and spirit functioning properly. Whether or not a run would dispel the weirdness she had sensed even before the alarm had gone off, however, remained to be seen.

She tugged her hair into a haphazard pony tail, grabbed a water bottle, and bolted out the door.

Less than an hour later, having given up on the run after only fifteen minutes, she was showered, out the door, and locking her bike to the rack outside the police station.

Not only had she arrived way too early for work, but she couldn't shake the grim feeling of foreboding closing in on her, almost as if it were something physical. True, it was starting out to be another hot and muggy day, but this felt entirely different than a weather phenomenon.

It felt ominous.

Grace logged in, then checked with the Sheriff's office for non-emergency messages, only to discover that Gunny Spriggs had called six times in the last hour. "Some 'floozy,'" the SO dispatcher said, "is sitting on her front porch and won't leave." Other than those, not a single call had come in.

"Floozy?"

"Direct quote."

Grace's dread grew.

She checked to see who was on graveyard. Cameron Taylor. A nice guy, but near the end of his shift, he might not put his best face forward for a little old lady reporting a floozy on her front porch.

No one else coming in at eight was likely to volunteer to respond on the Spriggs's call, either. Gunny's disease made everyone too uncomfortable. Grace climbed on her patrol bike and pedaled over to her old teacher's house.

She was in no damned mood to find Hamm Starr, jammed into Gunny's rocking chair, dead as a road-crossing possum, all duded up like his best friend had been a week earlier.

"Shit, shit, *shit!*"

Early-morning crows lined up on the porch railing. As obnoxious as ever, they *caw, caw, cawed*, taking flight over Grace's outburst.

Grace appealed to a power higher than her own to recall the unprofessional response, but her hopes were dashed when two of Gunny's neighbors stepped outside and at least two others stood at open windows, peering out at her.

"What's up?" the man across the street hollered.

Grace improvised. "Flat tire. Sorry I bothered you."

"Young ladies shouldn't talk like that," someone else yelled. "Especially over a flat tire."

"I know, and I'm sorry," Grace yelled back, certain her mother would hear about this lapse before the morning was over. She bent, pretending to exam the tire, wondering if any of Gunny's neighbors could out her lie from a distance.

Not that it really mattered. In short order, they'd have an inkling something was up. The street would be jammed with patrol cars, an ambulance, the Deputy ME's car, the call car, hoards of reporters and TV news vans. "Shit!" she muttered again, keeping her voice low.

What a fucking nightmare!

She wheeled the bike up to the side of Gunny's house but didn't bother to lock it up. At this point, she almost dared someone to steal it. At least stealing bikes was a normal kind of crime.

Moments later, she stood grim-faced, staring up at the remains of what once had been a living, breathing hunk of man.

At least now, the presentiment engulfing her like a damned wet blanket had a name: Death.

With a wave behind her to anyone who still watching her every move, Grace climbed the steps and knocked. Gunny answered instantly.

"See her?" the old woman whispered. "She's been there all night. I didn't want to wake her up, but now, I want her to go home and she won't listen to me."

"I see her," Grace said, gently steering Gunny back into the house. "I want you to wait inside while I talk to her."

For once, Gunny didn't argue. She allowed Grace to lead her to the kitchen, where one of the burners on the stove glowed bright red. Grace lifted the tea kettle from a cold burner and ascertained it had been filled. She placed it on the hot one, adjusting the knob to LOW. "You wait right here," she told Gunny again, speaking slowly and with authority. "Until I get back, okay?"

A multitude of thoughts raced through Grace's mind as she went back to the porch, the first and foremost being that she should have had Montoya bring Frey in the day before, whether the chief had okayed it or not. If she had, Hamm Starr might be home in bed with one of his many lovelies right now, instead of dead in Gunny's rocking chair.

An artist's canvas, propped against the rocker, had the words *Now I am like them* painted in bold red strokes across the front. Blood red strokes. This killer really knew how to make a statement.

Starr was dead, no doubt about it. Pasty white skin, blue lips. Bit of bloody froth at those beautifully chiseled lips. Still, she approached his body and put her fingers against his carotid artery.

His blue, blue eyes, now dull with death, were open. No seductive or contemplative spark remained as they stared vacantly, and maybe accusingly, at her. Grace had a desire to close them, but knew better than to alter even that small aspect of the crime scene.

Muttering all the way back to her bike, she pulled her cell phone out of the saddlebag and dialed the chief. With an eerie sense of déjà vu, she said, "We can cross Hamm Starr off the suspect list in Clausen's murder."

After a slight pause, Aidan, his voice husky from sleep, said. "Jesus. Tell me you're not calling to say he's dead."

"Believe me, I wish I wasn't."

The brooding silence on the other end of the line seemed far worse than if the boss had bellowed out obscenities.

"Chief?"

"I'm just thinking about Dylan. I don't have day care exactly lined up yet and he's still sleeping. Hell, *I* was sleeping!"

Grace's first thought was that the boy was old enough to stay by himself for a few hours, but she refrained from suggesting it. She didn't know the chief well enough to offer parenting advice, never mind that she wasn't even qualified to give it. Instead, she offered up another solution, which under normal circumstances she would have discounted because of her mother's propensity to play matchmaker. "Pop can pick him up and take him back to the house."

"I don't know…."

"It'll give him a chance to meet Kyle, too."

"You're sure your folks won't mind?"

"They're grandparents. I'm sure."

She could almost hear him grappling with the idea over the phone line. "I don't like to impose, but I guess I'll have to this time."

Aidan Cruz apparently wasn't a man who like being beholden to anyone, ever. "I'll call Pop now. He'll probably be there by the time you get dressed." She sighed. "I'll call Tina, too. Unfortunately, we all know the routine by now."

"Do we need to call in the Major Crime Team?" Grace asked the chief.

"Maybe," Aidan said. "A single homicide is one thing, but two pretty much stretches our ability to give this everything we've got."

"You think it's a serial killer?" Deets asked.

"At this point, it's hard to say. It has some of the markings." The chief studied the fancy taffeta-and-chiffon dress, the messy blonde wig, the tilted tiara or crown or whatever the hell it was, the dyed-to-match satin heels. "Whoever's doing this definitely has a pattern." He frowned. "Deets, as soon as you finish lifting prints, take Wozinsky and bring Frey in."

"I should have questioned him yesterday," Grace said, "but I wanted to check with you first."

"We don't know that he had anything to do with either crime," the chief cautioned.

Grace gritted her teeth. *Then why bring him in?*

"Go on about doing what you need to do with the scene," Aidan said. "I'll get on the horn to Tina to call the MCT and DA's office out here."

An instant later, Melody radioed that the neighborhood crowd was growing larger and the press had begun to arrive. "I don't know if Felix and I will be enough to hold them back."

"*Tina!*" Aidan barked into his hand-held, "Call everyone in for duty. I'll be damned if we're going to let this turn into a media circus."

"I think you're too late," commented a new voice, in a dry tone.

"Hi, Jade," Grace said. She introduced the deputy ME to the chief.

"I hope you're not planning on calling me out here every Sunday for one of these formal events," the Deputy ME said, shaking Aidan's hand. "Although I have to admit, last week's *haute couture* fit a little better than this week's."

All three gazes shot to the dead artist. Olive-skinned with a masculine amount of body hair, his features looked somehow obscene against the feminine lemon-colored gown that looked as if it had been cut open in the back and tucked around him. His ponytail must have come loose because hanks of black hair straggled from beneath the wig, finishing the bizarre picture with an almost macabre whimsy.

"He's definitely not as neat as our first stiff," Jade commented.

"It all seems more hurried." Grace bit her lip. "Hamm was a bigger man, for one thing. He's got some bruising, too, which Clausen didn't have. And lividity down his right side. He wasn't killed here."

The chief nodded tersely. "I agree. Mrs. Spriggs's front porch doesn't exactly offer the obscurity of a mint field outside of town. Wherever it happened, Starr fought his killer." He scanned the surrounding area. "Plenty of neighbors close by who might have heard or seen something while he was being placed here, though." He motioned Deets over. "Start canvassing the neighborhood. Get Montoya to help you." He turned to Grace. "Who's missing?"

"Amaka and McPherson are on their way in and reservists Reiker, Trudeau, and Wright are at the station suiting up now."

Deets frowned. "I thought you wanted me and Montoya to pick up Frey."

Aidan scowled at him. "Well, now I want you to canvas."

"Whatever you say, boss." Deets looked down at the fingerprint brush in his hand, then back at the chief. "I mean, Chief."

"Finish up, then get going." He hit the button on the hand-held again. "*Tina!*"

"Yeah, Chief?"

"Hand-held only to McPherson and Amaka. I want them to bring in Frey, and I do not, I repeat, *do not* want them to extend him any special courtesy. If he gives them any shit, they are to use restraints. Understood?"

"Perfectly," Tina said. If a voice could ooze satisfaction, hers did.

Aidan panned the area and uttered a sound that came out like a growl. "Reporters everywhere."

"They're hoping for a glimpse of the corpse," Grace said. "They couldn't get close enough with Clausen."

"Shit! *Double shit!*" The chief activated his hand-held one more time. "*Tina!*"

"Yeah, Chief?"

"Anyone hanging around there yet who doesn't have

anything to do?"

"Not yet."

"Anyone coming in who lives by Home Depot?"

"Just a sec." After a few tense moments, Tina said, "No."

"Damn. Never mind then."

Grace braved Aidan's wrath. "What do you need at the Depot, Chief?"

"Plastic sheeting to put up around the porch to obscure the view. Something that's not a dark color, so it won't cut our light."

"I think Rocco can help us out with that. He keeps a roll of painter's plastic in his garage for painting and other projects."

"Good. Call him."

Grace hit her brother's number on speed dial and firmed up the deal in less than a minute.

Aidan stared at her, his expression contemplative. "Both bodies were in plain sight. The killer didn't even try to hide his crimes."

"Yesterday, Gunny told me that her rocker was missing from the porch."

"Is this the same rocker, back again?"

Her glance went to the chair. "Looks like it."

Aidan's eyes narrowed on her. "What do you think that means, Gabbiano?"

"He's completely confident that we won't figure out who he is?"

"Try this on instead. He knows your routine and he wants to make it easy for you to find the bodies."

Where the hell did that come from? "He wouldn't know I'd be the one to respond to Gunny's calls."

Aidan's eyebrow shot way up. "You're kidding right? Everyone in town knows you have a soft spot for the old lady."

"Not *every*one."

"Don't bet on it," Deets said, pulling off his latex gloves as he approached. "*Every*one already knows you hollered 'shit' three times when you found Starr's body this morning."

Grace couldn't defend herself on that count, but that didn't stop her face from turning red. News really did make the rounds quickly in a small town.

"Hey," Jade said, winking at Grace, "I said a lot worse when I got the call this morning."

"Yeah, well, I'm thinking of asking for Sundays off so I can start going to church again."

Jade grinned. "You've called in the MCT?"

Grace nodded, grateful for the diversion.

"Guess I'll make myself at home while we wait, then." She stepped up to the victim, felt for a pulse with her gloved hand, shrugged, and said, "He's dead."

Grace shook her head, amused. "The mistress of understatement."

Jade grinned again, peeling off her gloves.

The front door opened and Gunny timidly stuck her head out. "Angelina?"

To the three surrounding her, Grace explained, "She gets me mixed up with my mom."

"Angelina," Gunny said again, "the whistling won't stop. I tried, but I just don't know how to make it go away."

"Oh, my God!" Grace cried, hurrying toward the door. She'd completely forgotten about the tea kettle, and if truth be told, she'd forgotten about poor Gunny, too.

With Jade Riordan on her heels, Grace bolted for the kitchen. The weak noise from the kettle told her the thing had nearly boiled dry. Reaching for a potholder, she removed it from the burner, then turned off the knob, thankful the old woman had not been burned. "I'm so sorry, Gunny. I completely forgot about the tea kettle."

Gunny considered the stovetop with uncertainty. "I don't remember…."

Jade put her arm around the old woman's bony shoulders. "I'm Jade, Mrs. Spriggs. Why don't you have a seat and I'll fix you some breakfast and a nice hot cup of tea. Are you hungry?"

"I am," Gunny began, "but there's that woman on the porch."

"I'm taking care of her," Grace said. "And I'm going to

call Jasper right now and see if he can come down for lunch. Would you like that?"

The old Gunny, the one with sparkling, intelligent eyes, smiled at Grace. "You're a good girl, Angelina. Can we take the jitney into town?"

"Sure," Grace said. She put a hand out to Gunny's face, stroking the wrinkled skin with intermingled fondness and despair. Would her former teacher be able to tell them anything viable at all about what had happened on her front porch in the middle of the night?

And had anyone besides Grace and the chief noticed that Hamm Starr's penis had been skewered on a rusty garden stake and shoved into a pot of ivy geranium?

CHAPTER 37

AS SOON AS the body was bagged, the neighborhood canvassed, and the members of the MCT and DA's office disbursed, Felix and Deets took off to assist McPherson and Amaka in the search for Jimmy Frey. Unlike the week before, he had not shown up to intercede in Starr's death investigation. Grace completed recording the scene, though not much surfaced in the way of evidence, with the exception of the penis-kabob.

Jade Riordan abandoned whatever Sunday morning plans she had, helped Gunny dress after she'd eaten, and waited with her until Jasper showed up to take his mother out of the house. Grace and the chief shouldered the depressing task of informing Zelda Starr her only son had been murdered.

"Murdered? Who'd want to murder my boy?"

Neither the chief nor Grace had an answer.

"I would'a thought that Yeager did it," Zelda said, crying softly, "but the bastard's already dead and unless there really is such a thing as ghosts, somebody else killed my boy." She wiped her nose with the hem of her blouse. "Did he die just the same as that Yeager, or different?"

"It looks like drug overdose, but we won't know for certain until after the autopsy."

"So, is that the same as with Yeager?"

"We think so," the chief said.

"My boy used to do drugs, but no more." She shook her

head sadly. "His poison was women. Always women."

Something he had in common with his best friend, Grace noted in silence. "The autopsy will probably be tomorrow. It can take up to a week or so to get the lab results back, but the ME will have a preliminary on the cause of death and probably release Hamm's body to you by Tuesday."

Zelda shuddered. "I don't like to think of them cutting my beautiful boy up, but they haf'ta, don't they?"

"I'm afraid so," the chief said, his voice soft with regret and empathy. Grace hadn't known he had it in him.

"I guess I'd better see to getting him a funeral together." She used the hem of her blouse again. "Hamm said Pastor Grimes did such a nice job for Yeager, so compassionate…."

Grace avoided exchanging glances with the chief, who'd read her notes on the interview with the "compassionate" minister. She put an arm around the woman's narrow shoulders. "We'll do our best to keep you informed during the investigation, Zelda." She gestured toward Aidan. "The chief and I, and our whole office, we're very sorry for your loss."

"Thank you, Grace. You're the only one down there who ever treated me like I was in my right mind. I appreciated that then, and I appreciate it now."

"Is there someone I can call for you, or anything I can do?"

"No, honey. It was just Hamm and me for family. I got some friends, though. I might call one of them to come over for awhile." She stared at them helplessly. "I need to go over and see to Blackie, too."

Grace had forgotten about Starr's dog. "May I ask you one more thing, Zelda?"

Starr's mother sniffed. "Sure, honey."

"The car crash that caused Hamm's hand injury, when was that?"

Zelda thought a moment. "It was the summer before he changed schools, I think. That's right. He was still in Colorado." She squinted red eyes at Grace. "Why?"

"I don't know," Grace admitted. "I thought maybe it was somehow connected."

Zelda stared at her, rather shrewdly, Grace thought. "You

was thinking my boy killed Yeager over that accident."

"It crossed my mind."

"More likely it would'a been over that upstart, Ellie Clausen."

Grace had no response to that.

"But now my boy is dead, too."

Grace nodded. "Yes, so the point is moot. Hamm didn't kill his friend."

"Well, maybe someone did have an ax to grind with Hamm over that crash, but that don't explain why Yeager was murdered, now does it?"

"They were both in the car."

"Maybe so, but Hamm was doing the driving."

Grace called Ellie immediately upon returning to the office. The widow herself answered. "I tried to reach you yesterday," Grace said.

"I took the girls to Portland to shop for school clothes, then we put Cait on a plane to San Francisco. She has to be at freshman orientation tomorrow." She paused a moment. "Why, what's happened?"

For once, Grace thought she sounded like the old Ellie, confident, self-assured. "Did Jimmy Frey go with you?"

Ellie laughed, apparently genuinely amused. "Grace, I told you, he's traveling a one-way street. I have absolutely no interest in him, or any other man, for that matter. I think I've had enough of that gender—of both genders—for a good long while."

Ellie seemed in good humor about her new life choice. Maybe getting out of town for a day, spending money, had been good for her. "I need to talk to you, face-to-face. I'm coming over." She hung up before Ellie could tell her not to.

Within five minutes, Grace asked Ellie, "Have you seen Hamm recently?"

"Not since the memorial service. I thought about calling and giving him a piece of my mind, but it seems I can't afford to be without all of it, so I decided not to." She half-smiled at her own wit, then sighed. "Besides, he seemed like the only person at the service who actually cared that Yeager was dead."

Grace had to agree, but contrary to Ellie's purported new philosophy, she had slept with the man, and she had done it with her emotions, as well as her body. Was it possible she'd killed him in retaliation, because she thought he'd used her? How would they ever know now if he had?

"Someone murdered Hamm last night or early this morning, Ellie. The same way Yeager was killed."

Ellie went completely white and swayed on her feet. Not the reaction of a guilty person, for sure. "Ohmygod! *Ohmygod, what's going on?*" Ellie began to sob uncontrollably.

Grace was glad to see the woman had cared about someone, even if that someone was a louse. "That's what we're trying to find out. May I speak to Lindsey, please?"

"Verifying my alibi?" Ellie choked out.

"Yes." No sense beating around the bush.

"What the hell is going on?" snarled Jimmy Frey as soon as Grace and the chief walked into the conference room. He leaped up, only to be restrained by McPherson and Amaka. Deets and Felix stood backup. "This isn't fucking funny."

"It's not supposed to be fucking funny," Aidan said. "You're a suspect in two homicides and I expect you to plant your sorry ass in that chair and keep it there while you answer my questions."

Aidan leveled a look at Frey that should have scared the shit out of him, as far as Grace was concerned, but the arrogant LP glared back. "If I'm a suspect, then I want a fucking lawyer. Right now." He jammed his index finger against the top of the table.

Chief Cruz leaned forward, his palms flat against the same surface. "You don't need a fucking lawyer. I haven't arrested you, I haven't Mirandized you. I just want some answers. If I don't get those answers, then you can call your scumbag lawyer, and I'll get my answers anyway."

Frey belched whatever he'd had for lunch in response.

"Tell me where you were last night," Aidan said. Only by the barest expression of disgust could Grace tell he'd been affected by the odor of Frey's breath.

Belligerently, Frey folded his arms over his chest.

Amaka smacked the back of his head.

Frey whirled around. "I'll have your fucking badge for assault!"

All innocence, Amaka asked, "Did you see me assault him?"

The other three officers shook their heads. All of a sudden, Frey didn't seem so cocky.

"I repeat, where were you last night?"

"With my girlfriend."

"Which one would that be?" Grace asked. "Ellie, whom you're going to marry? Or Dagne, whom you've turned against a certain co-worker with your lies?" Next to her, the chief started at the mention of the student worker's name, but Grace ignored him. "Which one, Frey?"

Frey resumed his slumped position, arms still folded. "Neither."

Aidan stalked around the table. "I'm going to give you fifteen seconds to start talking, then I'm booking you." He leaned down to within an inch of Jimmy Frey's nose. "You think when you get fucked down at the jail, it'll feel as good as whoever screwed you last night?"

"She's underage," he said, whining. "I don't want to get her in trouble."

Without warning, Aidan reached out and grabbed the Corporal by the shirt, lifting him out of the chair. "If you're screwing an underage girl, you piece of shit, *she's* not the one who's in trouble!"

"It was that Sousa chick. The one with the big tits. Jennifer."

Grace closed her eyes in dismay. Good lord, the girl did get around. She'd alibied Hamm Starr, and now she'd probably alibi Jimmy Frey. "You weren't with her last night."

Aidan released The LP and in a gesture she guessed was unconscious, wiped his hands down the legs of his jeans.

Frey turned toward Grace, his tone menacing. "What

makes you think I wasn't? You been watching me?" His eyes traveled an insulting path down to her crotch. "You got a *thing* for me?"

"Yeah, I do have a *thing* for you, Jimmy. It's called *disgust.*"

Either McPherson or Deets snickered, infuriating Frey even further. He came up out of his chair again, lunging toward Grace. Even as Aidan moved, four officers pounced on Frey. Deets whipped out his cuffs and used them to secure him to the chair arm. Felix followed suit on the other side. Grace figured it for a wasted effort. The dickwad had so much adrenaline pumping, so much meanness and stupidity running through his veins where there should have been blood, he'd take the chair right across the conference table with him just to get at her.

She considered wiggling her fingers at him in a *bring it on* motion. She hadn't fired her weapon recently, except at the range, and she'd never willingly shoot another human being, but at that moment, she wasn't sure Frey qualified as *homo sapiens* anyway. It might feel good to take him down.

"To answer your question, you dumb ass jerk, I know exactly who Jennifer Sousa *was* with last night, but he's dead now, and I think you killed him."

CHAPTER 38

AIDAN FOUND A judge to sign a search warrant for Frey's apartment. It was small studio and surprisingly tidy. After two hours, they came up with nothing. Almost. A huge bowl of M&Ms sat on the kitchen counter.

"Chocolate freak," Deets said. "He eats these by the pound at work, too. Millions of people eat M&Ms."

"Yeah, but how many of them are killing someone at the time?"

Deets shook his head. "You think Starr's got some shoved up his ass, too?"

"I'd be willing to bet on it." Grace put her hands on her hips, surveying the small quarters. "How can the guy have no personal effects?"

"Beats the hell out of me. If he didn't have his bathroom shit, and his clothes weren't in the closet, it wouldn't even look like anyone lived here."

Grace's eyes swept the apartment one last time. They hadn't even found a dust bunny lurking in a corner. "Something's definitely odd here." She gnawed on her lip for a moment. "Let's get back to the office. I want to take a look at his desk."

Once there, Grace read every piece of paper, pulled out every drawer, checked the backside of every file folder. "Nothing," she finally said in defeat, "except more M&Ms." Frey had a drawer full of individually wrapped bags.

Deets shook his head at her. "Something incongruous about a guy like Frey being an M&Ms junkie."

It wasn't the candy that bothered Grace so much as the complete lack of anything personal to be found, either at his apartment or in his desk. "Isn't one of the reservists a computer geek?"

"Yeah. Ruby Trudeau."

Grace went to the staff phone list, picked up the phone and dialed.

Within minutes she had arranged for Trudeau to come back in and start going through the computer Frey used on the job, see if she could find anything in his emails, or if he'd done any incriminating web surfing. The latter wouldn't hold up in court, probably, because staff shared the few computers in the office, but there might be something to help make a connection between Frey and the murders.

In the meantime, the chief had released The LP as soon as Deets and Grace returned from searching his apartment. Without any concrete evidence, they couldn't hold him, and you couldn't arrest a guy just because you didn't like him.

"Go home, Gracie," Deets said at the end of their long day. "Relax, get a good night's sleep. Maybe Trudeau will come up with something and we'll figure this out tomorrow."

"I have to be at Surgery 10 first thing."

"Sorry you have to do Cappland *and* Starr." Deets put a hand on her shoulder. "You gonna be okay?"

Grace shrugged, cursing the burning sensation in her eyes. "I have to be. There's no other option."

"For tonight, just have some sweet dreams about busting Frey's balls."

I'd rather have sweet dreams about someone else's balls. "Not worth the effort," she said instead. Much as she disliked her co-worker, Jimmy Frey didn't feel like the right candidate for the two homicides. On the other hand, she still had a bad feeling about him. Normal people didn't live so…sterilely. And he was so damned brazen about his sexual harassment and the way he'd grabbed and bruised her arm right in front of the chief. She'd heard from at least three people that Aidan had warned him he'd better never lay a hand on her again, and yet he still acted like he could do whatever to whomever and get away with it without fear of retribution.

Before she could dwell on it further, Tina peeked around the doorframe. "Fax coming through!"

"Finally!" Grace muttered, racing into the other room. "I can't believe you're still here, Tina. Go home."

"I am, right now. See you tomorrow."

"I'll walk you out," Deets said. "'Night, Grace."

Grace waved, then reached for the cover sheet. Thank God, it was from Michaela. Her sister's message on the cover page was short but compelling: *Holy shit!!!!* She had underlined it three times.

Grace wanted to strangle her sister. If the information was that important, why hadn't she waited to ensure it faxed? Or better yet, called to relay what she'd found?

Grace almost ripped the second sheet pulling it from the machine. Her eyes scanned the text in disbelief. "Oh, my God." She collapsed into the chair and began to reread in earnest.

No wonder there'd been a sense of familiarity about the Clausen murder.

Alone in the office, she had no one with whom to share this new development. Deciding on a long shot, she sat down at the computer and searched the Internet for Houston PD contact information.

Once she had the number for the Violent Crimes unit, she picked up the phone and dialed. In a city the size of Houston, someone was bound to be in the office working a case.

It might even be a homicide that occurred less than a year earlier, involving an electronics magnate named Jack Dellenbach. He'd been found dead of a drug overdose, dressed in an salmon-pink silk evening gown, dyed-to-match satin pumps, a blonde wig, and a rhinestone tiara.

Grace changed into civvies, ready to head home. She was reaching for the pushbar on the half-glass door when she noticed Jennifer Sousa racing up the station steps. Grace opened the door and stepped outside.

Rivers of tears ran down the girl's face. She wrung her hands together, barely able to speak. "Please tell me he's not dead. Please! *Not Hamm! Please!*"

Grace punched in the code on the keypad and took the girl inside. Was there a woman Hamm had screwed who hadn't fallen in love with him? She settled Jennifer into a chair and got her a bottle of water and a box of tissues. She sat beside her, giving her what details she could, knowing it was never enough when you lost someone you cared about.

"Did you see him last night?"

Hiccupping and congested from so much crying, the girl could hardly speak. "He called me around ten and said not to come over. He's never done that before. I thought he was seeing someone else, but he swore he wasn't. I didn't believe him, so I went over anyway."

Grace went on alert. "Did you see who was there?"

Jennifer shook her head. "His place was dark. I could hear Blackie barking, so I knew he wasn't home. Blackie never barks when Hamm is home. He must have called me from somewhere else, but I didn't have a clue where that was, unless he was with that Clausen bitch." She gulped down more water and used several tissues.

"I thought he was cheating on me. I tried calling him. I wanted him to admit it, tell me who he was fucking. I could hear his phone ringing inside the house." She looked at Grace, her expression agonized. "Why didn't he tell me something was wrong? Maybe I could have helped. Maybe he'd still be alive! Ohmygod, my beautiful Hamm dead. I can't believe it. What am I going to do without him?"

It was a rotten thing to do, while the girl's defenses were down, but Grace had to seize the opportunity. "Did you decide to pay him back?"

Jennifer gaped at her. "How…how did you know?"

Grace couldn't believe she'd scored a bull's eye. "I need to know who you hooked up with, Jennifer, and tell me the truth."

She hiccupped again. "Are you going to tell my parents?"

"Not if the truth comes out of your mouth."

After a moment or two of hesitation, she said, "Jimmy Frey." She lowered her eyes and when she raised them, her torture was apparent. "I thought if I fucked him, it would make Hamm jealous and he'd never shine me on again."

So much for Frey's alibi being a lie.

And for silly girls who didn't know how to play men's games.

Grace knocked on Uncle Vito's door, then realized he was probably out back, working in his vegetable garden. She followed the narrow brick path around the house and found him elbow-deep in the string beans.

"*Ciao, Zio Vito*."

"*Ah, buona sera, Grazia. Come sta?*"

"*Bene, e tu?*" Grace knew a little Italian. Enough for short conversations, anyway.

Uncle Vito snapped the beans from the stalk at an amazing rate and tossed them into the basket at his feet. "Couldn't be better. This heat has been perfect for my crops."

Grace eyed the tiered vegetable garden that was the envy of anyone who had the privilege of being invited into the backyard to see it. Word of not only the garden's beauty, but the quality of its produce, had spread throughout the Northwest and *The Oregonian* had done a feature story on it right after early planting. The reporter and his photographer were scheduled for an end-of-season visit the following week.

"Got any ripe First Prizes?" Grace asked hopefully. There wasn't anything she liked better than a flavorful tomato, fresh from the vine.

"Absolutely. I had two for lunch." He kissed his fingertips. "*Delicioso!*"

"Your plums are looking good," Grace said as she veered toward the regular tomatoes.

"Your mama picked some yesterday for tonight's sauce. I think these are the best plum tomatoes I've ever had."

Grace rinsed a First Prize under the hose took a big bite.

Juice and seeds dribbled down her chin. She rolled her eyes with pleasure. "Heaven, Uncle Vito. Pure heaven. I am so glad you found this variety—it's your tastiest ever."

Finished with the beans, her uncle lifted the basket and proceeded to the squash. He pulled several really nice looking crooknecks from the jumble of leaves. "These should be good for Angelina's veggie lasagna at the shop." He straightened, scrutinizing the cucumbers. "I heard about Hamm Starr."

"Yes. His mother took it pretty hard."

"Poor Zelda. She has no other family. Her life revolved around that boy. I think I'll run over there before dinner, see how she's doing. I have some cannelloni from last night. She might like that."

"I'm sure she would. She looks like she hardly ever eats. Gunny doesn't eat well, either."

"I feel bad about Gunny. Beautiful woman, incredible mind. Now this Alzheimer's. I stop over there twice a week. She remembers me, I think, if I wear the collar, so that's what I do."

"She always calls me Angelina." Grace sighed. "It's such an ugly disease."

"These murders are ugly, too, people taking other people's lives. Bad stuff."

Grace filched another tomato, rinsed it, and took a bite. "I wanted to talk to you about that. Is now a good time?"

Down on his knees, Uncle Vito picked several cukes, laying them carefully in his basket. He leaned back, studying her thoughtfully, his big, aged hands on his thighs. "I always have time for you, Grazia."

Grace took a seat on the edge of the raised garden bed closest to her uncle. "We found a file in Yeager Clausen's office. It was labeled DEAD WEIGHT." She explained to him about the companion files labeled DELINQUENT TAXPAYERS and FINANCIALLY INSOLVENT. "Those two are pretty self-explanatory, but the other one, well I don't get it."

Vito stood up and stretched, then sat down next to Grace. "Dead weight usually implies that someone isn't carrying his or her share of the load, that they're a burden."

Grace frowned, thinking. “That’s the way I read it, too.”

“So then the next question is, why are you talking to me about this? Don’t the police like to keep information like this to themselves, discuss it with each other?”

“Generally,” Grace said, reaching down for her uncle’s hand, “that would be the case. But this time, because your name is included in the list he compiled, I have to talk to you.”

Vito Santarelli started so violently, he almost fell over backward into the squashes.

Grace helped him right himself. “Your reaction tells me this might mean something to you.”

Uncle Vito shook his head and stood. “You want to tell me who else is on that list?”

“No, but in the interest of finding out what it’s all about, I will. I need your word that you will keep this confidential.”

“You have it.”

He began to pace as Grace recited the names. Former Police Chief Harmon McCrea, Zelda Starr, Ellie’s father Patrick McCormick, four farmers—Tracy Howard, Abner Nelson, Edward Crane, Bud Crockett—and his own accountant, John Peck. There were at least a dozen other names Grace didn’t recognize.

“*Dio santo!*”

“So this means something to you?

”I know we’re all Catholics.”

“Nothing more? This isn’t an Opus Dei kind of thing, is it?”

Uncle Vito gave a bark of laughter. “Grazia, you see too many movies.”

“I didn’t see the movie,” Grace retorted. “I read the book.”

Her uncle gave her a *look.* “Seriously,” he went on, “we are all Catholics who were trying, behind the scenes, to raise enough money to buy the land adjacent to St. Anthony’s with the hope of keeping out an industrial plant Clausen was trying to woo to Coburg.”

“What kind of industrial?”

“Chemical. Manufacturing janitorial compounds.”

Grace groaned. She didn't need more motives for people wanting Clausen dead. "You really think he had a chance of getting that through?"

"He had an option to buy, but we convinced the property owner to give us until the end of the year to come up with the money."

"Who's the owner?"

"A company called SeaTac Development out of Washington."

Grace stood up, slapping her hands in anger against her thighs. "Great, just great!"

"I take it you know about SeaTac."

"Apparently not everything."

"You know, Grazia, there's an underlying reason why Yeager Clausen wanted that plant next to St. Anthony's."

Grace felt like screaming. "Which is?"

"He hated Catholics."

She gaped at him. "His wife and her family are Catholic."

"Begs the question of why he married her, doesn't it?"

Grace had a pretty good idea why, and it started with the letter M and ended with O-N-E-Y. She hugged her uncle. "Thanks for the info. I gotta go take a shower and cool off before dinner."

"About ready to blow your top, are you?"

Grace couldn't suppress a rueful smile. "About."

She encountered Uncle Sal on her front porch. "Hi, sweetheart," he said, hugging her. "Thought I was going to miss you again."

"You're looking good," she said. Everyone in the family was worried about Uncle Sal. He'd had a minor heart attack about a year earlier, but he'd changed his lifestyle to include more exercise, red wine as his only alcohol, and pretty strictly, a Mediterranean diet. He'd even given up his pipe.

"I feel great. I just wish everyone would quit looking at me like I might croak at any minute!"

"Well, I for one, am sure you're going to live to be at least ninety."

"Fine by me, as long as I don't end up like my father, with the Alzheimer's."

Grace hoped so, too. She hoped they all escaped that fate.

"Guess you saw me talking to your new boss last week at dinner. I've been wanting to tell you what I told him. Unless he already passed it along?"

Grace shook her head. "I've been meaning to ask either one of you, but somehow, well, this has been a crazy week. I never got around to it." She grinned. "Those were some pretty wild hand gestures you were throwing around that night—I figured Chief Cruz must really be getting an earful."

Uncle Sal nodded, somber. "He was."

"Are you sure you're not Pop's brother, instead of Mom's?"

Uncle Sal laughed. "Gracie, it's because you *are* so much like your papa that I tell you this. Your Aidan asked me about Yeager and I told him what I thought."

"Now you *do* sound like Mom's brother," Grace admonished. "He's not *my* Aidan."

Her uncle shrugged, all innocence. "In a nutshell, I told him that Yeager was a dirty dog and that if Ellie killed him, we should gather up a collection to buy her a trophy."

CHAPTER 39

FRESHLY SHOWERED AND changed into clean clothes, Grace realized, as she took the path toward her parent's house, that she hadn't eaten anything all day, except for the tomatoes. That might explain the raging headache and the constant rumble in her stomach.

Kyle, Cassidy, and Maddy were in front of the TV watching the *Happy Feet* DVD, again. A boy whom she presumed to be the chief's son, since he looked like a miniature of his dad, had curled up on the couch. He stared at the screen, a ferocious scowl on his face. Grace stopped to introduce herself, surprised when he nodded politely, gave his name, and said, "Nice to meet you."

She found her father in the kitchen, watching her mother prepare dinner from his perch against the counter. Jason sat on a barstool, sipping what looked to be a straight bourbon. Angelina didn't tolerate much help when she cooked, but onlookers were permitted. "Hi," Grace said. The three of them greeted her in return. "Where is everyone?"

"Out back," her father said. "Rocco got the bright idea to have homemade ice cream for dessert, so Sal and Loretta are supervising. Dante, Aidan, Vito, and Rocco's friend, Josh, are pitching horseshoes."

"No cousins?"

Aside from Gina, Sal and Loretta had four other children. "Gina and Nico are coming. She had to go pick him up from band practice. Cara and Dino are at a swim party."

"I see Nico got a gig at the Grange," Grace said.

Joe grunted. "Teenage bands are a dime a dozen, but I think maybe the kid's got some talent. I actually like some of the music he writes."

"They kind of sound like that Pink Martini orchestra out of Portland," Angelina said. "All they need is a good singer."

Jason stood, taking his empty glass to the sink. "I thought they were trying to talk Gina into being their vocalist."

Angelina laughed. "Gina tells them she's saving herself for *American Idol*, but really, that girl has a plan to finish college in three years, and singing with her brother's band just isn't on her agenda."

Grace moved closer to the bubbling pot of spaghetti sauce.

"The sound—or lack thereof—of horseshoes hitting metal is calling me," Jason said, heading for the back door.

Grace leaned over the pot to give her smeller better access.

"Rough day?" Joe asked.

"Rough week." Her stomach rumble extra loud.

"I take it you haven't eaten today." Angelina studied her daughter as if she suspected a case of starvation in progress.

Grace shook her head. "Uncle Vito let me pilfer some tomatoes."

"How about some sauce and bread?"

"I'd love it. And maybe you could throw in a meatball?"

Angelina pointed her wooden spoon at her daughter. "Just like your father. Work, work, work. Everything else comes second."

Grace shared a look with Joe, who grinned. "That's why we only have five bambinos," he said, "instead of eight or ten."

Her mother blushed and swore softly at him in Italian. She handed Grace a small plate and informed her, "I had all those bambinos before I was thirty."

Ignoring her mother, Grace sliced a piece of bread from the loaf on the cutting board and spooned red sauce on top of it. Then she went digging for a meatball with a fork. "Hey,

Pop. Can I talk to you for a few minutes?" She reached for the parmesan, sprinkling it over her spaghetti sauce sandwich.

"Sure, Gracie."

"You can run, but you can't hide," her mother interjected.

Joe walked around the counter and pinched his wife on the butt. "I like you when you're sassy," he said, nuzzling her ear. "Between that and the new haircut, you're really turning me on this week."

"Joe!" Angelina rounded on him with the wooden spoon. Marinara went flying in an arc across the room. "Get out of my kitchen, right now!"

Grace made sure she was close enough to the door to escape before she said, "Gee, maybe you two will make another baby and I won't have to worry about having one of my own."

"*Cacasenno*!" her mother shot back, waving the spoon at the fleeing father and daughter.

Grace laughed. Smart aleck or not, she loved getting the last word on her mother-the-matchmaker.

Joe put his arm around her shoulders, laughing. "Your mama, she has spirit."

"She does."

"Like you."

"Maybe. I got a double whammy—your genes, her genes. All of us did."

Joe kissed her cheek. She eased into the wicker settee on the front porch, sitting cross-legged. Her father took the other chair and put his feet up on the ottoman. "So, what's up?"

"Murder."

"Yeah, too much of that," he agreed. "Unbelievable and in Coburg, no less. What do you think's going on?"

Grace brought him up-to-date on the Starr death, then speared the meatball with her fork and took a big bite, chewing thoughtfully. She swallowed and said, "I had a vague recollection of something similar, so I called Mikey last week and she thought it sounded familiar, too. She did some searching and faxed me an article she dug up." She put down her plate and dug a copy of Michaela's fax out of her back pocket.

While her father read, she finished off the bread and sauce, disgusted afterward that she was wearing a spot or two of red on her white shirt. One of these days, she'd remember not to wear white to Sunday dinner.

"Same MO, but what's the connection?"

"Dellenbach, Starr, and Clausen were buddies in high school. Went to college together at the University of Colorado until the summer before senior year. Then the happy trio split up, moved on to different schools." She flicked futilely at one of the red specks, succeeding only in smudging it. "Hamm Starr was involved in a car accident that summer. Maybe it had something to do with the friends' split-up, maybe it didn't."

"You're facing a lot of maybes."

"I know."

"What does Aidan think?"

"He was gone when the fax came in. I haven't discussed it with him yet."

Joe shook his head at her. "It's nice you want to brainstorm with your old man, Gracie, but Aidan Cruz is your boss. He's the one you should be talking to."

"I need to talk someone right now, Pop, and Chief Cruz isn't available."

"He's only in the backyard. Go get him."

Grace's face scrunched up. "You think he'd appreciate me bothering him about this when he's not working."

"He's the police chief. He's always working."

"It's true," Aidan said, pushing open the screen door with his hip. "McCrea informed me when he made the job offer, 'The chief signs on for a twenty-four hour day, every day.' Kind of sucks, doesn't it?"

He put down two glasses of wine, keeping a bottled beer for himself. He settled his butt against the porch rail, studying Grace. "You got sauce on your shirt."

A hot flush of embarrassment flooded her cheeks. "Tell me something I don't know."

Aidan quirked that damned eyebrow at her. "So, what's

up that you need to talk to me about?"

Grace filled him in on Jennifer Sousa alibiing Frey.

"Shit."

She nodded her agreement and put down her plate. She retrieved the article from her father and handed it to the chief.

He scanned it with a squinty eyes. "Well, it's about goddamned time," he said, almost under his breath. "This might be the break we're looking for." He looked at Grace. "I know you're off, but we should contact Houston PD. Any chance—"

"Already done," Grace said. "The lead detective is back tomorrow morning and I left a message for him to contact me. I'm waiting for a police report from Boulder County SO on Starr's car crash, and now that we know Jack Dellenbach's whereabouts, we can find out what he's been up to for the past twenty years. Well, before he died, anyway."

Aidan took a long swallow from his beer bottle. "You know, there's one thing I can say about you, Gabbiano. Whether I like it or not, you're always one step ahead of me."

CHAPTER 40

AT SOME POINT in their married life, Joe and Angelina Gabbiano decided if they wanted to host Sunday dinners for the Santarelli–Gabbiano clan, they needed more space. They tore down some walls, added on some square footage, and bought a old farmhouse table they couldn't afford, but which turned out to be good investment.

As Grace helped her mother pile food on that table, she thought it fortuitous that the table seated fourteen. The dining room also had room for the smaller, narrower kids' table. On this Sunday evening, the junior table was only half full, if you counted Dylan.

Grace caught her mother watching the children with a look of both affection and longing. Clearly, she loved the grandchildren she already had, but being greedy, she wanted more.

None of the chairs around the tables matched, and most of them squeaked, but every single one was comfortable. Beyond that, no one cared anyway. They came for the family, the camaraderie, and the food. Angelina always had plenty of the latter to go around at the table. The rest just came naturally, and tonight, Uncle Vito had brought six bottles of four-year-old Dago Red wine. "To celebrate this year's bountiful harvest," he said, uncorking two of them.

Grace sat with her back closest to the kids' table. She almost choked on her spaghetti when she heard her oldest niece, Cassidy, inform Dylan that she planned to marry him when she grew up. Dylan was heard to reply, “You won’t even like me when you grow up, squirt!”

Grace found that hard to believe. Little did Aidan’s acorn realize he was destined to break a few hearts. Sitting directly across from the boy’s father, she glanced up to find Aidan watching her, an amused smile on his face. Flanked by Aunt Loretta to his right and Jason Knox on the other side, he nonetheless had a father’s ear tuned to his child.

Few words were exchanged once everyone began to eat. Forks and knives clattered against stoneware, sighs of contentment wafted around the table. Chief Cruz finally said to Jason Knox, “I hear you have an aviary over at your place.”

Jason washed down a bit of Italian sausage with a sip of wine, savored it, took another sip. “Yes, I bought the Thompson place a little over a year ago, did some remodeling, added the aviary.”

“He has tons of cool birds,” Kyle contributed from the kids’ table.

“Tons,” agreed Cassidy, who went on to explain to Dylan just exactly what kinds of birds.

Maddy, using her fingers more than her fork to shovel spaghetti into her mouth said, “Neighbahs don’ like buhds.”

Jason laughed. “She’s got that right! I mistakenly thought they would appreciate the sound of nature next door.”

“They haven’t complained to us,” Grace said.

Jason finished off his wine. “It’s a civil war, so far.”

“We found one of Jason’s birds in the van of the guy who led us on that merry chase down the Interstate on Friday.” Grace reached for a piece of bread. “Jason had reported it stolen on Monday, but because of our work study’s error, none of us knew until the bird showed up, on the fly, so to speak, that his missing animal had feathers.”

Rocco aimed a smart remark at her about her propensity for puns. Grace responded by sticking out her tongue.

Joe asked Jason, “Which one?”

“The blue macaw.”

“The baby bird?”

Grace and the chief shared an incredulous look. “You’re

kidding?" he said. "It's at least three feet high."

Jason laughed. "And still growing."

"Your aviary must be huge," Grace said. "I'll have to come by and see it."

"Bring the children. They love the birds, and I swear, the birds like them."

"Are you retired, then?" Chief Cruz asked. Grace gave him points for interrogating in a conversational manner. A quick glance around the table told her that no one but her noticed, except maybe her father, who narrowed his eyes at the chief.

"I am. My family's gone now, and I've always loved the Northwest. I drove this way a few years ago and decided this is where I would live once I retired."

Aidan didn't break his stride on either eating or asking the next question. "What kind of work did you do?"

"I had an import/export business—that's how I got interested in the birds, through travel to Central and South America. I was blessed with success, I guess you could say, and I did very well when I sold the company."

He said it in such an unassuming way, it invoked admiration. Rather incongruous, Grace thought. From the day she'd met him, Jason Knox had seemed a little bit full of himself.

The chief congratulated him on his accomplishment, then asked for the meat plate to be passed. He turned to Aunt Loretta, inquiring about her quilting class. Grace almost fell off her chair.

Rocco had brought his friend Josh this week, someone Grace remembered from high school. Someone who had tormented her unmercifully. He seemed all grown up now. Grown up and pleasant. And good looking.

She glanced over and caught her mother giving Josh the eagle eye. Grace didn't know whether to kill her brother or thank him, but she definitely owed him one. She started to give him a thumbs up, when the front door flew open.

In breezed Mikey.

After dinner, Grace took a breather on the front porch. A

few minutes later, Jason joined her, carrying two cups of coffee. Curious, Grace asked, "How do you manage my mother's match-making?"

Jason chuckled. "Believe me, some days it isn't easy."

Grace leaned forward, interested in who her mother thought was the perfect woman for Jason. "Who has she tried to hook you up with?"

"That woman over at the beauty shop, for one."

"Marilou? She's a little...." Grace trailed off before she finished with either *young* or *flamboyant*. Or both.

"I haven't met her, but your mother assures me I could use some excitement in my life."

Marilou could sure offer that. "Who else?"

"Rose Callahan."

"*Rose*? What was Mom thinking? Rose has been in love with Uncle Vito for years."

Jason set his coffee cup down, surprised. "Your uncle's a priest!"

"Retired, but yes, and Rose has had a crush on him since high school. For some reason, she has it in her head that retirement equals giving up the vows."

She thought Jason would smile, or even laugh, but he didn't. "When you love someone more than life itself, Grace, you don't just forget about it when the other person is unattainable. I think it's unutterably sad. Rose and Vito may be soul mates, but they'll never find out." He picked up his cup and drank deeply. "Maybe in another lifetime."

His face and voice were overcome with such heartbreaking sorrow, it brought tears to Grace's eyes. "You loved your wife very much."

"Even more than you can imagine."

"Did she die from cancer, or...?" His features twisted with grief and she wished she'd kept her mouth shut. "I'm sorry. It's none of my business."

He swallowed deeply, striving for composure. "No, it's all right. Helen's only diseases were alcohol and despair. She took her own life after our daughter died."

Grace's heart broke for him, his pain was so obvious. "I'm so sorry, Jason," she said, putting a comforting hand on his arm. “I didn’t know you’d also lost a child.”

He jerked away and reached for his cup. Grace got the message loud and clear. He didn’t like to be touched.

Jason cleared his throat, once again in control of his emotions. “It’s something I’ve learned to live with,” he said, “but not something I talk about.” He glanced at his watch and said with a smile that seemed forced, “It’s getting late.” He stood. “Please say goodnight to Joe and Angelina for me, will you? And tell them thanks again for the wonderful meal.” He patted his stomach. “Your mother is an amazing cook.”

He walked the path to the driveway and climbed into his Lexus SUV.

Grace crossed her arms over her chest, warding off a sudden chill. It must be horrible to be in that much pain. Losing a wife was bad enough, but to lose a child, too.

CHAPTER 41

MICHAELA STEPPED OUT onto the porch, a dishtowel in her hands. "Come in and dry what won't fit in the dishwasher."

Standing at the sink a minute later, both sisters looked out the kitchen window. Gina and Nico had come and gone. Cassidy, Kyle, and Dylan were playing croquet. Aunt Loretta reclined in a chaise with a glass of wine, watching the men play *bocce*.

"Where's Mom?"

"She took Maddy up for a bath. She had spaghetti from her hair all the way down to her cute little toes." Mikey rinsed a pan and handed it to Grace. "Your Chief Cruz is pretty damned hot."

"He's definitely easy on the eyes." Grace tore her gaze away from the window and glanced at her sister.

Michaela's eyes roved Aidan's backside, as that was the part of his body facing the window. "I give his butt a ten."

Grace felt her face grow warm. Gamely, she entered into a life-long scoring debate she'd had with her sister since they were old enough to care about boys. "Or a ten plus."

"Umm. Great pecs. He must work out."

"He must."

"Nice legs, too."

Grace glanced out the window again, though she didn't need to. His dark coloring against the deep, rich tones of the purple shorts and the white polo made every inch of him look good. Better than good. Disgusted with direction her thoughts were headed, she said, "He didn't get one drop of spaghetti sauce on his shirt."

"Admiring that nice wide chest of his, were you?"

Grace colored furiously, at a loss for a quick rejoinder.

Her sister laughed. "Is he taken?"

"Geez, Mikey, you're as bad as Mom."

"Who says I'm asking for you?"

That stopped Grace short. She didn't particularly like the little green jealousy worm wiggling around inside her. "What about the guy you went away with last night?"

Mikey shrugged. "Okay, so I was asking for you. You can't be a sex hermit for the rest of your life."

"Wanna bet? I'm not interested."

"You'd have to be dead not to be interested," Michaela countered dryly, "and you're as alive as I am, Grace Gabbiano. You can't bullshit a bullshitter."

Grace couldn't sleep. The little fan she had set up in her bedroom seemed ineffectual against the day's leftover heat. Coupled with the fact that she couldn't stop thinking about the police report being faxed from Texas, she felt like she'd taken a No-Doz. Besides, when she *did* close her eyes, all she saw was the very tempting backside of Chief Cruz. What the hell was the matter with her, anyway?

Grace flopped over on her side, disgusted with herself. She forced her brain back on the puzzle of three related murders. Morning seemed too far away, either to wait for a drop in the temperature, or to read the report.

Michaela had already gone off to bed after an hour of discussing the three homicides. Regardless of Grace's warning that nothing new would be announced at the news conference the next morning, her sister was determined to have a front-row seat. "How often do I get to do a story like this when a guy like Aidan Cruz is answering the questions?" she had asked, toothbrush in hand. "I can't believe I never ran into him when he was at Portland Police Bureau."

"You still haven't told me about what's-his-name that you spent last night with."

"His name is Connor and he's every bit as hunky as your Aidan."

"He's not *my* Aidan," Grace had replied through gritted teeth. This was getting to be an irritating refrain.

Mikey had grinned and closed the bathroom door in her face.

So, after an hour of tossing, and resigned to a sleepless night if she didn't get dressed and head over to the station to get that fax, Grace climbed out of bed, pulled off her short cotton nightie, and scrambled into a pair of cutoffs and a D.A.R.E. TO SAY NO TO DRUGS T-shirt. She slipped her feet into sandals, captured her hair in an elastic band, and grabbed her house key. A few minutes later, she was pedaling toward the office.

Cameron Taylor sat at the computer entering case notes.

"Busy night?" Grace asked.

He shrugged. "Little stuff. Kids throwing rocks at the trailers in the mobile home park, dogs baying at the moon, silent alarm at one of the antique shops."

Grace moved toward the fax machine. "Burglary?"

"Near as I can tell, a cat fight set it off. Fur balls everywhere."

Grace chuckled. Cats were not her favorite four-legged creatures, especially when they were yowling and fighting.

"What're doing here so late?"

"Looking for a fax, but it's not here."

Cam rolled his chair over to the machine. "Maybe it's out of paper." He pulled out the tray. "Yep."

Grace didn't consider herself mechanically deficient, but she must have been more tired than she realized not to notice the flashing red light. He replenished the tray and pushed it in. The machine began to print immediately. "Thanks."

"No problem," he said.

The Houston PD detective had put a note on the cover sheet indicating his department might send someone up for a look-see at the evidence gathered by CPD. Grace welcomed another opinion.

With the last page off the fax, she went to the photocopier and ran three sets, placing the original in the Clausen file, another in the new Starr file, and the last one on the chief's desk. She put the original in a manila envelope to make it easier to carry on her bike. "See you later."

Cam, logging off the computer, raised a hand in farewell.

So intent was Grace on the fax in her back pocket, she didn't hear the low murmur of the vehicle coming up behind her with its lights off.

Later, she would think it had only been by the grace of God that she'd sensed movement behind her and swerved at the last moment, landing mostly on the grassy strip bordering the roadway when she fell, rather than directly on the shoulder of the road, which was scattered with sharp pieces of gravel and who knew what else.

Despite her training, Grace barely got a glance at the vehicle. It was an SUV. That's all she knew for sure. No color. No model. No plate number. Great!

The sound of footsteps pounding across the roadway cut through the night air. "You all right?" Cameron Taylor asked, out of breath.

"I think so. Did you see who did it?"

"Did what? I heard you scream just as I went out to get in my vehicle and came running."

Grace hadn't realized she'd screamed, but then everything had happened so quickly, she still wasn't sure what had gone down. "A car came up behind me with no lights on and forced me off the road."

Taylor's flashlight swept her from head to foot. "Jesus, you need some medical attention."

Grace looked down. "I do?"

"Your head's bleeding, for one. And your arm and leg are scraped and bleeding, too."

The moment he told her where she hurt, Grace began to feel the pain.

"I'm going to call the EMTs."

"No, don't."

He looked uncertain for a moment, then said, "You're a police officer. Everyone in this town knows you. If someone came up behind you in the dark and ran you off the road, that's assault and possibly attempted murder of a police officer. The chief'd have my ass if I didn't get you some medical attention and write this up."

Cameron was newly out of the marine corps, having served two tours in Iraq. He was enrolled in the criminal justice program at Lane Community College. His military background and his fervent desire to eventually end up a detective for the Eugene Police Department put a steely quality to his voice Grace wouldn't have recognized in the dark, had she not known who was speaking.

Resigned to her fate, she said, "Just give me a ride to Urgent Care."

"No one will be on patrol, if I do that. I don't think the chief would approve."

"Call LCSO. They'll cover."

Taylor opened his mouth to argue.

"You can wait there for me, complete your report while I'm being treated, and give me a ride home."

He aimed the light at her head. "Here." He pulled a handkerchief from his back pocket. "It's clean. You need to stop the bleeding. I think you're going to need stitches." He frowned at her. "You should've been wearing a helmet."

"Thanks." Grace accepted the hanky with shaky fingers. "And you're right, I should've." She pressed the cloth against her wound and winced. "I'm going to be doubly pissed if my bike's damaged. I still owe two payments on it."

Cameron righted the bike, shining his light over it. "It looks okay. Maybe a scrape or two."

"Would you mind wheeling it back to the office? I didn't bring my U-lock, so I'll have to leave it inside."

"No problem. You make it okay?"

Grace murmured a *yes*, but hobbling along behind him, she became more conscious by the second of how sore she was going to be in the morning.

And she couldn't get rid of the strange image in her mind of the person who had run her off the road.

His glowing head had made her feel like she'd entered some kind of *Ghost Hunters* episode.

Grace came to a screeching halt. *Glowing head!*

What the hell?

CHAPTER 42

GRACE WAS GLAD she'd set the alarm for thirty minutes earlier than usual. With two stitches in her forehead and three in her arm, she wasn't her usual expedient self. Each morning ritual took twice long as normal to complete. Maybe longer. So much for landing on "soft" grass.

Her sister wandered into the kitchen where Grace sat drinking a cup of coffee, trying to decide the best means of getting to work, since her bike was still at the station house.

"My God! What happened to you?" Michaela cried.

Grace told her.

"If you had to go out that late, why didn't you wake me? I could have gone with you."

"My bike's not a two-seater," Grace said.

"Don't be a smart-ass. You could have been killed!"

Suddenly sober, Grace said, "I know." Still, in a town like Coburg, who would have thought...?

"Give me fifteen minutes and I'll drive you." Michaela started to leave the kitchen, then turned back. "Do Mom and Pop know yet?"

"No, and—"

"Haul your butt over there right now, or I'll pick up the phone and call them."

Grace knew her sister was right, but dammit, she'd come back to Coburg, in part, to help her parents out, not to be coddled by them.

"I know what you're thinking," Michaela said, "and you're way off base. Letting your parents who live practically in your backyard know that you were injured is not asking them for help. Do you plan to avoid them until the scars fade?"

Grace held up her uninjured arm, palm out. "Okay, okay, you've made your point. Honk when you're ready, but hurry. I've got two autopsies this morning and I have to be there by eight. Traffic is a bitch this early in the morning."

"*Two?*"

"Yeah, the second murder victim and the guy with the bird on the freeway."

"I think you forgot to tell me something," Michaela said. "I'll hurry. You can fill me in on the way."

Grace shuffled into the station, intent on finding the ibuprofen bottle. The Urgent Care doc had given her a few pain killers, but she couldn't risk taking any while at work.

Mikey promised to connect with her later in the day so they could have lunch together, compare some notes. Grace looked around, glad no one else was in yet.

No one, that is, except the chief, who came into the kitchen area when he heard her rummaging. Dylan was close behind him.

"What happened to you?" Aidan demanded.

By the time the chief asked, Grace was weary of the concern, having been inundated with solicitudes by six family members already that morning. She hated being a spectacle. As succinctly as possible, she filled in the details for him. "After Cam dropped me off at home, he was going to drive around, see if he could find someone cruising the streets with no lights."

"Were you wearing dark clothing?"

"White T-shirt, cutoffs. The moon's waning and the streets aren't that well lit. It could have been an accident."

"Driving with the headlights off?"

Grace shared his skepticism, and in the middle of the night, drifting off to sleep after allowing herself one little white pill for pain, she'd had an absurd thought that maybe someone had deliberately run her off the road.

He considered her with narrowed eyes. "At that hour, you should have been home in bed. The fax could have waited until this morning."

Grace's face grew hot from his chastisement. She squared her shoulders. "I've already heard that lecture this morning. Three times."

"How many stitches did you get?" Dylan asked.

Grace told him.

"Wow. Did it hurt when they stuck the needle in?"

"Absolutely," she said, nearly looking him eye-to-eye. "There's no honor without pain."

"That sounds like a load of crap," the boy declared.

"Dylan...." The warning in his father's tone was clear.

Grace grinned. "It is a load of crap. It hurt like crazy and I wanted to belt the doctor right in the puss for hurting me worse than I already hurt."

"I would'a kicked him in the balls if he'd done that to me."

"Dylan!" Aidan roared. "That's enough."

"What's the big deal?" his son demanded. "She's a fucking cop like you—she's heard a lot worse than that on the street."

Aidan towered over the boy, his body taut with anger. "Regardless of what Officer Gabbiano has heard on the streets, you're an eleven-year-old kid and she's a person deserving of your respect, and you will *not* speak like that to or around her again. Got it?"

Dylan glared at his father.

"Got it?" Aidan repeated, glaring back.

"I got it," the boy mumbled defiantly. "The big tough cop daddy speaks again and the kid gets to cower in fear."

Aidan's expression altered uncertainly. "What's that supposed to mean?"

"You wanna hit me, don't you?"

Aidan recoiled as if *he'd* been hit. "I've never hit you in my life!"

The boy blinked rapidly.

"Are you *afraid* of me, Dylan?"

Watching the interaction, Grace wondered if Aidan was too absorbed to catch the fleeting expression on his son's face that shouted, *Mission accomplished*.

"Hell, no, I'm not afraid of you! I don't care enough about you to be afraid of you."

The chief's jaw clenched, not with anger, Grace noticed, but with pain. His son had just dealt him a fierce blow.

Helpless, embarrassed at having witnessed the confrontation, and knowing any contribution she could make to the conversation would not be appreciated, she stood by hurting for both of them.

The second autopsy went just about like the first one. Yeager Clausen and Hamm Starr, compatriots even in death.

Doug Hacker, ME, found the star tattoo between the middle and index fingers of the left hand, the white ribbon folded neatly in the deceased's mouth, not one, but two puncture marks in the crook of Starr's right arm, and a boatload of M&Ms crammed up his butt.

Hacker also found a golf ball-size lump on the back of Starr's head. Once his scalp had been peeled back, the cracked skull revealed by an X-ray was fully visible. "Hairline fracture," the ME said, "but it didn't kill him."

He went back to the crook of Starr's arm. "Two needle marks probably means something was injected into the victim's body in addition to the heroin. He's heavily bruised around his forearms, wrists, and hands, so he didn't go out submissively."

Hacker motioned Chick to lift the body. "He's got lividity on his right side, but you found him sitting in a rocking chair?"

"Yes. It looks like he was killed somewhere else and moved later. The gown was slit up the back and arranged around him once he was in the rocker."

"You have your work cut out for you, Grace." He glanced at his diener, then back at Grace, grinning under his mask, if the crinkled eyes beneath his safety visor were any indication. "Chick and I both thank you for providing us with job security."

Medical people. Always with the dark jokes. Grace chuckled and said, "Happy to oblige." She told him about the Houston connection. "The tox results there confirmed heroin overdose."

He nodded. "It'll be the same on both the boys here." He motioned for Chick to lower the body. "I've been working Surgery 10 for a long time, and Cleveland for a number of years before that. I have to admit, I've seen a lot of weird stuff, but this is right up there at the top."

"Lucky us," Grace murmured.

"Did everything else match up with the autopsies?"

"Everything," she confirmed, "right down to the last piece of candy and the excised penis."

"Crazy weird," Chick said.

Hacker nodded his agreement. "I'll release the body to the family this afternoon."

"His mom's been in the lobby since seven," Chick said.

"I'll go talk to her," Grace volunteered. *Right after I visit the bathroom.*

After that, she still had autopsy number three to attend. With her mouth tasting rank, she pulled a travel toothbrush out of her pocket and loaded it up with toothpaste, thankful she'd had the foresight to plan ahead this time. She prayed to some obscure saint she remembered being a favorite of her grandmother's that the next autopsy—the one on the crazy van driver who'd stolen the bird—wouldn't send her running to the bathroom afterward.

Bent over the toilet later, she accepted with resignation that some prayers just never got answered.

CHAPTER 43

WITH NO CHIEF to greet her outside the hospital following more than half a day of marathon post-mortems, Grace went directly to Gunny Spriggs's house. Although the old woman suffered from Alzheimer's, she had her lucid moments.

Gunny sat on the front porch in a brand new rocker. Grace greeted her and said, "Nice chair."

"My boy bought it for me." She frowned. "The other one walked away, then it came back and that woman sat in it, and now it's gone again."

"I know," Grace said with empathy. It had been a hard call, but after talking with Jasper, they decided to tell Gunny the truth. Keeping the information from her, especially since she frequently walked about the neighborhood, would have been impossible. Still, she apparently hadn't accepted the facts of her late-night visit for what they were. Hamm Starr, as far as Gunny was concerned, was a woman.

Grace eased down on the top step, considering Gunny's words, taking them literally. "Do you remember anything about the night the chair walked away?"

Gunny nodded her gray head. "I heard noises." She frowned. "I hear noises a lot at night," she admitted, "but this time it was loud. I looked out the window. We have some fine summer picnics out in the park across the street. Glenn Miller was going to come once." She frowned. "I don't know why he didn't make it."

"Did you see anything the night the rocking chair walked away?"

Again the old woman nodded. "A man. Tall. His head glowed. I thought he wanted to dance, but he walked my chair away, instead."

Grace started. His head *glowed*? Gunny with her Alzheimer's, and Grace knocked off her bike and sprawled on the ground. Both had the same impression of someone. Did that mean something, other than neither one of them had been in full control of her wits?

"Did the man take the chair down the street?"

Gunny fidgeted with the bow of her blouse. She still dressed every day as if going off to teach school. "No. He had one of those cars that's not a car."

"A truck?" Grace ventured.

"No, no. Closed in at the back, but they look like a truck in the front. Sort of. One of those drive things with…" —she paused for several moments in a heart-breaking struggle to search her mind for the right words— "four wheels."

Grace thought a moment and interpreted the garbled descriptive as four-wheel-drive. A cold chill ran down her spine and the gash on her forehead began to throb. "A sport-utility vehicle?"

Gunny squinted toward the street, pointing a thin finger toward a silver-colored Grand Cherokee easing up to the curb in front of the house down the block that had been converted into an antique shop. "Something like that, but darker. The moon only smiled that night," she said almost whimsically, "so I couldn't see it all that well, but it was a darker color than that one." The old woman sighed, returning her gaze to Grace. "I miss my old chair, but this one's nice. It doesn't squeak. I kind of miss that squeak. Squeak, squeak, squeak."

Grace didn't have the heart to tell Gunny her chair had been sent to the OSP lab for a thorough going-over, or that she might never have it back again. "Can you remember anything about the night when the chair came back?"

"That funny-looking woman was sitting in my chair. She looked like a harlot! *A floozy!*"

"She did look strange. Do you know how she got into your chair?"

"Of course," Gunny said, as if she was talking to an idiot child.

"Did the man with the glowing head bring her?"

Impatient, Gunny waved a thin, shaky hand through the air. "No, no! The man with no eyes brought her. I opened my door and asked him what he was doing."

"No eyes?"

Gunny nodded, her eyes sparkling with excitement, and maybe a little fear. She leaned forward and whispered, "His eyes were *gone*."

"Gone?"

Gunny nodded. "He had dead eyes."

Grace thought hard, trying hard to interpret the older woman's observation. "You mean, like he had no emotion?"

Again Gunny nodded, then took a deep breath and her fingers fluttered through the air. "With his dead eyes right on me, he told me to go back to bed."

She smiled at Grace with such trusting sweetness it nearly broke Grace's heart.

"I wasn't worried," Gunny assured her. "He said you'd be over in the morning to take care of things, Angelina."

Grace met her sister for a late lunch at Buon Gusto.

"Your chief really knows how to handle the press," Michaela said, digging into her antipasto salad with a vigor Grace could hardly stand to watch.

The chief must have put on a helluva show if Mikey thought he had a way with the press. "I wouldn't know," Grace said. "Both times I've been at Surgery 10."

"Well, he comports himself really well. No one pulls anything over on him and believe me, these small-town news people are as good at trying to trip him up as anyone from a metro paper."

Grace took that to mean Harley had been in top form. "Careful, your big-city snobbery is showing."

Mikey grinned. "Bite me." She pointed at the piece of

foccacia on Grace's plate. "Is that all you're having?"

"It's all my stomach can handle right now."

Her sister stopped eating long enough to offer her a look of commiseration. "How did the autopsies go?"

"Gruesome. Gory. Interesting, if you like seeing bodies cut up."

Mikey frowned at her salad. She appeared to have lost some enthusiasm for her food. "Did you learn anything?"

Grace took pity on her. """Nothing new."

"So, Starr died the same way?"

"Probably."

"Aidan said someone is coming up from Houston."

"He must have gotten confirmation this morning. Last I heard, that was a maybe."

"*You* sure don't have his way with the press," her sister grumbled, stabbing a plump black olive with her fork.

"I thought I was having lunch with my sister," Grace shot back, "not a reporter."

"Sorry," Michaela said, obviously not.

Grace gave her a look.

Her sister shrugged. "I got what I needed this morning anyway. Aidan kindly granted me a personal interview."

"That was nice of him."

"I guess it pays to be your sister."

"Don't count on it."

Mikey laughed. "You're right—he's as close-mouthed as you are. He didn't give away a single case secret."

"I promised you I'd let you know when the case broke."

"So you did." Michaela studied her salad intently, pushing the bowtie pasta around, apparently looking for something. "I set him straight about Seattle."

Grace went cold all over. Her head began to pound. "You had no right to discuss that with him."

Michaela looked up. "You're my sister. Men are basically idiots and just in case he was leaning that way, I wanted to set him straight."

Grace groaned. *Why do I have to have a matchmaker for a mother and an armchair psychologist for a sister?*

CHAPTER 44

JOHN AND LILA Peck, Clausen's accountant and office manager, respectively, looked well-rested from their month-long vacation. Tan and fit, they had spent the majority of the last four weeks on some remote Caribbean island.

Yeager Clausen had apparently paid well for services rendered.

Grace was beginning to wish she could spend the next four weeks somewhere equally obscure.

Doubtful of what the Pecks might offer about Clausen's financial situation or his business practices that would put some forward motion into the triple-murder investigation, she nonetheless began her interview. Helpful information sometimes came from unlikely sources, but more often than not, it came from those closest to the victim.

"This is so shocking," Lila said.

Her husband murmured in agreement.

"Do you remember seeing anything in the office related to Jack Dellenbach or Hamm Starr?" Grace asked.

Lila crossed her long, tan legs. Despite being on the other side of fifty, she was one terrific looking lady. "I've never heard of this Jack person before, but Hamm came around or called once in awhile, and I know that Yeager sometimes met him for lunch or dinner. They also played racquetball and golfed together."

"Were things going okay for him in his business?"

Lila shared a look with her husband. "Ellie told us that we could tell you anything you wanted to know about Yeager. I worked for the man, but personally, I didn't like him. He cheated on his wife, treated his children like they were alien creatures, and screwed people on a daily basis."

"Why did you stay with him?"

Again, Lila glanced at her husband. "John is an excellent accountant. Yeager paid him handsomely to handle his financial matters. If I questioned his ethics or quit, he might have fired John. At our age, it wouldn't be that simple for either of us to find work elsewhere."

"You don't have other clients, Mr. Peck?"

"A few," he acknowledged, "but if Ellie chooses not to continue to run Yeager's business or to keep me on, I'll need to take on more to compensate. As you might have guessed, one of the reasons Yeager paid me so well was to keep overpayments to the IRS to a minimum."

Grace doodled in her notebook, then zeroed in on Lila. "I think it's a given that Mr. Clausen wasn't a very nice man. What aren't you telling me?"

Lila's hands clenched together so tightly, the knuckles whitened. Her lips became a thin, grim line, almost as if she were in pain.

John stepped over to his wife. He squeezed her shoulder gently and she responded by turning her head slightly so that her cheek rested against his hand. "I made a bad investment decision for one of my other clients," he said. "Yeager bailed me out."

People made bad investments every day, it was part of the money game they played. "Something illegal, I take it."

"Borderline."

"How much?"

"Two million…."

Grace waited for what he'd left unsaid, wondering if Yeager Clausen or his ilk ever dealt in anything less than million-dollar increments. Finally, she prompted, "And?"

John Peck swallowed convulsively several times. For late fifties, he was still a handsome man. Silver feathered his dark brown hair at the temples, giving him an aristocratic look that was not unlike a younger Sean Connery. By contrast, his attractive wife's gray hair had been professionally hidden.

"Mr. Peck?"

When he couldn't speak, his wife opened tear-filled eyes and said, "He wanted me."

Grace hesitated for a moment, then asked, "As in, if I give you a million dollars, will you let me sleep with your wife?"

Lila Peck nodded jerkily.

Grace wondered what kind of business deal Clausen had bailed his accountant out of. At this point, she didn't think she wanted to know, but she had to ask.

"It involved a start-up manufacturing company. Personal drones."

The only thing Grace knew about drones involved war and Amazon delivery. She asked for clarification and Peck provided a technical account of the details that basically boiled down to the start-up packing it in over a patent violation. How could it have been so bad that the two of them had agreed to sell Lila's body to save their hides?

"I tried to get the money back, but the partners of the start-up had already spent every dime setting up their facility."

"And there was no other way to redeem the loss?"

Peck grimaced. "The machinery to tool personal drones is not in great demand. Even at auction, we were able to recoup only pennies on the dollar." He sent his wife a tortured look. "I had my reputation and my career to protect…."

Personally, Grace thought there were other ways to do that besides selling his wife's body to Clausen. What the hell was the world coming to? "I hate to tell you, Mr. Peck, but what you've told me sounds like a good reason to kill another man. Exactly where were you a week ago Saturday?"

"I'm disgusted," Grace said, sticking her head in the chief's office.

He looked up from the case file on his desk. "Join the

club."

Her eyes fell to the file. "Is that the stuff from Houston?"

Aidan nodded. "The file isn't as thick as I thought it would be, considering the guy's standing in the community and the nature of the crime." He tapped the stack of papers. "Looks like they just ran out of leads—not that they really had any to begin with. I think we're ahead of them on that."

Grace doubted that was possible. "Did you see anything that indicates Dellenbach was a dirty, lowlife sonofabitch?"

"No, as far as I can tell, he was well respected in the business community and throughout the electronics industry. He'd built his company up to be worth triple-digit millions. His wife and children should be set for life." The chief tapped the file. "You've read the report. Why do you ask?"

She related her interview with the Pecks.

"Some guy wanted to trade money for sex with my wife, he'd be picking his sorry ass up off the floor."

"Some guy wanted to trade my husband money for sex with me, and they'd *both* be picking up their sorry asses off the floor."

Aidan lifted that one eyebrow at her, his eyes dancing with humor. "So, we have three birds lined up on the wire for the kill. Dellenbach, on the straight and narrow, respectable, monogamous, a pillar of the community, comes first. In the middle is Yeager Clausen, bastard, asshole, and rotten father, screwing women and senior citizens behind on their mortgage payments with equal fervor. On the other end, we have Hamm Starr, a moderately successful artist who liked women, married or underage, it didn't matter, but who didn't really bother anyone, one way or another."

Grace dropped into a chair. "That about sums them up."

"Besides being friends, what did they have in common?"

"Twenty years ago, a lot. They were three wild boys. Drank, did drugs, whored around. Then something happened. Summer before senior year in college, they went their divergent ways. Dellenbach apparently straightened up totally, Starr made some attempt at it, and Clausen chose the Mr. Potter route."

"Mr. Potter?" Aidan asked.

"You know, the nasty old curmudgeon from *It's a Wonderful Life*. He tried to screw Jimmy Stewart over?"

"Right."

"I'm sure that car crash is related somehow."

"Have you heard anything from Boulder County SO?"

Grace sighed. "Not yet. I hate to hassle them because I know how hard it is to help out other agencies when you're drowning in work. I'll give them until tomorrow."

"This sure would've been a helluva lot easier if our killer had been the guy in the van."

Grace agreed. "I'm going to do some further checking on his background. That blue feather in the wig says he was tied to this somehow."

"We know for sure the wig feather was from that particular bird?"

"Ashland faxed a report this afternoon confirming it." Grace bit her lip. "What's happening with Corporal Frey?"

Aidan scowled. "He called in sick today."

"Little weasel." She quickly filled the chief in on her discussion with Gunny, complete with Gunny's account of the man with the glowing head, who had stolen the chair, and the man with no eyes, who had brought it. She quickly debated the pros-and-cons of whether or not to tell the chief her own glowing head story. At the risk of coming across as a nut job, she came clean.

For several moments, Aidan stared at her like maybe her elevator didn't go all the way to the top. "I don't like this," he finally said. "An old lady with Alzheimer's tells us some guy with a glowing head stole her rocker, and I think she's off *her* rocker. *You* see a guy whose head glows, and I start to think we have something more going on here."

He considered Grace with narrowed eyes. "How much of Uncle Vito's Dago Red did you have to drink last night?"

"For crying out loud!"

"Don't go ballistic on me, Gabbiano. We've got to amend the assault report on you. I know you had a glass of wine before dinner and one at the table, but I'm not your keeper. Maybe you drank a whole fucking bottle after I left. I just want to be sure, if we put this 'glowing head' thing in, that sometime down the road, whoever did this can't come back and say you were so sloshed, you wouldn't have recognized your own mother if she'd been driving that SUV."

Grace cooled off, silently conceding he had a point. "That's all I had. After dinner had a coffee."

"Okay, good." He jotted down some notes on the pad he kept on his desktop. "When you walk out that door, be cognizant of your surroundings, of who's around you. More than you normally would be."

It was a fair warning, but Grace resented it, not quite able to come to terms with the fact that someone had deliberately tried to hurt her. Maybe even kill her. "I'm sure I'm not in any danger."

"And I'm sure that's what you thought when you left your house last night." His gaze pointedly went to her head, then to the bandage on her arm. "Look where you ended up." He considered her a moment. "Don't forget, Mrs. Spriggs got an assurance that *you* would be the one who came to get that body off her porch yesterday morning."

Grace didn't like to admit the chief was right. The killer knew her schedule. The killer was messing with her.

"What do you make of the 'dead-eyes thing'? Same guy as the glowing head or different?

"Same guy. It's dark on the porch at night. Everything about him would have been in shadow."

Aidan nodded. He closed the file, stacked it on top of another one, and pushed them both across his desk. "Time to review everything again." His mouth curved up a little. "That should keep you off the streets and out of trouble."

"You're so funny, you could guest-host Jimmy Fallon's show."

"Sometimes my witty human self makes an appearance."

"Surprising even you."

That got a laugh out of him."The Houston detective's plane arrives at 12:58 tomorrow afternoon. I want you to pick him up."

"Okay. Did you contact the Major Crimes Team about backing off?"

"I did and they will, but they're there if we need them."

Grace rose and picked up the files. She'd been contemplating a little white pain pill, a tall iced tea, and some soft music to cover the sound of the fan after she laid down for the night. Her hip was killing her, in addition to the renewed throbbing in her head and elbow. So much for going to bed early.

"And Gabbiano?"

She turned at the door. "Yes?"

"Be in my office at eight sharp tomorrow morning. We're going to get this Seattle thing resolved between us once and for all."

Grace left his office, but turned around and went right back in. "I forgot, I only have my bike here for transport home. My sister dropped me off this morning. Can I snag a ride?"

"Get changed. I'll load up your bike and wait for you in the lot." He took the files from her.

"Thanks."

Grace swore silently all the way home. As her other paternal grandpa had grown older, he used to say he "hurt like a bastard" whenever he got aches and pains. For the first time in her life, she understood exactly what that meant. The only part of her that didn't seem to hurt was her nose.

Aidan remained silent on the short drive to Grace's house.

She dozed, awakening only when he lightly touched her arm. Grace jerk, surprised she'd even fallen asleep. By the clock on the dash, they'd been parked in front of her house for nearly half and hour.

"Get some sleep and take one of the pain pills they gave you if you need it." He hauled her bike out of the truck bed and secured it to her front porch.

Grace thanked him again. She unlocked her front door before turning to wave him off. He waved back, but didn't drive away until she was safely inside.

CHAPTER 45

THE PAIN PILL would have to wait. Instead, Grace poured a glass of milk and downed a couple of ibuprofen. She toasted two slices of bread and filled small bowl with blueberries.

She put everything on a tray and headed for the living room, planning to watch TV while she ate. Pickens were slim. Sitcom reruns, Hollywood entertainment shows, reality TV, or political commentary.

Bored, she picked up the remote and began to imitate her father and brothers by channel surfing. She landed on the local news, where a live report was being given from outside Gunny's house. "The Coburg Police Department has no new leads in the two recent murders plaguing this small town. Police Chief Aidan Cruz said at a news conference this morning that even though his department is small, he has experienced investigators who have worked major homicide cases in Seattle, Portland, and Los Angeles."

The screen cut to a news clip of the chief with several microphones shoved in his face. "We want the public to know that, even though there are similarities in these deaths, we are certain they are not the work of a serial killer."

"What about the Houston killing?"

"The three victims were friends. Beyond that, we don't have a connecting factor. We're working with Houston PD, and for now, that's all the information I can provide. Thank you for coming."

Television news editors in big cities never included personable closures to press conferences, but Eugene was a smaller city. The camera loved Aidan Cruz, and so, apparently, did the news editor. The on-air reporter concluded by providing a phone number people could call if they had information concerning either local murder.

Grace reached for the phone and dialed a number she didn't recognize. A recorded message, made by Chief Cruz, thanked her for calling and asked her to leave a name and phone number. An officer would call her back shortly.

It was a few seconds before Grace realized she hadn't hung up, so surprised was she by the chief's forethought on how a small department might solicit and accept information on homicide investigations. How had he managed to get another phone line installed so quickly? Did people always ask *How high?* when he said *Jump!*

Grace rinsed her dishes, poured a glass of iced tea, and sat down at the kitchen table. She dismantled the contents of the investigation folder on DELLENBACH, JACKSON BRIDGES, careful to maintain the order, and began to read.

Making her way through the lab and pathology reports, questions cropped up that she'd like to ask her father, but Monday nights, her mother worked the late shift at Buon Gusto, so Pop was baby-sitting.

By the time Grace heard her mother's van drive past, she had finished the police and medical examiner's reports. She glanced at the clock and decided her parents wouldn't appreciate her showing up after eight to talk crime. And, if she was honest, Pop had already admonished her to discuss her theories with the chief, not him.

Grace took a breather to slip into her pajamas before examining the photos in the file. Apparently, Houston PD had emailed color jpgs and someone, probably Tina, had printed them out, most likely at the fire station. If this kept up, Rocco would start billing CPD for services rendered.

Jack Dellenbach had been a big man, larger in stature than his friend Clausen and even better looking than Starr. Nearly a year before, his body had been discovered on the south side of Memorial Park in Houston, in an area known as

Buffalo Bayou. The body had been propped up against a tree and discovered by a pair of bicyclists early on a Sunday morning.

The salmon-pink evening gown, like the ones found on Clausen and Starr, had a halter top. As with Starr's, this one had been slit up the back, then tucked around the body, probably after death. With his wide chest and muscular arms, Dellenbach looked something like a buff football player dressed up in sequins. His "suicide" note had been keyed into his smartphone using the MEMO function and left in the bodice of the gown. Like the notes of his two buddies, his also said, "Now I am like them."

A family photo had been included in the file. Dellenbach's wife, Carol, was a pretty redhead, and his sons, all four of them, had her red hair and his facial features. They were beautiful children.

Grace's emotions surfaced, despite her ongoing resolve not to let personal feelings interfere with her work. She straightened the pages and reattached them to the prongs inside the manila file folder. The photos were put back into their respective labeled sleeves.

She pushed away from the table, ready to call it a night. A total of six children without a father, two women without their husbands, and a mother without her son. She popped a pain pill, plagued by a single question that just kept repeating in her brain: Why? Why? Why?

From out of nowhere came three synonymous responses: Pay back. Retribution. Revenge.

But what had the killer of the three amigos been avenging? As young hell-raisers, had they done something horrible to someone?

Grace's thoughts raced back to the car crash over twenty years earlier. Who else had it involved? And had it occurred on a Saturday night or early Sunday morning?

Grace no sooner turned out the light than the phone rang. It was not yet ten and she'd been hoping for a full eight hours of sleep. "Hello?"

"Gracie, it's me."

Thanks to the pain pill, Grace forgot she had injuries. She jumped out of bed, reaching for the lamp switch. "Jesus, Delfina, where are you?"

"How are my kids?"

Just like her older sister to evade a direct question by asking another one. "Why don't you call the house and find out?"

A muffled sob preceded, "I...can't."

"Why the hell not? Is Bobby standing there holding a gun to your head?"

"Bobby's not here right now."

"Of course not." Bobby might not be there, but someone was. A lot of someones, if the background noise meant anything. Grace pushed a hank of hair off her face. "Your husband is bad news."

"Don't talk about Bobby that way, Gracie!"

"Why not? Tell me what he's done for you and the kids that makes your lives better."

"I don't need another lecture right now, especially from you."

Delfina had once called Grace a "nosy bitch cop." That day, Grace hadn't been sure if drugs or alcohol had been doing the talking. She'd let the name-calling pass, but the hurt had been inflicted, nonetheless. *And now, out of the blue, I hear from you?*

"Are my kids okay?" came the repeated, slurred question.

Grace took momentary pity on her sister. "They're fine. Kyle and Cassidy are registered for school and Maddy will go to preschool two days a week. They're healthy and happy, but they miss you. Where are you, Delfina? Why don't you come home to your children? We can help you, get you into rehab."

Her sister's began to cry softly. "Stop hassling me you nosy bitch cop. I can't. Bobby…."

"Your husband is a piece of shit, Delfina, and he's dragging you down with him. What's he using now? Coke? Meth? Brown?"

"He's speedballing."

Grace heard the tinkle of ice in a glass. Delfina was downing a long sip of something. “For God’s sake, are either of you working? Where are you getting the money to buy all this crap?”

“I’m working,” her sister said. “Bobby’s making me.”

Grace could hear a deep voice over Delfina’s softer one say, “Come on, baby.”

“I gotta go, Grace. I gotta...work.”

“Delfina, come home! You should be here watching your kids grow up. *You* should be taking care of them, not Mom and Pop.”

“I know.”

“Are you all right?”

“No….” The line went dead.

“Delfina!” Grace shouted, knowing full well the effort was futile. “*Damn!*” She thumbed quickly to the RECENT CALLS log and hit SEND on the last number. The guy who answered didn’t know anyone named Delfina, wouldn’t give his name, but did say he was in a pay phone outside a bar called Cactus Pete’s in Tucson, Arizona.

Grace thanked him and disconnected. *At least I know she’s alive.*

Tucson. Hot, dry. Exactly the type of climate Delfina craved, and so unlike the Willamette Valley, where rain and humidity dominated the weather nine months a year. Also close to the Mexican border, it no doubt offered Del and her worthless husband a steady supply of cheap drugs.

One of Grace’s former co-workers in Seattle, someone she kept in touch with because she was friends with his wife, had also hated rain. He had transplanted to Tucson PD the year before.

Grace was not above calling in favors, but the reason Travis Loew owed her a big one...well, asking him for help deserved a second thought.

CHAPTER 46

HAD GRACE BEEN prone to lying, she would have told anyone who asked that she'd lost no sleep over her eight o'clock meeting with Aidan Cruz. Of course, no one knew to ask except the chief, and if he noticed the dark circles under her eyes, he probably attributed them to either the case or her injuries.

Per his instructions, she arrived right on the hour. Interpreting his finger-waving, she closed the door behind her as she entered.

"I reread your supervisor's report," Aidan started off, gesturing her to sit, getting right down to business, "and your partner's. I've also read your rebuttal, which, by the way, was not part of the Seattle file, just as you suspected."

Just as I suspected, Grace parroted in sarcastic silence.

The chief leaned back in his chair, arms folded over his chest. "Tell me what happened."

He'd read the file, but this was his playing field, and he was her boss. She didn't have to tell him anything, but for some reason, Grace wanted him to know that she was a damned good cop, that she had not broken protocol. She had stood by her partner, to her own detriment.

She forced herself to sit upright, but didn't relax enough to get too comfortable, despite his seemingly inviting demeanor.

"My partner and I responded to a call downtown. Shots fired, one man dead, another seriously wounded."

"Start at the beginning. According to your report, the two of you were taking a lunch break. Your partner went one way at Pike Place Market and you went another."

She nodded, resisting the urge to ask, *Who's telling this story?* "Raston radioed that he'd meet me at the scene. We were only a couple of blocks away, but it was all uphill. I arrived in just under two minutes. Whoever fired the shots seemed to be long gone."

Aidan arched a brow at her. "Seemed?"

"Raston and I were both at the same location initially. He'd left me less than five minutes earlier, but he was already at the scene." She chewed her bottom lip. "I hadn't heard any shots when I was running up that hill, but he had a gunshot wound to the arm. He was conscious and coherent, but he wasn't panting or sweating like I was. For some reason, he hadn't called in an officer down, so I did it."

Grace shifted in her seat, which suddenly felt as if it had the proportions of an electric chair. "At first, I didn't think too much of it, that I was soggy and breathless and he wasn't, but it kept coming back to me that I'm a part-time runner and he's not. Raston never exercised off the job. His recreational activities leaned more toward guzzling beer or having sex with any woman he could get to leave a bar with him. He was soft, more than overweight, but I'd seen him exert himself before. He should have been drenched with sweat and doubled over, gasping for air."

Grace took a deep breath, concentrating on remembering the exact events. "The ambulance arrived right after about twenty patrol cars. The EMTs were directed immediately to Raston, so I called for another ambulance and stayed with the subject who was still alive. A couple of rookies were put on crowd control. It was the middle of summer, so hundreds of people swarmed around to gawk. The other uniforms hovered around Raston."

She shifted in her chair. The motion caused discomfort to her sore hip. "The subject came around briefly and was trying to talk. He grabbed my wrist and forced me closer." Unable to suppress a shudder at the memory, Grace said, "He scared the shit out of me, because I had broken the first rule of survival. I hadn't checked him for weapons and his hand had skimmed right over my holster."

To his credit, the chief refrained from admonishing her for a major screw-up, but his flexing jaw indicated he might have been thinking about it.

"I frisked him, then tried to make out what he was saying. At the time, it seemed nonsensical." She sighed, overcome with the resignation that engulfed her every time the futility of explaining herself surfaced. "He died desperately trying to tell me something, and I couldn't figure it out."

"But eventually you did."

"I thought about it all night. 'Rasdit, rasdit, rasdit.' It's not even a word. I kept repeating it over and over to myself and finally I started saying it out loud: 'Rasdit, rasdit, ras d'it, ras did it.'" She leaned forward. "Until the day I die, I'll believe he was saying, 'Razz did it.'"

Aidan's expression grew grim. "You can't be sure of that."

"But, don't you see? It all fit. Razz—that's what we all called Raston—wasn't sweating or breathing hard because he hadn't run up that hill—he was already there. And the gunshot wound to his arm? Remember the Diane Downs case? She tried to kill her children and claimed a 'bushy-haired stranger' was responsible and had also shot her? The DA proved her gunshot was self-inflicted." She paused briefly. "Razz had that same kind of wound."

The chief regarded her with an intensity that might have been frightening if she had read it as disbelief. "You're saying your partner shot himself?"

"What would you think if you came across someone who had an entry wound a couple of inches above the left elbow, dead center in the upper arm, and—"

"—and an exit wound slightly off center and to the left. Had he fired his gun?"

She nodded. "He said he'd fired back once after being shot. Only one shell had been spent."

He considered her in silence. "What about his spare?"

"He had it strapped to his ankle."

"And the two subjects? They both had weapons?"

"Yes, but there was also the third guy who got away. Supposedly, he's the one who shot Razz."

"You went to your CO about this?"

"For all the good it did. My partner had already changed the story, said I'd gone off into the market on my own and left him in the vehicle."

"You said you ran up the hill? You left your vehicle near the market?"

"Yes. It was locked and it didn't make sense to drive that two blocks in Friday afternoon traffic, when I could make the scene in just a couple of minutes on foot."

"So, Raston walked directly to the location of the shooting when he left you."

"Either that or he got a ride. I never once considered that he wasn't actually going to get his lunch." She shifted again in the chair. "Later, he said he heard the shots-fired call, that he radioed me that he'd meet me there but *I* hadn't responded. He flat-out lied about that and about calling in the meal stop. He handed over both his weapons at the scene, but neither matched the caliber found in either subject."

"What about the shot to his arm?"

"The bullet went straight through and was never recovered."

"Convenient for him. If he planned ahead, he could've had a third weapon."

Grace nodded. "And he had help."

"What do you mean?"

"The kicker was, our patrol unit ended up being at the scene, not down at the market."

The chief mulled that over. "Why do you think he killed those two men? And who were they?"

Grace shrugged, feeling impotent. "I haven't got a clue. I ran them both, but neither came up in the system and AFIS never returned anything on their prints. I didn't have a starting point for why Razz may have killed them, so I went to Dave, that is Lt. Mackey, thinking he'd help me figure it out. Not only did he pull me off the investigation assist, but he had me reassigned to another area where I supposedly didn't need a partner. All of a sudden, I couldn't get backup when I needed it, and a couple of times, I thought I wasn't going to make it out of a call alive." She took a deep breath, trembling with remembered anger and fear. "It sucks when your fellow officers think the worst of you based on someone else's lie."

She met his gaze evenly, though her face grew warm when she admitted, "Dave Mackey and I were seeing each other—it started before he got his promo. I trusted him and he wouldn't give me five minutes after I went to him with my suspicions."

"At-work relationships never work," Aidan said with matter-of-fact certainty. "But as your supervisor, he had a responsibility to look into this."

"The next thing I knew, IA started in on me. They'd been investigating Razz and two other officers under Mackey's command."

"Your boyfriend was most likely being investigated, too. Having a personal relationship with him put you under suspicion, as well."

Again Grace nodded. "The ironic part is that the investigation came to a screeching halt almost immediately. It didn't take long for word to get around that I was an IA squealer."

Aidan tapped the top of the file folder. "They didn't take any of what you're telling me into account, but no action was brought against you."

"IA put a nice little note in my file clearing me." Grace tried, and failed, to keep the bitterness from her voice. "They condemned me and confirmed the squealer story in one fell swoop. I didn't apply for this job just to be closer to my family. I wanted to know when I got up in the morning that I'd live to see the end of my shift every day."

The chief did some more jaw flexing. "Do you know what's going on up there now?"

"I heard Razz turned in his badge and took off for parts unknown. Dave went on being an asshole."

"Raston didn't recant his story before he left?"

"Not that I heard." She gave a self-deprecating laugh. "I thought I could figure it out on my own, but not even detectives who owed me favors would let me near the evidence on the case. I was blocked from every angle." She fidgeted with the pocket on her cargo shorts for the space of several heartbeats before she looked up. "If he hadn't lied about the chain of events, if he hadn't tried to set me up for God-knows-what, or had someone move the vehicle, I might never have given a second thought to how things went down. I might have just taken his word for it."

Aidan leaned back again, his tented fingers tapping against his lips as he studied her. "You're here now and you're doing a good job on our two homicides, in fact, all the way around. I know you have a problem with Frey—"

"He's a slimy pig!"

"Yeah, well, if he ever shows up around the office again, I plan to have a talk with him about that."

"What do you mean? Where's he gone?"

"That," the chief said, closing her personnel file, "is the million-dollar question. You probably heard he called in sick yesterday?"

She nodded.

"Deets went over to have a word with him, off the clock. When he got over to Frey's place, his car was in his assigned space, but when Deets knocked on his door, no one answered. He talked the landlord into letting him into the apartment."

"He lives so close to downtown Eugene, he could have been eating out, walking, something."

"Yeah, he could've been, but that doesn't explain why his apartment had been tossed."

"I wonder what he's been up to that warrants that."

The chief pushed his chair back and crossed an ankle over his knee. It was obvious he had some kind of internal struggle going on in his mind. Finally, he said, "Frey drives a dark-colored SUV."

Grace switched gears, quickly assessing the implications. "What are you thinking, that he *did* kill Clausen, Starr, and Dellenbach?"

"I don't know about that," Aidan said slowly. "But I sure as hell think with that bleached blonde hair of his, if the amber streetlight or the illumination from the dash lights hit him just right, it might make his head looked like it glowed."

Grace felt suddenly chilled. "I think he dislikes me enough to try something like that, but what possible reason could he have for taking the rocking chair from Gunny's porch?"

"That's what we're going to find out. EPD is on the ransack, but Deets is going back over to talk to people in the complex." He tapped a second file on his desk. "I'm going to be rereading Frey's personnel file. I want you to have McPherson do a records search and have Tina do an Internet search on the QT. Something may come up." He glanced down at the file, his eyes narrowed in thought. "I don't want all my patrol officers on this, so let's get Montoya and Jenks—"

"Not Jenks," Grace cut in. "She has a history with Frey, so even though she's wise to him, it's still conceivably a personal conflict."

Aidan gave her a curt nod. "Okay, Trudeau, then. Have them review Frey's reports for the past year, see if anything jumps out—somebody issuing threats, someone just getting out of jail. Make sure they look for any tells that *Frey* might be the harasser, especially if the report involves a female. We might be barking up the wrong tree, but I don't know where else to start."

"Deets should check Jimmy's vehicle. The key might be in the apartment if his SUV is in the parking lot." She had a sudden thought. "We should have a look at his patrol vehicle, too."

"Good idea."

"You know, Deets told me once that he thought Frey had something on Chief McCrea."

"And he arrived at that how?"

"Jimmy always screwing up, not performing the duties of an officer, always getting away with it."

The chief drummed his fingers on the desktop.

"Should we talk to McCrea, see what he has to say?"

"Deets may have a valid point, but let's hold off questioning Harmon for the time being." He moved around to the front of his desk and leaned back against it. He was close, but not to the point where he encroached on her space. Still, Grace rose from her chair, straightening slowly as her muscles protested.

"I realize this Seattle thing is unresolved for you, Grace."

She was shocked he'd actually used her name. She liked the way it sounded when he said it.

"I'd advise you to send a copy of your rebuttal to Mackey's supervisor and ask for confirmation that it's actually gone into your file this time. Then you need to let it go."

As if I ever could.

"I don't do business like your boyfriend. If you see something that's not right, come to me. I want to run a clean department here and I don't do favors or cover for bad cops." He straightened, looking her directly in the eye. "Just so we're clear, I'm with you on this. Anything ever comes up on it again, I'm your best ally."

He hadn't said it with sympathy or syrup, but as a supervisor who not only believed her, but believed *in* her. Grace was horrified when she realized her eyes had watered. She held out her hand to him, in a gesture meant to show her appreciation. "Thank you."

He looked down at that hand and extended his own. They shook on it. "You're welcome."

Grace moved toward the door.

"Be cautious. I don't want any dead officers added to my two-week-old homicide stats. And Gabbiano?"

She looked back at him over her shoulder.

"How many more relatives do you have who might be feeling the urge to defend your honor to me?" He looked serious, but he had a wicked little twinkle in his dark eyes.

Grace flashed him a wry grin, turning away before he could see the two tears rolling down her cheeks.

CHAPTER 47

GRACE WENT DIRECTLY to the bathroom. Even though it was multi-stalled, she locked the main door.

She was not a crier. That was Mikey's job in the Gabbiano family, but dammit, the chief had believed her! He'd also accepted the eccentricities of her family, rather than mocking her for their interference, or ordering her to tell them to knock it off.

So, despite the fact that she was not a crier, she shed a few more tears before she vacated the stall and stood over the sink, splashing cold water over her red eyes and flushed cheeks.

Refreshed, she went to her office and closed the door. She needed a moment to think, to plan the rest of her day, without interruption. Civic duty aside, she needed to take care of some personal business.

She placed a call to Travis Loew. If Delfina and Bobby were involved in drugs, and doing something illegal to get those drugs, Trav would haul Del's ass off to jail faster than Grace could spell sister. He had lost a brother to a drug overdose. As a result of that loss, he'd gained a new determination and unerring ability to track down criminals involved in drug use and trafficking. He'd find Delfina and Bobby, no matter how well they thought they were hidden.

"Not a problem, Grace. I'd do anything for you, and you know that, but you have to be ready for the fallout, kiddo."

"I know." Kyle, Cassidy, and Maddy didn't understand being abandoned by their parents. Being young, they'd welcome them back in a nano second. However, if Del and her worthless husband ended up in the slammer, the kids might not forgive Grace for helping put them there.

I'm damned if I do and damned if I don't.

"Email me the photo you scanned. I'll start circulating it."

"Thanks, Trav. How are Megan and Natalie?"

He laughed with pleasure. "Natalie is growing like a weed. She'll be three next month. Megan's doing well, too. We're expecting another one in April."

"Congratulations!"

"Yeah, well, if not for you, Gracie, this life we have wouldn't have been possible."

"Anyone would have done the same thing."

"I don't think so, sweetheart. It takes a lot of nerve to cut a hole in someone's throat, then stick a ballpoint pen in so they can breathe until the EMTs get there."

"You can thank my brother for insisting I take the life-saving class," she said, embarrassed, as usual, by Trav's effusive gratitude.

"Since you're back home, give him a kiss for me."

Grace laughed. "I'm not sure how Rocco would take it when I tell him who it's from!"

Grace stared at the wall. Once she'd called Trav, her personal concerns—Delfina, the Seattle fiasco, the bike crash—had to be shoved into a deal-with-it-later compartment.

She pulled her narrow notebook from the pocket of her cargo shorts and began to write.

She had work to do that involved a grief-stricken mother and two widows. Zelda and Ellie she could see in person. For Carol Dellenbach, a phone call would have to suffice.

Jason Knox had to fit into the day's schedule somewhere, too. The loud-mouthed macaw made Grace uneasy. It was such an oddball connection. A canvas of Jason's neighbors was in order. She'd have to get some help with that.

Every word in the three murder files had to be gone over

again with a keen eye. Every piece of evidence had to be re-examined and reconsidered. There had to be something that would help solve these crimes.

She looked at her watch. No way could all of that be done by 12:30. There was no direct route from Coburg to the airport, and she didn't want to be late picking up the Houston detective. Damn, the chief hadn't told her his name.

God, she was exhausted just thinking about everything she had to do. *I'm twenty-nine! That's too young to be tired.*

She went back to the bathroom to splash more cold water on her face.

Staring at her reflection in the mirror over the sink, she couldn't quite get one niggling little issue to stay put in the corner of her mind. It was damned aggravating to entertain the notion that the chief might be right.

Someone had deliberately tried to hurt her.

The thought seemed incomprehensible—in all the years she'd been a cop, no one had ever purposely tried to hurt her. Escape from her, elude her, betray her, yes. But actually physically harm her? No way.

Ellie Clausen had nothing new to say to Grace. She seemed genuinely distressed about Jack Dellenbach, having known him during high school and college. "How bizarre! Yeager and Hamm haven't heard from Jack for years. This has to be about something that happened in college."

Grace nodded. "It's possible. Do you know of any trouble the three of them got into during that time?"

"They did everything together, but Yeager never said anything about trouble."

"What about the car accident Hamm was involved in summer after his junior year? Were Yeager and Jack in the car?"

"I don't remember Yeager saying anything about a car accident."

"It's how Hamm injured his hand."

Ellie shook her head. "That can't be right. He told me that he fell on the ice when he was in college."

"I'm pretty sure he lied to you about that," Grace said. "He definitely had a car crash." She put away her notebook. "If you think of anything else, let me know, will you?"

No one was more surprised or shocked than Grace when Ellie reached over and gave her a hug. "Thank you for everything you're doing to find this killer."

"I'm just doing my job, Ellie."

"You're going the extra mile. You always have, ever since I can remember." Ellie uttered a small, self-deprecating laugh. "Even though you were younger than me, it was always something I envied about you. Hell, maybe I even resented you. I took on a lot of ambitious projects, but I hardly ever finished anything."

She reached out and took Grace's hand this time, giving it a squeeze. "Seriously, my girls need this closure. They have a lifetime of unresolved father issues ahead of them to deal with as it is. They don't need his killer running free on top of that."

Every cloud has a silver lining, Grace thought as she climbed into the patrol car. In this case, the death of three men seemed to be having a startling, but positive effect on one woman's character.

Hamm Starr's death was having the opposite effect on his mother.

Zelda looked like she had aged twenty years in the past forty-eight hours. Her pale face got lost behind her unkempt hair, frizzing in every direction, as if she'd stuck it in the proverbial light socket. She still had on her pajamas, but they were buttoned improperly and soiled, and the top didn't match the bottom.

She needed some serious looking after.

"I talked to Pastor Grimes. He's agreed to do the service for my boy on Friday. Hamm wanted cremation and his ashes scattered in the mountains. 'Don't stick me in a jar and leave me on a shelf somewhere,' he told me after Yeager's funeral service. 'I want to fly with the wind when it's my time.'" Zelda wiped her eyes. "Kinda artistic, ain't it, just like my boy?"

Grace nodded. She put an arm around Zelda's shoulders and steered her toward the kitchen. Hamm's dog Blackie trailed after them. "I just want to tell you again how sorry I am for your loss, Zelda. I can't even begin to imagine how difficult this must be for you."

She guided the old woman to a chair at the kitchen table. "I'm going to fix you something to eat." Grace went to the fridge, Blackie on her heels. The only items inside appeared to be ready for a Petri dish. Sensing she wouldn't fare better at the cupboards, she reached into her pocket for her cell phone. "Excuse me a minute, Zelda."

Stepping outside, she hit speed dial. Blackie sat her feet, looking up at her in a pathetic, forlorn sort of way. "Mom, it's me. Food alert." In less than a minute, Angelina took charge of getting Zelda some food and TLC. Within the next thirty minutes, at least four ladies from St. Anthony's would swoop down on Zelda and get her bathed, into clean clothes, and fed. Then they'd clean her house and do whatever else they could to help out.

Back inside, she found Hamm's mother trying to brew a pot of coffee. Grace scooted her back into a chair and took over the task. While they waited for the maker to drip, Grace located two cups, then joined Zelda at the table. Blackie sat on his haunches and rested his chin on Grace's knee. She absently rubbed him between his ears. "We've discovered that Jack Dellenbach was killed in the same way as Hamm and Yeager, about a year ago in Texas."

"Jackie?" Zelda cried. "My lord, I haven't heard a word about that boy for near on twenty years. And you say he was murdered, just like my boy and Yeager?"

Again, Grace nodded.

"Dressed up, was he, like they were?"

"He was found in a pinkish evening gown—"

"Oh, my!" Zelda slapped a hand against her chest.

Grace leaned forward in her chair. "What?"

The grieving mother waved her hands in front of her, apparently dismissing some thought she'd had. "It's nothing. It just brought back a memory of Hamm and a picture he sent me when he was at CU. He'd taken a girl to the Valentine Ball and she was wearing a beautiful gown, not quite pink."

Grace took a stab at the color she'd read in the Dellenbach file. "Salmon pink?"

Startled, Zelda said, "That would describe it!" Her eyes filled with fresh tears. "They made such a handsome couple. He was tall, dark, and handsome—all the things that make a romance hero—and she was a beautiful willowy blonde, a beauty queen. So sweet, and smart, too, Hamm said."

Zelda blew her nose loudly into a paper towel. "I never did see how me and my rotten other half ever produced a boy as beautiful as Hamm."

Murmuring something politely reassuring to Zelda, it took Grace a moment to realize what else Hamm's mother had said. "A beauty queen?"

Zelda scrubbed at her eyes with the corner of the paper towel, nodding. "A real stunner. She'd been entering beauty contests since she was a little girl. That year, she was in the Miss Colorado pageant. Pretty blonde hair, like that little girl who got killed…what was her name? Oh, JonBenét."

She shuffled off to a hutch and opened the doors on the bottom half, extracting a photo album she brought back to the table. Flipping through it until she found what she was looking for, she turned it toward Grace, who leaned forward to examine the five-by-seven color photo.

Hamm Starr, twenty years younger, posed arm-in-arm with a beautiful young woman with miles of wavy blonde hair. It was hard to believe he could be better looking, but like many men in a tux or a uniform, he was incredibly attractive.

Grace's studied the face of the woman in the photo. Something about her seemed familiar, but what? And then her gaze fell to the gown and she gasped.

What the hell!

Without the file photo in front of her for an accurate comparison, she couldn't be one-hundred percent certain, but the dress in the photograph looked exactly like the one Jack Dellenbach had died in.

"I'd like to borrow this photo, Zelda. I need to have a

copy made, but I promise it won't be damaged and I'll return it within twenty-four hours."

Zelda withdrew the photo from it's protective plastic sheath and ran trembling, loving fingers over the image of her only child. "Maybe being a beauty queen ain't all it's cracked up to be."

"What do you mean?" Grace asked.

"Just like that little JonBenét girl, this one's dead, too."

"How do you know that?"

"Hamm told me. Years ago. Called me in the middle of the night, crying." Her expression grew pensive, her tone sad. "Hadn't heard my boy cry like that since the last time Cal—that was my husband—back-handed him but good, same day he left us. Hamm was only ten years old."

"I'm sorry, Zelda."

The older woman gave her a watery smile. "You're such a considerate, kind girl, Grace. I wonder if you could do me a favor?"

"I'll try."

"I can't handle my boy's dog. He's too big and my house is small and my yard ain't fenced. Any chance you could take him so's I don't have to hand him over to the dog pound?"

Grace opened her mouth to say no.

"It's obvious Blackie takes to you, honey. Even Hamm told me how much his dog liked you."

Given a moment to think about it, Grace decided she could help Zelda out in this small way. Her yard *was* fenced and she could take Blackie on runs to exercise him. She could enlist the little ones to make sure he was fed and watered while she worked and they might enjoy playing with him. "How is he with kids?" she asked.

"Don't know, but ain't black Labs supposed to be personable?"

Grace smiled. "Okay, you have a deal, but only until you find him a home." She put a hand on Zelda's shoulder and gave it a gentle squeeze. "You let me know if I can do anything else for you, okay?"

"You don't anyone who can help me do the right thing

with all Hamm's paintings and such, do you?"

"Actually, I do. My aunt Gabriella, Pop's sister, has an art gallery in Portland. Would you like me to have her contact you?"

"Oh, honey, would you? I don't really want to think about it right now, but maybe in a week or so, I'll be ready…."

"It's no trouble," Grace assured her.

"Thank you, Grace." Zelda used the sleeve of her pajama top to wipe her eyes this time. "Damned near broke my heart when Hamm told me his girl died in that car crash. I never met her, mind you, but if he loved her, I knew I would, too. She just looked so sweet, didn't she? Just like you." She held the picture out to Grace. "My boy was eaten up with guilt over that girl dying." She stroked the photo one last time. "I don't know as he ever got over it."

CHAPTER 48

BLACKIE RODE SHOTGUN in the patrol car. His food, doggie dishes, and leash were stowed in the trunk.

Half-dazed by her latest discovery, Grace was anxious to get the dog settled and head back to work. Finally, thank God, they were getting a break in a double—no, a *triple* homicide.

She took Blackie to the backyard and went about filling his food and water bowls, both of which were plastic and looked as if they'd been through the war. She dug a long-abandoned tennis ball out of a drawer in the kitchen and threw it for him for a few minutes. Finally, she squatted down to have a conversation with him.

"I have to go to work, big guy. There's plenty of shade in the yard and you've got both food and water, so don't tear things up before I get home, okay?"

Blackie nuzzled her in response, his rear end energetically propelling his tail. Or vice versa.

"Good boy," she said, giving him a hug. Blackie followed her to the back door. He settled his butt against the patio stones and watched her expectantly. "Don't give me that hangdog look, Blackie. I have to go to work. Remember our deal."

Blackie *woofed* and she could have sworn he gave her a doggie grin.

Grace closed the door, hoping she hadn't made a whopper

of a mistake. She pulled her cell phone out and speed-dialed her dad. Quickly, she explained the situation. Rather than chastise her for a bad decision, Joe suggested, "Why don't I run down to the pet store and pick up some dog stuff?"

"Thanks, Pop. That would sure save me some time. He needs new doggie dishes and will you get him some doggie treats and maybe a chew bone, too?"

"Don't worry, *cara*, me and the little ones will get everything you need. You don't mind if I take them over to play with him when we get back, do you?"

Grace laughed. "Not at all, but I don't know how Blackie will react. He's never been around kids before."

"We'll take it slow, and I'm sure they'll all be fine."

"Thanks, Pop! You're the best."

He chuckled. "A dog. You never cease to amaze me, *cara*."

The tires of Grace's patrol car spewed gravel as she rounded a corner and raced the last half-block toward the police station.

According to the back of the photo Zelda had given her, Sarah Mays and Hamm Starr had gone to the Valentine Ball in February of his junior year at the University of Colorado. Five months later, according to Hamm's mother, the girl, a beauty queen, had been killed in a car crash.

Impatient with even the short time spent clearing out her gear and locking up, Grace hit her head against the door jamb when she climbed out of the patrol vehicle. For several moments she saw stars, but worse, she cracked herself a good one right where her stitches were.

Grace cussed a blue streak and sank back into the seat of her car, waiting for the pain to subside.

A short time later, her head throbbing unmercifully, she asked Tina, "Did the fax come from Boulder County SO?"

"In your box," Tina answered.

Grace waded through several pieces of mail, haphazardly shoving everything but the faxed police report back into her cubby. Deets looked up from the community computer and said hello. Grace returned the greeting, her eyes on the fax. "Any word on Frey yet?" Not that she cared if she ever saw him again, but he did work for her, and she ought to know his whereabouts when he was supposed to be on the job.

"Not a peep. He's in deep shit this time."

Grace did look up then, to see if Deets happened to be rubbing his hands together in delight. He wasn't, but he had an anticipatory gleam in his eyes.

Chief Cruz called out, "Gabbiano, in my office. *Now!*"

Ah, crap.

"Close the door," he growled. "I can't get a anything done around here! Every five minutes someone from the media is calling to find out where we are in the investigation. In between, the mayor or one of the city councilors is calling. And in between those, the DA hammers me. The only person who leaves me the hell alone is the Police Commissioner." He gave her a look. "I suppose I have you to thank for that.

"Sorry, Pop must have thought of leaving you alone all on his own. Speaking of Pop, guess what—"

"Have you made *any* progress since this morning?" he snapped.

Feeling as if he'd just slapped her silly, Grace retorted, "It's too bad you have your tits in a tizzy—again! Why don't you just shut up and hear me out?"

He blustered into silence, looking about ready to explode. Finally, he said, "I believe the correct terminology is 'tits in a ringer.'"

Beet red, and hoping to salvage her job, Grace stammered out, "I'm sorry. Ohmygod, I am *so sorry*! I—"

His glacial expression silenced her. "I'm okay about the tits, since I don't have any, but in the future, Sergeant Gabbiano, watch your mouth when you're talking to me." He leaned over, his palms flat against the paper-strewn desk. "I am *not* one of your other co-workers, that you can get cutesy with me."

Cutesy! His supercilious, nasty tone rankled her like little else had since she'd been at CPD. Her Italian temper got the best of her and she couldn't resist giving him a snappy salute. "Aye, aye, sir. Permission to *speak,* sir, since you apparently called me in for that exact purpose."

Aidan straightened and stared hard at her for several seconds. "Some day that smart mouth of yours is going to get you into trouble, Gabbiano."

"Yes, *sir.*"

"Can the 'sir' bullshit. I called a press conference for nine a.m. tomorrow morning. Every radio and TV station from here to Portland, and for all I know, the goddamned world is coming."

"You don't like the media much, do you, *sir*?"

"One more time and you're automatically demoted to fired," he snarled.

For just an instant, she considered challenging him to see if he'd really do it.

"What have you got?"

"You called me in, remember? *Sir.*"

"You're fucking hopeless," he said.

Grace praised whatever foresight had caused her grab the Houston file. She placed it on the chief's desk and foraged for the photo of Dellenbach in the pink gown. She put it side-by-side with the photo Zelda had given her of Hamm and the Mays girl at the Valentine Ball.

Aidan's dark eyes darted back and forth between the images. "It looks like the same dress."

"I'd bet you a week of my former salary on it."

The chief sent her a warning glance.

"And get this" —she tapped the Valentine Ball photo—"the girl in this picture was a beauty queen and according to Zelda, she died in that car crash."

"I'll be damned."

He was quick, Grace would give him that. Even if he was pissy. "Look, I need to work on nothing but this if I'm going to make any headway. You still have me on two hours of bike patrol, plus I need to get to the airport. I can't be everywhere at once."

The chief muttered a string of obscenities under his breath. "That's why I called you in. Get Jenks to do your bike patrol. I want this bastard, sooner rather than later."

"I'll do my best."

"Do better than your best." His gaze went back to the photos. "Go through all the paperwork again. Find out who this girl is."

"The report just came in from Boulder County SO, but I haven't had a chance to read it yet. I also want to talk to Jason Knox again, and I'm going to send two officers out to canvas his neighbors, see if any of them saw anything the day the bird was stolen."

"I don't think the bird will be a substantial lead."

Grace disagreed. Had she pressed her luck with the chief as far as she dared? One way to find out. "If you recall, there was a macaw feather in the wig Clausen wore."

After a moment of jaw-flexing, he said, "Put Deets and Montoya on it. They work well together and Deets has the experience to teach Montoya."

"I agree. Anyone come up with anything on Frey yet?"

"No." He picked up a pen and tapped against it the blotter. "Okay, let's meet again around three, go over what you have."

"Three?"

"Is that a problem?"

"I have to pick up the Houston detective at" —she glanced at her watch— "oh, shit, I have to go or I'll be late. What's his name?"

He looked down at his notes. "Luz Quintana."

"I'll check in at three, but I don't know if I'll be able to meet. I'm planning on taking him directly to the crime scenes first."

"Okay, see if you and he are at a point where the three of us can sit down at five."

Grace opened the door. With a grin on her face, she couldn't resist saying, "Yes, *sir*."

"Get out of here, Gabbiano."

She could have sworn she heard amusement in his parting order. Either that, or the squeak of his chair sounded a little like a chuckle.

Grace rushed back to her office to grab her cell phone and a red-rope folder to hold the files she needed. She gave

Deets and Montoya their assignment, thankful they didn't need instructions on how to carry it out.

Deets crossed himself, grinning. "Saying a little prayer to protect you from big bad police chiefs."

"Agnostic, my ass," she retorted.

CHAPTER 49

GRACE RESISTED THE urge to hit her lights and siren on the way to the airport. She arrived with five minutes to spare, only to learn the flight had been delayed because of a security breach in San Francisco.

The new estimated time of arrival didn't leave Grace time to go back to Coburg and return. She headed for the coffee bar, where she ordered an iced latte.

She picked a corner table to sit and read the Boulder County SO report while she ate. What she discovered stunned her.

Sarah Mays had not died in the Saturday-night crash, but she had arrived at the hospital in a coma. Nothing in the few faxed pages said what had happened to her after that, but all three murder victims were listed as passengers in the car owned by Hamm Starr. Had he been too drunk or drugged out to drive?

She had other questions, too, but the fax was missing a couple of pages, and for some reason, one page was only half there. *Damn!*

Grace moved on to reading the Houston file. Carol Dellenbach carried on her husband's business out of an office suite he'd rented in a pricey downtown high-rise. She had been a prime suspect in his murder—a five million dollar life insurance policy had sent the detectives and the insurance company sniffing in her direction. On top of that,

Dellenbach's company was worth easily a hundred times the value of his life insurance.

Eventually, the investigators had begun to look elsewhere for suspects, but Carol remained number one on the list. The theory was that she'd hired the killing done. After nearly a year, however, the case was stagnant.

Until now.

Grace moved outside where she could call Jack Dellenbach's widow without her conversation being overheard.

"Sergeant Quintana said you'd be calling," Carol Dellenbach said. "I understand you've had two similar murders there in Oregon."

Grace grimaced, as she always did when someone outside the state called it Ora-gone. Carol's soft drawl didn't soften the mispronunciation. "Yes, two men who were friends of your husband's throughout high school and college were killed by someone using the same MO. Yeager Clausen and Hamm Starr."

"I recognize the names, but we never met."

"Did your husband ever tell you anything about them?"

"He referred to them as Hamm 'n Yeggs. They drank together, smoked together—and I'm not talking cigarettes—and dated together. They were three horny drug heads, to hear Jack tell it."

"Until summer before their senior year in college."

An uncomfortable silence seemed to pulse over the phone line. "What do you know?" Carol finally asked.

"Why don't you tell me what you know," Grace said, "and I'll let you know if it agrees with what I know."

Clearly, the other woman wasn't comfortable with that arrangement, but she apparently respected Grace's position of authority. She gave a big sigh, full of resignation, and said, "They were doing drugs pretty heavily by the time they made junior year. All three of them had earned scholarships, but Jack said their grades were suffering. Hamm had quit painting, Yeager had quit investing, and Jack had quit doodling with electronics. Up until then, they had all earned extra money with their respective skills."

"Money for drugs and alcohol?"

"Yes. When the grades started to slip and the scholarships became endangered, their folks threatened to cut them off, except for Hamm, who also had a part-time job as an art tutor and no parental financial support."

"Summer before senior year, they partied pretty hard. The three of them took off one night and headed up to a cabin owned by the family of Hamm's girlfriend. They drank all night, did some coke, some heroin, had some sex."

"They shared Hamm's girl?" Grace asked.

"Jack and his friends were drunk on booze and drugs," Carol Dellenbach said in a neutral tone that indicated she'd long ago come to terms with her husband's youthful behavior. "They were young. That accident sobered him up. Jack thought it sobered all of them up."

"So they all had sex with Sarah."

Another pause. "Was that her name? Jack said she was willing."

"And you believed him?"

Carol sighed. "It's not a matter of what *I* believed."

"She had a blood alcohol level of 1.3 and enough heroin in her system to do her some serious damage."

Carol Dellenbach's responding silence was punctuated with a soft sob of emotion. "Look, I'm not making excuses for my husband. He really did turn his life around after that night. He transferred to UTEP and spent nearly two years making up lost credits and rebuilding his GPA. He came to Houston after that and got his electronics business off the ground. We met a year later and married a year after that. Jack told me all of this before he asked me to share his life with him. Not a day went by that he didn't regret what happened that night. He told me many times he wished he could go back and do it all over again, keep that girl from climbing behind the wheel of that car, ending up in a coma."

"Your husband told you Sarah Mays was driving."

Another silence, telling in its duration, condemning because it occurred at all.

"No, but that's what they told the police."

"And it's what the police report shows."

"Jack said it was really Hamm." Her voice, lowered to almost a whisper, had roughened with emotion. "Jack couldn't abide what they'd done, the lie they'd left as that girl's legacy. He couldn't betray his friends, either. They'd taken a blood oath as boys to forever stick by each other, but he never spoke to them again after he left Boulder. Both of them tried to contact him in the early years of our marriage, but he'd never return the calls."

Given that Zelda had also told her Hamm had been driving the car, Grace had no reason to doubt Carol Dellenbach's second-hand version of the same story. "Had your husband received any threatening calls or mail before he died?"

"Are you kidding?" Carol demanded incredulously. "Everyone loved Jack. He gave back to this community, Sergeant. He donated huge sums of money to drug rehab centers, paid for hundreds of thousands of dollars in alcohol abuse prevention materials for children, funded an intervention program for at-risk adolescents—the list goes on."

A real belated saint, for all the good it did him.

As if reading her mind, Carol said, "Jack carried a lot of guilt that he worked hard to assuage."

Grace sighed. Sometimes she forgot it wasn't her place to pass judgment. Jack Dellenbach, Yeager Clausen, and Hamm Starr were in another place now, where, if the majority of the world's population was to be believed, a higher authority had already assumed the role of both judge and jury concerning their final fate. "One last thing. Did Jack ever tell you what became of the girl, Sarah?"

"He checked once, about a month later. The hospital where she'd been treated told him her family had put her in a care facility somewhere. At the family's request, they wouldn't say where."

They talked for several minutes more, then Grace thanked Carol Dellenbach and hung up. Her cell rang almost immediately.

"Grace, it's Tina. Quintana's flight is held up in San Fran. The security breach hasn't been resolved yet. He's going to try and catch a seat on a later flight. He'll call back."

"Rats!"

"You know, we have so few flights into Eugene, his chances of getting here today are probably slim to none."

So much for my day off tomorrow. She asked Tina to let the chief know she'd be available at three after all. She also asked her to try and locate the whereabouts of Sarah Mays.

Before she left the airport parking lot, Grace dialed one last number. After a quick greeting, she asked Zelda, "Are you positive Hamm told you the girl in the car crash had died?"

"Of course! How could I mix up a thing like that?" A moment of silence passed. "Why are you asking, Grace?"

"Because…Sarah Mays didn't die in that accident."

"You're mistaken."

"No, I have the police report in front of me. The girl was hospitalized for a week, then moved to a long-term care facility. She was in a coma."

"Why would my son lie to me about that?"

That is exactly what I'd like to know, especially since he didn't lie to you about who was driving.

Grace went back through the entire file on both Clausen and Starr, then reread the paperwork from Houston. If asked, she could probably repeat all of it verbatim.

Since she had time, she entered her case notes into the computer, then composed the *CliffsNotes* version for the chief. With little more than she'd had earlier, she hoped it would appease him.

Tina was at the photocopier when Grace entered the room where the copier and printer were housed. "I think your three o'clock with the chief is off."

Grace retrieved her single-sheet print job. "Oh, yeah? Why?"

"He left about ten minutes ago and said not to expect him back for a while."

"You're kidding!"

"Nope. Felix saw his kid walking over on Coburg Bottom Loop. When he realized who it was, he went back to pick him up, but he'd disappeared. Felix called Aidan, and the next thing I know, the boss is out the door, smoke pouring out of his ears."

"I thought your mom was watching Dylan this week."

Tina pulled out the final few pages and straightened her pile. "Mom thought so, too, but she got a very convincing call this morning. Dylan pretended he was speaking to his father, relaying what Aidan was saying word-for-word, that he wouldn't be coming over today." She shrugged, an impish grin on her face. "Needless to say, Mom won't be so gullible in the future."

"I'm guessing Dylan is going to be learning a lesson of his own today."

Tina quickly pulled stapled groups from the fifteen bins. "Yeah, and the boss was already having a rough day before that because his ex called."

"This morning?"

Tina nodded and started loading her next copy job.

That, at least, explained Aidan's surly behavior earlier, beyond his peeve at being hounded about the recent homicides. "Thanks for the heads-up."

"Any time."

Within minutes, Grace was on her way.

She had to see a man about a bird.

CHAPTER 50

GRACE ARRIVED ON Jason Knox's doorstep unannounced, so she wasn't surprised he didn't answer the doorbell. She stepped back from the massive two-story Tudor-style structure and looked up. After Clausen's, this had to be the next largest house in Coburg.

Her parents' friend must not have been exaggerating about the success of the business he'd sold. Sitting on almost an acre, the landscaping was of the variety featured in one of those coffee table books—everyone envied it, but no one could afford it. Except Ellie Clausen. Maybe they used the same gardener.

Grace turned and followed the flagstone path around to the back of the house. There she found the aviary Jason had told her about. Enclosed in glass about ten feet high, with half-inch chicken wire for another four feet above that, it was replete with trees and a waterfall feeding into a small pond. Grace counted a dozen brightly colored birds. Given the hundred thousand dollar overall value, she assumed more were hidden by foliage.

The obscenity-shouting macaw with the brilliant yellow rings around its beady black eyes perched on the branch of what looked to be a giant leafless madrone. Its feathered buddies ranged in size from about twelve inches in height to slightly larger than the macaw. Some flew, some sat, but they all seemed to have an eye on her and several squawked up a storm, probably at her intrusion.

"What do you think?"

Despite the raucous cacophony, Grace jumped and spun around. "Jason! You startled me."

"Sorry."

"I rang the bell, but no one answered."

"I was running some errands in Eugene."

"I should have called."

"No need. I don't keep any set schedule. Usually I'm here and I'm not big on formalities." He put the palm of his hand up against the glass as one bird flew close and landed on a branch that didn't seem strong enough to hold its weight. The colorful creature put its head against the glass, apparently trying to nudge Jason's hand. He glanced at Grace. "They're quite gentle and loving. Would you like to go inside and see them up close?"

Grace didn't really have time to tour a bird zoo, but said, "Sure."

"What happened to your head?"

"Fell off my bike," she said, slightly bemused as she hurried to keep up with his long-legged strides through the house and into the aviary. He appeared not to listen or care about her answer. Competing with Jason's birds apparently took some doing. If her mother-the-matchmaker ever found a woman who possessed a fondness for boisterous winged creatures, Jason would be married off in no time.

The Hyacinth macaw remained on its perch, but several other of the birds swooped down, coming within inches of Jason and Grace's heads when they entered. "Rowdy, aren't they?" She forced herself not to flinch.

"I like to think of them as playful."

Grace shot him a doubtful glance. "I've always preferred dogs with paws to birds with claws."

Jason chuckled. "The birds grow on you."

Still dubious, Grace was glad Blackie was a dog and not a three-foot-high bird. "The macaw doesn't seem to have suffered any ill effects."

"Cyan's always been a little quiet, but," he added with some humor, "she now speaks with forked tongue."

As if to prove her owner right, the magnificent macaw screamed, "Fucking pigs!"

"Bet the neighbors really love you now."

"No doubt."

The bird, seemingly tired of obscenities after just one round, immediately broke into "Blue Moon."

"Ella Fitzgerald, eat your heart out," Grace murmured.

Jason laughed. "Would you like a glass of iced tea?"

Sweating in the environs of the aviary, Grace said, "That sounds wonderful."

An intelligent, cultured man, Jason was an impeccable host and he had a lovely home. He indulged in beautifully executed oils, Aubusson carpets, Loetz and Tiffany art glass, and furniture at least two centuries old. No wonder her mom had tried to pair him up with Rose. Pop had also told her Jason was a prolific reader and owned an impressive collection of first edition books. Those she would have liked to see, but he didn't invite her into his library. His home was comfortable and welcoming, which made the absence of family photographs all the more surprising.

By the time he led Grace through to the front of the house thirty minutes later, she hadn't learned anything new connected to the theft of the macaw that might help her find a murderer. She hoped Deets and Montoya, who were out on the street now, gleaned something from one of Jason's neighbors.

Near the front door, an iridescent jade green vase with gold aurene threaded gracefully around the rim captivated Grace.

Jason caught her interest. "It's a Steuben, made around the turn of the last century."

"It's lovely," Grace said, resisting an urge to reach out and touch the delicate piece.

"My housekeeper has a fit because I keep M&Ms in it."

For the first time, Grace fully registered the colorful bits inside.

"Help yourself," Jason encouraged, dipping his hand in.

She followed suit. "They definitely taste better out of Steuben."

Jason laughed. “I hope so.”

Grace reached for a second helping, remembering belatedly that the killer had shoved some of these same candies up where the sun don’t shine on all three of his victims. She suddenly lost her appetite for chocolate.

“Get anywhere?” Grace asked Deets as soon as she walked into the office.

Her fellow officer threw up his hands. “I just got back from a call over at the Interstate. Got a hooker doing business at the truck stop again.”

“Do I take that for a ‘no’?”

“I went door-to-door with Felix and couldn’t find a single person within a two-block radius of Knox’s who saw squat.”

“Do I still take that for a ‘no’?”

“Yes, it’s a no. Montoya and I want to take a ladder over there. Maybe the bird thief went in through that chicken-wire stuff he has around the top of the bird house.”

Grace wondered what Jason would think of Deets calling his aviary a bird house. “Jason told me he doesn’t keep the door between the aviary and the house locked. I suppose it’s conceivable Cappland cut the wire near a tree he could climb down. Once he grabbed the bird, he could have easily left through the house, then gone around and retrieved his ladder. Did you see any impressions?”

“Nah, the landscaper had been there. Anything we might have had last week was gone.”

“However it happened, the ruckus would have been incredibly loud. I’m surprised no one heard the birds, especially since Jason says his neighbors complain constantly about the noise.”

“Beats me, but not everyone was home today. Maybe we need to go back out.” Deets pulled the CPD cap off his silver head and wiped his brow with the back of his arm. “Freaking hot outside.”

Grace agreed.

“And humid, too. I think it’s going to rain.”

She folded her arms over her chest and tried to look stern.

"Oh, you're the weatherman. I mistakenly thought you were Corporal Deets Mallory."

"Goddamned smart aleck," he mumbled under his breath.

Grace turned to Tina. "Were you able to locate Sarah Mays?"

"I got a few phone calls in, but it was a long time ago, Grace. Memories are short."

Grace slumped down into a chair. "Someone must know what happened to her."

"Deets has a cousin in Boulder who works in the county recorder's office. He's checking death certs for me."

Grace gave Deets a thumbs-up for helping out. "She died?"

"Too soon to know yet."

"Does your cousin have any connections we can use?" Grace asked Deets.

"His daughter works at the newspaper office."

"Tell me she'll run the morgue for us."

"For a story."

"Apparently extortion is part of the curriculum now in all journalism classes."

Deets laughed. "Hey, my cousin's kid is a senior at CU J-School. She'd like to give 'em a story that will tie in to a past Boulder event and knock their socks off. She needs a job come next summer."

"Okay, tell her I'll give her a personal interview if she can come up with what happened to the girl. And," she added for good measure, "if it helps us find the killer, I'll get her a personal interview with the chief, too."

Deets blew out a breath. "You like living dangerously, Gracie."

"Hey, the chief told me to get this case solved. He didn't say how or put constraints on my methods."

"He hates the media."

"Technically, your cousin's kid isn't media yet."

Deets shook his head. "Just warn me before you tell him. I plan to be out on patrol right about then."

"I'm not worried. You said a prayer for me, remember?"

He grinned. "So I did."

Grace took hope. If Deets had enough confidence in his cousin's kid to be worried about the chief's reaction when she hooked him up for an interview with a budding reporter, they must be on the right track.

"Grace," Melody called out. "Phone for you. Line one."

Grace punched the blinking light on her desk phone and said, "Gabbiano."

"Grazia, *cara*, are you getting off on time today?" her father asked. Laughter and barking could be heard loud and clear in the background.

"Bite off more than you can chew, Pop?"

He chuckled. "Maybe just a little, but the kids love Blackie and he's really good with them."

"I'm glad to hear it. So, what's up? You want some relief?"

"No, no. I was trying to reach Aidan, but he's out."

"His kid pulled a fast one on him. I guess he's getting it straightened out."

"Well, that's the thing, Gracie. Dylan is here and I wanted to ask Aidan if it's okay for him to spend the night." He blew out a deep breath. "I guess if he's done something he shouldn't have, now is probably not the time to ask."

"Probably not. I'll see if I can track the chief down and have him call you."

A vigorous burst of squeals and more barking ensued. "Never mind, Grace. Aidan just got here. Talk to you later."

Grace pondered what kind of punishment would be doled out to the clever little acorn for his audacious stunt.

CHAPTER 51

GRACE WALKED NEXT door to the fire station and asked Rocco to scan the photo of Starr and Sarah. "Can you print me off four copies?"

Rocco gave her a stern look. "You do realize that this is not the police department."

"You have more money in your budget than we do, ergo, you have the scanner and the color printer." She smiled sweetly at him. "Anything we have that you need or want, Roc?"

He barked out a laugh. "Not likely, but I'll let you know if things change."

She gave him a cheeky grin.

Within ten minutes, Grace was back at CPD. Chief Cruz sat in his office, an unhappy Dylan at the table in the corner. He was eating bread and lasagna that had to have come from Buon Gusto. Aidan seemed almost relieved to see her. Grace guessed the request to let Dylan spend the night at the Gabbiano hotel had not been granted, if it had even been asked.

She waved a greeting and stopped to invite Dylan to join her and her nieces and nephew for lunch and an "animal safari" on Thursday.

"Maybe," the sullen youth said, keeping his eyes on his food.

As she ducked into her own office to update the three

homicide files, Grace belatedly realized the boy might be grounded over the day's escapade, and perhaps she should have checked with his father first.

Knowing she'd find out before she left for the day whether or not she'd overstepped, she inserted the photos into clear plastic sleeves and added them to the binders. Then she began to reread everything, starting with the crash report. She had a strong feeling that incident was the impetus for the recent killings. Somehow, it all revolved around the beauty queen, Sarah Mays.

No matter how many times she read through the pages, the facts remained inalterable. Excessive speed, drugs, and alcohol had contributed to the crash. The three males claimed Sarah was driving, even though the vehicle was belonged to Hamm. Investigating officers couldn't prove otherwise, despite one eye-witness account to the contrary, leaving the blame to remain on her.

Stymied as to why the young men's blood and urine hadn't been tested like Sarah's had, Grace searched for family information, wondering what the girl's parents had to say. The last contact showed Jason and Helen Mays living in Highlands Ranch, Colorado. Dad owned a lucrative business called MaysCo, mom was involved in numerous local organizations, and sister Nicole, two years younger, had just graduated high school.

The last notation, dated three months after the crash, indicated the investigating BCSO officer had attempted to return a gold necklace to the family—an oval locket with two black-and-white photos inside, which had been recovered at the scene. The package came back as undeliverable.

Grace drummed her fingers against the fax. No photos had been sent of the crash scene, but she had an uneasy feeling she needed to see them. She dialed Boulder County SO. "Dana Roberts faxed me an incident report yesterday." She read off the case number. "Pages three and four are missing and six is only half there. Can you fax them to me again?"

"Not a problem."

"Also, can you scan and email as jpgs, the photos that

were in the file, or if that's not possible, color photocopy them and have them overnighted to me? We'll reimburse expenses." Grace paused a moment, giving the clerk time to take down the information.

"We do have a scanner, so it won't be a problem. What's your email address?"

Grace gave it to him. "One last thing. I'm interested in a gold necklace with a locket that should still be in the evidence box, maybe in a sealed envelope."

"I'll have Dana call you back tomorrow on that."

Flies, honey, be nice. "We're investigating the murders of three of the four people who were in that car crash. I'd really appreciate it if you could help me out here."

"We're so back-logged right now…."

Flies, honey, be nice! "Believe me, I know exactly what you mean. Other than our chief, we only have six paid officers on our entire police force."

"No kidding?" The *clickety-clack* of fingers on a computer keyboard broke the momentary silence. "Okay, I sent an email down to evidence. I cc'd you, so he can contact you directly."

Grace gave the clerk a heartfelt thanks and disconnected.

Dylan stuck his head into her office. "This place really sucks."

Grace looked up from her paperwork. "I guess it depends on your perspective. I used to hang out at the Oregon State Police Forensics Lab with my dad."

The boy's expression remained disdainful. "Yeah, but you're old."

Grace resisted the urge to run to a mirror and check her face for wrinkles. She didn't *feel* old, but to an eleven-year-old…. "I was your age at the time."

"And you *liked* it? Your dad didn't *force* you to go with him."

Ah, the punishment. "I loved it, and I used to beg Pop to take me. He couldn't do it very often, but when I was allowed along, it was great."

Dylan scowled. "If it was anything like this place, you must have been one big geek back then."

Grace smiled at his back-handed compliment. "I've had an interest in all things criminal from the time I had my first cap six-shooter and tin sheriff's star, when I was about five. Rocco and my sister, Delfina, and I played cowboys and cattle rustlers using old brooms for horses. I used to chase them around the farm." She grinned. "I loved arresting them."

Dylan eased through the door and leaned on the jamb. "I wasn't allowed to have toy guns. Mom wouldn't even let me have a Star Wars light saber. How lame is that?"

Grace could see where that ought to be an exception. Even Kyle had one. But then, she wasn't Dylan's mother, so she kept her mouth shut on the subject.

"I think Mom takes it out on me because Dad's a cop," he continued, disbursing a pearl of wisdom Grace thought unusually insightful for a boy his age.

"Maybe things will be different now that you're living with your dad."

Dylan scowled. "This town sucks as bad as this place does. There's nothing to do. And everyone who lives here is an old geezer."

"Really?" she asked, amused.

He narrowed his perspective to exclude her nieces and nephew, but his tone remained defiant. "I did like your dog, though. And he liked me. He kept licking my face."

"He's not really my dog. I'm just dog-sitting him for a while, until he finds a new home."

"Why does he need a new home? He seems to like your place okay."

"His owner died recently and, honestly, I didn't have plans for a dog right now." She leaned her elbows on her desk and stuck her chin in her hands. "I guess things might seem quiet—"

"*Quiet*?" he scoffed. "Try *boring*!"

"Boring if you don't give it a chance. Me, I had the mini crime lab when I was growing up. I spent hours examining bugs under the microscope." She grinned. "I even took samples of hair from everyone in the family and all our neighbors so I could compare them. After that, I moved on to Mom's spice cupboard. Drove her crazy, but spices are really interesting under the microscope."

"I don't have a crime lab," he said, moving a few steps closer.

"Do you like to read? There's the public library in Eugene and the Knight Library on campus."

"They're too far away."

"You could check the bus schedule. If he doesn't want you to go all the way downtown, there's a branch library at Sheldon Plaza, right next to the McDonald's."

He looked doubtful. "I think I'm going to be punished for the next ten years for ditching Mrs. Reese."

"I'm sure your dad will be more reasonable than that," Grace said dryly. "What kinds of books do you like to read?"

"Fantasy and science fiction," he admitted. "History. Mom always gets mad at me 'cuz she says I spend too much time reading and daydreaming about what I'm reading."

Grace didn't like contradicting the boy's mother, but she did it anyway. "You can never read too much. They've done studies that show the more you read, the longer your brain functions properly, even" —she couldn't resist teasing— "when you're an old geezer."

"Hunh," the boy scoffed, but Grace caught the hint of a smile tilting lips so like his father's.

"Do you like to write?"

He inched forward. "I got an award for a short story I wrote last year."

"Wow! I'm impressed."

"I won free tickets to OMSI...and a dictionary and a thethesor—"

"Thesaurus," she supplied.

"Yeah. The synonym book. My tongue always gets twisted on that word." He hurried on, warming to his topic. "I liked OMSI."

"It's fun. Lots of neat scientific stuff to look at."

"I guess. Mom took me and we practically ran through the place. I didn't get to see much."

"That's too bad. Maybe you can get your dad to take you sometime."

"He's too busy."

"Maybe he won't be as busy on his new job here."

"Yeah, right," Dylan said bitterly.

"Do you have a computer?"

By now, he was leaning against her desk. "Mom couldn't afford it and Dad won't buy one because he says I'll just play games all the time."

"Maybe you could strike a deal with him."

Dylan cocked his head at her.

"Well, if you like to write, maybe you could spend a certain amount of time on the computer writing stories and doing some of your homework when school starts, and a certain amount playing games."

Dylan's lip curled. "Writing just to write sounds boring."

"Then write for a reason. When you go to the library, ask the reference librarian to help you search for some youth writing contests." She tapped her pen against the desktop, wondering if anything she had to say would actually stick in the kid's brain. "You could investigate those just like Kyle examines his fingerprints."

"Yeah, Kyle told me about that, but it's not exactly the same, is it?"

"Not exactly," Grace had to admit, "but a lot of writing contests pay cash prizes and I think they always publish the winner's work."

He perked up slightly at that possibility. "Maybe. I wanna play soccer, when school starts."

"That sounds like fun."

"Maybe."

On that note, Grace pushed herself away from the desk and stood. She gave Dylan's shoulder a squeeze, knowing he'd resist her ruffling his hair even more than Kyle did. "Let's go raid the snack machine. I have a terrible craving for something sweet."

They turned, both surprised to find Aidan standing in the doorway watching them.

CHAPTER 52

DAY OFF OR not, Grace couldn't sleep in. She tried, but her internal alarm woke up her internal self, even if the clock radio on the bedside table remained silent.

Besides, she had two murders to solve and a detective coming in from Houston. She had to be prepared to collaborate with him without looking stupid or unprepared.

On that note, she padded barefoot to her laptop and logged on to her work email, pleased to see the jpgs had come through. By contrast, the missing fax pages had still not come through before she'd left work the night before.

She downloaded the jpgs and briefly reviewed them on her screen. Rocco had switched shifts with someone taking a long weekend, so she forwarded them to him for printing at the fire station. She might have to buy him two koi after this.

She took a leisurely shower—with the day she had ahead of her, Grace thought she owed herself that much—and washed her hair, trying not to disturb the stitches at her hairline. Technically off the clock, she decided to wear a sundress in a cheery periwinkle print.

She fed and watered Blackie, who was more interested in her breakfast than his own. He padded after her to the front porch, where she took her meal.

Two newspapers lay neatly on the top step. The media had shown an incredible amount of interest in the two Coburg deaths. Even to the small community's knowledge, no one had been murdered in Coburg for years and years—maybe since the turn of the 20th century or before.

Of course, the fact that the male victims had been dressed in glittery evening gowns had a little something to do with all the notoriety.

Grace was thankful the *Policies & Procedures Manual* mandated that Chief Cruz had to field all media inquiries.

Today, three articles appeared in the Eugene paper. The one on the front page criticized Coburg City Council's lack of budgeting for experienced officers. The editorial page chronicled CPD's "lack of experience in handling homicides."

Grace shook her head in amazement. Even though the chief had mentioned it at the news conference, neither the reporters nor the editor had done their homework. The CPD officers had over sixty years of combined experience among them, including the new chief, who'd spent ten years in the Portland Police Bureau's Person Crimes division.

The third article, in the City-Region section, thoroughly scrutinized Yeager Clausen and Hamm Starr. Clausen had warranted several derogatory quotes from Coburg residents, while Starr had been glorified by the local arts community.

No wonder cops disliked the media.

At least none of the articles had mentioned the Houston tie-in. Thank God for small favors.

Grace set aside that paper and unfolded the *Coburg Herald Weekly*. Harley had done a nice job covering Hamm's death and the subsequent investigation. Unlike the Eugene paper, he cut Coburg PD some slack, even offering a little praise regarding the caliber and quality of the officers on staff.

Grace reached for her coffee. Harley knew which side *his* bread was buttered on.

Laying at her feet, Blackie growled.

"Good morning, Grace."

She looked up, surprised to find Jason Knox coming up the walk. "Hi, Jason." Blackie growled again. "Quiet," she shushed him, putting a hand on his head, petting him.

"Did I come at a bad time?"

Grace refrained from saying *yes*. Geez, it wasn't even seven o'clock yet. On her days off, she liked being alone in the morning, enjoyed having her breakfast, and reading and cursing the paper in solitude. Remembering her manners and feeling petty for so selfishly guarding her free time, she said, "Not at all. What brings you out so early?"

"Your father and I have a golf date."

"Umm." She took a sip of her coffee, then remembered her manners and the fact that Jason Knox was a coffee aficionado. "Would you care for a cup?"

Jason glanced at his watch. "Sure, I guess I have time. I'm a little early."

"Have a seat. I'll be right back." Blackie let out another growl. "Okay, buddy, in the house you go," she said, grabbing hold of his collar.

When she returned, Grace got the impression Jason's gaze was intent upon her, even though he wore expensive sunglasses and she couldn't see his eyes. He drummed his fingers rapidly against the top of her bistro table.

"Thanks," he said as she poured from the carafe. "How is it being home again? Your parents tell me you've been gone for quite some time."

Puzzled, because she'd had virtually the same conversation with him at Sunday dinner, she said, "I have. It's good being back."

"And you like your job?"

"Yeah, though it's been anything but quiet lately."

"How's the investigation going?"

She shrugged. "It's going. There are a lot of leads to check out, a lot of people to talk to. It definitely would have been easier if the guy who'd bird-napped your macaw had been the killer, but he wasn't, so we just keep plugging along."

Jason frowned. "I still don't understand how he got in the aviary." His fingers continued their steady tap, his coffee remained untouched. "So, did your people find anything?"

"No, but Cappland had an extension ladder in his van. A couple of officers are going by your place this morning to see if he cut through somewhere up high where it couldn't be seen from the ground."

Jason removed his sunglasses, revealing troubled eyes.

"Since you don't lock the door between the aviary and the house, he may have just walked out through the house."

He leaned back in his chair, his expression anxious. "Good lord." He rose, shoving his sunglasses on rather haphazardly. "I've been thankful he only wanted one of the birds and now you've got me worried that he pilfered something else I don't even know about yet. I need to get home and check."

"Jason, I'm sorry. I didn't mean to agitate you."

He held up a hand to stave off her apology. "No, no, I'm glad you told me your theory. I should have thought of it myself. What time will the officers be there?"

"I think Deets said around nine."

Jason glanced again at the sleek gold watch on his wrist. "Nine. We won't be back from the golf course by then."

"You don't need to be there. They're only checking the wire from the outside."

"Of course, of course." He pulled his cell phone from his pants pocket and hit a couple of keys with his thumb. "Joe?"

He hurried away without saying goodbye or ever having touched his coffee.

"Let us know if you find anything missing," Grace called out as an afterthought.

Jason didn't acknowledge that he'd heard.

Even stranger was that he had never acknowledged Blackie, who made no secret of disliking him.

Grace went up to her parents' house to chat with her cousin Gina, who was baby-sitting. She finalized arrangements to pick up her nieces and nephew the following morning, after she dropped the Houston detective back at the airport.

Next, she stopped at CPD to see if her fax had come from Boulder. No such luck. Because she didn't want to be late picking up Luz Quintana, she assigned Tina the task of contacting Dana Roberts directly for the missing pages.

Grace found a nice end space in short-term parking in the airport parking lot, where she hoped not to get any door dings in her VW Beetle. The apple-green Bug still had one year owing on it and so far, remained in pristine condition.

The heat-reflecting asphalt left a sheen of perspiration on her as she crossed the parking lot, heading for the terminal building. The display board showed Quintana's 9:19 flight to be on time, so Grace grabbed two cold bottled waters from the gift shop and waited for him in the lobby just past the escalator.

A few minutes later, a scratchy voice over the PA system announced the plane's arrival. A number of passengers disembarked before Grace focused on the man she guessed to be the Houston detective.

About five-five and around fifty years of age, he had started to bald and his belly had a middle-age roundness to it. His countenance projected fatherly warmth.

Grace eased toward her Texas counterpart and introduced herself. The man to whom she spoke smiled and said, "*¿Que?*"

"Luz Quintana?" she repeated.

The man shook his head and waved his hand in tandem. "*No, no. Humberto Gallegos.*"

"Sorry," Grace said. She stepped back and collided with another passenger.

"Don't be sorry, *chiquita.* It's hard to tell us Hispanics apart."

Grace froze, her face burning with embarrassment. She turned slowly, ready to apologize.

The man who stood before her, looking as if he'd just stepped off the big screen, grinned engagingly. His beautiful teeth so were white against his bronze skin they could have had a sparkle star. His sun-streaked hair was on the longish side, thick, and wavy, the kind a woman would love running her fingers through. And his eyes—they were so blue, she could have gone for a swim in them.

Her mouth opened, but the only thing that came out was a strangled, "I'm so sorry!"

His handsome face immediately wrinkled with concern.

"Hey, don't go all politically correct on me, Sergeant Gabbiano." He took her elbow to guide her away from the last few departing passengers. "I'm the one who owes you an apology. I'm a displaced class clown. Sometimes, all I do is open my mouth to change feet. My mum says it's my least appealing feature."

He delivered that last rather like a dry punch line. Grace didn't doubt his sincerity, and she couldn't help grinning at his doleful expression. She extended her hand. "Let's start over. Luz Quintana?"

He nodded, swallowing her hand up in his. "Grace Gabbiano?"

Grace couldn't believe it when an unfamiliar shiver of excitement coursed through her body. "Yes, it's nice to meet you, Sergeant."

"The pleasure is all mine, *Sergeant*."

His playfulness made Grace smile. She'd heard Australian accents on infomercials and home improvement shows, but never in person, and certainly never expected it from a Houston detective with the surname of Quintana. There was definitely something kind of sexy about a voice from Down Under.

"I'm a paradox, I know," he said with good humor. "Dad's grandfather immigrated to Australia from Brazil in 1896 and before that, his grandfather had immigrated from Spain. Dad was a big brute of an Australian who came to America to buy some Longhorns to breed with his Herefords. He met Mom, a gorgeous Texas rancher's daughter, right off the bat. They had a short courtship, and as soon as he made arrangements to ship his Longhorns home, they were married and he carted her off to Australia. I'm the oldest of six, said to be conceived in a flurry of passion in the great state of Texas." He gave her a devilish grin. "I decided to go to university in the state of my conception and stayed. That's it in a nutshell."

"Wow." Grace couldn't help comparing Luz Quintana to her boss. She'd learned more about the Houston detective in sixty seconds than she had about Aidan Cruz in almost two weeks. "You must have some big nuts down in…." She trailed off, mortified and coloring furiously at her unintended sexual innuendo.

Luz laughed and with a wink, tweaked her on the chin.

Suddenly self-conscious, Grace asked, "Uh, do you have a bag to pick up, or just your carry-on?"

Still grinning, he said, "I travel light. Good thing. I had to hop a flight to Denver last night to get in to Eugene this early today. Didn't know I was going to hit so many states on this trip. Quite an adventure." His blue gaze skimmed her. "And well worth it."

That grin was so rakish, so delightful, so sexy, Grace didn't know whether to relax or run for cover. "Your transportation awaits, Sergeant."

"Luz," he said.

"Grace," she countered.

Holy shit.

CHAPTER 53

GRACE CALLED TINA about the missing fax pages before leaving the airport parking lot. Dana Roberts was out sick, Tina said, but the records clerk Grace had spoken to the day before *swore* he had faxed the pages and *promised* he'd do it one more time.

Either the guy was full of shit, or some higher power didn't want Grace to see those pages.

She speed-dialed Rocco next. He confirmed he'd received and printed out the jpgs. Grace beelined for the fire station to pick them up. Quintana followed her and the two men had a bonding experience over the classic fire engine Coburg Rural Fire Protection District had on display at the fire house.

She let Quintana choose whether he wanted an early lunch or a late breakfast. He chose lunch, so Grace headed for Buon Gusto, where her mother spent half an hour fawning over him and interrogating him about his long-term plans with Houston PD.

Later, he said with amusement, "Hey, I have a mum just like yours. Six kids, remember? Only two married. She's about ready for the Funny Farm over it."

Grace was glad he understood, but she decided it might be time to have a serious sit-down with her mother over trying to recruit Grace's co-workers for a son-in-law.

They spent an hour at each crime scene.

Once back at the office, Melody and Dagne lost their

powers of speech in Quintana's wake, but Tina popped up with, "They sure grow 'em cute in Texas."

Quintana wiggled his eyebrows at Tina over his shoulder, and said in his sexy Aussie voice, with a definite undertone of Texas twang, "Why, thank you, ma'am. I think y'all grow 'em pretty cute up here in Orygun, too."

Charmer, Grace thought, admiring his ability to finesse the ladies with his diverse language skills. And he knew how to pronounce Oregon, too, regardless of where he came from.

Munching on Angelina's fresh-baked almond cookies, they discussed and compared cases, studying the had files and photos spread across the table.

"These have got to be revenge killings," Quintana said.

"I think so, too," Grace agreed.

"I think so, three," Aidan said, entering the room. "Sorry to keep you waiting." He introduced himself to the Houston detective, then searched for the file Grace had labeled STARR, HAMMOND RAY. He pulled out the Valentine Ball photo and held it up for Quintana's inspection.

"Revenge connected to the sheila." Luz glanced at Grace. "I recognize the dress."

"Sheila?" Grace asked.

"That's what we call the ladies Down Under."

Grace nodded. "My gut says the car crash was the pinnacle point." She studied the photo, wondering again why Sarah Mays seemed so familiar. She wracked her memory, but nothing came to her. "What about Dellenbach's penis?"

"He didn't have one," Quintana said with a straight face.

Grace threw him a look. "You forgot to mention you're a comedian in addition to being the class clown."

He grinned at her and winked.

Blushing, Grace glanced at the chief, who stared at her with a slight frown.

Quintana shrugged. "His donger had been shorn like the other two, and left dangling at the end of a charging cord from a low-lying branch over his head."

The chief winced.

Grace refocused her attention back on Quintana. "So, the

fact that Dellenbach and Starr had their joysticks left close by, and Clausen didn't, means Clausen's probably did get carried off by a crow, and that all three of them were maimed for a specific reason, probably to do with sex."

"Again, back to the girl," Aidan said.

Grace related Carol Dellenbach's second-hand version of the events preceding the crash."She told me they'd all three had a go at her."

Quintana shook his head. "I can't believe the information you got out of that sheila. I must have interviewed her a dozen times and I never heard any this." He scratched his chin. "It's not unusual for smackies to cop a group root—or mates, either, for that matter."

Grace did some quick internal translation. Smackies, druggies. Cop a group root, group sex. Those Aussies sure had some interesting slang. She opened the conference room door. "Tina, any sign of that fax from Boulder yet?"

"No, sorry. I'll call them again."

"Go for a supervisor this time. We need that report right now."

She closed the door and went back to the white board. With a sigh, she said, "Too bad so many people like M&Ms. The cigarette ashes, by the way, were Abner Nelson's brand."

"Marlboro, right?"

Grace nodded.

Quintana's chair creaked when he leaned back. "Candy might be important, especially as it was freckle candy, but I don't like your farmer for the killer. Millions of people smoke Marlboros."

"Freckle?" Grace asked.

"Anus," Luz clarified.

"Abner did hate Clausen, but he had no reason to kill either Starr or Dellenbach." She glanced from the chief to Quintana. "Clausen and Dellenbach were so cooperative, they must have known the killer."

The chief took a seat at the table. "Starr definitely knew him, and because of that, he knew what to expect." The three of them stared at the pre-autopsy photo of Starr, the one that clearly showed his many bruises. "Knowing what happened to Clausen, he didn't give one inch of cooperation."

Quintana tapped a finger against the file folder. "Clausen was found in a more obscure location, or at least one that wasn't traveled at night, but Starr was left near your main drag. Does that make the killer more brazen, or is he taunting you?" He stood and began to pace in front of the windows. "Starr was a big guy, like Dellenbach. The killer either had to be big and strong, or enlisted some help."

He stopped in front of the white board where Grace had listed the suspects and put his hands on his hips. "I'm not liking *any* of the sheilas, Grace, but on the other hand, you don't usually see guys cutting off other guys' doodles unless it's a sex crime. The problem is, this isn't adding up to a sex crime, but it is a crime of passion, which usually indicates a sheila, if the donger is gone." He lifted a shoulder. "It's a Catch-22."

In a fit of frustration, Grace erased everything she'd written on the board and started over. She labeled four columns as SUSPECT, ALIBI, MOTIVE, EVIDENCE, and in a fifth, she made a big question mark.

Between the three of them, they quickly established Ellie Clausen as the number-one suspect. She had no alibi, plenty of motive, black-and-blue marks on her fist, and a garden shed that might lead to some sort of cutting tool with blood evidence on it. Only problem was, she had no reason to kill Dellenbach.

Aidan stood. "I'll see about a search warrant for that shed."

Grace held up a hand. "Let me call Ellie first." Within minutes, they had permission to search "any damned place you please, including up my ass!"

Deets and Montoya were notified to hit the Clausen garden building after they wrapped up a DUII stop underway on Pearl Street. Grace crossed Ellie's name off the list for a second time and slammed the marker back into its holder. "This is driving me nuts!"

For another two hours, Coburg's finest poured over every shred of evidence, every alibi, every police report with their counterpart from Houston.

Midway through the session, Deets and Montoya reported in. "Sorry for the delay," Deets said. "Our DUII gave us some shit during the field sobriety test and again at the jail."

"Nice black eye," Grace said to Montoya.

Montoya grinned ruefully. "Gee, thanks, Sarge."

"The Clausen garden building is basically a potting shed," Deets said. "The gardener brings his own tools, but Mrs. Clausen apparently pots her inside plants and some of the ones on the patio, so she had a few hand tools hanging over the potting table. I bagged two pairs of small pruning shears, like you'd use for trimming off dead leaves and blooms. Frigging building was so clean, you could eat off the floor."

Grace sighed. It wasn't any more or less than she'd expected. "What about the aviary?"

Montoya said, "No cuts in that chicken wire anywhere, so we asked him, could we look at his exterior doors. Knox followed us around like a bloodhound. No sign of any forced entry there, either. He finally took off, so we hit the neighborhood again, talking to folks who weren't home the last time we canvassed. Got nothing different this go-round. The van was in the neighborhood at the end of last week and the only vehicle anyone saw at Knox's house was the Lexus SUV he drives."

"For all intents and purposes, this Cappland guy walked through the walls, took the bird, and split," Deets said.

"How did he even know about the aviary? You can't see it from the street." Grace propped her elbows on the table, her chin in her palms. "Jason says he never met Cappland."

"Who is this Knox bloke?" Quintana asked. "His name keeps popping up in this investigation."

Grace shook her head. "Only in relation to the macaw Cappland stole."

Quintana frowned. "Have you run a CHC on him?"

"No."

"What do you think, Chief?"

Aidan rapped a knuckle against the table. "He is a newcomer to town."

"Over a year ago," Grace inserted, "but maybe we should

do a criminal history check on him. Anyone else while we're at it?"

When neither man responded, Grace suggested, "How about Jimmy Frey?"

"That's already underway," the chief said.

Once Deets and Montoya had gone off to run a criminal history check on Knox, Quintana asked, "Any other odd behaviors you've noticed, or unusual events?"

"No," Grace said, at the same instant the chief said, "Yes."

Quintana looked from Grace to Aidan. "Come on now, mates, play nice."

The chief said, "Someone tried to run Grace down one night while she was on her bike."

"You don't know that was related," Grace protested.

"You and old Gunny Spriggs both coming up with the glowing head makes it related."

"Glowing head?" Quintana asked. He raised his big body out of his chair and walked around to Grace. "Tell me, *querida*, what have you been withholding from old Luz?"

Grace quickly recounted the events of the previous Sunday evening.

Quintana *tsk-tsked.* "Grace, assume everything that happens is related in a case like this."

Appropriately chastised, Grace glanced toward the chief, who gave her an I-told-you-so look.

"Just be watching over your shoulder," the Aussie advised.

"Exactly," agreed the Chief, as if he hadn't already given her the same warning.

Grace had the urge to tell them both to shut the hell up.

Luz said, "Whoever the mongrel is who killed these blokes, he or she must have come across as fair dinkum." At their quizzical looks, he said, "Sorry. Someone trustworthy."

"Clausen may have been an asshole, but he wasn't stupid. The killer had to be a really smooth talker." She drew a line through Frey's name. "He's about as smooth as a dried corn cob."

Chief Cruz moved around the table. "Who the hell did

Dellenbach, Clausen, and Starr have in common after all this time?"

The three of them stared at the board in brooding silence.

Finally, Grace said, "Only the girl, if she's still alive."

The two men nodded in agreement.

Grace threw up her hands. "What if our killer *isn't* finished? What if there's someone else connected to this triad we don't know about yet?"

"The killer *is* done," Quintana said with quiet confidence. "Let's go over the possibles one more time."

"Why bother? The yellow brick road always leads right back to Ellie." She erased Ellie's lined-through name and rewrote it.

"For good reason," Aidan said. "Cunning can be a lethal substitute for strength."

They went back to staring at the white board. Frustrated, Grace picked up the eraser and cleaned it off for the third time.

Aidan leaned back against table. "I don't like Frey for a suspect," he said, just as Deets burst through the conference room door.

"Me, either," Grace admitted reluctantly.

Breathless, Deets said, "You're not going to like him much better as the victim of a homicide."

CHAPTER 54

THE EUGENE HOMICIDE detectives were having a love–hate relationship over the discovery of a CPD officer face down in the poison oak at the bottom of Spencer Butte. With a bullet hole in his head.

Murder suspect or not, Frey's death was being taken personally by the neighboring police department to the south.

Secretly, Grace was relieved the investigation had landed on their doorstep. EPD had top-notch homicide investigators and she had enough on her plate trying to figure out who killed Clausen and Starr.

When Chief Cruz, Grace, and Quintana were politely told to butt out, that was exactly what they did. Right after the three of them endured a rigorous questioning by the lead EPD detective on the case.

"So, you think this is linked to your two homicides?"

Grace opened her mouth to respond, then promptly shut it.

The chief did the talking. "It's entirely possible."

The sun had begun to set, and they'd worn out their welcome. The LED lights the forensics unit had set up began to work their twilight magic.

Quintana stood between Grace and the chief, all a good distance away from the corpse, and said, "In this light, it looks like his head is glowing."

Studying the dead Jimmy Frey's bleached-blonde dye

job, Grace and the chief had to agree.

"The question is, who was he helping if he stole that rocking chair off Gunny's porch?" Grace asked.

"More importantly," the chief corrected, "did he run you off the road, and why?"

Grace silently concurred and another thought flitted through her brain. Was Luz wrong about the killer being done? Was she next on the list?

The office was buzzing when they returned. Everyone had hung around, eager to hear the details of Jimmy Frey's demise.

Dagne Nelson sat in a corner, sobbing, even as she glared nonstop at Grace. Tina finally told the girl to go home and instructed her not to return until the following week.

Once she was gone, the chief gave out assignments. "This is an EPD investigation," he reminded his officers and reservists. "We have our own homicides to investigate, but Frey's death may be linked to them. Don't step on any toes, if you can avoid it." He glanced down for a moment. "Mallory, I want you at the autopsy in the morning. The doc has all his slabs full right now, so apparently, he's going to start at six a.m. and do Frey first."

Deets nodded, his expression grim.

As Grace knew first-hand, no one liked going to an autopsy. Or at least not as much as Doug Hacker and his diener.

Grace, Aidan, and Luz conducted a follow-up interview with Ellie, but she had nothing to contribute that brought them closer to knowing the identity of the killer. Or killers.

Afterward, Quintana asked Grace and Aidan to join him for dinner. Grace accepted before learning that the chief had plans with Dylan for the evening.

They climbed into her car and headed to her house so she could change clothes.

Quintana settled into the wicker chair on the front porch with a beer. Blackie kept him company. He flashed her a lazy grin."Wear something sexy." His gaze wandered down her sundress and back up. "Not that I don't like what you're wearing already."

"This isn't a date," Grace protested, a little flustered.

His expression suggested otherwise. "Just you and me and no chief? I beg to differ."

"Be still my heart."

Quintana laughed. "Hustle up, Gracie, and I'll take you to the best place in town."

They got Quintana checked into his hotel in downtown Eugene. Grace waited in the lobby while he went to his room to freshen up, then they walked the two blocks to a recently renovated restaurant near the train depot. Quintana insisted that a visit to the Northwest wasn't complete without a fresh salmon dinner. Grace agreed and he ordered for both of them.

They talked about their families over drinks and a stuffed mushroom appetizer, then moved on to their jobs. Quintana had been on homicide investigation for seven years and said he wouldn't trade it for double his annual salary. By the time the entrée arrived, Grace found herself confiding her trouble in Seattle and felt a rush of emotion when he became indignant on her behalf. "It's behind you now, Gracie, but you need to send a certified letter with your rebuttal to the police chief up there and insist it be included in your file."

Grace sighed. "Chief Cruz suggested the same thing. Common sense tells me you're both right, but I don't know if I have the energy to pursue it right now."

Quintana slid his hand across the table and captured hers. "This case has got you down, *querida*. That's understandable."

His compassion warmed Grace and she squeezed his hand back. "In my wildest dreams, I never imagined that I'd ever work a homicide in Coburg, let alone two of them. I don't want to make a mistake."

"You won't."

"You can't know that."

He shrugged, threading his fingers with hers. "You're smart, you've got good instincts. How can you fail?"

Grace shook her head, smiling ruefully. "Luz, if that's a

come-on line, it's the best one I've ever had."

Quintana grinned, extracting his hand and placing it over his heart. "Grace, you wound me. I'm saving my come-on line for later, when we get back to the hotel."

"Finish your tiramisu," she instructed, fighting back the fresh wave of excitement coursing through her body.

On their walk back, they passed several couples who had apparently attended a performance at the Hult Center. Quintana uttered a low whistle.

"What?" Grace said.

"Glowing head."

Grace turned to watch the foursome. In the streetlight, one man stood out. His silver head appeared to glow.

"You know, I've been thinking, Grace. That bloke I met today—Deets?—he has silver hair."

"Deets wouldn't—"

"You don't know that for sure about anyone. The only person you can trust is yourself. Don't forget that."

"My father has silver hair, for pete's sake! So do half his friends and both my uncles."

"Just be careful," Quintana warned. "Sometimes the people closest to us are the ones we overlook. Think with your brain, not your heart."

"Don't go chauvinistic on me," Grace said dryly.

"Never."

Before she knew what was happening, Luz maneuvered her into the darkened doorwell of an art gallery. His arms went around her and he lowered his head. When his lips took hers, when his tongue dove into her mouth, Grace didn't think twice about her response. She went up on tiptoe and slid her arms around his neck, giving back as good as he gave.

Luz lowered one hand to cup her ass and pull her firmly against the blatant evidence of his desire for her. Grace almost melted, but he held her firm and she pressed herself even more tightly against him. The hand against her back moved around to the side of her breast. A lightning bolt sizzled all the way down to her womanly parts. Grace couldn't suppress a moan. Was it longing? Desire? Loneliness? She couldn't tell, and didn't care. Everything Luz did just felt so damned good.

"I like you in red, love," he murmured against her lips. "It's so very hot, like you."

When they finally eased apart, both were breathing hard. "Come up to my room, Grace. We'll pour a little wine, turn out the lights, enjoy the view of the city at night."

"Luz—"

"*That's* my come-on line, *querida,*" he said softly, seductively. He cupped her face between his big hands, lowering his mouth again.

CHAPTER 55

THEY SKIPPED THE wine and undressed in the dark. The city lights probably were beautiful from the eighth floor, but neither cared.

"This feels so…decadent," Grace whispered, stroking his chest. "I'm…I'm not a one-night-stand kind of girl."

"I know." He nuzzled her neck, nipping at her ear lobe. "Me, either."

Grace knew what he meant. He'd sent her up to the room while he visited the hotel gift shop to buy condoms. If he'd been a one-night-stand kind of guy, he would have had a supply in his wallet.

"You are so beautiful, my lovely Grace."

"Ditto," Grace uttered on a sigh. The sheers were drawn at the windows, affording them both just enough light to get the particulars of the other's body. He gave her ass a gentle squeeze before he moved on to her breasts. Grace's hands dropped from his chest and roamed around to his buns. They were so taut, she couldn't resist saying, "Your buns are made of steel."

A chuckle rumbled in his chest. "And your titties were made in heaven." He bent, dipping his head so his mouth could sample them.

Grace's knees buckled. He saved her from collapsing and scooped her up in his powerful arms. With one arm still holding her, he grasped the bedcovers and pulled them back with one yank. He placed her gently on the bed and followed her down. His mouth went back to her breast and his hand roamed down between her legs. His fingers slid across her wet opening, then eased inside.

"So ready for me already, Gracie."

She whispered an invitation in his ear.

He opened the small package and sheathed himself. Within seconds he was inside her. "I had planned to go slow, sweetheart, but…."

Grace understood. She arched her body, sliding her legs up around him, digging her heels into his steel buns, meeting him, taking his hard, wild thrusts like she'd never done before. When the orgasm rippled through her, her moan of pleasure came out more a scream, but she didn't try to stifle it. Moments later, she felt his already engorged penis grow and pulse as he filled the rubber with his ejaculate. The muscles of his neck corded, his face became a grimace of pleasure, and then he collapsed on top of her, his entire body trembling.

His heart beat furiously against her bare breasts. Grace felt sated, but she wanted more. Much more. As if he read her mind, he rolled off of her, careful to hold the rubber so it wouldn't leak. He dealt with it in seconds, then pulled her to him, working her legs apart.

"What are you doing," she asked, her voice sultry, soft. She almost didn't recognize it as her own.

"I want to hear the sounds you make again when you come," he said, his own voice thick with desire. "I want to hear them again and again and again. They are amazing." He shoved two fingers up inside her. "*You* are amazing."

And then they had no words. His fingers played their magic and after that, he kissed and licked his way down the length of her and let his mouth take over.

Grace woke up moaning, her body shuddering with the remnants of yet another orgasm.

She could still feel his hands on her, feel his lips on her mouth, his tongue *down there*.

Dear God, if she felt like a woman well-loved from a night of nonstop sex dreams, what would it be like to spend hours actually making love with him?

Her eyes flew open. Orgasms while she slept? That had never happened to her before. In fact, she'd never had explicit sex dreams before. At least nothing on this level, with such intensity, such intimacy. Such heat. Such erotic detail.

Her body began to hum. Her breasts grew heavy, the tips pebbled. Then the tingling started. It culminated in a pulsing at her core.

Somehow, Grace managed to climb out of bed and into the shower. In dreamland, she'd been well and thoroughly washed in his hotel room shower. Just thinking about him touching her, remembering how he sudsed her, made her come in that shower….

Instead of cooling her horny jets, she got even more hot and bothered. She considered pleasuring herself to the memories of his tongue *down there*.

But Grace was nothing if not dependable and she had made a promise to four kids. She readjusted the water, yelping when the cold spray hit.

She tried, she really tried, to rinse her horniness down the drain.

When she began to shiver from the chill, it hit her that even in her nocturnal fantasies, she'd practiced safe sex.

Grace laughed until tears streamed down her cheeks.

Conscientious me, even when I'm dreaming scintillating, erotic sex.

Right about now, Grace figured Luz was sitting in the airport, pouring over the medical examiner's reports, rereading the Clausen and Starr files. Last night, he'd insisted he could catch the hotel shuttle to the airport. With one last lingering, toe-curling kiss, he'd encouraged her to sleep in on her day off—all the better to have sweet dreams of him.

If he only knew….

By this afternoon, her promise to her nieces and nephew for their "animal safari" fulfilled, he'd be half-way back to

Houston.

Just thinking of those kisses caused Grace's innards to jingle. Man, oh, man, could that Aussie kiss.

Aside from his magnetic charisma and sex appeal, Luz Quintana was a nice guy and obviously good at his job. Unfortunately, he hadn't brought anything new to the investigation except more doubts on her part.

Did he really have to throw fat on the fire by pointing out that a glowing head could just as easily have been silver as blonde? Talk about opening another can of worms!

Grace forcibly pushed aside feeling guilty over the few hours she'd spend with the kids, recognizing that sometimes a short break was all it took to regroup and revitalize. In spite of being her day off, she'd still be back in the office by mid-afternoon and probably work late into the evening.

With that schedule in mind, she put out an extra dish of water for Blackie and gifted him with the large chew-bone her father had purchased. The Lab circled and rubbed her knees with gratitude before he loped off with his treasure.

All thoughts of the four murders temporarily shoved into whatever part of her brain housed the law enforcement piece of her life, she headed to her parents' house.

At the kitchen counter, she listened over a second cup of coffee as Kyle, Cassidy, and Maddy recited their agenda suggestions for the safari.

"Okay," Grace said, mentally paring the list down. "First, we'll go to the llama ranch, then over to the agritainment farm to the petting zoo. We'll have lunch after that, then head to the fish store. We'll finish up at Jason's aviary." She took a deep breath, tired already. "Sound okay to everyone?"

The kids nodded their agreement, but Maddy said, "We gots to buy a goldfish."

"If we do that," Grace explained to her youngest niece, "we'll have to skip the aviary, because it will be too hot to leave the goldfish in the car."

In typical big-brother fashion, Kyle informed her bluntly, "He'll be belly-up by the time we finish."

Maddy frowned. "Belly-up? What's that."

"Dead," Cassidy said, her big-sister tone somber. "We'll

have to flush him down the toilet like the other one."

Tears welled up in Maddy's big brown eyes.

"Don't worry, sweetie," Grace said, hopping off her stool to comfort the little girl. "We'll buy a goldfish another day, okay?"

Maddy nodded, but it was obvious she wasn't happy about it.

"Okay, guys, everyone to the bathroom, then we'll go get Dylan."

"I like Dylan," Cassidy informed her. "I'm going to marry him when I grow up."

Grace eyed her mother suspiciously.

Angelina raised her hands as if in self-defense.

For once, Grace believed her. Cassidy had fallen for Dylan over spaghetti and meatballs almost two weeks ago.

Grace just got the kids loaded into her mother's van, when her smartphone rang. Deets. Since he still had to be at Surgery 10, she knew something crucial had been found.

"What's up?" she said in greeting.

"Good morning to you, too, Gracie."

She glanced at Cassidy, who had tucked the shoulder strap of the seat belt under her arm. "Hold on. Cass, put your belt on properly, or you're staying behind."

"Gracie," the girl whined, complying.

"Sorry. Good morning, Deets. What's up?"

"The doc went in and extracted the slug. Looks like a .40 caliber."

"Okay."

"But get this—he had the white ribbon folded up in his mouth."

Grace walked away from the car. "You're shitting me! Was there a note?"

"Not exactly the same as the others. His said, 'I should have minded my own business.'"

Grace's pulse hammered. "So it *is* connected."

"Looks like."

She wondered if she should cancel the outing, then

glanced at the anxious faces staring at her. Hadn't they had enough cancellations in their short lives? "I should be back at the office by two. No matter what else gets accomplished, I want the rest of that fax from Boulder County SO by then."

"Got it," Deets said. "Look, Gracie, try to enjoy these few hours with those kids. You deserve it."

Compartmentalize! Can the guilt. Can the call to duty. "See you this afternoon."

By the time they finished up the outing at Jason's aviary, Grace really was exhausted. Chasing bad guys was nothing to minding four children aged eleven and under.

If I had one-tenth their combined energy, I could work seven days a week and sleep only two hours a night. I'd have these murders solved in no time!

Jason answered the doorbell on the first ring. "Right on time," he said, favoring the children with welcome smile.

"We saw llamas," Cassidy said excitedly. "Tons of them."

"And piggies," Maddy added with a giggle. "Piggies *squeal*." And she proceeded to imitate the porkers quite accurately, sending her siblings and Dylan into gales of laughter.

Laughing right along with them, Grace hoped Dylan's relaxed manner carried over into his home that night. He hadn't been surly or smart-mouthed once.

"They have the coolest fish in the salt water tanks at Fins," Kyle said, getting in his two bits.

"I liked the puppy we saw at the petting zoo," Dylan said. "I'm gonna ask my dad to buy us a dog."

Jason stepped back, rubbing his chin thoughtfully. "I don't know if my quiet birds can compete with all the other animal wonders you've seen today."

"Quiet?" Kyle hooted. "You've got the noisiest birds in town!"

"Well, according to my neighbors," Jason admitted, "you may have a point." He glanced at Grace. "Rough day?"

"Tiring, but fun." She grimaced. "Except for the stupid

llama that spit at us."

"Gross!" four young voices agreed.

Grace trailed behind as Jason lead his youthful troupe into the aviary. Her cell phone rang before they'd heard a full accounting of the first bird, one he identified as an African Grey parrot. "Sorry," she said in apology to the others. "Hello."

"Grace," the chief said, his voice so urgent that she felt a cold chill run down her spine. "Can you talk?"

Grace slid a glance toward Jason and the four children. "Not really. Can you hold on a sec?" She lowered the phone. "Jason, will you be all right with the kids for a few minutes? I need to take this call." Fearful Chief Cruz was calling with bad news about one of her family members, she added, "Privately."

The warmth he'd shown toward the children vanished when he looked at her, only to be replaced by one she interpreted as concern. "Certainly. Why don't you step back inside the house? We'll be fine."

"Thanks." She directed a no-nonsense look at the four youngsters. "Enjoy yourselves, but don't cause Jason any trouble, okay? And don't tease any birds!"

Not that they were actually paying any attention to her—the now-famous Hyacinth macaw chose that moment to verbalize a string of profanities, then immediately began to belt out its favorite song, "Blue Moon"—but Grace took the various murmurs that turned to giggles and howls of hilarity to be consent.

She made her way out of the aviary and back into the house. "Okay, what—"

"Where are you?" Aidan demanded, cutting her off.

"We're bird-watching. Is something wrong?"

"The complete report just came through from Boulder County SO. You need to get in here right now. We have our killer."

CHAPTER 56

GRACE GLANCED AT her watch, calculating how much time it would take to gather the kids and drop them off. "I can be there in about twenty minutes."

"Where the hell are you?"

She sighed with impatience. "I just told you, we're looking at the birds at Jason's—"

"*What?*"

Grace started to repeat what she'd said, when the chief bit out, "Then take care of it, goddammit! I'm on an urgent call here!" She realized he was talking to someone in the office. She wandered toward the interior of the house and veered into what appeared to be Jason's library.

"Grace, did you say you're at Jason Knox's?"

"Yes, he's giving us a tour of the aviary. What's…?" She trailed off, staring in horror at the three portraits above the fireplace situated between the floor-to-ceiling bookcases.

"Grace?"

"Ohmygod."

"*Grace?* Goddammit, pay attention!"

She lowered her voice, unable to take her eyes from the painting on the left. The lemon-colored gown, the gold locket around the girl's throat. No wonder Sarah Mays looked familiar.

"Grace, get the kids and get the hell out of that house. *Right now!*"

Startled by a noise behind her, she spun around.

"Disconnect the call, Grace."

Jason stood in the doorway, pointing a gun at her. A semi-automatic that indicated he meant business. Was it a .40 caliber?

"Now." He didn't raise his voice or issue a specific threat. He didn't need to. Her first consideration would be for the children and he knew it. She would do whatever he told her.

"I have to go, Mom," she murmured into the phone, cutting off Aidan's, "*Grace, goddammit—*" with a subtle movement of her thumb.

"Put the phone down."

"Mom says 'hello,'" she said, unobtrusively activating the RECORD function.

For a moment, he looked disconcerted, uncertain, Grace noted with relief. Under no circumstances did she want Jason to know she'd been talking to the chief. "She wanted to know when to expect me back with the kids," she went on improvising, hoping against hope that he would abandon whatever foolish plan he had in his mind and let her leave with her charges safely in tow. "Dad's not feeling well and she thinks he needs to see a doctor."

"Your mother is a fine woman," he said.

"She's a wonderful mother and grandmother," Grace said. She waited for a response from him, but none came. "She would be devastated it if anything happened to one of her children or grandchildren."

He merely stared at her, his expression registering obvious turmoil. Finally, he said, "The children are fine. The birds won't hurt them."

As if I think they're in danger from the goddamned birds when a cold-blooded killer is holding a gun on me.

Funny how everything made so much sense, once the final piece was in place. The evening gowns, the crowns, the white ribbon in each victim's mouth. Clausen instructing his daughter, *Tell your mother I picked up her crowning glory, the red dress.* If only she'd known before Hamm Starr's death about the beauty queen he'd dated in college, and that Jason Knox was her father.

If only. But Jason knew. Somehow, he'd found out about the group sex. That would explain the missing penises. Had he befriended Clausen, listened to him brag about M&Ms and female orifices? She'd never even thought to ask Jason if he *knew* Yeager. How stupid was that? Some investigator she was.

After all these years, the grieving father finally had decided to exact his revenge. Why had he waited? Grace decided to stop pretending. She set her phone down on a nearby side table.

"You're Sarah Mays's father," she said, easing her purse off her shoulder, taking a moment to fasten it closed.

Unlike her peers, she never carried a weapon during her off-duty hours; after today—if she survived—she planned to reconsider. In the meantime, her purse was much less effective, but it was leather and inside were her wallet, her badge, Kyle's inhaler, and some other odds and ends. Zipped up, she might be able to use it against him, throw him off kilter for just a moment.

With her heart pounding harder than it ever had before, she said, "You killed those three men because of what they did to your daughter."

Jason reached behind him to close the door and with the same hand, locked it. Grace allowed her gaze to leave him briefly, searching the room for a means of escape. With him blocking the door, the windows remained the only option.

"They were responsible for the deaths of my entire family," Jason said, his voice wavering with emotion, even though his expression remained stone cold.

"Your whole family?" Grace repeated, feeling like one of his captive parrots. She continued to back away from his steady approach.

So matter-of-factly it almost seemed canned, he said, "Hamm took Sarah and showed her a side of life she should have never known. Sex. Drugs and alcohol. Perversity. He and his trashy friends. And they weren't satisfied with ruining Sarah's life, they had to have Nicole, too. They got her hooked on drugs, you know." He stopped for a breath.

"She called the night she first overdosed, bragging that

those boys had shared her and Sarah. Helen and I forced her to go into a treatment center, and when she came out, we thought she was clean. She *swore* to us that she was! We believed her. She didn't want to live in the dorm, so we helped her get an apartment set up, enrolled her in college."

He briefly closed his eyes, obviously anguished. "She must have connected with a drug supplier almost immediately. After that, it was a downward spiral. She dropped out, went to the streets, selling herself to get money for a fix. She contracted AIDS from dirty needles." He took a deep, gasping breath. "Can you imagine watching your daughter wither from such a horrible disease?"

Finally, his voice broke. "My little girls." He choked back a sob, swallowed several times, and finally regained his composure. "My beautiful little girls."

He moved a step closer to Grace, putting out his free hand to steady himself against his desk. "Nicole disappeared, you know. We tried to find her, wanted to help her get some medical treatment. They didn't have the advances then that they do today, but there were drugs, legitimate drugs, she could have taken." Tears coursed down his cheeks. He let them fall. "The police phoned one morning, asking us to come identify a body they thought was Nicole. They'd found her in an alley, dead. The needle was still in her arm. Helen and I buried her four years after Sarah was in the crash."

"Oh, Jason, I'm so sorry," Grace said, meaning it.

"After ten years of being in a coma, the doctors said we had to make a decision about Sarah. You know, to pull the plug? Our beautiful Sarah. So beautiful she won beauty pageants. She had shriveled up to nothing. The doctors said her brain was dead. It was cruel of us to keep her alive, I know, but we just couldn't kill her." He gazed upward for a moment. "One day, God took the decision out of our hands."

He moved closer, his hand not quite steady as he held his weapon waist-high and aimed at Grace. "Our Sarah, she was always strong. She lasted in that care home for over fifteen years. My beautiful girl was a vegetable, but she held on."

"Jason, I…." Grace couldn't find the words that might ease his grief.

"My wife started drinking even before Sarah died. I couldn't abandon her after all we'd been through. I loved her, tried to get her to stop drinking, but she wouldn't. Then she started taking sleeping pills. Sarah gone first to the coma, then Nicole...." He raked the fingers of his free hand through his silver hair. "Drinking like that for so many years, Helen's mind wasn't right anymore and then when Sarah finally died...." He choked on a sob. "Helen was dead inside years before she ever swallowed those pills."

Grace's heart ached for Jason's loss, and she cursed the stupidity of Jack Dellenbach, Yeager Clausen, and Hamm Starr in their youth.

But as a cop, despite any personal feelings she might have about why Jason had done what he'd done, she was bound to uphold the law. His victims had wronged Sarah and Nicole, providing them with drugs, taking advantage of them sexually. Immoral if not illegal, but by law, it didn't justify killing three men two decades later in a well-planned scheme of revenge.

"Jason," she said quietly, "no matter what happened, you can't be a one-man vigilante committee."

"Can't?" He smirked at her. "Really? I believe, Grace, that I have already proven I *can*."

He had her there. "Do you think killing me will get you out of this?"

"Maybe not, but it will give me time to disappear."

"What about the children?" she asked, suddenly afraid of how far he'd actually go to ensure his escape. "You wouldn't hurt them?"

"Of course not!" he said stridently, his tone disgusted. "I exacted revenge where revenge was due, but I don't hurt innocents."

"That's not true," Grace said softly. "There are four Dellenbach children who have no father. And the Clausen girls? They're without their father, too. They're all innocents."

Again, his expression registered uncertainty.

"And for the record, Jason, I haven't done anything to you, either. My parents befriended you. They won't take kindly to you killing me."

A look of regret creased his features. "I'm sorry for that. Your parents are wonderful people."

But not wonderful enough to keep you from murdering their daughter. Grace was nearly close enough to a window to do something about her plight. The lamp on the table between two highback chairs in front of one of the windows was plugged in, making it useless. But between the other two windows, if memory served, there'd been another table, one supporting a good-sized and probably expensive piece of art glass.

"What about Jimmy Frey? Why did you kill him?"

Jason waved his hand dismissively, not even denying her assumption. "He was a pimple on the ass of humanity, Grace. Don't tell me he never harassed you sexually, or made your life or the lives of others down at CPD miserable in myriad ways."

"How do you know what he was doing?"

"People talk. Clausen and Starr talked at the end. I knew all about Frey and his sexual escapades, doing to other young girls what had been done to mine."

"So, you killed him for that?" Grace inched back as discreetly as possible, hoping she wouldn't stumble or trip over anything.

Jason grunted a sound that sounded like a laugh. "I killed him because the idiot tried to blackmail me. He was always snooping around and he overheard me dealing with Cappland. He knew I'd bought the heroin from Cappland, so he figured I'd given Cappland my bird." This time he did laugh, a sound that came out half-maniacal, half-crazed. "Did that imbecile think I would pay him to keep quiet, that I would pay *two* blackmailers?"

CHAPTER 57

GRACE SURPRISED HERSELF by defending the obnoxious Jimmy Frey. "Blackmail doesn't deserve murder."

"He cried like a baby, begged me not to kill him." Jason's expression became one of satisfaction. "In the end, they all begged for their lives. That was something Sarah and Nicole and Helen never got the chance to do."

"Maybe you can call Mom and Pop and apologize afterward for killing me."

Once more, he faltered, closing his eyes briefly in apparent torment. Perhaps he did have some conscience left.

Grace took the opportunity to move closer to the piece of art glass that she hoped was a heavy as it looked.

"I've come too far to back down," Jason said, opening his eyes. With his gaze trained on her and his right hand trembling as he gripped the pistol, he moved around behind his desk and pulled a plastic bag from the top drawer. It contained drug paraphernalia.

"If you're not ashamed of what you've done, why run?" Grace persisted, fear pounding through her veins at warp speed.

The question stopped him cold. His shoulders slumped; he lowered his gun hand and stared at the floor.

Grace tried to be unobtrusive as she moved closer toward the second window.

Jason seemed to snap out of his momentary funk. One-handed, he emptied the contents of the bag unto the top of the desk, his gaze downward.

Grace seized her golden opportunity. She hurled her purse at him, then swung around to grab the heavy piece of art glass from its perch. She flung it with all her might through the window.

The children's excited voices could be heard through the broken window, which Grace hadn't realized faced the aviary. She stood her ground and screamed, "*Run, kids! Go for help!*"

"You actually think they can hear you?" Jason's laugh was full of scorn. "Or that they can get out of the aviary? Grace, Grace," he chastised, "They'll never be able to figure out where the secret door is or how to open it, if they do."

Grace realized in that moment she was in danger of losing her mind. The aviary had an outside exit? Had Deets or Felix found it? Would they be able to free the kids or had Jason effectively trapped them with the birds? Being children, would they think to find something heavy enough to break the glass so they could escape?

Her strategy changed. Whatever she had to do to take Jason Knox down, to keep the children safe, that's what she would do.

He laid his weapon on the desk within easy reach and quickly prepared the syringe. He picked up the gun again, glancing toward the window. Confusion had etched wrinkles into his face. Gone was the handsome Jason Knox. In his place stood his crazed doppelganger.

He seemed suddenly discombobulated. Grace calculated rushing him to get the gun away—or the syringe—but realized that success in removing one weapon from him could still result in him using the other one on her. "If you think I'm letting you put that needle in my arm, you're crazy."

"Ah, crazy," he said, his eyes back on her. "I think I am a little crazy, but who wouldn't be, experiencing the losses I have?" Without waiting for a response, he went on smoothly. "Come closer, Grace, and put your arm out for me."

A silver tongue to match his silver hair. Why hadn't she seriously considered him a suspect before? Luz Quintana's words echoed in her head. *Sometimes the people closest to us are the ones we overlook.* True, she wasn't close to Jason. Her parents had befriended him, welcomed him into their home, but hadn't she always noticed what a smooth talker he was? "If you want me, Jason, come and get me."

Even as she taunted him, Grace's life passed before her eyes, including missed opportunities. For a moment, she regretted not being a one-night-stand kind of girl. Making love with Luz might have been a memory worth taking to the grave. In an absurd moment of clarity, she realized her dream lover had been dark-haired not surfer blonde. For an instant before she pushed the revelation aside, it staggered her. "How did you get them to cooperate for you, Jason?"

"With the first two, it was easy. I simply convinced them that I wanted to humiliate them in their own community for what they had done to me." His lip curled with disdain. "I managed to persuade both those fools that they were self-injecting a tranquilizer and would awake with nothing more than a groggy headache and a tarnished reputation."

God, sometimes it sucked being right. "And Starr?"

"Ah, Hamm was more of a challenge." He closed in on her. "I enjoyed killing him the most—he was the one Sarah fell in love with, you know. He was the one *really* driving the car that day." He stopped and stared up at Sarah's portrait for several moments. "I had to kill him outright and worry about getting him into Sarah's dress and that rocking chair afterward. She was beautiful, wasn't she? Like Nicole. Both of them beautiful like their mother."

"Beautiful," Grace agreed, keeping her eyes on him. "How did you manage to catch Frey unaware?"

"That cocky buffoon! He saw me take the rocking chair off of Gunny Spriggs's porch. Said he'd do me a favor and not tell anyone if I made it worth his while." He shook his head in disgust. "I can do without *favors* from a filthy pervert blackmailer. He'd bleed me dry." Jason reached up and wiped his eyes with the knuckles of his gun hand. "I set up a meet at Spencer Butte. He was greedy and gullible enough to show up. Even bragged about how he'd run you off the road. He wanted you dead, you know."

From a distance, Kyle and Dylan screamed for her, then the pounding began on the door between the house and the aviary, so loud she could hear it from where she stood. More screaming, and were the girls crying? *Please, God, help me find a way to keep them safe.* Moments later, silence reigned from the aviary. Not even a bird squawked.

"I hope they haven't let the birds out," Jason said.

"The kids wouldn't do anything to harm your stupid birds." Grace gasped. "You said they'd never be able to find the secret exit."

"I'm sure you're right."

Which told Grace that Jason was full of shit. Somehow those brilliant kids *had* found the door. "How did John Cappland really know about your macaw?" Grace pressed on, hoping to learn the exact why of the bird-napping.

"When I purchased the heroin from him, he followed me home." He grimaced. "I should have dealt with him then. He saw Cyan, did some research, and decided he wanted her instead of the cash."

"The macaw is worth quite a bit more than the heroin you bought." Grace visually swept the room, looking for another way out of her predicament.

Jason chuckled without humor. "He was a vagabond. As fate and misfortune would have it, he was in Houston at the time of Dellenbach's death and when he heard about Clausen, he put two and two together."

"So, he was the other one blackmailing you."

"Between cash and birds, the bastards would have taken me for a great deal." At Grace's questioning look, he went on. "The day he robbed the truck stop, he'd already collected Cyan. I was supposed to meet him there with one hundred thousand dollars and two more birds." Beneath his aristocratic silver eyebrows, his eyes gleamed with satisfied malevolence. "I never showed up, so I suppose he became desperate. He got what, a couple hundred dollars from the truck stop heist, and ended up dead for his trouble. Too bad you can't prosecute stupidity."

"Not very smart of him." *Please keep talking.*

"Greed itself is a killer," he went on. "Cappland and Frey

sealed their fate with their greed."

She still couldn't hear the children. Kyle and Dylan were clever. They would have found a way to escape. *Please let them be far away from the house by now.*

"I still have my money and my birds," Jason said, his head cocked toward the aviary as if he, too, were listening for the sound of childish voices.

Grace began to inch around toward the door. "Why do you care about the birds if you plan to run?"

"I love my birds. I've made arrangements for them when I'm gone." He turned back. "Now, be a good girl and put out your arm."

CHAPTER 58

JASON KNOX REALLY was crazy if he thought she would comply. Less than five feet separated them. Grace spared an instant to take her gaze from him to search the room one more time for a weapon.

From the next room came a bellowed, "Grace, stand away from the door!"

Without taking time to think, Grace dove between the leather sofa and the wood-and-glass table in front of it, flipping over as she hit the floor. A clap not unlike thunder reverberated through the room. A moment later, two things occurred simultaneously: the door slammed open with a crash against the wall and Jason Knox fell on her, his gun forgotten, the hand clutching the needle aiming for her neck.

Grace had trained for this moment, never expecting it would arrive. Her knee went up to Jason's groin, leaving him in obvious agony, yet he did not relinquish his hold on the syringe.

She grabbed his left hand with both of hers, praying for strength she wasn't sure she had. Voices—shouting, angry, and loud—registered in the peripheral of her consciousness, but every ounce of her was focused on keeping that hand, that needle, away from her body.

Jason's weight pressed against her, crushing the breath from her lungs. For several agonizing seconds, Grace feared she was in a battle she might lose. What was taking the chief so long? The needle was so close, she could almost feel the sting of its metal tip penetrate her fragile flesh, the heat of the lethal drug make its way into her system, killing her.

"Grace!" someone shouted. Aidan? Deets? Or was it Luz? No, that was crazy. Luz was long gone back to Texas.

An almost inhuman wail filled the room. Totally unexpectedly, Jason pushed himself away from her, nearly wrenching her shoulder as he half-carried her with him. She fell back to the floor and watched in horror as he plunged the needle into his arm, depressing the plunger.

He made a gagging sound and his eyes looked startled. He toppled sideways against the glass table, shattering it.

Grace threw up her arms to protect her face from flying shards.

For several seconds, the total silence deafened her. She lay frozen, half-trapped by the dead weight of Jason's body.

"Grace! Jesus, are you all right?"

"Did he get her?"

Grace cracked open one eye, imagining Luz was in the room saying, *Did he get her?*

Aidan holstered his Beretta and bent to pull her arms gently away from her head.

"You're bleeding."

"Glass," she croaked.

"Did he get you with the needle?"

Grace had to think. She had only *imagined* the needle in her neck, hadn't she?

"Grace, goddammit, did he stick you with the needle?"

She managed to shake her head. "I don't think so. Can you get him off me?"

Aidan barked orders at Deets and Felix, who still had their weapons drawn. "Montoya, go check on the kids. Make sure they stay outside. Mallory, radio in with a status report and find out where those EMTs are!" Both men slammed their weapons into their holsters and ran from the room to do as the chief instructed.

"I'll lift him up," Aidan said to the apparition of Luz Quintana standing beside him. "You ease her out."

"You okay, Grace?" Luz asked.

"I think so. He—I don't think he got me with the needle," she said again, not really sure he hadn't. Her arm hurt, but it was the same one she'd fallen on in the bike accident….

Her gaze flew to Jason's inert form. Her parents' friend. The last person in the world she would have expected to be a killer.

The chief checked for a pulse at Jason's neck. Quintana helped her stand.

Grace swayed and the room began to spin like a carousel out of control. "Frey and Cappland were blackmailing him," she mumbled. "Frey ran me off the road. He wanted me dead." A shiver wracked her body. Twice. Someone had come close to killing her twice.

Quintana pushed several straggling wisps of hair off her face with a gentleness that belied his size. "Oh, *querida*, I thought I came up here to *help* you. I never expected you to capture our killer single-handedly."

"Texas isn't the only state where they do things bigger," Grace managed to tease. "Why are you still here?"

"Aidan and I had coffee, then he got the call that the fax came in and I was curious as to what it said. I decided to re-book on a flight tomorrow."

Grace read a message in his eyes, but couldn't quite assimilate it. Maybe because a spinning top was about to implode in her head. Her stomach didn't feel so good, either.

"Sit down," Aidan ordered.

"Are the kids all okay?"

"They're fine. Sit down."

Grace finally obliged. "The fax?"

The chief shook his head in disgust. "Every goddamned thing came together just about half an hour ago. Those missing pages named Jason Knox Mays as the father of Sarah Mays. We also learned that the gun Cappland used was registered to Jason Mays." He planted his hands on his hips. "Mays bought another gun three weeks ago, which I'm assuming is that one." He inclined his head toward the weapon Jason had discarded at the last moment.

"I set my phone to record," Grace said, waving in the general direction of where she'd left it. "He confessed…to everything, but he didn't mention anything about guns." Her stomach heaved. *So close to death....*

Deets reappeared. "Montoya is taking the kids over to Gabbianos."

"Make sure he lets Joe and Angelina know that Grace is fine," Aidan said. "We'll get her some medical care, then she'll be home. Tell Dylan I'll be there as quick as I can."

"Bathroom," Grace mumbled. "I'm gonna be...." Before she had time to think about the humiliation of it, she bent over and tossed her cookies all over her new boss's feet.

Quintana handed her a handkerchief, and laid a comforting hand on her back.

"Thanks." She groaned, embarrassed to have barfed in front of anyone, ashamed of her delayed reaction to the danger she'd faced. "I'm sorry," she said, unable to tear her gaze away from the mess she'd made on the chief's shiny black boots.

"Don't worry about it, Gabbiano," Aidan said. "You'll have plenty of time to clean them up later."

Over twenty media people crowded into the small conference room. Cameras flashed, video cameras whirled, several laptops had been set up, and dozens of hands were poised, notebooks at the ready.

Outside, the promised rain had finally arrived. It tapped gently against the windows.

Chief Aidan Cruz took his place at the head of the room, not quite scowling, but not exactly friendly, either, as he spoke into half a dozen microphones. "At approximately 1:45 p.m. yesterday, Sergeant Grace Gabbiano apprehended the alleged killer of local residents, Yeager Clausen and Hamm Starr, and Houston resident, Jack Dellenbach, formerly of Coburg. The alleged killer's name is—*was*—Jason Knox Mays. He had been living in our community for just over a year as Jason Knox. Mr. Mays, a former Colorado resident, had two daughters...."

Grace leaned against the door jamb, listening as Aidan spoke, succinctly relating the details of the investigation and the ultimate standoff. He held the media captive with his charismatic demeanor. Not one of them knew how he actually felt about journalists.

Except for maybe Michaela, who sat up front. With the chief's approval, she'd already gotten her story first-hand from Grace the evening before. Her version had been written and sent to the news desk long before the press conference had started. *A promise*, Grace thought, *is a promise.*

She allowed herself one small smile. *Wait until Aidan finds out I promised Deets's cousin's daughter a personal interview over the phone right after he finishes here.* A promise is a promise.

Once the chief made his statement, he gave Luz a chance to speak about the first murder in Houston. A detective from Eugene PD spoke next concerning the related death of Corporal Jimmy Frey. The chief then opened the floor to questions. Mikey, ever persistent, went first. "Chief Cruz, what do you mean, *alleged* killer? Either Mays was, or he wasn't."

Aidan's expression remained stern. "As you know, Ms. Gabbiano, we live in a country where a person is presumed innocent until proven guilty. Since Mr. Mays is dead and can't stand trial—"

"With all due respect," Michaela interrupted. "Didn't Mays admit to committing the murders?"

Aidan nodded. "He gave a full confession to the deaths of Dellenbach, Clausen, and Starr, and also admitted killing Corporal Jimmy Frey. Fortunately, Sergeant Grace Gabbiano had the foresight to activate the recording function on her smartphone, capturing events as they occurred."

"And didn't Mays try to kill Sergeant Gabbiano, one of your best officers?"

The corner of Aidan's mouth lifted in amusement. His gaze shot toward Grace as he nodded. Half the room craned their necks, trying to see who he was looking at.

Grace wondered if he'd been in agreement with the "try to kill" part of the question, or the "best officer" part. She grinned and gave him a thumbs up.

"You're gonna get your butt in big trouble with the boss one of these days," Deets whispered in her ear.

Grace straightened. "Ya think so?"

"Chief," Michaela persisted doggedly, "do *you* really think 'alleged' is the correct term to use in this case?"

Aidan's eyes swept the small gathering. "Legally, I can't say anything but 'alleged.' You folks, however, have the First Amendment behind you, the mighty pen at your disposal, and a company lawyer on retainer."

That drew some chuckles.

He continued as if he had no clue he had them eating out of the palm of his hand. "I can't *force* you to print an adjective in front of the word 'killer' when you write your stories, nor can I make you *omit* it."

Michaela sat back in her chair and Grace read triumph in every inch of her sister's posture. It would be accompanied by a satisfied smirk.

Grace had little time to bask in her own self-satisfaction before Tina tapped her on the shoulder. "You have a call from an Officer Travis Loew in Tucson, Arizona."

Delfina!

Aidan went on to the next question, as if he didn't hate the media.

Grace left the room smiling as she listened to him tactfully try—without much success—to wind down the press conference.

Poetic justice, she thought, *is sweet.*

Author Note

A book like *Dressed to Die* involves a lot of research. I owe a debt of gratitude to Dennis Ross, former Police Chief of Coburg, Oregon for his read of my early-days manuscript and for sharing his insight, not only on the day-to-day activities of being a police officer in a small town, but also on his days as an undercover cop and serving as a detective with the Lane County Sheriff's Office. Thanks, Denny!

In addition, I want to thank retired Lane County Deputy Medical Examiner Frank Ratti, who spent hours discussing murder with me—and trying to convince me that there are a lot of other interesting ways to die besides being the victim of a homicide. He was right. However, *Dressed to Die* is all about murder, so manner of death was predetermined, but who knows if some of those other suggestions will come in useful down the road? Thanks, Frank!

I would also like to thank Lt. Mike Hurley, former head of the Oregon State Patrol Forensics Laboratory in Springfield. The idea for Grace Gabbiano was born in the Forensics class I took from Mike and he was an invaluable resource for me. I still don't get the mass spectrometer, but I loved the tour of the Forensics Lab. Thanks, Mike!

Coburg, Oregon really exists, but I have taken liberties with the town because this book is a work of fiction. For example, I gave Coburg PD a brand spanking new building next to the fire station. All the characters and businesses within these pages are fictitious, and any variations or errors in law enforcement or emergency services protocol are mine alone. I have a fertile imagination and sometimes, I just can't help myself...

Watch for **SLICED TO DIE**, *the next book in the Grace Gabbiano Mystery series, coming in 2015.*

Preview the first book
in the upcoming
Andi Comstock Paranormal Mystery
series by Ann Simas...

HOLY SMOKE

~ CHAPTER 1 ~

FROM THE FIRST day Andrea Comstock started her new job as a software engineer at eFuture, she got a whiff of smoke.

The scent was neither pleasant, nor unpleasant, but Andi couldn't identify it, regardless. It didn't smell like cigarette smoke, or electrical wiring gone bad, or the aftermath of someone's burned toast.

It vaguely reminded her of burnt hair, like when the intake on her blow dryer had sucked in a few strands too many, or maybe of scorched meat on the barbeque, but even that was not quite right. One thing she was sure of, she had ever smelled anything like it before, but it was definitely smoke.

She had one weird moment as she sniffed. The sound of amused laughter filled her head. It was so clear, so contagious, Andi laughed, too. Then she got up to look outside her office door, which fed into a small common area with casual seating, to see what her co-workers found so funny. No one was in sight.

Puzzling over what her nose could not deny, Andi went back to her desk. The smoky smell soon dissipated and with it, the remnants of the mysterious laughter. She immersed herself in the coding project her boss Brent Hathaway had assigned earlier and soon forgot about anything else.

Andi considered herself perfectly suited to software engineering. She had the ability to block out external influences, to intuit problems and solve them, and to be creative—all positive assets for writing computer programs.

She expected to work overtime some days, but being single and having no significant other to focus on left her free to work long days if necessary. Besides, the extra dollars on her paycheck would help build a nice savings account.

Even though she'd only been on the job for a few hours, she loved it already. The coworkers she'd met so far were friendly, she had a small office of her own rather than an open cubicle, her boss was a dream, and the work promised to be challenging, fun, and interesting.

Andi hadn't been at her desk for more than an hour on her second day before she smelled the smoke again. When she went to the break room to fill her coffee cup, she asked several co-workers chatting at a small table in the corner, "Do you know what that smoke smell is and where it comes from?"

Lacey frowned. "Is someone smoking in the building? This is a smoke-free workplace!"

"Smoke, what smoke?" Ted asked. "I don't smell any smoke."

"Are you sure you didn't walk by someone smoking outside and the odor is hanging on your clothes?" Susan asked.

Andi sniffed the air. "Can't any of you smell it? It's quite prominent today."

The others sniffed as well, but no one, including two other coworkers who passed through the room, said they could smell anything unusual, including smoke.

Andi went back to her office. She sat down at the double-monitored keyboard, baffled. How could she be the only one with a nose sensitive enough to smell smoke?

Andi, it's just you. No one else can smell it. Lucky girl!

Startled, Andi got up and went to her open door. No one was in sight in any direction and all the other doors were closed. What the heck? She gnawed on her lower lip for a few moments, then shrugged and went back to her desk. The smoky scent had all but disappeared and she soon became engrossed in her coding project.

By noon, satisfied with her progress and inexplicably feeling rejuvenated, even though she'd been sitting for almost three hours straight, she saved her work, a program she had named ELWAY, then checked her email and the network calendar that notified of meetings and other events.

She used the restroom, then went back to her office to retrieve her purse. The scent of smoke had returned, and as she started to pull her door closed, someone spoke to her. Indistinguishable as to gender, the person clearly said, *What a beautiful day for a walk, Andi. That's one of the many things I'm going to miss. Enjoy!*

Andi faltered, releasing the doorknob as if it were red hot metal. She spun around, looking for the source of the voice. What in the world was going on? Was the smoke an after-effect of some kind of hallucinogenic drug someone outside the building was smoking? Was it somehow seeping into her office, and only hers? Was she on some kind of acid trip without knowing it?

Andi pondered the smoke and the voices as she made her way to Trattoria d'Italia. Inside, she took a small table by the window and ordered an sausage sandwich. Though she smelled only delicious Italian cooking aromas, she couldn't shake off thoughts of what now numbered three unusual experiences at work.

Back at her desk an hour later, she pulled up ELWAY and got back to writing code. Not ten minutes later, the scent of smoke filled the air, followed immediately by, *Congratulations on your new job, Andi! You have a lovely office.* Andi gasped, but this time, she didn't jump up to see who was speaking outside her office door.

Twenty minutes elapsed before her fingers stopped trembling. Andi wiped her sweaty palms against her denim skirt and forced herself to concentrate on ELWAY.

The following day, she smelled smoke just after arriving at work. The vocal accompaniment was, *Your job looks like fun, Andi, but remember, there's more to life than work.* On Friday, the smoke arrived late morning with a voice that said, *Have a wonderful weekend, Andi. I loved spending mine in the garden.*

Andi wasn't much of a drinker, but after five days of smoke-and-voices, she seriously considered having a liquid lunch at the bar two blocks up.

The voices didn't really creep her out. They were friendly and wished her well, but why did she hear them? Were they caused by something in her environment or did she have some weirdness going on in her brain? Did people develop schizophrenia when they were almost thirty years old? She hadn't experienced any headaches, but what if she had a brain tumor?

The thought caused Andi's stomach to clench painfully,

even as goose bumps raced up her arms. Brain tumors could cause dementia-type symptoms. She'd witnessed it in her grandfather. He'd been in incredible pain and completely nonsensical at the end. She didn't want to end up like that.

That's not what this is, she told herself. She was smart, with an above-average IQ. She was not nuts. She did not have cancer. There was a rational explanation for this...this phenomenon. Genetics were *not* rearing their ugly chromosomes inside her!

Once outside, she abandoned the idea of imbibing her noon meal and decided to do a little sleuthing instead. She circled the L-shaped eFuture complex, which ended up being a challenge. A two-story high cinderblock wall, which her office window faced, ran the length of the back of the building. At each end, gates had been installed to keep out vagrants. Nonetheless, she peered through both chain-link gates, trying to determine if anyone had scaled the fence and taken up residence in the six-foot width of landscaping, armed with a crack pipe or a camp stove or whatever paraphernalia drug users needed to make-and-partake. Nothing.

At that point, she realized there was no longer a trace of smoke scent in the air, either. She went on her way, perplexed.

On her way to Soup Station, Andi sidetracked into the office supply store to purchase a small journal with a pen attached to it.

After a hearty bowl of chicken noodle soup and two fresh-baked wheat rolls, she walked several blocks out of her way to get back to eFuture. She perused without really seeing the delightful window displays of the shops she passed by. Her thoughts were on the last five days.

In the small courtyard at the inside corner of the corner of the eFuture building, she sat on a bench beneath a shade tree and opened the journal. On the first lined page, she recorded each smoke-and-voice event, beginning with the laughter she'd heard on Monday.

Once back at her desk, she worked for two hours straight before taking a short break to retrieve one of her Diet Cokes from the fridge in the break room. Easing into her chair again, she got a whiff of the now-familiar smoke. Her boss walked in and asked how things were going.

"Great," Andi replied. "ELWAY's almost finished and I should have my written evaluation ready for you first thing Monday morning."

"ELWAY?" Brent asked.

Andi laughed. "Sorry, I always name my projects. Since this software is for a sports memorabilia company, I named it after John Elway."

Brent grinned. "One of my favorite quarterbacks! You seem to have taken to this job like a duck to water."

Andi smiled. "I love everything about it." *Mostly*, she added silently.

"Any problems or concerns, or any questions?" Brent asked.

She debated whether or not to mention the *mostly* part. "Maybe one question, and really, it's not about work."

Her boss tilted his head slightly. "Okay."

"Do you smell the smoke?"

Brent frowned. "Smoke? Like cigarette smoke? No one's supposed to be smoking in the building."

"No…no, not from cigarettes." She sniffed the air. "I don't smell it constantly, but I smell it right now." She shrugged, embarrassed, and tried to make a joke of it. "Since you don't smell it, I must be having olfactory malfunction."

Brent's expression registered concern. "If it bothers you—"

"Oh, no, it doesn't. It's just…odd. No one but me seems to smell it." *And that's enough on that subject,* she thought, *or he'll think he's hired a loony and I can kiss this job goodbye before I complete my three-month probation.*

Brent seemed uncertain. "Well, if you're sure, but if it becomes a problem, let me know. This isn't a new building, you know. We've had a leaky roof during the rainy season, and maybe what you actually smell is mold. We can have an air test done, maybe isolate the problem."

"I'm sure that won't be necessary," Andi assured him.

"But you'll let me know if it gets worse?"

"Of course."

"Good. Don't want you going somewhere else because our building stinks." His face screwed up like he'd been eating lemons.

Andi grinned and took it as an encouraging sign that Brent was happy with her work so far. A permanent position loomed on her horizon, which was a good thing, because she was ready to move out of her studio and into a two-bedroom apartment. "Thanks. And don't worry. I really do love this job. I can't imagine going anywhere else."

"See you Monday morning then. I'll put you down for ten, if that works for you."

She nodded.

Brent gave her a thumbs-up and left the office.

Andi turned back to her keyboard, sipping from her soda can.

What a lovely man. He has a beautiful wife and three darling children. Someday you'll find a man like that, Andi, and then your life will be complete.

Andi spewed Diet Coke on both her monitors.

. . .

HOLY SMOKE, coming soon!

About the Author

Ann Simas lives in Oregon, but she is a Colorado girl at heart, having grown up in the Rocky Mountains. An avid word-lover since childhood, she penned her first fiction "book" in high school. She particularly likes to write a mix of mystery-thriller-suspense, with a love story and paranormal elements. Her books are available in both digital and print format, with autographing and free shipping directly from her website for paperback books.

An award-winning watercolorist and a budding photographer, Ann also enjoys needlework and gardening in her spare time. She is her family's "genealogist" and has been blessed with the opportunity to conduct first-hand research in Italy for both her writing and her family tree. Some of her Italy photos are displayed on the home page of her website, **annsimas.com**. The genealogy research from century's old documents, written in Italian, has been a supreme but gratifying and exciting challenge for her.

Contact the author via:
Magic Moon Press
POB 41634
Eugene, OR 97404-0386

Or visit:
annsimas.com
and
Ann Simas, Author
on Facebook

Thank *you* so much for reading **DRESSED TO DIE**!
I'd love to hear what you think about it.
You can email me at **ann@annsimas.com** or post a comment on my **Ann Simas, Author** page on Facebook.
I hope you'll "like" me while you're there, and if you are so inclined, please leave a review on Amazon.com, Goodreads.com, iTunes Bookstore, or on my Facebook page.

And just for fun, if would like to submit a picture of yourself reading this or any book by me, please send your jpg to **ann@annsimas.com** and I'll post it on my FAN page!

Made in the USA
Charleston, SC
31 May 2016